VACANCIES IN TIME

Vacancies in Time

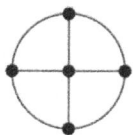

Ashley Godschild

This is mostly a work of fiction. Names, characters, places, and incidents are either products of the author's imagination or are used fictitiously… unless regarding historical figures or locations in which case gross artistic license was used. Any resemblance to actual persons, living or dead, events, or locales is not entirely coincidental but mostly is.

Vacancies in Time
Copyright © 2022 by Ashley Godschild
Corrected First Edition

All rights reserved. No part of this book may be used or reproduced in any manner whatsoever without written permission except in the case of brief quotations embodied in critical articles or reviews. Pirates are only cool when they are named Captain Jack Sparrow or Bootstrap Bill. If you pirate this book or read a pirated copy, you suck. No cap. May Z-library remain dead for all of eternity and the creators rot in whatever prison they were taken to.

The text of this book is set in 11-point Times New Roman Text. The headings are 22-point Algerian.
Hardcover ISBN: 9798367102482
Paperback ISBN: 9798366995443

TW/CW:

blood, mass shooting (blood & bodies described on page, gunshots described), discussions of slavery and racism, elements of suspense (enough to give my grandmother a literal heart attack), cancer. This book contains elements that might be disturbing for a younger youth audience, I'd suggest no readers under the age of 13. I consider this a NA book (16-26), not a YA per se (13-18). There is little to no vulgar language and no sexual content, but mature themes are discussed. Please be advised these 'mature' themes continue through the trilogy (especially in book 3).

Historical science fiction romance adventure (yes it's a mouthful but the most accurate description of the trilogy)

DB

To my Avery, reach for the stars and don't worry about the fall (I'll always be there to catch you). Thank you for inspiring me to finally giv'r.

And to Oma, you said at the rate I was going, you wouldn't get to read one of my books before you keeled over and while this book played a role in hospitalizing you, you have read it… so there.

(written three months before her death)

TABLE OF CONTENTS

CHAPTER 1: SLEEPLESS BUT NOT IN SEATTLE

CHAPTER 2: PERVERT

CHAPTER 3: SHEEP FARMING IN ITALY

CHAPTER 4: RATS NOT WELCOME

CHAPTER 5: 9-1-

CHAPTER 6: NOT MY IKEA TABLE

CHAPTER 7: A PROPER HOSTESS

CHAPTER 8: KICKED PUPPY

CHAPTER 9: TIED UP WITH STRINGS

CHAPTER 10: LITTLE SHARK

CHAPTER 11: STEP OFF BRO

CHAPTER 12: PERPETUALLY 24

CHAPTER 13: HE DOESN'T BELIEVE IN FAIRIES

CHAPTER 14: THE TRAP

CHAPTER 15: DR. RACECAR

CHAPTER 16: I AM NOT A RACIST

CHAPTER 17: ENDLESSLY HONOURED

CHAPTER 18: CASUAL CANNIBALISM

CHAPTER 19: YOU MAKE ME FEEL SO YOUNG

CHAPTER 20: THE BUTTON

CHAPTER 21: ADULTS ONLY

CHAPTER 22: FAT LARD

CHAPTER 23: GONE LIKE THE WIND

CHAPTER 24: TAKE CARE

CHAPTER 25: DR. MAMA

CHAPTER 26: THE IMPALER

CHAPTER 27: TO MY LIZZY

CHAPTER 28: SUPERTATOR

CHAPTER 29: GLORIOUS PURPOSE

CHAPTER 30: I SEE

VACANCIES IN TIME

"The most effective way to destroy people is to deny and obliterate their own understanding of their history."

~

George Orwell

CHAPTER 1: SLEEPLESS BUT NOT IN SEATTLE

How many ramen noodles does it take for a student with mountains of debt to explode? Emma laughs to herself, grateful no one else can see her in the empty condo. Subsisting entirely off a diet of boiled cardboard, while being subjected to nightly cramming sessions, is tearing apart her sanity and palate.

Not to mention the hot steam burning her fingers!

Emma hisses, scandalizing the succulents in her kitchen with a couple choice words. She waves the seared digits around in the air as if the action can save her from the damage already done. Refusing to be conquered by an instant noodle bowl, she rips the lid off in one swift movement. Her socks slide easily on the kitchen tile to escape the plume of scorching heat, but the burn does not fade from her pinkened fingers.

Grabbing an ice cube from the fridge tucked into a corner, Emma slides it over her fingers and glares at the offending Styrofoam container. The ramen continues to expel steam, creating waves over the faded, yellow backsplash of her tiny, outdated kitchen. "Moe warned me impatience would be my downfall."

Sighing, she reaches for the phone plugged into the wall beside the sink and taps in her password. A picture of her little sister's grinning face pops up surrounded by apps. Avery balances precariously on Emma's back, a trophy in one hand and the MVP medal in the other. Mud covers her freckled face, but she wears it proudly, along with the biggest smile Emma's ever seen. Her team is on the way to win their second championship in a row this year.

To this day, no one knows who took the picture—at least her family claims they don't. Someone saw Avery jump on Emma, heard their laughter, and decided to immortalize the moment.

The piggyback ride ended up giving Emma bruises but they faded. A temporary reminder of their closeness in a terrifyingly finite world... and then she saw the photo and Avery's smile. Like any older sister, she'd embrace all kinds of pain to keep her *schatje* smiling.

Finding Avery's contact in her phone, Emma throws herself on her bed and presses the icon for the video call. She watches her ramen in quiet yearning, now too comfortable to leave burrowed between her pillows and fluffy blanket.

Her resolve breaks when the call rings out. Eyebrows drawing together, Emma stands and walks back through the hallway to grab her dinner. The bowl warms her hands against the cool temperature of her condo. *Chopsticks or fork?* She ponders the question, slipping glances at her silent phone on her bed. When no call comes, she grabs a used plastic fork from beside the sink and forces herself to walk past the comfy, warm bed.

Neon lights bleed from outside past rain covered windows. The precipitation is as much a part of the cities infrastructure as the buildings and streets. Everyone who lives here knows to expect the stormy ambiance for eighty percent of the year, leaving a little space for the occasional sunny day or the rare snowy one.

Emma takes her seat in the wide office chair, avoiding her own reflection in the mirror to her right. It leans against the wall, floor length and gold, too big for her apartment but where would she be without it? As a working woman, she prides herself in the care of her appearance, and refuses to leave the apartment if she looks anything less than her best.

Right now, 'best' is a foreign concept. Emma eyes her textbook with quiet disgust, shoveling noodles in her mouth. She excused herself from her studying session to make dinner two hours ago. Looking at the forgotten notes and the blinking cursor on her laptop screen brings a flood of guilt. It's hard to study on days like this.

Someone honks outside. Laughter trickles in from the window. A siren goes off further in the city. All noises she used to start for, but now they are part of her life. Like the ivy hanging down from her shelves, trying to tickle her nose. Like the forever opened drawer of her desk filled with loose paper. Like the silence inside her home while the world outside stays loud.

The chime of Emma's phone saves her from the slippery

slope of introspection. Reaching for it, expecting to see Avery's shining face, she instead reads the text with a scoff. **I have soccer practice, what do you want?**

I was going to invite you over to hangout but not with that attitude… it's not raining out there?

Standing again, she leaves her desk and books behind, wandering towards her south wall. Glass panes make up the entirety of the wall. Awful for insulation, but city dwellers pay to experience downtown in all its glory. Droplets of water roll down the windows as if the city itself is mourning Emma's lack of a social life. Running her finger in time with a drop, she almost leans her head against the cool glass. A single speck of grease ruins the perfect view into the world below and above, imagine a forehead of oil. Besides, washing her windows is an even more pathetic way to spend a Friday evening in her early twenties in the heart of her city.

The text notification breaks the silence, interrupting her internal debate of turning on the TV to fill the void. **We're in the city. Indoor stadium.**

She could go watch Avery play. Despite her personal favourite sport being volleyball, she never minded soccer. Especially at her parents' side with her other siblings cheering loudly enough to burst her eardrums. However, the junior league plays in a stadium on the outskirts of the city. While riding a motorcycle in the rain holds a certain appeal to some, the reality is less glamourous.

And Moe might lecture her... a threat grave enough to stave off the desire to escape her Hobbit hole.

Emma's work outfit sticks to her still-damp, olive skin. She does not need to look in the mirror to know her hair resembles a clown's wig. By the time she changes into appropriate soccer-watching attire, and fixes her hair, Avery's game might be over. **Kick their butts. Tell Moe and dad I said you earned a treat.**

No Avery then. Her sigh fogs up the glass, rapidly dissipating as the cold from outside claims her breath. Orange and red lights glow from Chinatown below, where people walk and laugh though night fell hours ago. The acupuncturist clinic across from her shines near-blinding light through the window. People mill about within, although the frosted glass and curtains protect patients from being viewed by half the city.

Emma averts her eyes, careful not to stare too long into the building across from her. God only knows what kinds of things they protect her from seeing by hanging those dark curtains. Studying medicine herself, she's seen a fair share of naked bodies and explicit diagrams but those were textbook illustrations.

The reminder of her studies draws her eyes back to the desk but they quickly find something else to focus on. A group of people her age wrestle outside the library down the street. One young man ducks past the others and launches onto the lion statue, roaring so loud, she can hear it. *I love the library.*

Emma marches back to her bed, flopping onto it as she searches her contacts. Cody, her oldest brother, is a lost cause, and yet the first person her finger clicks on. Maybe it is because she forgets he lives in a different country now, or maybe she desperately hopes he will come to his senses and remember the family he left behind. When was the last time he even responded to a text? She scrolls through the one-sided conversation, returning to her desk chair and throwing herself into it with a loud huff.

Three months ago—The text takes up an entire screen. She stopped messaging him multiple times a week and opted instead for updates on school and work all at once when necessary. **Hey Cody coyote, haven't heard from you in a while! I know you are kicking butt and taking names with your residency. Just make sure you aren't taking drugs ;) I am learning all about them with this new course. Narcs, stims, hallucinogens…. my prof told me a statistic of how many surgeons were/are on drugs or are alcoholics. Big number.**

No response for four hours. The blank time between adds to the pressure building in Emma's chest, returning her to the first stages of mourning. No one talks about the grief accompanying the transition into adulthood. Watching the life you know, morph and change, leaving you to recognize nothing. Not your friends, not your family, not the place you sleep, the clothes you wear, the person you see in the mirror, not even your heroes.

Not that I think you would take drugs! God knows Moe would want to conduct an exorcism on you and she'd probably drag us back to the Orthodox church just to do it. My boss told me to 'can it' the other day because I was talking about you too much. What can I say? My brother the brain surgeon!!! The first deVries to be a real doctor... I guess this is just my long-winded way of saying I love you and I miss you. You make me proud every day to be your sister!

His succinct response, eight hours later? **Thanks sis.**

It hurts being the proud sister sometimes. She wants nothing more than every happiness and success for her siblings. Except watching them climb their ladders to success often means being at the bottom, holding it in place.

Emma brushes a thicket of messy, black curls away from her face, trying to smooth the braid they are supposed to be contained in. The humidity encourages chaos. Normally her hair toes the line between a bird's nest and Greek goddess waves. She does nothing to tame them either way, preferring to keep her hair in braids when it does not want to be kind, and out for everyone to see when it does.

Pulling at one of the golden hoops in her ear, she stares at the pictures on the shelves above her desk. Most of the space is taken up by her books, but she wanted her family with her, no matter how close or far. Cody stares at her from the thrifted frame, half-smiling while the rest practically split their faces in joy. Avery's hair finally grew long enough to be styled, and her joy touches Emma every time.

Cody and Oliver didn't want to take part in family photos. One felt 'too busy' with college prep and the other loves to imitate his eldest brother. Cody, being the oldest at 24, never enjoys the comments made by people when the family comes together. People asking if their parents have hobbies, or if they are Mormons, or if they are all 'actually' related.

The comments come from ignorance and prejudice, so it's easy for Emma to ignore. Moses, her older brother and one of her best friends, embodies his namesake. Perpetually unbothered and free-spirited like water. Both take after their father's calm temperament though.

Cody and the others inherited Moe's countenance. Their mother, a full-blooded Dutch woman, has a temper worthy of any tradesman (in the opinion of their electrician Father). Henny deVries: the perfect example of a high-strung Type A personality… though her sweet demeanor and heart of gold makes her crushing expectations bearable.

Emma loves all seven of her siblings equally. Despite her resolve not to show favoritism, Moses, her 22-year-old brother, understands her in ways no one else can. At times, Moe mutters about the two of them sharing one mind. Emma can think of no greater compliment, considering how clever they are. And Avery, her 12-year-old sister and youngest of the deVries clan, embodies everything Emma wishes she were brave enough to be.

Cody, Oliver, the twins Summer and Winter, and Joseph may be deeply loved but are entirely different from her two closest friends.

Moses will not go out. A hermit (or introvert as he says) to a T, Moses rarely wants to go out on the town. Especially after a week of work. His idea of the perfect Friday night consists of videogames on his expensive PC or playing with a complex puzzle. Not the kind used to form pretty pictures but blocks with bright colours and moving pieces. When dad figured out Moses enjoyed the little blocks, he found every X cube in town and didn't wait for a special event to hand them over. Now, Momo solves the puzzles in mere seconds.

Emma's finger hovers over 'Basket Boy' in her phone. Sometimes, it is nice to be thought of. With that in mind she shoots off a text, tearing her eyes off the phone to look at the clock hanging between her shelves and desktop. The night is young—Her final option is Carter.

Work best friend, and one of the oddest people she knows. He may be one of the funnest too, but fun also means unpredictable. She cannot guess what adventure waits on the other side of her phone. They both need to be at the clinic tomorrow at 6 am to open. Neither one of them are naturally morning people as it is.

Carter shoots energy drinks like shots on a typical day...

then again what is a typical day for Carter? He once called in to work from Arizona two hours after his shift started to let them know he'd be gone for a week. The piles of uncompleted coursework are enough reason *not* to play the game of 'what will Carter convince me to do tonight'. No late nights on a school/workday.

Staring at her stack of schoolwork, she stabs the noodles with her fork and brings them towards her mouth. For good measure, Emma blows on the noodles and broth. The lukewarm food sticks to her mouth as she catches a drip one inch from touching her turtleneck.

What to do with a Friday evening? She considers watching one of her comfort rom coms or even rereading one of the classics seated above her head on the raw-wood shelf, but nothing piques her interest. Moe calls it her 'dangerous mood'. The quiet desire for something new. Something exciting. The kind of mood nudging her eyes towards her phone, where Carter is a click away.

Rapping the fork's plastic stem against her tooth, she turns to face the windows again. The library does not close for another hour. A new book might be the perfect cure for a heart gripped by wanderlust. Really, anything to avoid working on the essay due in a week. What are equations and formulas to love and adventure?

Spinning in the office chair, she surges onto her feet and walks straight for her door. It takes all of two seconds to slip her black rain boots back on and don her long raincoat. Beads of water roll off the sleeves, disturbed by the motion. Reaching for her umbrella, she flips the switch to the lights in her apartment, and steps into the dimly lit hall.

"Hey Emma," Trevor, her neighbour, greets with a wide smile. He pauses with his grocery bags, fighting with them to release his shaggy, brown dog, Chewy.

Dropping to her knees, she greets the chocolate lab/retriever mix with a quiet squeal of delight. "If it isn't my favourite little guy."

"Ouch, that hurts," Trevor jokes, pressing a hand to his heart. He leans a shoulder against the doorway, halfway into his apartment already. Chewy didn't give him the chance to change out of his paramedic uniform, leaving his owner to soak in the rain on their daily evening prowl to find sufficient dinner. When he works night shifts, Emma gets the great honour of taking her favourite dog out for his walk. "We are leaving this week."

"No," she gasps, holding Chewy's ears to his head. It'll be embarrassing for both of them to hear her beg. "Trevor—"

"Not permanently. Just for the week." Trevor massages the back of his neck as his eyes begin to drift close. Anyone in the medical industry knows the increased pressure during the first half of the year. Post-Christmas, New Years, Valentine's Day, and the many holidays in between where tourists come to visit the beach and islands. The pharmacy fills dozens of new prescriptions within this bracket of time. Chewy, sensing his owner's distraction, lunges for the bag potent with the smell of Korean barbeque.

"Chewy!" Emma admonishes, apologetically smiling when Trevor jerks awake. He glares playfully at the dog, patting him on the muzzle with a loud yawn.

Trevor shakes his head as his eyes glaze over. "They already own my soul; they aren't getting the rest of me too."

"Spring break."

He offers a weak smile in response, lowering the bag of food to the ground so he can remove his fluorescent jacket. Chewy eyes the food but stops when Emma scratches underneath his ear with her long nails.

It used to mean more before. Children see spring break as a magical week free of responsibility. Free to do whatever they desire. Between work and school, Emma rarely gets to be free. Yet, she manages to find ways to dawdle and procrastinate between the two.

"The last thing I need is a bunch of horny, stupid college kids drinking on the beach. You have the one guy with something to prove who decides to jump off the pier." Emma offers a nod and soft smile in solidarity but cannot begin to imagine the frustration of dealing with the same easily avoidable problem. "In the dark. It's always in the dark. Into the ocean. I wasn't that stupid at their age. How some of these guys get into college I'll never understand...."

"Sounds delightful," she retorts, laughing quietly as her furry friend tries to lick her. Avoiding the stretch of his tongue, Emma jumps to her feet. His tiny, brown hairs begin to cling to her grey slacks like magnets. The pattern hides it but she hoped to be able to wear them again next week without taking a trip to the laundromat. Oh well, the snuggles are worth every nickel. "You know I am a college kid too, right?"

"Not a stupid one though, that's what counts," Trevor reassures, clicking his tongue. Chewy shoots to his side and then into the apartment at the fling of his owner's hand. "Make good choices."

"I normally do," she laughs, walking backwards, until he disappears behind a solid wood door.

She could be one of the librarians. The thought draws out a snicker. No longer alone in her condo, Emma catches the attention of a couple looking at the NA section. Waving politely, she turns back to the classic literature, tempted to go and say hi for the sake of human contact.

I need to ask her where she got that skirt, Emma decides, watching one of the library assistants swish past her. The piece looks so comfortable matched with an oversized white sweater and layered jewelry. Both girls look like Ivy League students or historians, except Emma's frizz ruins her attempt to appear composed and put-together.

"Do you need help finding anything?" the assistant asks, cocking her eyebrow when she notices Emma watching.

"No! No, not at all, I was just admiring your skirt." Emma confesses, laughing as she slides her hands into the pockets of her jacket. Wrappers from this afternoon's lunch crinkle underneath her hands. "It looks incredibly comfortable."

"It is," the girl responds proudly, sliding her hands into the skirt's hidden pockets. Both grin, sharing the joke all women know, as the assistant drifts towards her. "I thrifted it though. Someone must have loved it a lot because the tag is worn out. Trust me, I tried to find the brand. Even scanned a couple of second-hand websites to see if anyone listed similar skirts. Lucky for my wallet, I didn't find their store."

"A not too long, not too short, not too tight, not too loose, pencil skirt with pockets?" Emma lists, tapping her fingers with every positive attribute. They nod together knowingly as Emma drags her eyes from the plaid skirt. "They'd sell out in an hour."

"What kind of book are you looking for?" the assistant inquires, staring at the classical literature with bright eyes. She steps away and scans the aisle with breathless intrigue. "I spend most of my time reading about mythology and witchcraft; the only one I remember reading is To Kill A

Mockingbird... and only because my grandma forced me to."

"That's a good one, but I need something new," Emma admits, realizing with growing sorrow every book on the shelf is one she has read. Between her obsession in high school and her desperate escapism in junior high, not one book provides a new world to escape into. "I am Emma by the way."

"Elena; it's nice to meet you," she responds, accepting Emma's handshake. Despite how uncommon it is between younger people, neither think much about it. Traditionally kindred. "Do you enjoy Jane Austen?"

"She is one of my favourites. I don't think anyone can read *Pride and Prejudice* and not get attached." Emma runs her fingers over the spine of the book. The library's version is not as nice as her copy at home. Clothed in satin with golden embroidery. An expensive graduation present from her Oma. Her finger wanders further down the centuries old books to the classics from the 2000s. "Is this a new one?"

"New to the library," Elena announces, watching her grab the Shakespeare adaptation from the shelf. "I think it is based on *Midsummer's Night Dream*... but I am more of a Macbeth girl myself."

"Sounds interesting," Emma murmurs, flipping the book to read the summary hidden within the book. The other young woman smiles politely and slips away with a soft *adieu*. As she finishes reading the blurb, she lifts her head expecting to see the girl and instead stares down an empty aisle. "Next time."

Finding girls with similar interests and personalities is akin to the needle in the haystack conundrum. When she was younger, Moses stood at the center of her friendship problems. Most of the girls in their church wanted to get close to her for him. Throughout school she barely trusted most of them to be near her, let alone her older brother. College took her away from them. Most of her high school acquaintances wanted to stay in the suburbs while she ran to the city.

She never realized how much she took for granted until she ended up living alone in a tiny apartment with a half-functioning fridge. Dad helped her out of her first apartments' lease, and she found a better place to live. God knew she needed someone like Trevor and he was the first person she met when touring the space. While the other neighbours are kind, he makes it his business to know everyone and be a presence in the condominium. For that reason, and likely countless others, he gets to be the only occupant with a pet… it took a couple months to get over the jealousy.

Leaving the classical section, she finds three more books before coming to the checkout desk. No one goes to the library for one book… well, they might. She scrutinizes her haul, knowing she may easily grab a dozen more given the chance. It doesn't matter how strict she is, she ends up with double what she came for every time.

"Did you find everything okay today dear?" the librarian asks as Emma scans her card. Nodding with a smile, Emma glances at the museum outside. The city finished it a week before the week of sleet in November. Now, white shines from within the completely glass building, assaulting the night and all its dwellers. "Have you seen the new exhibit yet?"

"Not yet," Emma sighs, playing with a damp curl as she watches the lights flicker from people wandering within. "I need to find someone who will stare at art with me for an hour and pretend we are refined and sophisticated."

The librarian laughs, holding the books. "A pretty girl like you should have no trouble with that. Did you want a bag today?"

"No, thank you."

She takes the books, slipping them into the waterproof pockets on the inside of her trench coat. Opening her mouth to compliment the librarian back, Emma almost steps into the couple from the NA section. They smile politely, nodding at her when she smiles back but then they are sliding their books onto the counter and the librarian is occupied.

Leaving the library chases away all her warmth and comfort. Cold rain slams into Emma's body as she struggles to open her umbrella. She closes one eye and turns her face away from the downpour, ready to sing a praise song when her shield expands. Cowering behind the plastic cover, she reties the waist of her jacket, and sets off down the street.

She should return to the condo. Especially with the gloomy night sending so many people inside but thinking of going back leaves a hollowness in her chest. Here on the street, with cars driving past and girls shrieking as a bike rider swerves to miss them, peace finds its home.

Instead of going home, Emma takes the scenic route around a network of buildings. As she walks, the museum light follows her. She walks into the free gardens, staring at the glass footbridge above. People dress for the celebration of the new opening. Shimmering dresses. Suits with dark fabrics and proper ties. Jewelry sparkling bright enough to blind under the illumination of white bulbs.

She makes it to the end of the diagonal path, finding a lamppost to lean against. Directly across from her, separated by thin glass panes, patrons view a sculpture of a former Queen with serene expressions. Most museums know better than to display their art through transparent walls, but this one does not care. They understand the art is simply one part of their appeal. Decadence, the *gezellig*, the atmosphere and renown are part of what draws people in.

There is little sophistication to be found, watching from the outside in cold, dreary weather, while others bask in classical music and free champagne within.

Emma slides her hands into her pockets, holding her umbrella with the nook of her elbow. A light flickers on the second level. It is rarely illuminated and mostly hidden by the curved ceiling. The building reminds her of a peach ring candy. Such an eloquent way to think; displaying her refinement and sophistication, along with the frizz of her hair and how she eats out of a Styrofoam bowl most nights.

Intrigued by the flickering light, she leans forward, as if that will help her see into the enigmatic second story. Nothing shows. Someone, in one of the convenience stores, mentioned it will be an industrial center, for more dentists or optometrists or even pharmacies; but Emma thinks it'll ruin the air of sophistication the museum demands. Why give space for the public when it can be used for the offices of the artists, critics, and collectors—people who preserve the elevated atmosphere?

"Sorry!" Emma apologizes moments before the person collides with her. She pulls her shoulder back, nearly hitting the lamppost as the person barrels past. "I am sorry sir!"

He grunts back, turning enough for her to see the displeased curl of his lips. Everything else remains partially hidden behind a hood of black. For a moment, she stands with her mouth open, no air coming in or out. Not because of his rude behaviour, which is completely uncharacteristic for the country, but because of his appearance.

Between the flickering of the upper room's light and the lamppost, she caught a glimpse of his shadowed face. She might have called him out for being impolite, despite her hatred of confrontation, if he didn't look like Adolf Hitler's *doppelgänger*.

The thought fills her with guilt enough to apologize to God because she cannot apologize to the man. It is a very cruel thing to look like someone known for such heinous crimes. No wonder he was so rude.

CHAPTER 2: PERVERT

"Good morning bestie," Carter greets with his normal flair, waltzing into the clinic as if he is not ten minutes late. Then again, he arrives ten minutes 'late' every shift. Has he been early before? Emma wracks her memory but comes back with nothing. "I brought a coffee. I know it won't be as good as your Italian beans put in a French press whatever, but it does the trick."

"You seem awfully chipper for the morning," Emma responds, shaking her head when she sees the travel mug in his hand. Their boss, Dr. Pepper, shared his disapproval of drinking liquid caffeine. Coffee is acceptable, but the energy drinks Carter chugged every day raised his brows. Eventually, Carter realized three cans fit into a nice, professional metal mug. The perfect disguise to avoid lectures from the middle-aged doctor.

"Being awake at six is bad enough, but on a Saturday morning? It's a crime. A sin even." Carter claims, grinning at Emma's failed attempt to hide her affectionate smile. Born to Catholic parents, Carter knows every one of 'their' sins like a child memorizing the alphabet. Despite wearing a crucifix gifted to him from them, he does not adhere to most of their beliefs or the ideology itself. "You look rested... no big spring break party?"

"On the contrary, it was a total rager. Me, ramen, and

Shakespeare."

"Sounds like one," he remarks sarcastically, throwing himself over the counter instead of walking through the gate. The end of his lab coat catches on the lock, earning an annoyed huff. Emma takes Carter's drink before he spills it on himself in the ensuing struggle. "Did you know they theorize that Shakespeare wasn't really William Shakespeare?"

"Do 'they'?" Emma inquires, organizing the pick-ups on the computer as he stumbles into the enclosed space. A couple early birds intend to come right at opening, 6:30. While most show up a minute or two early, Emma recognizes two names on the list. They always arrive five minutes before opening, watching them through the glass doors. Mina, their other co-worker, petitioned the boss to get curtains to avoid the glare of impatient clients. He refused. "Well Dr. Friesen you have two pickups scheduled for six-thirty... you should probably fill those up."

"One theory, my favourite one, is that Shakespeare's greatest rival Christopher Marlowe wrote most of his plays."

"And why would his *rival* want to give Shakespeare's name renown and glory?"

"Because who doesn't want to live a secret life? Christopher Marlowe supposedly died when Shakespeare first became popular, but why live your own life when you could be someone else entirely?" Carter questions, shaking his little ponytail. Most of his hair is contained by a small black elastic, but some dirty blonde strands cling to his damp face. Emma removes his rain jacket in a bid to get him to the back of the clinic, except Carter's eyes are brightening with excited obsession. "William Shakespeare came from a poor family. He was illiterate—"

"*Dr.* Friesen I would be more excited to hear about this, if you were filling up prescriptions," Emma reminds, trying to be as stern as their employer. She grabs the two bottles he needs from the drawer below and holds them out, refusing to meet his eyes. They are the colour of the sea, with a tide strong enough to pull her in. Her lips twitch in response to the pressure of his raised eyebrow.

Carter sighs and accepts the container, winding down the aisle made by drug-filled shelves. He grins at her from behind a section of paper bags, encouraged by the hidden smile he sees now on her face. She shakes it off, handing him gloves when he slides to her side.

"As I was saying. The guy was illiterate. He came from a poor family and historically he was mentioned as an actor, *not* a writer."

"And is that what you spent your Friday night doing?" She inquires, prepping the pens for Dr. Pepper. There are many things he wants perfectly in place for when he comes in... things her best friend can't care less about.

Carter works the odd shifts when the practice owner needs time off. A new graduate, and not one for a normal human calendar, Dr. Friesen never worries about his hours, or consequences. Luckily, his charm and wit keep him safe from punishment—most of the time.

"No, RedPanda69 uploaded new footage of behind the scenes at the 'moon landing'."

"And you still believe it was faked?"

"It was faked," Carter promises, crossing his arms as he follows her to the shelving unit she stands in front of. Humming in response, she moves back to the front counter, watching the blinking light from their telephone. One person calls every morning hoping to cancel an already filled prescription and a hundred more attempt to get theirs filled before expiration. Saturday mornings follow an unsaid script.

One person called to ask if the pharmacy sold cocaine once… that was an interesting shift.

"C'mon Em. Nineteen sixty-nine the first moon landing took place and nineteen seventy-two the last one did. *Eighty* years ago. America is less advanced than China and Russia, yet, neither have managed to repeat the technology and actions of those a century ago."

"I do remember from the binder you showed me," Emma vows with a smile, following his hand as it smooths down baby hairs. She pointedly stares past him at the abandoned bottles waiting in the back of the clinic. The doctor jumps into action as Emma drops onto the desktop and silences the ringing phone. "Tell me again how you got into medicine?"

"Medicine is proven. We can *see* the effects of drugs and monitor the reactions they have with other materials and the human body." Carter scoffs, dropping the bottles into their respective bags. He tosses them to her, emptying his drink, as Emma checks the dosage and request forms. "Most importantly, it can be recreated."

"And the moon landing can't," Emma echoes, listening to the first voicemail as she pushes the pills into their time slot. A congested woman relays monotone information on the line, pausing to cough, as Emma opens the healthcare system's website. Typing in her practitioner ID, she takes down the information needed, sends the request for evaluation to Dr. Pepper, and deletes the voicemail.

"See, now you understand."

Her laugh makes no sound as she smiles regretfully at him. Screams sound on the phone as a man struggles to pronounce *methylphenidate*. The call ends prematurely but she keys in the request and deletes his voicemail.

"Have you been giving yourself overtime?"

"I am here anyway," Emma dismisses, scratching the back of her ear. Technically, they aren't on duty until 6:30 but she prefers to be organized and ready for the doors to open. Helps minimize the morning rush... although no one should be up at six in the morning in the first place, particularly on a Saturday.

"I will make a believer of you yet," Carter declares,

restocking what Mina and Dr. Pepper did not last night. He collects a pile of boxes and ends up buried underneath them as his foot catches on a rug.

"You are not a believer Car; you are a questioner."

"Is that a bad thing?"

"Definitely not, but there are many things I believe you do not," Emma counters, deleting the next message. Listening with half an ear to the person complaining about the rash in their nether regions, she watches Carter unearth himself. Knowing her best friend means staying clear of the warzone or they'll end up on the ground making 'pill angels' while ailing people wait at the door. "And I am not going to revoke those beliefs because of RedPanda69—who is probably a fourteen-year-old boy spending all his time in his family's basement and laughing every time he sees his username because it's a sex joke."

"Nineteen sixty-nine was the first moon landing, MaMa." An empty box flutters close to her head in time with his admonishment. "Pervert."

Emma gapes, twisting in the chair to defend herself. 'Dr. Friesen' hides his smile poorly, running away with arms full of empty boxes, as she tosses the one used as his weapon into the recycling.

VACANCIES IN TIME

"No way!" Carter exclaims, tripping over her feet to get back to his place at their little patio table. He drops into his chair, phone in hand, eyes glued to the screen. Even the sun, returning in a beautiful but fleeting moment, cannot draw Carter's eyes from the device.

Emma picks at her salad, less than enthused, as she watches his pupils dilate. His hair glows like a halo around his head in the discreet rays, drawing the attention of a nearby table. A young woman leans back to see Car around her friend, freckled face flushing when Emma catches her. *Please talk to him, catch his attention while you still can*, she tries to relay with a warm smile.

Unsuccessful in catching the embarrassed girl's eye, Emma grabs her bottled drink and begins to shake it vigorously. The pupil dilation, bated breath, little giggles... Carter hit the jackpot. She crosses one leg over the other, trying to get comfortable in the aesthetic little seat. "Do you know who Lieutenant Robert Smith is?"

She stares at him, twisting off the lid of her drink as his eyes snap up to meet hers. The answer is plainly written on her face. As much as she'd love to share in his excitement, she cannot imagine who he's talking about. "Have you told me about him before?"

"He was the war prisoner from the 1800s, the one who was caught on photo and looks like that old actor, Nicolas

Cage."

A memory tugs at her. It's hard to keep track of his theories sometimes, binders or no. "I remember hearing something about Nicolas Cage being a vampire and Bruce Willis being a commander from the American Civil War—"

"World War II."

"My apologies," Emma chuckles, sipping at her juice. Carter excitedly scrolls through his phone, blue eyes moving faster than ever. Even her interest is piqued as the silence stretches. "Carter?"

"Right, sorry," he apologizes, shifting his metal chair closer to her. It grinds over the wet cement, drawing attention to their table. Emma pretends not to notice the peering eyes as she leans over to see his phone. "See that?"

"The grainy picture of someone walking down a street?" Emma asks, sucking in her lips at his unimpressed expression. It *is* a grainy picture of someone walking down the street. Carter's trained eye may see more but she's struggling to differentiate the person from the sidewalk. "How about you tell me what I am supposed to be seeing?"

"That's Benito Mussolini!"

"Or it's a bald man with poor posture," Emma quips, trying to smother her smile in her hand. He narrows his eyes on her, holding the phone expectantly.

"Open your eyes."

"Yes, of course."

She stares at the phone, still unconvinced of what she is supposed to see. The man faintly resembles the Italian dictator. Moe, an English Major with a minor in history, pinned pictures of different dictators on her office walls at home and created posters for her university classroom with puns and famous quotes. She taught a class once alongside a renowned sociologist about the personality types of dictators and why they became so popular for a time. After listening to her practice her lectures in the mirror for months on end, Emma knows more than her fair share about absolutist regimes and their leaders.

"It does look like him," Emma relents, keeping her mouth in a firm line as mirth fills her eyes. Carter flicks her curls playfully as he harrumphs. He enjoys spiraling. Enjoys the thrill of pulling apart existence. Some people have the time and energy for it. Emma prefers the comfort of a familiar world. One without complications and unanswerable questions.

Her adventures come from storybooks. He tries to make them reality.

"Exactly like him!" Carter cries, throwing himself back into the hipster seat. He nearly hits a waitress who apologizes as she slides right past. "Oops, sorry."

"You know, now that you mention it… no, that's crazy." She whispers to herself, playing with one of her layered gold necklaces. The owl. Expanded wings, caught in mid-flight. Her fingernails catch in the miniscule cuts used to define its feathers. Carter watches the movement briefly before he clears his throat and leans forward expectantly. Unused to being the one with something exciting to say, she plays with her braid and shrugs.

"What?"

"I am telling you it is impossible, Car."

"Dude, it's just you and me. Come on!"

"Okay. Last night, I was walking back from the library. And I saw this person and they... looked like Hitler." Carter's eyebrows shoot up in shock as Emma presses her lips together. His hands shake excitedly around the phone. As she takes another sip from her juice, he begins typing on it. Probably uploading the sighting to the conspiracy thread or messaging RedPanda69. He stops when he notices the curve to the side of her lips. "He did look like Hitler."

"You are messing with me."

"The guy looked a little bit like the awful German dictator. That is punishment enough without the added suspicion of people on the internet." Emma laughs, forcing herself to eat some of the salad she ordered. Try as she might, there is nothing interesting about leafy greens. No matter the dressing used to disguise them. "He probably got bullied in school Car—"

"If he attended school in this time period."

"I suppose," Emma muses, grateful when he offers his plate of fries to her. Moe's voice plagues her mind. Reminding her to eat every food in the pyramid. Potato = vegetable. The more French fries she eats, the happier her mother. "How is one supposed to deal with that? Say for instance, dictators *are* reincarnating."

Carter pauses, uncertain of how to answer the question. This is what she brings to the friendship. Little questions to spark the creativity in his mind. Emma grabs one last pinchful of fries, resolving herself to the salad she ordered. Back home a bag of chips and a case of blueberries call her name. "We should go looking for them."

"The post said he was seen in Seattle," she points out, eyebrows drawing together. "We do not have the time for a road trip."

"The library, then. Tomorrow." Carter declares, grinning proudly. He puts his phone down, turning to face her fully. "The dream team back together? We can find them all in a week."

"Can't... it's Sunday. Church, dinner at my parent's house. Dad is barbequing." She answers, although the idea holds merit. While she is fully aware there are no dictators to find, spending time with Carter guarantees fun. Despite their different personalities, she and Carter get along as effortlessly as her and Moses. "Every Sunday. You know how it works."

Eyes rolling, he watches the streets. As if he expects Vladimir Lenin to walk out with a gang of devoted disciples following him. "I am more exciting than church or a barbeque.

Stop being boring. Live a little."

"Burgers," she begins, raising one hand. "Dictators."

She raises the other one, weighing them against each other. He follows the motion with obvious interest. He must know which one she is going to choose. Too many Saturdays are filled with the same debate. Though it is not always dictators. Sometimes it is vampires, or old queens, or trolls—that was an especially interesting evening.

Lifting the burger hand, she shrugs apologetically. "Dad's burgers win every single time."

"Burgers? Burgers! Where is your sense of adventure Emma!?" Carter demands, his eyebrows shooting into his hairline. When he slaps the table, others stop to watch. Emma smiles when he unapologetically drains his cup of water and slams it onto the precariously balanced glass table. "His burgers have nothing on—"

"My definition of adventure is different than yours, Car. Hiking, exploring a waterfall, going horseback riding, skydiving, all of them adventures. Trying to track down dictators in 2050? Not my idea of adventure." Emma responds quietly, grateful when he hands her another fry. He would not notice, or care, if she cleaned the entire plate.

"You are one of the most boring people I know."

Laughing, Emma forks a pile of leaves into her mouth. Behind her poker face, a tiny bolt of hurt shoots through her body. Boring? Life feels a little boring. To the point she cannot watch her favourite comfort movies without feeling tired. Going to the library. Taking out books. She didn't take the time to consider thinking less of her simple life, but Carter reminds her constantly of everything waiting outside the mundane.

"I wish I could be as excited as you."

"You need to open your mind to the possibilities."

"I am a realist, Carter. An optimist when I allow myself to be." She explains with muted pain. Keeping herself neutral and light, she finishes off the fries at his invitation.

CHAPTER 3: SHEEP FARMING IN ITALY

Emma yanks the front of her motorbike up, shooting over the driveway to her parent's house. Trees flank either side of her, leading her home. All her stress melts away when she sees the white building peeking out from the trees. Her bike stutters over the brick laden driveway, shying in comparison to the shiny cars tucked into the three-car garage.

Moses' truck hides by the side of the house—knowing Moe, she wanted the dirt-covered thing to stay far away from the house's white wooden exterior. Emma's motorcycle, covered in dirt thanks to the country road, fits nicely beside the large vehicle.

Laughter trickles in from the backyard, distinctly feminine. *The twins.* Even the sound of her sibling's laughter manages to soothe the anxiety carried over from yesterday. She's been sensitive her entire life, but Carter's words struck a chord. The taunt of being 'boring' followed her through every attempt at distraction. Emma gave up trying to make cue cards when she ended up writing boring instead of *bortezomib*.

Removing her helmet, and the frustrating thoughts from her mind, she cuts the engine. Her legs burn as she slides off the bike, punishing her for taking the scenic route. The faster road is paved, well-kept, and better on her tires and body.

It cannot compare to the sights of the countryside.

Storing the helmet away in the bikes front hump, Emma collects her hair and throws it into a high ponytail. Her nails and rings catch on the hairspray used to preserve the curls she put in for church. With the fight done and her scalp smarting, she tugs out a couple pieces to frame her face. They stick to the sweat on her brow.

Grey clouds hide the high humidity and heat clinging to greater city. Unzipping the leather body suit gives her brief relief from the sticky feeling. She rolls it into a bundle and pushes it into her trunk as a breeze rips newly sprouting leaves off the tree in front of her.

A scream sounds from the backyard, followed by a shouting match as Emma shakes her head fondly. Removing the skirts of her dress from between her legs, she grabs the large watermelon from the back of her motorcycle. Seeing as the surface of the fruit is more brown than green, the plastic bag she used for protection failed in its purpose.

Holding the oblong fruit as far away from her satin dress as possible, she makes her way to the front door. Moe's *International Women's Day* decorations cling to the black front door. Prominent women from history stare at Emma as she struggles to open the door while keeping the watermelon away from her front. She tries her best not to look Queen Elizabeth II in the eye when she stumbles through the door.

"Honey, I'm home!" Emma calls as she kicks the door closed behind her. No one calls back to her, likely too busy with the shouting match happening outside. As she struggles to find a place to put the watermelon, she trips over a pair of shoes. The front landing is a minefield of boots and shoes. With the season's shifting, Winter must cycle in her season appropriate retire. Unfortunately, this leaves a weeklong period four times a year where the house becomes hazardous.

Dropping the watermelon onto the top row of muddy work boots lined by the door, she fights with the zipper on her heeled boots. Something crashes in the house. "Are you okay?"

"In here," her Mom calls back, the sound of clatter in the kitchen drawing her attention. Emma shoves her muddy boots beside her Dad and Moses', dragging the hoarding twin's own shoes into place. She takes a moment to adjust her dress in the mirror hanging on the coat closet doors before grabbing the watermelon again. "You found the biggest one, *ja*?"

"As instructed," Emma responds with a grin, sliding into the kitchen. She carefully rolls the watermelon into the sink as Moe murmurs something more in Dutch. The black turtleneck she layered underneath her dress did not survive the encounter. Streaks of faded dirt run up her arms and chest. Most of them disappear as she rolls the sleeves up. Removing a couple rings from her fingers, she pushes them onto the marble hand sticking up beside the faucet. "It got a little messy on the road."

"*Je hebt een auto nodig,*" Moe remarks underneath her

breath, tossing her salad. Emma pretends not to hear, grabbing a *doekie*. Rubbing the watermelon with the cloth, she rinses it and walks briskly over to the cabinet filled with kitchen linens. "*Iets veiligers dan dat* death machine."

"I like my death machine."

"You cannot come visit in the winter," Moe counters, though she is careful to keep her tone light and considerate. "We do not see you enough when it snows."

"I spent two weeks here for Christmas, Moe. The motorcycle and snow are not the only things keeping me in the city—"

"You could have stayed here to finish school," Moe argues, turning to stare at Emma as she puts the tongs down. Frustration claws at the nape of her neck. How many times can they have this same argument?

Moe crosses her arms, leaning one ample hip against the counter, and waits in tense silence for Emma to meet her eyes. *Honour your mother. Honour your mother.* She drags her eyes from the watermelon to meet her mother's. Both shine the same green colour, shaped with the same pinch on the inside and wing on the out. The similarities end with the emotions welling behind their soul's windows.

Silent pleading bleeds from Moe's. Exhaustion from Emma's.

"We did not want you to leave, we did not expect you to," Moe insists quietly, reaching for Emma across the kitchen. She reluctantly steps around the island, squeezing her Mom's hand affectionately. "You can come home."

Despite her desire to please her mother and the hatred of confrontation twisting through her stomach, Emma shakes her head. Neither give an inch in these arguments. Her natural serenity hides the stubbornness so natural to the Dutch.

"I know Moe and I appreciate your consideration, but I am an adult. Baby birds don't learn to fly by staying in the nest." Emma states, finding a butcher knife. Moe watches her make the first cut, scrutinizing the action. There is nothing quite as nerve-wracking as your mother watching you cut fruit like she expects you to chop off your hand. "I am twenty-years-old."

"Practically a baby."

"You got married the moment you turned eighteen." Trying to inject playfulness in her tone, Emma smiles up at Moe. A wistfulness enters the woman's eyes. "You left Holland on your own at sixteen."

Her mother shared so little about Holland in the twenty years of Emma's life, leaving a distinct impression not to ask about it. Oma, her grandmother, hurt Moe. She cannot explain when or how or why but Moe fled the Netherlands to escape her family. While the deVries kids stay in contact with their grandparents, the mention of Moe and her teenage escape to Canada remains forcibly forgotten.

One thing Emma knows and will never forget is Moe felt

unprotected and alone. Naturally, she found the largest, strongest, most stable man available and clung to him as soon as she had the chance. She and Daniel deVries within months, and Daniel took his wife's name because his parents didn't 'deserve a continued bloodline'.

No one mentions them either.

"And? I am trying to make it better for you. So you do not need *te rennen* en *het gevoel* te *hebben dat je* fend for yourself *moet*."

Moe's voice drops as her desperation reaches its pinnacle. She pinches at the bridge of her nose as if she can force the pressure away. The action pulls Emma forward, compelling her to take her mother's hand.

"I know. I know you want to protect me and give me the life you couldn't have. *Ik heb uw liefd* and I appreciate everything you do for me. I'm not being stubborn as a punishment." Emma squeezes Moe's hand in emphasis, hoping the words will find their way to a permanent home. Moe and Dad weren't this controlling at first, but their lives predisposed them to fear. Fear when triggered bred control and control bred children who need an escape. Like Cody. "The world is dying, Mom. I walk where I can but the bike puts out less emissions, it uses less materials, and it is *goedkoop.*"

"*Pah*," Moe dismisses, waving a hand by her shoulder. Collecting the condiments for the barbeque, she pins Emma with an all-too-familiar look. "I care more about saving my daughter than the world."

"And it is that kind of mindset that gets it into trouble in the first place," Emma counters, smiling as she brushes a strand of hair behind her ear. She recognizes her mistake when Moe's lips pucker. A disapproving noise rattles up her mother's throat as Emma flushes. "I did get another piercing—"

"I can see that," Moe says, clicking her tongue. She begins to wash the corn for the evening, her expression failing to conceal distaste. It is Emma's least favourite expression. Her mom knows not to nag (too much) and tries her best to keep quiet on matters that "are not a threat to *mijn schatjes*". Except the expression of "not trying to nag" resembles a baby's face the first time it tries a lemon.

"Moe."

"I didn't say anything."

Emma forces her sigh back down, not wishing to rehash another age-old argument. The sound of her blade cutting through the watermelon and meeting the wooden cutting board showcases her frustration well enough.

Growing up in the Dutch Orthodox church poisoned her brilliant mother. Five years into their marriage, Emma's father decided he could not attend the church anymore. Every gathering they made mention to his lack of shared ancestry and attempted to pry the newlyweds apart. Then Henny met a Pentecostal preacher at a charity drive hosted by her university, and the Holy Spirit found its way into her stone heart.

Despite the freedom God gives, the routine and 'rules' were forced into her mind from childhood. Her dad prevented Emma, and the other children, from being born into the same doctrine. Shallow 'relationship' filled with legalism, law, and devoid of any true experience. In Moe's mind, tattoos, piercings, even the dress Emma wears (despite the turtleneck and nylons), and the motorcycle are all symptoms of a greater problem. The disease of the world. The sin of secularism.

Imagining Moe's reaction to the new tattoo on Emma's left wrist causes her to tug her sleeves down. Her mother looks up from her collection of bottles, eyebrow raising. She is not ashamed... only aware of how the family matriarch will react. A new piercing is one thing. A new piercing and a new tattoo? A tattoo with a *snake*?

No need to bring unnecessary strife to Sunday family dinners.

"Do you want these on a tray?" Emma inquires, pausing when the weight of Moe's stare falls on her arms. She opens the cabinet of serving trays, pushing back on the guilt threatening to spill over. *It is honouring to know she is not in a place to see this tattoo... right?* As an image of God laughing from above flashes through her mind, her mother's gaze snags on an older tattoo. She got the cross on her 18th birthday, right at the base of her thumb. The two orange tulips on the back of her left arm were her 19th birthday present. Moses joined her in January, a couple weeks after her 20th birthday, to get his first tattoo while she got the RX symbol on her wrist. The snake curled around a bowl stares into the soul with one green eye and one red. "Or would a plate be better?"

"A tray will be fine," Moe answers, eyes snapping away from Emma. By the time Emma chooses one and turns around, her mother is standing within an inch of her. Their eyes lock as Moe takes the tray. She zips back to the condiments, murmuring to them in Dutch. While Emma manages to catch a couple words, she chooses to go to the back door and pull on a pair of Winter's boots. Better to feign ignorance than argue. "Are you going to get more?"

"Maybe." Did Winter's feet get smaller or Emma's bigger? She shifts in the boots, debating whether to remove her wool socks. The warmth may not be needed with the humidity. "We will have to see."

"Please no nose things. I raised a young lady, not a *stier*."

Emma withholds her laugh, reaching to grab the filled tray. Once she steps outside into the meek sun, she chuckles. Better to laugh than be annoyed. Who can be annoyed on such a beautiful day? She closes her eyes to bask in the muted warmth and listen to the sound of the creek. A scream ruins the otherwise peaceful environment.

Oliver, her closest younger brother, wheels away from Summer, left by the bank of the creek, as she begins to throw mud at him. "Hey! You know what Moe says about ruining our Sunday best."

"I wouldn't worry about your clothes, son," her dad shouts, grinning from his place beside the grill. Oliver, facing Summer, misses her twin sneaking up behind him in the bushes.

"No mercy for your own son." Emma and her father grin at each other as the scream comes from Oliver this time. With one twin on his back, smearing mud into his face, and the other launching for his feet, Oliver needs all the help he can get.

"My Emmy," her dad murmurs warmly, opening his arms widely. Emma places the tray onto one of the counters and walks happily into his embrace. Pressing a kiss to the top of her head, he crushes her close with one arm, as the other keeps his greasy metal spatula away from her. "You look beautiful sweetie."

"Thank you." He leans down for a kiss and smiles as she loudly drops one on his cheek. Joseph, her youngest brother, appears from the brush in a surprise counterattack against the girls. They all disappear down the bank. "What started them off this time?"

"No clue," he shrugs, laughing as she does. "Want a sip?"

Her dad likes craft beer. The fancy kind where they do not sell it in liquor stores. Moses enjoys the brew well enough but none of the three other adult children can stomach it. "No, thank you. I drove here."

"You know you can stay over," Dad offers, facing her as she makes her way over to Moses. He salutes her with his mug of hot chocolate and a knowing look. Taking the seat at his side, she accepts a sip from his drink. "We've got an air mattress and your room is sitting here waiting—"

"I have obligations back home."

Obligations to that adaptation of Shakespeare's play she borrowed from the library. Try as she might, classical literature doesn't hold a candle to nerdy fantasy stories anymore. She grew out of the classical literature phase after the brief obsession in high school.

… There is also the stack of schoolwork needing to be finished. Half-completed cue cards, a blank outline for an essay, but can any of this compete with mind-numbing tv and daydreams of a handsome man coming to whisk you off to an incredible adventure?

Boring. She forgot to toss away the offending slip of paper last night. The first order of business when she gets home is ripping the card and throwing it in the trash. Emma chides herself as her younger siblings return from the forest laughing and covered in mud. Carter would never say something to hurt her.

"Motorcycles are dangerous enough without alcohol," Moe remarks, stepping outside. She clucks her tongue, tossing a glare over her shoulder as she places watermelon in front of Emma and Moses. "I cannot believe you offered her *beer*."

He laughs sheepishly, pretending it's a cough when Moe levels him with a proper glower. "You must have worn the cat suit. I hope you didn't ride in that dress."

"You will catch a chill—"

"I wore the suit," Emma assures, glancing between the two of them. Playing off each other's concern leads to smothering and the humidity already presses on her chest. She glances at Moses helplessly, shifting a fraction away from her parent's. Shrugging, he offers her another sip of his hot chocolate. Their eyes hold as Moe and Dad continue in their lecture. A smile teases her lips as Moses rubs his thumb over the dimple in his cheek. "How's it going?"

"It goes," he answers, shivering when the clouds cover the sun. The cold wind comes with a vengeance, drawling a squeal from Winter. She rushes towards the house to change as Moses hands Emma his mug. With free hands, he throws the end of his large flannel blanket over her covered legs. His body heat seeps into her legs, showing her how cold she was. The early March weather never fails to remind Canadians Spring has not *yet* come. "How about you?"

Emma hands him the mug back, trying not to laugh at the way he curls around the heat. His long fingers clutch the green porcelain like a gremlin with its treasure. "Always going."

"Amen." He rests the hot mug against his chest, relaxing back into the chair as she plays with her newest piercing. She got the daith piercing as a Christmas present to herself. After a long year in school and working at the clinic, she deserved a reward. Though the gift scandalized Moe.

Moses' phone vibrates on the table, showing a wall of unanswered texts and neglected notifications. Grabbing the device from the table, she holds it up to him with feigned disappointment, one long nail pointing at the text from **Pea Two.** "You didn't even read my text."

"I saw it... I just lost track of time with building our next campaign. You know the duties of a DM are never-ending." Moses laughs, tugging on one of my curls as I toss the phone into his lap. *Brothers.* "Did you expect me to respond?"

"Expect? No. Hope? Yes."

"I'm not the worst brother." Moses closes his eyes as if to stop himself from seeing Emma's reaction to the blow. She keeps it contained behind a frail nonchalance. "Sorry."

"Cody's has his own life now. No worst or best, we all have different lives. Different paths." Emma shrugs, playing with the new piercing and getting a shot of pain for it. Part of her rationale for moving out included an insight into Cody's thought process. What appeal does an empty apartment in a busy city have to a house filled with laughter and love? Two years later and still clueless. Though sometimes the small, empty apartment is better than the poking and prodding of Moe and her accomplices. "Have you heard from him?"

"I got a 'can you tell Mom to send me the care package to my new apartment'?" Their combined efforts at appearing unaffected fail when their eyes briefly meet. Emma pulls at her bare hands, wondering if she should run inside to get her rings, and wipe the moisture from her eyes. Moses squints into the sun as the younger siblings return in varying degrees of dressed. For the first time, Emma notices the absence of the youngest deVries.

Panic shoots up her spine straight from her stomach. It grabs at her heart from behind in an iron grip. Breathing through the knot, she inhales steadily. Avery is probably playing upstairs on the computer. She likes games as much as Moses, if not more.

"I can suggest he make you the messenger?" Moses offers, a muscle in his jaw ticking. He picks at the callous' on his hand as Moe returns from the house to finish the last touches on the table set.

"That would be inefficient," Emma counters, smiling apologetically at the rare flare of irritation in Moses' green eyes. Little touches the gentle giant, but people who use other people ruffles his feathers. Especially when it involves his older, less considerate, brother. "I do not live at home anymore."

"I am working on it," Moses confesses, almost like an afterthought, as he picks up his mug. She holds back what might be a shout of surprise or joy. He showed no interest in moving out when she last suggested it. Moe made jokes about him being the one who lived in the basement for the rest of his life. The one who will take care of them in their old age. "Like a tree planted by the water", Moe liked to joke, making sure to affectionately tug his ear or ruffle his golden curls. She admires Moses' stability and calm demeanour, so similar to her husband's, but often fails to see the ox in him. Moses is the kind of man to build his own path, even if it means using his bare hands and working them to the bone.

"We could live together," Emma proposes excitedly, images of a townhouse filled with computer equipment and books playing through her mind. Although... Moses works in their father's company and as a senior member on the team must be nearby in case of a power outage or other emergency. "Somewhere close but not too close."

"About that—"

"Oh, you're not a new guy," Summer whines, coming to the deck out of breath. Flopping into the seat across from Moses, she flips her dark blonde hair over her shoulder. "I thought you finally brought a man home, Em."

"Just a watermelon," Emma responds with a tempered smile on her face. Her older brother snickers to himself, sipping at the last dredges of his hot chocolate. For reasons she cannot figure out, they never bother *him* about his prospects. Or Oliver, the newest deVries adult, for that matter. He breezes past the table with a smile reserved for his father, stopping to stand beside him with his chest puffed out. Newly eighteen and past six feet tall, he's beginning to tower over Dad. All of them are tall, even Joseph at fourteen is taller than Emma's 5 foot and 9 inches. "You better watch out Dad. You're going to end up being the shortest deVries man."

"Because he is not deVries by blood," Moe points out, wrapping her shawl tightly around her shoulders. She glares up at the sky as if trying to scare the grey clouds away. "No Dutch blood runs in his veins."

"What do you mean? I get taller every day." Dad assures, elbowing his youngest sons when they try to stand over him. Both end up doubled over as he smirks. "See?"

"Like magic," Winter murmurs sarcastically, sitting beside Emma. She smiles grateful when Emma extends a bit of blanket to her.

Joseph and Oliver share one wicked look before spinning with fists raised to face Dad. Armed with a barbeque covered spatula, Daniel deVries fearlessly fends off the fiends. Gloop comes flying off the metal utensil, falling short of the table, but nothing stops Summer from squealing in worry. Moe tends to her and marches towards the boys with a barely restrained smile. "When *did* they get so big?"

"Don't get too sad," Moses murmurs, watching Summer leap to the other side of the table to cower against her twin. "They are still young... and dumb."

"Not ready for Oliver to join the taskforce?"

"Oh, I was ready... before Dad told me I would be the one training him." Moses sighs, brushing his hands through the short curls. They stretch between his grip but bounce back into place at their release. How nice it must be to have obedient hair. Poor Moses' distress doubles when Oliver sends their father careening towards the grill. "He will electrocute me and laugh about it."

"I am sure he would not laugh… if you get seriously injured."

"What a comfort," Moses murmurs, picking at a chip in his empty mug. He stops the moment Moe notices the imperfection from her spot lecturing the boys on fire safety. Before he can hide it, she snatches the mug and disappears inside. "You're old too, kid."

"I feel like I have been old since I was born."

"Don't let yourself get old. It's all a mindset." Moses promises, watching the group of men laughing. Moe comes out again and with a single snap of her tongs, summons the lanky boys away from the grill. One look is enough to calm their hyper father. "How's the good doctor?"

"Embracing the forever young mindset," Emma answers, curling her feet underneath her. Another gust of wind pulls goosebumps to the surface. Winter burrows into her side in a murmured conversation with Summer. "He invited me to go hunt reincarnated dictators today."

"You manage to find the weirdest people to hang out with."

"Says the man who wanted to get into LARPing."

"I still would... I just don't have the time with Dnd and work and obligations to my guild." Moses laughs, shaking his head as the sides of his eyes crinkle. Emma's do the same as she smiles back. "I am one of the weirdos. Yet, you are one of the least weird people I know."

"Is that your way of saying I am boring?" Emma inquires conversationally, though she knows he can see the emotion disguised by her light voice. They have no secrets. It is impossible to have them when you are two peas in a pod as their dad used to call them. *Why do I want to be interesting?* Emma clears her throat, rubbing her cross tattoo. Old insecurities. It's hard to face tragedy when the others your age think the world limitless and filled with endless happiness. "Carter says I am boring."

"Carter believes aliens walk among us." Moses scoffs kindly, the dimple in his cheek deeper in the new sun peeking out. "You did say he invited you to hunt dead dictators today."

Oliver and Joseph take a seat at the table, momentarily still before Joseph cannot stop himself from pulling one of Summer's boots off. She attempts to kick him and they interrupt in a light arguing match. All of this witnessed by their parents standing in the outdoor kitchenette. Yet, neither of them say anything. A serene smile replaces Moe's normal expression of discontent as she leans over and kisses her husband.

"All I am saying is his opinion may not be valid."

"He is one of the smartest people I know. I don't exactly lead a life of intrigue." Where is Avery? The thought tugs at her mind as she scans the deck and then the backyard. She shifts in her seat, careful not to disrupt Winter, as she looks at the windows facing the backyard. Her bedroom light is not on. "I would probably be an easy target for a serial killer."

"Boring people don't know that."

Emma smiles gratefully, ready to ask where Avery is when Summer interrupts, "are we talking about Dr. Yummy?"

Somehow the sixteen-year-old says the nickname shamelessly whenever Carter comes up in family conversation. Moe, Dad, and Emma have on different occasions told/asked her to stop but she doesn't care. She shuffles closer, stealing part of the blanket and exposing both Moses and Emma to a temporary flush of cold air. They squeal at the same time.

"Has he asked you out yet?" Summer continues, sitting on Winter's lap. She ignores Joseph as he delves into a teasing song about her obsession with Emma's best friend. "The only reason I'd join medical school is to meet a cute doctor."

God forbid. "Carter doesn't love Jesus, Summer. And while he is not technically my boss, his name is partially on the clinic." Emma points out, trying to imagine a life romantically involved with Carter. It is not disgust but the feeling of something being wildly wrong that makes her shiver. Or perhaps the cold air Summer rudely let into their warm cocoon. "He is my friend and that is all he will be."

Both by his admission and her own. The discussion about feelings could have been mortifying if Carter didn't outright exclaim randomly, during a shift, that he "thought of her like a stray cat". Neither knew where to go from there so they laughed.

"What about another guy?" Summer prods, grinning broadly. "Maybe that's why you moved out. Any other doctors?"

"Yes Summer, I have a secret doctor hidden in Italy. Once I leave here, I am running right into his arms and we are going to raise sheep together." Emma describes, closing her eyes as if living in a dream. Her voice takes on a soft, romantic lilt. "Never to return to Canada. When we eventually have children, they will ride the sheep and each will be named Ewen."

Winter chortles, leaning against Moses. He rubs her mess of locks with a smile on his face. "Summer Beatrix deVries," Moe snaps, elbowing her way between the boys to put food on the table. "Armrests are not for butts and old men are not for young girls. Find a proper seat or I will."

As she hurries to return to her previous spot, Joseph and Oliver help Moe with the food. Their father brings the plate of burger patties and the family begins to settle around the table. Grace is second nature to them as heads drop and eyes closed before Dad commands it. Then Moe lifts her head with a smile. "Supper is served."

Without Avery? Emma tries to get Moses' attention but his pupils dilate as they land on the corn. He and Oliver duel silently for a particularly roasted piece. "Momo—"

"You know Emma, Lorraine from church has a grandson your age. Andreas. He is a plumbing apprentice—"

"And Dutch?" Oliver asks, smirking at Emma. He sits in the chair directly across from her, wearing the same goofy grin Cody mastered when they were kids. Something aches in her chest. Avery is not the only one missing from this table. "Emma wants a good boy from the motherland."

"Moe wants a good boy from the motherland for Emma," Dad corrects, pressing a kiss to his wife's head as he brings a patty to her plate. She mutters something in her first language, rolling her eyes to emphasize her displeasure. "No boy is good enough for my girl."

"All I am saying is that you only have so much time, *liefje*," Moe remarks innocently, beginning to dress her burger when she sees the juice pitcher sitting on the kitchen counter through the window. Moses stands up to grab it but she's already out of her seat and rushing back into the house.

Andreas. Emma's nose scrunches at the thought as she meets her brother's eyes. They share a look again, using their best form of communication: silence. It is important to be discreet in matters of a sensitive nature, especially with Summer, the nosiest sibling, sitting in front of them. Luckily, her interest gravitates more towards her phone than the conversation she started.

"You are not getting any younger." When did she get there? Moses chokes on his laughter as Emma jumps from the nearness of her scolding. Their father chuckles with him, dishing out some coleslaw before passing it down to Joseph. "You too, Moses. Emma's very active in her church and puts in the effort to meet new people."

"Great points, Moe. I will get right on that." Emma promises, sharing a covert smile with Moses. The two of them know this routine well enough.

"And by 'that' she means a man," Summer jokes, laughing even when Moe gasps. Summer's amusement ends the moment her mother begins in a stream of Dutch so fast and think even Emma cannot understand a word. Dad nods his head in agreement for his wife's sake, expression serious. It begins to crack when Joseph and Oliver snicker and someone snorts like a pig.

Normally this is where Avery says something like 'Moe we all know the end result of your matchmaking' and because she is Avery no one does anything but laugh. The girl could commit murder and maintain her innocence through sheer charm and wit. "Where is Riri?"

At first no one appears to hear. Moe gives Dad a look and suddenly he is telling the boys to stop laughing and telling Summer about how inappropriate the comment was. Winter pulls out her phone and scrolls through it under the table. It is

Moses who finally leaves over and says, "Dad said something about how she couldn't get famous off streaming her sandbox games… Last I saw her she was stomping up the stairs crying about how no one in this family understands her. Typical teenage girl stuff."

"But not typical Avery stuff."

"She is basically a teenager now. Or so she insists."

"No one has checked on her since?" Emma questions, shaking her head when he shrugs. Pushing away from the table, she gives her warmed blanket to Winter, and marches inside.

CHAPTER 4: RATS NOT WELCOME

Emma's parents never wanted pets but after Avery came home and asked for a ferret, they could not think of a reason to say no. Now her room smells like animal poop and sawdust. Clear tubes run over the length of her ceiling, multiple exits leading onto the ground and wooden shelves for her furry friend. Her bed, bigger than Emma's queen, sits on top of a raised platform with a net secured to ceiling above it. No one else shared concerns about the falling poop risk.

Chocolate, her aptly named brown and yellow ferret, greets Emma with a little chitter. He watches her from one of the tubes with beady black eyes. She forces herself to smile though the rodent does not appreciate it—not rodent, "weasel" according to Riri.

Fairy lights surround Avery's bed, casting light onto the lilac walls so they glow. Her main lights are not on, but one does glow from underneath her bed in the reading nook built into the wooden base. Mirrors reflect Emma from the South Wall, surrounded by the closet doors. Photos with lights hang around the doors and mirrors. Hundreds of polaroids of her friends, soccer teams through the years, and even schoolmates. Emma's favourite one, a picture of all the siblings the Christmas before Cody left and after the worst year of their lives, creates a center to the web.

The ferret launches himself from a platform onto Avery's bed, running down the short stairs built against the wall. Shelves filled with her books cover the walls beside her bed and the staircase. Her line of bookcases morph into a desk covered in paper and little trinkets. Beside it, a large video game creature stands, green against the rest of her delicate, flowery room.

Emma jumps away from Chocolate as he scurries around her socked feet. He snickers to himself, disappearing into a wooden hut.

Why a ferret? Why not a fluffy cat? Emma keeps her eyes on her feet as she ventures further into the room. Avery is nowhere to be seen. Not at her desk with its powered down gaming system, or daydreaming in her closet, where Emma can see the outfits she's keeping for her award shows. One of the dresses is probably bigger than Avery will ever be but she saw it in a thrift store and announced she'd walk the red carpet in it one day. No one dared to challenge her.

Little *scratching* sounds come from the darkest corner of the room. The ferret peeks his head out, eyes reflective in the low light of the bed. One moment Chocolate perches on his net and the next, he launches. Throwing her arms out, she drops. The 'weasel' collides with Avery's bed instead of her, chittering unhappily. "Your rat tried to attack me!"

"He's not a rat."

The little voice comes out muffled as if in a different

room. Emma spares one last glare at Chocolate, to ensure he knows what she thinks of him, before wandering away from the bed.

"He's a long rat," Emma counters with veiled amusement. Lips twitching, she waits for a response, but none comes. Running her fingers lightly over the soccer posters stretched across Avery's free wall, she reaches her closet. The half-packed suitcase vomits clothes onto the white carpet. A dangerous choice with a long, destructive rat. "I wonder where she could be? Do you know Chocolate?"

Avery snickers, her voice almost stolen by the wooden confines of the reading nook. Crouching beside the suitcase, Emma pushes around the different items. Toiletries. Pajamas. Five books. A picture of their parents with Dad's face bent away. Scratching her ear around the golden hoops, she stands slowly.

"You know, I wanted to be a spy when I was younger," Emma declares, reaching the platform of her little sister's bed and the gated entrance into her reading nook beneath it. Sliding slowly down the surface, she gathers her legs to her chest. Chocolate sniffs her fingers as she plays with her hoop earrings. The feeling of his little whiskers against her ear elicits a shiver. "At recess I would run off into the trees and practice my somersaults and cartwheels. I used this stick like it was a gun. I really did think I was the coolest kid at that school."

Avery laughter stops short when she hears Emma run the back of her knuckle against the closed door. She drops her hand when the silence stretches and the ferret goes back to its adventuring. Outside the family laughs loud enough to rattle the windows. Emma laughs herself. It was a silly notion. Being a spy. Yet, she truly thought she would be overseas, collecting intelligence, and bringing it back.

"Dad told me I could never be one. Canada doesn't have the same agencies." Emma explains, brushing her hair behind her ear. She leans her forehead against her arms, watching the wavering light coming from within the nook. Another minute passes. Turning slightly to face the door, she knocks, and waits for her sister to open the gate. "Riri."

"Go away."

"I can't do that. It looks like someone is planning to steal some of your clothes and your favourite book." Emma announces, injecting as much solemnity into her voice as possible under the circumstances. She plays with the end of her long-sleeved shirt, eyes narrowing on a loose thread. "I think they are trying to go on a trip to Hawai'i. Obviously, we have to fight them, and likely die in the duel... it's the only way to protect your honour."

The lock on the reading nook slides out of place with a shrill whine. Red-rimmed green eyes, so similar to hers and Moses', peek out from the golden light. Splotches choke out the freckles on Avery's sloped nose, spreading all the way down to her exposed neck. Snot creates a reflective line down from her nose. She crawls forward, dropping her head against Emma's hip, effectively hiding her beautiful face. Emma tries to fortify her aching heart to withstand the sound of Avery's sniffles. Dropping her hand into the thicket of Avery's dark hair, she begins to lightly run her nails from the crown of her head to the nape of her neck.

"I am running away."

"And where are you planning to go?" Emma inquires kindly, twirling one of the waves around her finger. Avery bursts into body-wrenching sobs.

"That's the problem."

She crawls back into the reading nook, closing the gate before Emma can stop her. Muffled sobs fill the room as Chocolate scampers over and screams at Emma. Dismissing him with a wave, she opens the door and wedges herself into it. "You're not running away, Riri."

"Yes, I am. And I am never coming back."

"You are twelve years old. Most buses will not let you on by yourself. Do you even have the cash to pay for a ticket without asking Moe or Dad?"

Avery pouts, glaring into the closet. Twisting around, she scans her audience of stuffed animals and settled on a gigantic squish. She presses her face into the furry fox, running her fingers over the ears. Lights line the top crevices of the nook. Shelves, packed full with her favourite books, explode onto her console system and small screen below. Moe and Dad built this oasis for her. A safe space for her to be excited about school and life and new experiences after her hard-fought victory.

"Are you on spring break now?"

"Yes, and I wanted to start a channel because I don't have homework but Moe and Dad won't buy me the equipment. They paid for some of your schooling and cover Cody's house and they're paying for Oliver's tools."

"It feels really unfair," Emma agrees quietly, playing with the edge of her sock. Avery nods her head, face enveloped by the orange body of the squish. "Unfair or not, you're a young girl *schatje*. You cannot run away… but you can have a sleepover at my apartment if you want."

Avery's head immediately snap up. Her eyes double in size as she wipes away her tears. "Really?"

When she had her dreams crushed, Emma just wanted someone to hold her close and tell her they believed in her. Maybe not as a spy, but to do something amazing. Avery needs someone to see her. To appreciate her. Remind her she is loved and valued. "Your rat is not welcome to come, but yes, you can come stay with me… we will have to convince Moe. We both know she doesn't like my motorcycle—or my apartment."

"I don't need to ask them," Avery counters, grinning widely. She stands, brushing away her heart back as she marches to her suitcase. Chocolate launches himself onto her shoulders, wrapping around her neck like a scarf. "They are eating food—"

"We do, because I am not starting World War Moe because you tried to sneak away on the back of my 'death machine'. They would see you missing and run us off the road." Emma assures, laughing quietly. Avery's lips purse as she stares at the window to the backyard. "So, clean yourself up. Pack the suitcase. And let's work on a convincing speech to sway Moe into letting you come to my 'sardine can'."

"Where's the puppy?" Avery asks, glancing at Trevor's empty apartment. Emma smiles at her displeasure, fighting with her keys to open the front door. It fights against her until she slams her entire body into the wooden slab. Locked or not, the door refuses to budge unless opened in a specific manner. An attribute as annoying as it is useful. Break-ins happen often in the area, but she'd congratulate anyone able to get into her apartment with the door as it is.

"Chewy is somewhere in the Rockies by now," Emma answers, removing her boots the moment she steps inside. She shoves them off to the side, hiding them underneath her hanging coats. Avery fights with her sneakers as Emma stares out the glass wall of her living room. Red and orange light flood into the room from the streets below. The fickle weather of the day depleted the streets of their walkers, leaving more lights off on the street than normal. Now pockets of a hundred colours spread out as far as the eye can see in either direction. The sight takes her breath away and puts a smile back on Avery's face. "Trevor took him on a trip for Spring Break."

"Do paramedics get Spring Break?" Avery inquires, sitting in front of the windows. She wanders into the illuminated room as Emma struggles to balance the bags in her hands and turn on the light to the kitchen.

"I don't think so... but Trevor works holidays and overtime. He is a bit of a workaholic." Emma smiles to herself as her little sister squeals and throws herself in a flip onto the bed. Her fumbling fingers finally find the light switch but it takes a second for the dingy yellow light to flicker on and fill the outdated kitchen. She drops the bags of junk food onto the counter, checking the clock. As commanded, Emma went under the speed limit on the highway and added an extra half hour to her trip. As they were heading back into the city, she glimpsed stars for the first time in months.

Pulling her phone out of her bra, she rushes back into the kitchen where her charger awaits. The battery sits at 2%, but there is a text waiting for an answer. **Did you get home safe?**

Yes. Everything is ok. We got ice cream, I'll make sure she brushes her teeth before bed. Floss and all.

Plugging her phone into the wall, Emma slides the tubs of ice cream into the empty freezer and adds the bottle of pop to the fridge. She slides out what junk food needs to be easily accessed and stacks the paper bags left behind underneath her sink.

"Pick a movie," Emma suggests, removing the tight belt holding in her dress. She grins at Avery burrowed into the pillows as she walks to the dressers lining her far wall. Removing the dress, she tosses it into her laundry basket, and grabs the matching pajama set from where it fell on the floor. Avery's full-out assault on the bag displaced it. "And get into your pjs."

"Moe said I'm finally old enough to watch you-know-what."

Emma pauses on her way to the bathroom, setting her pajamas on the sink. She retraces her steps, leaning against the wall as her arms cross. Avery expertly avoids detection as she dives into her suitcase. Her innocence routine looks the same as every other sibling. All widened eyes and croaky voices. "Did she really now?"

"I am twelve years old!" Avery argues, rolling her eyes. Her face flushes as she throws her pajamas onto the bed. "I can handle a strip tease."

"How did you know about that?"

"The internet exists, *Emma*."

Avery throws off her shirt and pulls on her nightgown,

shimmying out of her jeans afterwards. She gives Emma a look so much like their Moe's that it steals her breath. *She'd tell Rome to burn and they would ask how quickly.*

Her satin pajamas slip over her skin like a caress. Washing her face to get rid of the mascara and eye shadow, she runs the cool cloth over the back of her neck and arms. If Avery were not here, she'd take a proper shower to wipe away the day and all its sweat, grime, and sorrow. Dropping her rings and extra accessories onto the pile of worn clothes, she returns to her bedroom, and a frowning Avery.

Despite her constant fight to be seen as older, the unicorns on her pjs remind Emma how young she really is. The weight of affection and protectiveness hurry her in the effort to find a suitable spoon size for their pints of ice cream.

"Where are you watching stuff like that?" Emma inquires, raising her eyebrow. The girl plays with the remote for the tv as she eyes the ice cream suspiciously. "Do Moe and Dad know you're watching stuff online?"

"Do they know about your new tattoo?" Avery asks coldly, her eyebrows raised as she curiously glances at the snake. Emma's jaw drops. For all the ways the two are similar, she never inherited Avery's 'don't care' attitude. They size each other up but Emma's the first one to break the staring contest with a laugh.

"Tell you what, you don't tell Moe about the tattoo, and I won't tell her about the movie."

Avery nods her head gratefully, melting with her relief. "Deal."

"You better watch yourself little girl," Emma warns good-humouredly, readjusting her mountain of pillows. Avery plays the movie with a triumphant *humph*. Curling against her body pillow, she meets her sister's eyes and shakes her head. "You're going to get yourself into trouble by extorting people."

"I just need to find a way to extort Moe and Dad." Avery drops gloomily back into the pillows, pinching the ice cream between her knees, as she organizes herself comfortably onto her side of the bed.

Familiar music fills her apartment as Emma considers shutting the blinds. She leaves them open 24/7. When the sun rises, she rises. The city's her favourite art project—Avery is biting her nails. Emma pulls her little hand away, trapping it in her own.

"You will grow warts."

"Maybe I like warts."

"You will not like them when they spread from your fingers to your face," Emma comments lightly, sucking on her ice cream filled spoon for emphasis. The flash of fear on Avery's face signals Emma to release her hand from its fleshy prison. "You don't look so nonchalant now."

"You have warts," Avery taunts childishly, pulling off the lid of her ice cream. She sticks her tongue out, the surface-stained blue by the ice cream. *Thank you, Jesus, for this beautiful little girl,* Emma prays with glassy eyes. "Shh, I am trying to watch a movie."

"I didn't say anything."

Avery shuffles closer, muttering to herself. She pulls Emma's pillow away and rolls into her, curling around the tub of bubblegum ice cream. Kissing the back of her youngest sister's head, Emma rearranges her hair comfortably, and hugs her ice cream to her chest as the opening credits roll onto the screen.

CHAPTER 5: 9-1-

Avery is already asleep. A soft smile curls over Emma's face as she pulls the comforter over her little sister's bare shoulders. Locks of dark hair cover Avery's face, drifting closer to her open mouth. It takes Emma a moment to realize how close her head is to Avery's mouth. She cannot help herself but to wait, suspended, holding her own breath, until she feels Avery's against her cheek.

Relieved, she brushes the hair off Avery's face, and reaches for the empty carton of ice cream beginning to slide off the bed. Quiet snores follow her into the kitchen as she discards Avery's empty container and slides her half-eaten pint back into the freezer.

Her phone flashes with a text, drawing her attention away from the ritualistic dance happening on the tv screen. Emma catches the last few letters of the texter and excitedly dives for her phone. Residency must be going well, or very poorly, if it takes two days to respond to a text. **Good, thx.**

A slow crawl of something works its way at the back of her throat as she reads the one line over and over again. The phone goes dark, reflecting her face back in the lights flashing from the living room. Emma quickly drops the phone onto the counter and waddles back to the bed as chants fill the living room.

On screen, two women dance around a fire as they beg for

fertility and blessing.

Off screen, something goes *bang*.

Emma pauses halfway into the bed as Avery shifts. A fist pounds into her chest as she glances down at her slumbering sister. *Don't be dramatic. They could be fireworks.*

People often set off fireworks during Chinese New Year on this strip. Canada Day and New Year's Eve are celebrated further downtown in a huge park. But none of those occur in March.

Grabbing the tv remote, she puts it on mute, waiting to hear another firework go off. Her eyes search the tops of the buildings in front of her and the reflections dancing on their glass panes for a sign of light. *Lord let it be fireworks.*

Emma's mind conjures a thousand tales as she inches towards her wall of windows. The cold from outside and the heat within meet, casting a fog across the glass as her breath comes out in pants. She clutches the remote in her hand as she finally braves a proper look at the streets below.

Light reflects from the puddles gathering on the sidewalks and roads. A car drives through a lake of orange, creating shards of light across the street. Rain drops cling to the window as Emma cranes her neck. Red and yellow divide her face as she lifts one hand to the glass. Between her breath and the heat from her hand, the view becomes hazy. Too blurry to make out anything besides large blobs.

Two years in this city and not once has she been a witness

to anything violent. Why would it be bullets? Still, she stands by the window and fidgets with one of her golden earrings. Nothing wrong with being vigilant.

After a minute of standing there, the silliness of this scenario wiggles in. Exacerbated by a young couple trying to dodge the rain as they laugh together. The man removes his jacket and lifts it above his girlfriend's head, disappearing around the corner at a jog. They were not panicking, why should she?

Rushing back to her bed, she slips in beside Avery, and turns off the tv. No more entertainment for the night. She fights a laugh as she settles in beside her little sister, stealing some of her warmth. Henny deVries' victory parade would marvel any holiday celebration if a shootout occurred the one time she allowed Avery to stay in the city with her older sister. Once the shock and panic wore off, of course.

Riri needed this. It is hard being so young and having big dreams. People find children with plans amusing. Scoffing, laughing, teasing, rarely encouraging them. Emma easily recalls the times she imagined a brilliant life rife with danger and intrigue. Moses, her partner in crime, and Cody, the villainous mastermind. The irony of her former musings settles into her mind as she lies on her back. Yet, she'd proudly name Cody as one of her greatest heroes if anyone asked.

Forcing the upsetting thoughts away, she gladly lets Avery cuddle up to her in sleep. The little hairs on Avery's head tickle her lips as she brushes a kiss there. *She needs someone in her corner.* The fierce protectiveness wells up in her chest as a quiet snore breaks the silence. Despite the entire family practically worshipping Avery as the deVries Princess, they view her as a naïve child. One they need to 'prepare' for a world of cruelty. As if she needs anymore reason to be bitter—has Avery not faced enough already?

She's fought battles of those twice her age. Twice her size. Twice her strength.

No... not her strength. Avery is and will always be one of the strongest people in the world.

It must be difficult. She was told by hundreds of people what she would never be able to do. The family got told countless times not to expect anything. Emma remembers the doctor's gentle, patronizing voice as he told them not to roughhouse with her. Not to run, to climb, to jump, but they *could* sit and read to her. They thought she might not be able to read. How many times did they tell Moe and Dad not to expect much academically? Most people, practitioners no less, thought she'd end up malnourished, tiny, and living a shell of a life.

Time and time again she proved them wrong. Even Emma.

Why must this time be the exception? Riri works her way to starting forward in every soccer league she enters. She wins MVP every year, including the year she began her soccer journey. Avery deVries holds the household record for longest streak of straight A's. She earns praise from teacher after teacher, coach after coach. Beyond performance, she pushes everyone around her to be better simply because of her heart to serve.

If anyone can turn streaming a children's game into a lucrative career, it is Avery. People find themselves attracted to her. Emma cannot remember one person who managed to withstand Avery's charm. She's adored wherever she goes. With a single smile she brightens up a room. She makes people feel special. Be it with her energy or spirit.

Women like Avery come once in a lifetime. The ones who can move mountains with a flick of their wrists. Emma's *schatje*. Her little treasure. Rare and precious beyond belief. Aiding brilliance to anyone near it and reflecting light in the darkest of places. She cannot fathom how anyone would doubt her.

Emma pushes down the urge to speed back home and yell at her parents for discouraging Avery. Well... not yell. She cannot remember yelling once in her life. Speak strongly... Perhaps sternly.

In their own way, they are protecting their youngest child. Trying to keep her from disappointment and heartbreak. Isn't that what the doctors were trying to do though? And she proved them all wrong. Avery will never truly live until she learns to face the effects of life on her own.

Her success and disappointments are between her and God. Her path laid by Him, not defined by any person. Doctor, parent, or otherwise.

Finally calm, Emma closes her eyes. They peel open at the sound of distant sirens. *Distant.* Maybe she needs something stronger. Her eyes drift to her Bible open from her morning devotions. Then to the TV. City noises rarely disturb her. Maybe having Avery here is putting her on high alert.

She knows the movie didn't make that loud sound.

Tying her hair back, Emma sits up, willing herself to see the solution waiting on the other side of the glass. Her paranoia almost tricks her into seeing something in the steady strobe of the streetlights. Avery shifts slightly underneath the blanket, letting out a quite huff onto Emma's arm. It might have been a fluke. A car backfiring.

Praying underneath her breath, she leans back into the wall and grabs the remote. The movie plays at her command, quietly filling her apartment with chatter. Already the sound of other humans lends her strength.

Bang.

She mutes the tv, pulse moving into her brain.

Bang. Bang.

Emma throws off her blankets, one leg out of bed. Her eyebrows draw together as she leans towards the window. Maybe it's construction, maybe a neighbour throwing a party with confetti—

Bang. Bang.

She cannot mistake the sound this time. Not after years of watching over Moses' shoulder as he plays first person shooters. Not after hunting trips and Remembrance Day ceremonies. Those are gunshots.

Emma jumps from her bed, bare feet thudding then slapping against the floor. She stops herself an inch from the windows, breath coming out in spurts. The streets are empty now. No one made to witness whatever monstrosity is taking place in the dead of night. No sirens sound off in response. A rare occurrence for a busy city. Where are the ambulances constantly transporting those in need? Patrol cars letting out a short *bleep* to notify naughty teenagers of their proximity. A firetruck driving near the roundabouts, waiting for the tell-tale *smash* of an accident. Surely someone else heard the bullets.

Lights flicker from the acupuncturist clinic across the street. A flutter of the dark curtains. Red and orange pulses from the sign but the building shows no further sign of life.

It could be thunder. March brings in a mixture of storms and sleet. She stares at the sky, holding her breath, praying a flash of lightning will come. Rain continues to pour but the dark clouds remain hidden in the night.

Her eyes strain against the dark and neon pockets of light, waiting to see something hidden in the shadows. Anything. Emma slides her hands down her satin pajamas, starting when they reach her empty pockets. *I left it on the charger.* She can barely make out the shape of her phone in the dark of the kitchen. She should grab it. Right now.

But what if I miss something?

Emma prays underneath her breath. She repeats it in Dutch and French as her eyes drift to the phone. What would she say to the police? She *thought* she heard gunshots on her strip? Penalties occur with 'prank' calls. What if it ends up being nothing and someone in real needs suffers?

Calm down. Your neighbours always watch TV loudly. Trevor is right next door.

Except Trevor left for Spring Break. He and Chewie were her comfort. Now, if something is wrong, it's up to Emma to hold the fort. "Dear Jesus, I need—"

Scat, scat, scat.

The coupling of gunshots come with a flash of light. She tries to find the source when someone murmurs behind her. Emma spins around, peering at Avery as she whispers into a pillow. With the reminder of her sister's vulnerability, she crouches and begins to pull down her curtains. She keeps her head between them, eyes scanning what little she can see from behind a wall.

Someone has a gun. She knows it now. After those last shots, she cannot dissuade herself. Once she knows a location, the cops are a quick dial away. The difficulty comes when she tries to look at the tops of the buildings in front of her. While she is high off the street, she is nowhere near penthouse level.

If this fight is taking place on the roof of a building, she will not see it.

Knots form in her stomach as the sound continues. Muffled. Unheard by so many as they watch their movies and tv and try to distract themselves from the work week starting tomorrow. She could too. The thought slithers into her mind amidst the panic, offering a way out. Her earbuds lie beside her abandoned schoolwork and her dozens of playlists begging to be used. Music will soothe her to bed. Or even turning up the tv. Avery obviously sleeps through anything.

Even with her heart in her throat and sweat gathering on her hands, it might be possible to go to sleep. To ignore the signs of some awful crime. For Avery's sake. For hers too.

Then she sees the body.

Head lulled to the side. Surrounded by a crawling darkness. Left in the stairwell of the glass museum at the very end of her street. The lower level is completely dark, barred walls drawn behind the glass. Above, on the industrial level, Emma begins to see more. More unmoving people.

Rising slightly, Emma moves towards the high table pressed into the corner of the hallway wall and the row of windows. She considers moving it but fears waking Avery and subjecting her to this massacre. Her face comes flush with the glass, the cool of the window ebbing away at the fog of her breath.

Lights from the street, from the medical centers and

stores, pour through unprotected, unobstructed windows. The occasional car disturbs the constant cast but there is no mistaking the sight before her naked eye. *Bodies.* Strewn across the glass floor. Blood seeking to gather in one place like a macabre installation

Slapping one hand against her mouth, she uses the other to search her pockets. *Not on me.* Her eyes shoot to the kitchen, pitch black save for the occasional flash from cars unknowingly driving down the street without a care. As if knowing she needs it, her screen bursts to life, finally at 100%.

Instead of running to grab it, she scans the museum. Waiting for movement. For a glimpse at the person doing this, so the police get a proper description.

Her breath pauses at the distinct feeling of being watched. As if someone were standing behind her. Stalking her. She spares a quick glance into her empty apartment, light-headed. With a curt reminder to breathe, she begins to draw away from the window.

No new gunshots. No yelling. Nothing. Perhaps it is a trick of the light or a new exhibit they are setting up. Construction began on the top-half of the museum a few weeks ago. The top half of the museum is a silly place to hold a gunfight. There is nowhere to hide. Or there wasn't a few days ago—

Something flashes, illuminating the bodies, and even from so far away, making it clear the pools spreading out from underneath them is blood.

Bang. Bang. Bang.

She squeaks involuntarily. The sound is too big in the silent apartment. Avery mumbles. The tv screen plays the strip tease Avery desperately wanted to see. Another gunshot rings out.

Emma forces her eyes to remain open. Glued to the museum. Even if she wanted to move, she cannot. Her feet are stuck to the ground. Cemented into place. Forcing her to bear witness to the growing light from within the supposedly empty museum.

In fact, she can barely move her hand away from her mouth. The ends of her fingers grow cold as her neck begins to burn. A scream, or cry, lodges itself in her throat. She tries to breathe around it but it becomes more and more difficult as she catches shadows moving within the glass building.

This cannot be happening. This cannot be happening.

Over two years of living in this city, a year in the downtown area, and her entire life in its greater reach, and not once has she even heard stories of a mass shooting. These kinds of things don't happen anymore.

One voice, her own panicked one, screams at her to grab her phone. Her mind wants to listen but her body cannot. Especially when she sees someone press themselves against a glass pane of the museum wall. Hands flattened, leaving prints along the glass.

The streetlights may be enough to see the bodies but they do not show the finer details. She cannot see who they are. What they look like aside from the mask on their face and hard hat on their head. From so far away she cannot hear them banging against the glass but she feels it. Her shoulders flinch with every shake of the glass. Their last desperate call for help, and no one there to answer.

I am here, she whispers in her own mind. Too afraid to say the words aloud though no one can hear. *God please save them. Help me to save them.* Avery makes a sound. Loud enough to split her attention for half a second.

When it returns to the museum, someone is standing behind the person beginning for help.

Why is no one reacting? Surely someone else must be witnessing this too. Where are the cries of concern from her neighbours? From the insomniacs wandering the streets endlessly at night.

Her breath catches as a group stumbles out of an underground club, laughing and hanging off one another. Finally.

Someone steps into a town car, folding their umbrella. The acupuncturist across from her turns off their lights for the night, dimming the clinic sign. Yet not one scream pierces the night. Do none of them see this? Do they not care?

How can no one care when a human being presses themselves into glass to escape the gun pointed at their back?

VACANCIES IN TIME

Panic and fear wind through the streets, bleeding into Emma. In the fluorescent lights of the fleeing town car, she sees dark, exposed skin. Curling around the trigger of a silver pistol. As if the shooter does not care about remaining hidden.

They are not wearing a mask like the victim. In the fading light, she cannot differentiate between flesh and the black tactical gear they wear. Emma catalogues every detail, running it through her mind, so she knows what to tell the sketch artist.

Another innocent car passes, giving her a momentary peek at the person's physique. A man. A tall one.

She cannot hear their conversation, but with the aid of the light, Emma can see the hostage tensing. Their mouth moves quickly as she glances at her phone on the counter. Will they be dead by the time she returns, phone in hand? No one should die alone.

Moe is right. A gated lot in the heart of a rural region will always be safer than an apartment in the middle of a busy city.

She glances guiltily at Avery, cursing the moment she decided to suggest this sleepover. Her vantage point is not good enough, but there is no better place to stand and see within the building. She needs faces. Defining features like a tattoo or scar. *There must be others watching. Close enough to see what's really happening. I am not the only person in their poorly insulated apartment on a Sunday night.*

… but she could be. With Spring Break, tourists normally stay in hotels or cabins. Others want the Air Bnb's by the water. Many natives travel to the mountains like Trevor, trying to avoid the influx of students.

What if this is a college kid in the wrong place at the wrong time?

They make the person stand. A man she sees now, wearing a suit. An odd combination with a mask and helmet, but that might be a hint for the police. The gunman keeps the pistol level with the first man as two people are pushed beside him. Emma's blood rushes through her head, trying to tally the number of people already dead.

A shot rings out.

Then another.

Both bodies crumple to the ground as the man remains utterly still.

He gives off no reaction. No flinch. Not a shout.

Emma flinches when a sound comes from within her own apartment. Light comes from the kitchen as another text comes in. Probably Moe worrying, checking in, knowing with her instincts something is wrong.

This cannot be happening.

She pinches the fatty part of her upper arm to try and wake herself. Thank the Lord Avery is not a witness to this.

Maybe she is hallucinating. After months devoid of candy and sweets, she could be in a sugar coma. It explains why her body cannot move. How her feet turned to led and legs to stone.

Then the man plastered against the glass begins to turn around.

He keeps his arm up in surrender as more people in tactical gear rush forward, guns raised. These are not the standard-issued guns police officer's use. While she may not be well-versed in gun knowledge, she knows what an assault rifle looks like.

She hoped it could be a police matter. Part of her still does, even though she can see there are no letters sewn into their bulletproof vests. The military must identify themselves as well... right?

Emma pulls at her earrings, watching the group close in on the man as she gets to her knees. Maybe this is where it ends. They take him to a secondary location. A true hostage. She pulls back the curtains, staring at the time on her oven. *At 12:49 AM, on Monday morning, I witnessed a shooting. They made off with a single male Caucasian in a black suit from the—*

A shot rings out.

Her heart stops.

Blood splatters against the glass wall where a human being had been standing only moments prior. This time she cannot contain her scream, though she silences herself when Avery moves.

I just witnessed a murder.

Tears gather in her eyes as she forces herself to look back

at the museum. The man in the black suit, the murderer, is no longer where she left him. He inches closer to the window, not shy of the light pouring into it. Half his dark face obscured by a film of red blood, part of it illuminated by the golden light of the street. Instead of cleaning the blood obscuring his view of the street or running, he stares up.

At her.

No way, no way, he cannot see me. Not from this far away. He could not have heard me!

Still, he stares.

Heat rushes through her head as her heart slams back into place. Her frozen state edges away, replaced with stony disbelief.

The space between them almost seems to contract. She comes to know, intimately, that he has black eyes the colour of onyx and a face cut from dark rock.

And then he disappears.

Her breath catches as she throws herself against the glass, sure he had been standing in front of the body a second ago.

Now, the body lies across the floor of an empty room, encased in his own blood. All movement ceases on the industrial floor of the glass museum.

Where did they go?

Like a broken spell, her panic subsides, replaced by adrenaline.

In the span of a breath, she springs to her feet and sprints towards her kitchen. For her own sanity, she pauses in the hallway, staring at her locked door. The metal shines between the door and the wall. Just for good measure, she surges forward and runs her fingers over the chain. A silver bar crosses the width of the door, along with a twisted deadbolt and the extra security lock her Father made her use.

It does not matter. He could not have seen you.

Despite her own rational voice attempting to soothe her, panic returns with stakes of ice. Her cold hands shake so much that it is difficult to hold her phone. In the dark, she fumbles to remove it from her charger, too afraid to turn on the light. Maybe in the dark they cannot distinguish her apartment from any other.

He could not have seen you! The museum is at the end of the block. It is one in the morning. Breathe. It will not serve anyone if the operator cannot make out what you are saying between the tears and gasping.

Emma closes her eyes, forcing herself to be grounded. Her prayer is quick but enough to remind her to breathe through the shock. She fights with numb fingers to press her phone app and begin dialing.

9-1-

She stops.

Heavy footsteps sound down the hall. Far at first but getting louder.

Not possible

CHAPTER 6: NOT MY IKEA TABLE

Her finger hovers above the final 'one', eyebrows knitting. Between the pounding of her heart and the panic shooting through her brain, the sounds coming from the hallway may be an adrenaline-induced hallucination.

They could not get here so quickly.

Panic gives way to reason, for a brief second, before she edges away from the counter and hears it again. Marching. Not running but in perfect unison stomping towards her apartment. No rush, no hurry, no concern about the cops being notified or a neighbour complaining... because they are fast enough to dispose of the person and get away.

Emma pops her head out of the kitchen, staring at the door. It shakes with every step outside. None of this makes sense. He could not have seen her. The buildings are a block away from one another. He could not, yet he did. They could not have gotten here so quickly... and yet their steps shake the floor and send tremours into her legs.

"No way."

Emma erases the numbers from her phone with shaking fingers. Every hair on her arms and the back of her neck stands up. All the panic drops from her body in a mass exodus, leaving a cool numbness behind. On the rare occasion when God endeavours to give her this supernatural peace, it means danger ahead.

She cannot know they are outside her door. And yet there they are and she *feels* it in every fiber of her being.

Emma covers the distance between her bed and the hall in one jump. Throwing herself over her little sister, she wraps the blanket around her body with a small hole for breathing. She whispers prayers in whatever tongue she can manage, halfway to tears as Avery remains asleep. Her chest aches as she says her goodbye, begging the Lord to disguise Avery, and praying the police will remove her body before Avery sees it.

The door *creaks* open.

Light pours into the hallway, obstructed by shadows. Her body becomes a stone wall around Avery as she closes her eyes. *Bang.*

She flinches, ready for the pain. Ready to see pearly gates and her Heavenly Father. Avery shifts underneath her, silent as the dead. Emma tries to restrain her from moving as something else *thuds.*

Another follows it.

Slow as a snail, she twists her head, watching as two women drop a large black crate onto the ground. Guns swing from their hips as they march in line back out of the apartment. The lights in her kitchen switch on, but not the one in the living room where a group of them are standing—completely silent.

Emma disguises her motion with pillows and the mess of

Avery's hair, stopping when a large man storms into the room. Her body tenses again but he simply places a small box on top of a crate and dusts off his hands.

Panic continues as a steady partner to the confusion welling up. Groups of men and women in black tactical gear march in and out of her apartment. One disappears down the hall and she hears the bathroom door *click* into place a moment later. Emma brings her fingers up to her neck, checking her rapid pulse. She has one... that must be a good sign.

A man and woman grunt loudly, holding up a bin the size of a motorcycle. One of them begins muttering, it is hard to tell from behind their helmets. Together they heave the box onto the small table tucked into the corner. It shakes under the weight.

That's an IKEA table, not made for weight. Emma bites her tongue, trying to ignore the inclination to lecture them about breaking other people's things. The long rifle strapped to the tall man's back humbles her. Quickly enough to chase away her lingering intrigue and confusion.

She witnessed a murder of five people. Watched them shoot three of them. There is no doubt these are the people from the museum. Bloodthirsty murderers who shot an unarmed man. They cannot leave her alive.

The more boxes brought in, the more people spreading across her apartment, the more she expects the bullet and pain. Her eyes drift to the stove, where the time flips to *1:00*. Ten minutes of excruciating tension and not a moment of acknowledgement towards her.

Not a word.

Not a glance.

They do not speak with one another either, save for the muttering pair responsible for her quivering table. Occasional grunts break the near silence. Her own laboured breathing assaults her ears. Distant sirens fill the room but not one soldier pauses.

Emma draws herself up, extracting herself from Avery's side. None of them spare a glance as she catches herself on Avery's limbs. Tumbling off the bed, she rearranges the blanket over the sleeping girls form and spins to face them.

Nothing.

Her confusion increases with every minute stretching by without answers. She expected an interrogation. A gun waved in her face. Death. Her soul prepared to meet its Maker.

Dazed, Emma watches her hands as the adrenaline fades entirely. Someone must have stuffed cotton balls in her ears and cranked the pressure to a hundred. Deep inside her mind a battle wages between her amygdala and pre-frontal cortex. The temptation to give in to curiosity and believe this a dream is enough to all worry.

Her brain wanders. Eyes roaming around the room, trying to see blurred lines at the edges of her vision. This must be a dream. It cannot be real life. She pinches the skin of her wrist, watching another group of people walk in. As time continues a slow trudge forward, Emma comes to the realization there are not hundreds of soldiers as she worried. In fact, there appears to be less than two dozen.

And they are soldiers.

Between the military gear, the guns on their backs, and their uniform march, it's difficult to label them as anything else.

Every single one of them looks like they could rip her head off. Muscular legs. Confidence radiating off them. Emma begins to see the difference in their uniforms though. They all wear black cargo pants, tapered at the bottom, right above their tall leather boots. Utility belts hide underneath bulletproof vests. The difference lies in their shirts. Some wear long sleeved turtlenecks. Others wear t-shirts.

The tall man who carried in the smallest box wears a muscle shirt. He leaves his helmet on one of the crates, glancing out the window as a woman squeezes between him to reach the table. In the dimmed orange of the acupuncturist clinic, he resembles a stone statue. Strong facial bones, wide lips, an indent in his chin most get fixed with cosmetic surgery. One bump interrupts the smooth plains of his face. A mole right on his chin.

An identifying feature.

She should grab her phone, lost somewhere in the sea of blankets, and dial the police. For all she knows, those sirens distant sirens are heading to the museum. At the very least, she should ask the soldiers what they are doing.

Then again, she watched them murder a man in cold blood fifteen minutes ago. He possessed no weapon. His arms were raised in surrender. They allowed him to turn around. Look into the face of his murderer. As if that's any consolation for being killed in the first place.

Why did you kill that man? The words play on the tip of her tongue as the soldiers begin removing their helmets. They kept him for last. Purposefully killed every other person, made him face them, and killed him. Although... a better question, less dangerous question, may be how they got into her apartment in the first place.

No longer interested in what they are throwing onto the four-year-old sad excuse for a table, she turns slightly towards the hall. Remaining in the safety of her bed, she leans forward, as if by doing so her neck will grow long enough to allow her a glance at the door.

Deadbolts are easily picked. However, the chain is reinforced. Her father changed out the standard one when he added the secondary bar to the door. No human being without a saw or large piece of equipment could get through the bar. The chain is too strong for bolt cutters. So how did they get in?

And without one sound of frustration. No grunt. No scream. The door opened like it wanted to invite them in. Most of the time when Emma opens it, she lunges forward to stop it from hitting the wall with her effort to make it budge. She heard the doorknob twist. Listened to the slide of the metal bar move out of place....

Despite knowing little about them, she surmises they are not people of brutality. A silly thought to have, considering the massacre below. They are polite. Polite enough to wipe their boots on the front mat. She hears it every time they step into the apartment. *Swipe, swipe, swipe.*

Their guns are stowed away. Boots clean as to not drag in dirt... or blood. She heard the water in the bathroom go off as someone washed their hands, so they have good hygiene. Not one of them bothers her or her sister. As if she and Avery do not exist.

It must be a dream. While she has never been one for vivid, life-altering dreams, it would not be the first time in her life weird things have happened.

She briefly considers taking a book from one of the shelves above her head and throwing it. Maybe not at the large people with scary guns, but into the hall. Just to see if they will flinch. Why are they waltzing through the apartment like they pay the rent? Emma has never witnessed a group of people so unperturbed and collected.

She searches for a badge or any other indication of identity but finds nothing. No S.W.A.T. No star badge. No logo on their vests or chests or anywhere she can see in the light coming from the kitchen.

Glancing at Avery again, she withdraws from the corner of her bed and reaches underneath her mound of pillows. Emma carefully keeps an eye on them the entire time her hand flails across the sheets. A panicked second stretches into a minute as she fails to find the device. They magically entered her apartment; maybe they managed to snatch her phone too?

Finally, she finds it trapped between the mattress and headboard.

"Not there," Avery gasps, her disgust breaking the sacred silence. Emma freezes, caught by Avery's arms as the girl fights with the blanket over her head. She smashes her barren face into Emma's back as the muttering ceases.

None of the people in black react. Not even a glance their way. As if they cannot hear her sister or see the movement from her bed. It is dark this far into the living room... but not dark enough to miss the figures on this bed. Not dark enough to consume the words being said.

It cannot be a dream. Avery's arm feels too warm against her numb body.

Emma fights with her sister's desperate cuddly arms to free herself. When she manages to disentangle herself, she hurriedly taps in the passcode to her phone, one eye on the soldiers. They continue to add more and more black cases on the tower they began. One begins to tip but a woman fixes it, sighing loudly as she glowers at the man with a mole on his chin.

For the first time, they look at her.

Emma meets the woman's eyes, heart rattling in her ribcage. In all her life, she's never seen eyes like hers. Melted gold gathered in a copper bowl. An odd sense of familiarity teases the back of her mind. Déjà vu.

The soldier lifts her chin slightly, pushing her people back. Emma scrambles to hide her phone behind her back, but the other woman noticed the movement. Yet, without a word, she marches out of the apartment.

No one stops her from using her phone. The text from earlier came from Carter. A message sent to show her how much fun she is missing on his Sunday adventure. What will he think of hers?

Blue and red lights flash from outside. They get brighter and then fade as the sirens blare past. Her saviours are heading in the wrong direction! While the police tend to the bodies in the museum, they may not know about the other two victims a block away.

One, Emma corrects stubbornly. She makes sure to shift in front of her sister's body as she opens Carter's text.

Guess who found Hirohito at the library? She might have laughed if she could afford to make a sound. While her fear rapidly subsides, her common sense knows better than to draw attention to them. The woman confirmed Emma is not invisible... it is only a matter of time before others acknowledge her. They must want something.

Unless the cases are filled with bombs.

The idea sounds ridiculous but then again, so does the thought of an entire group of people being murdered in front of her eyes in the museum at 12 in the morning.

His text about the dictator must have been sent right after she left her phone on the charger, because the second one is his last message. **Did not appreciate me making the comparison. Heading to the ER now to see if they can stick my tooth back in… could have used my handy dandy first mate.**

Joke or not, a bigger problem garner's her attention. She and Avery need help.

Emma begins to type out an SOS, but something white catches her attention. One of the cases being brought in has a painted symbol on its side. At first, she wonders if it a bike tire. The concept, given the circumstances, elicits a soft laugh. Perhaps they needed to settle a trike dispute.

Light from the kitchen causes the white symbol to glow. Emma inches forward, waiting for a lull in their processional to take a picture of the insignia. Her phone buzzes in her hand as she snaps the photo. If all else fails, Carter can show it to the police.

They could be covert government agents though. It explains their professionalism. Not their conduct, because last Emma checked, breaking and entering is illegal without due cause. The way they hold themselves is methodic. Enough to distract her as they work together to bring a long box into the room.

The golden-eyed woman returns bag in hand. Not a plastic grocery bag, but a laptop case. The same symbol is painted on the front of the black fabric. A circle, cut into eighths, with two dots on every spoke and one in the middle. Kind of like a bike tire with lights on it. People who bike at night use them to increase visibility.

Emma references back to the picture saved on her phone. The image quality is grainy at best… but Carter is smart. He may know what it is supposed to represent. If not, his internet friends might.

I witnessed a shooting. Bad guys with guns in my apartment. Attaching picture of their logo. Send police!

The front door slams shut. She jumps. Now trapped inside a room with two dozen agents, Emma reconsiders sending the text condemning them.

Her thumb hovers over the send. Fear grips her, making it impossible to move. The agents, outlined by the warm light of the kitchen, gather in a circle around her bed. Some clasp their hands in front of them while others leave their arms at their side. Inches away from their weapons. The woman with the fiery stare crosses her arms slowly as she slides into the circle. She must be their leader.

The thought vanishes when the mole-man steps forward, claiming the room. With blue eyes, icy enough to freeze her, and the face of a statue, he'd strike fear into any police officer. She suddenly begins to wonder who would win. Her captors or the police?

What does she have to bargain for Avery?

Still, none of them say anything. Her eyebrows draw together as she shuts off her phone. They may tie her up and throw her into the bathroom, the only isolated room in her apartment. Being alone would make it difficult to maneuver her phone behind her back but they may throw Avery into the room too. With her eyes and Emma's hands they may be able to call the police!

"I—" She begins but stops when they look away from her and towards the door. Every single one of them. Even the scary woman with the stare of golden fire.

For some reason, she knew he was large. Not in height or stature, though he is both, but in stature. Watching the Black man enter her small apartment makes it feel like a prison cell. An odd thought rushes through her head at what they think of her quaint space. She remembers the dirty dishes beside the sink and lack of food in her apartment. Insecurities pour out from the woodworks. Her hand left streaks on the windows. The shower needs a cleaning. Her school desk is a mess of papers and old mugs. Odd things to worry about at a time like this, but her mother taught her what it means to be a proper Dutch hostess.

He and the other men were cut from different boulders by

the same sculptor.

This is the one who shot a surrendering man with little more consideration than that of a bug. Her lips quiver despite her resolve, and even though she wants to buckle under the weight of their gaze, she keeps her chin up and her eyes open.

Between the commander's dark suit and the colour of his skin, he blends into the shadows of her apartment. For a moment, she loses where his torso ends and his head begins. When she finally meets his eyes, she sees black voids surrounded in a white cloud. Up close, his eyes are doubly powerful. Compelling and magnificent enough to reach out with invisible hands and steal her breath.

He extends the large, dark hand she saw holding the gun. Half-expecting to get shot, she tenses, waiting for the sound. Instead, she sees his open palm face up, level with her chest. "Let me see your phone."

CHAPTER 7: A PROPER HOSTESS

Trying to figure out where his accent is from should not be Emma's highest priority, and yet she does not relinquish her phone. Instead, her eyes narrow slightly as the familiarity tugs at the back of her mind. *Not entirely British but similar. Somewhat Germanic too…*

"Your phone," he repeats, adding an emphasis onto his words this time. Emma slaps it into his hand, meeting his eyes with fear. Their leader would tower over her brothers. His hands must be twice the size of hers. Veins cover the surface and she needs to stop herself from telling him about the gauge of needle she could insert into them.

Mr. Tall, Dark and Handsome steps away from the edge of her bed, tearing his eyes from her. His hand engulfs the little metal device, broad, muscular shoulders illuminated by the glowing surface of her phone. The distant light from the kitchen casts half his body in golden light. Enough to reveal a darkened patch of skin teasing the edge of his turtleneck—a tattoo!

Light bursts from above her. Emma raises her hand against the blindness, holding back a groan at the assault. It appears they found the right light switch.

Despite facing down a dangerous man who she watched murder someone, Emma turns to make sure the light is not disrupting Avery. She adjusts the blanket over her little sister's head, hoping the giant did not see her. He seems more perplexed by the phone than her presence.

"Do you need... here let me help," Emma offers, eyebrows drawing together when he starts at the sound of her voice. As if *he* should be scared of *her*. She offers her hand, palm up to him, watching the way his fingers curl around her phone. He scans her over skeptically, eyes narrowing when they reach her face. The other agents lost interest when she put up no fight; rifling around her apartment as if they own the place. She would have... if they would put their guns far out of reach. "You need to get into my phone, don't you?"

A loud siren blasts past as the red and blue lights outline his body. One of the agents finds the metal cord hanging down beside the wall of glass and pulls it. Curtains shoot out from either side of the wall, colliding together in the middle. They are white and see-through and do little to hide bodies walking along the window. However, Emma is not going to tell them about the little button on the cord or about the blinds it will bring down to close off the room.

Clearing her throat apologetically, she stands up and presses her finger into the back of the phone. It unlocks, dismissing her messaging app to display the homepage. The draft of her SOS will be saved in the send bar though. Will she be punished for almost sending a text to Carter?

Maybe not... but the picture on her phone will not be

appreciated.

"What are you looking for?" Emma asks as the curiosity grows beyond her control. The silent giant continues to stare down at her but she keeps a doe-like expression on her face. He's holding the phone like a foreign object. As if it will grow legs and try to run away or explode if he presses the wrong button. An adorable confusion furrows his brow as she refrains from asking again. "I can help you."

He raises his eyebrow at her, full lips firmly shut. Undeterred, she drops back onto her bed, holding his stare. The urge to check on Avery comes and goes as she forces herself to maintain eye contact with the handsome, armed man. Suspicion evaporates from his gaze but something deeper remains. Emma begins to squirm, pressing her thumb into the pulse on her wrist. *Calm down,* she urges as her stomach flips.

The longer Emma keeps their attention on herself, the better. Avery might wake up in the morning to find her sister missing... or dead. It will be traumatic. Not as traumatic as watching Emma beg for their lives or dying herself.

"Call history."

Emma relaxes, careful to keep her hands calm. Too eager and he will wonder why. It takes her a moment to get to her call history. Offering the phone to him, she leans forward, reading what he can see. *He smells good.* The soldier presses his finger against one of her missed calls, panicked when it starts to redial.

"It's just Thai takeout," Emma remarks, hanging up before the first ring fully completes. What kind of soldier doesn't know how to use simple technology? It's 2050... and this is an older model of phone. While his onyx eyes appear timeless, he does not look older than thirty. She runs her nail along the ridges of her earrings as she stares at him. Memories of the blood spattering against the glass pane bring her back to reality. "I did not call the cops."

He nods slowly, though he continues to scroll. What could he possibly be looking for from seven months ago? Her eyes move from the phone to the lack of blood on his bare hands. Emma continues her silent appraisal as he scrolls, reaching his mouth before she realizes what she is doing. Blood flushes her face as she tears her eyes away. *I was looking for proof he killed someone.*

Sirens overwhelm the night as the lights fight against the glass wall and curtains. The man with eyes of ice walks towards the window and pushes apart the curtains to watch the road. He mutters something in a thick Russian accent to the woman who reminds Emma of molten lava.

A Russian and a Germanic Brit. Not two people typically found in a single agency together. They could be Canadians; but then other accents sound. German. Spanish. Australian. Vietnamese. Korean. Canada is rampant with diversity. Fugitives, refugees, immigrants, and everyone who came before. Most adolescents lose their accents as they get older when they live in the West.

"If you let me know what you are looking for... I can help you," Emma suggests kindly, realizing her state of undress. The silk set is one of the most luxurious things she owns, a gift from Moe. He allows her to leave his side, a gracious thing, probably because he noticed the material first. The fabric leaves little to the imagination as it clings to her chest. The shorts cover nothing for goodness sakes! Grabbing a soft fur robe from the high cabinet beside her desk, she slides it on and ties it quickly. Her flimsy armour against prying eyes, though the agent did politely duck his head when she scrambled away.

He manages to exit out of the call history and tries to press on her messages. A jingle begins instead from the app he wrongly chose and it earns a couple jumps from the group of soldiers.

As she extends her hand, he slaps it into her palm. Thanking God underneath her breath, she fights a little laugh at the scandalized expression on his face. They do not know technology as well as they should. Years of screentime trained her for this moment. She angles the phone enough to hide it from his view well enough and slams her thumb against the messaging app.

A crash draws the leader's attention as the agents shush one another. Emma glances worriedly at Avery, relieved to see her fast asleep and silent. Her relief burns away as she notices the other agents glancing at her sleeping form too.

They are trying to keep her asleep!

Her mouth drops open as she watches the Russian man berate two younger agents. She almost forgets to delete the message she intended to send Carter. They kill people, evade the police, break into her home... and respectfully keep silent so a little girl can sleep. How odd.

When she remembers why she is holding her phone, she swiftly erases the picture and message.

"Which conversation first?"

He takes the phone back wordlessly, pressing onto one conversation and scrolling through it. Not Carter's. Read but without a response, Carter's text stream moves to the bottom. He is staring at Cody's username, unamused at the added coyote emoji. Emma smiles to herself, playing with the wispy curls at the bottom of her neck. She stops the moment he looks up at her.

It takes her a moment to remember this is not a nostalgic trip down friendship lane. This man killed at least one person already. He could kill her and Avery and not blink an eye. These facts become harder to remember as she realizes their closeness. His warmth. The distinct smell of wood and campfire smoke but fresh like the sea... she imagines batting the thoughts away as he says something. What *did* he say? Who is he?

Emma searches his chest, looking for a single sign of his name. He wears no name tag or badge. No military plates on a chain around his neck. Emma searches for anything else. Scans the other soldiers to see if one of them wears dog tags or a patch with even their last name. Not one. No badge or threaded code name. Then again, none of them are marked with the white dotted circle.

"Who is this?" The man repeats, his eyes narrowed slightly. "Mom or is his name Moe?"

"Mom," she answers, peering over his hand. His understanding of Dutch confirms her theory on the origin of his accent. South African.

She steps back from the agent as he shifts towards her. He may seem… friendly, but his gun swings against his back with every movement. The dangerous weapon comes intimately close to her nose. They can operate heavy artillery but cannot figure out a phone? Mr. Tall, Dark, and Handsome struggles to look through her other text conversations, blowing out a frustrated breath. Obviously, he cannot find what he hopes for.

"What are you looking for?" Emma inquires when his lips purse in irritation. *Do not look at his lips.* She tries to put her attention on the phone instead of his lips, newly glistening from where he wet them in a huff. "You can see I didn't call the police. I have not texted anyone."

"Social media."

Nodding silently, she grabs her phone out of his hand, opening the first app. He takes the phone right back. With her heart rate back to normal and the panic subsiding, she allows herself one moment to admire how attractive he is. The strength of his jaw and the smoothness of his skin. He smells divine. If she were senseless, she would ask him what his cologne is... or even his skincare routine. Is his face naturally so smooth and dewy or does he take the time to care for his skin? He seems like the kind of man to. His hair is cut perfectly. Obviously, he works out....

"Do you need help?" Emma inquires softly, reaching up to touch his arm. She fights the urge to jump away when his eyes shoot up from her phone. Instead of cowering, she meets his eyes calmly. "You want to make sure I did not message anyone through it or post about it? I can show you I did not."

His lack of communication offers little guidance about what he wants. When she reaches for the phone, she notices blood crusted on his sleeve. The same blood from the person he shot. Careful to avoid the blood as she snatches the device back, Emma begins to scroll through the messages. He has no idea what he is looking for. Or what it would look like to find what he thinks he wants. She swallows back the swell of sympathy for the perpetually confused man.

Moving to the other apps, she scrolls through them for him. He barely pays attention to the rows of pictures and group chats. Eyes of stone watch her instead, now too close for her to ignore. It takes every ounce of her self-control not to shiver. "That's everything."

He takes the phone back, holding the power button. The

screen goes back. Silence reigns as he removes the SIM card. The man cannot navigate social media or even her call history, but he knows enough to shut it off and remove the only thing she can use to contact others.

While her fear begins to well up at why he's shutting it down, she understands a key thing about her family. If she does not respond to even one of her mother's texts, Moe will take the hour-long drive to the city at twice the speed limit. Henny deVries is many things, overprotective and terrifyingly intense being two of them. Avery is her *schatje* too. Moe cannot go a day without contacting Avery. It's been that way since she brought Riri home from the hospital.

Avery deVries is their mother's Benjamin. She may not claim a favourite child but all the siblings know. Emma's breath catches. Whether in horror or amusement she cannot tell. In this story she is the 12 brothers… who sold the youngest into slavery. For a terrifying moment she considers they could be a trafficking ring. The idea fades away when she stares at an agent hidden behind the others. One of the quiet ones. She keeps her head down, eyes focused on the computer screen she sets up. The girl looks younger than Emma. They cannot be traffickers. None of them look like they would be possible of something so awful… even the Russian.

Laying aside the murder that is….

Emma gives it two days internally. Two days before Moe kicks down the door with the entirety of the military and their church. Pitchforks and torches at the ready. If Avery were awake, they'd begin betting. How many days until Moe comes with smoke pouring from her nostrils?

Mr. Tall, Dark and Handsome steps away from her, talking lowly to his agents. They jump into action, opening the cases and boxes. Emma steps away from them, returning to Avery's side. The woman with golden-eyes snaps at a group of three men as they begin to assemble a metal frame. Whispers fill the apartment as it begins to gain height and takes shape. A camera.

Her eyebrows draw together as she reaches down to brush her hand over Avery's face. Deep, quiet breaths slip through her nose as her eyes move in sleep. The kid slept through a hurricane once. Moe nearly had a meltdown because she thought Avery would never wake up. The girl woke up chipper as ever four hours later to a doctor flashing light in her eyes.

Ask him questions.

A million shoot through her mind. So many questions and no idea where to begin. The terror returns.

None of them put their guns down. One wrong word and they might kill her. What if they kill her and take Avery? Pulling at her earring, she begins to entertain the idea of returning to bed. A good night's sleep… if she can fall to sleep with strangers in her apartment.

Her pulse rattles down her legs. It trickles into her fingers as she struggles with what to do next. Emma's bravada lasted long enough to throw herself over Avery and offer help to a group of murderers.

Sleeping in a room filled with strange people carrying guns? Impossible. Leaving? Not a chance. Questions? Too dangerous. She lowers herself onto the edge of her bed, resting her hands in her lap. The leader organizes the soldiers into teams, calling them by militaristic names like Beta and Delta. From the outside, they appear entirely untouchable.

No one spares her a glance. Not a fake smile so normalized in the culture of this country. They continue unpacking the boxes and briefcases, expanding on the camera, and adding telescopes. Are they... watching the acupuncturist?

Her curiosity grows until it can no longer be contained. None of them have threatened her... or yelled at her. Albeit the tall, handsome one is not alone in having blood on him. Blood splatters cover one's neck. The golden eyed one swipes at some crusted into a strand of her braids. Mr. Russian makes no attempt to hide the blood soaked into his hands and up his bare arms. It's foolish to underestimate the danger they pose to her, and stupid not to try and get answers.

Yet, when the lead agent looks at her, Emma is left reeling. Her mind goes completely blank. No thoughts. Where did all the good questions go? "Do you want tea?"

Tea?

Tea!?

She keeps her face neutral as her mind roars at her. Heat

builds up on her neck, touching the tips of her ears. They have blood on their bodies, weapons attached to their backs, and they broke into her apartment! Instead of asking anything about that, she wants to give them refreshments...

Moe raised a good Dutch lady, tattoos and all.

Stunned silence greets her. From all angles as the agents stop what they are doing to stare at her. They make a fearsome group with their blood-covered uniforms and weapons. Especially the Russian man, though he might be the most shocked of all. His eyebrows practically crawl into his hairline. Shifting from one foot to the other, Emma places her hands on her hips. "Do you?"

"You offer us tea?" The iceman inquires, his heavy Russian accent smothering the words. Straightening his shoulders, he laughs a little, glancing at the other agents to see if they are experiencing the same bemused delight. The Asian woman with long black braids shouts one command, clapping her hands together to get them moving again. "What are you?"

"Dutch," Emma answers softly. Moe would be proud and appalled. Both by her offering armed intruders tea... and because of the lack of suitable refreshment options. "We know how to be proper hosts. You always offer your guests food and beverage."

"Guests?" The two men look at one another. Emma briefly considers tucking tail and hiding. Except Moe told her unwelcome guests are still guests. Anyone who comes into the house. It's a witness. To your family, to the Lord, to everything. Finally, the tall dark one smiles and looks at her. "I would love Earl Grey, if you have it."

"Do you have coffee?" The other one asks, crossing his arms with a secretive smile.

"Yes."

She twists on her heel, marching to the kitchen. The coffee pot sits in the sink, surround by an entire pile of dirty dishes. *Just breathe,* she thinks as she twists the faucet. *They are not about to come shoot you in the back while you are making drinks.*

Bubbles grow from the hot water and soap mixing in the sink. She searches for her tea bags and coffee filters, tossing them onto the counter. Closing and opening the cabinets helps to distract her from the people muttering to one another in the living room. It occurs to her she left Avery alone in the room with them… but she can still see into the bedroom. None of the agents venture anywhere near her bed.

How can she get her out? The agents are not going to leave a witness by herself. While they are not watching her right now, it could change in a moment if she tried to escape. Her apartment is a newer build. One with the integrated fire-retardant system. There are no fire escapes or external ladders. The all glass, sleek exterior is what attracted her to the building in the first place. Now she curses the smooth, city-slicker aesthetic.

Trevor's gone on vacation. He might return while they are here but she only walks Chewie during his night shifts which are Thursdays and Fridays. Her next clinic shift is Wednesday. Carter will not be suspicious of her ignoring him, especially because he knows she took out new books. He sends her upwards of fifty texts a day... she doesn't get the chance to respond on a good day.

Their best bet is Moe and even then, she knows her mother's mighty temper poses little threat to dozens of armed agents.

"Where do you come from?"

Emma flinches, proud of herself when she does not squeak like the mouse she is. What's more intimidating? The gun on his back? The fact he towers over every single one of his agents? Or how grossly attractive he is? It's a silly thing to think of but with the acclimatization of her body, and his constant presence, she sneaks veiled glances to admire him.

The muscular arms perfectly emphasized by the dark, tight fabric of his long-sleeved shirt. Bright white teeth against wide lips, soft lips. Sharp, intelligent eyes with an ounce of warmth. The same eyes scanning her; taking in her fluffy robe and sizing up her kitchen. He makes it look smaller than ever. When he stands beside the fridge, it reaches his chin.

"What do you mean?" She inquires, filling the coffee filter. "I have lived here my entire life."

"Not in this apartment."

"In the city," Emma counters with a smile. She shoves the smile off her face. No smile. Not for the murderer. "Technically. We lived in a village in the outer rim."

"And your parents? Where is their place of birth?"

"My mom is Dutch. She came from Holland a million years ago. Dad's been here since the country started." Emma answers, the smile dropping off her face when his face darkens. Thunder roars in his eyes, severe enough to shake her. The terror returns, coiling coolly at the bottom of her throat. What will he do? Yell at her. Well… that sounds horrible. She never handles being yelled at well. Once her gym coach shouted at her in class and she broke down in tears. Junior High treated her poorly.

"A million years?"

"She was sixteen when she immigrated. Married my Dad at eighteen. They have been married for thirty years now." Emma explains, running her hand through her hair. She catches a tangle and almost groans aloud. Throwing the coffee filter in place, she pours the water to get it started and flips the switch. While it gurgles and the kettle heats up, she tries to work her fingers through the knots and contain it.

"When?"

"I do not remember the exact dates," Emma laughs, though she stops when she sees the look on his face remain scathingly intense. With no effort to appear friendly, his brows drop over his dark eyes. He looks like the kind of man to tear a person apart with his bare hands. "They married in twenty twenty. Moe's birthday is September twelfth, two thousand two. Dad's is May first, nineteen ninety-eight."

Leaning against the counter, his arms cross slowly. She catches herself, wondering when she began rambling, but he no longer watches her intently. Was that his desired response? Probably, cunning pairs well with beautiful people.

His eyes move over her kitchen, searching. There is little to see. A couple photos stuck to the fridge with fun magnets. Chinese takeout menu... Thai takeout menu... pizza menu.

With a stranger in the kitchen, scrutinizing it, she realizes just how unhealthy her lifestyle is. His stare does not end on the hundred different ramen packages or bowls stuffed into the overflowing trash can. It comes all the way back to her. Emma's not lazy. She considers defending herself, but he's a stranger. Emma cares more than him.

Between practicum, school, and reading, it is difficult to remember cleaning and proper nutrition. Half of her time goes to dreaming of different worlds. Living in characters' bodies. All energy left behind goes into her schooling and work.

"And you?"

"December twenty-fourth, twenty twenty-nine." Emma replies, tempted to turn the question on him. Except his cold mask slips firmly back into place. Taking a deep breath, she opens her fridge, searching for creamer or anything else. Something to doctor the drinks she offered to the agents.

Agents of what calibre, she still does not know.

"What is your dream job?"

Her eyebrows draw together as she twists to stare at him. Dream job? What kind of question is that? The other questions made sense. Personal information to be used against her... but dream job? He hasn't asked for her name, her SIN, or healthcare number. Unless he already knows!? "Sorry, what?"

"Your dream job," the man repeats, arms crossed as brutally as they were before. His fists push up his biceps as he crosses one ankle over the other. Does he do it knowing how big it makes his arms? If so, to scare or impress her? She refuses to consider the response it elicits.

Turning off the kettle the moment it begins to scream, she twists towards him.

"I am not sure adults are allowed to have dream jobs," Emma confesses, laughing slightly as she plays with her earring. His brow continues to lower over his eyes. She struggles with how to get the look off his face. Replace it with a smile maybe. Reading him is harder than Les Mis.

She's not talented at readying people though, not like Avery. Most of the time she goes off how often they smile and laugh at what she says. For the most part people like her. Emma makes herself agreeable so they do. Then again, most people are not murderers. "I wanted to be a spy for the longest time. I didn't think a better job existed."

"What changed?"

She almost laughs. Well, more a dry croak than anything else because he is being serious. Blinking cluelessly at him, she remembers what she's supposed to be doing. Multitasking cannot be considered one of her skills. There is a reason she cannot finish her schoolwork, read a book, and enjoy things at the same time. "I got older. My parents told me you cannot be a spy… and I found something better to do."

"Something better or something more mature?"

Dropping the mug onto the counter, she glances at him. "I'm sorry, what?"

"You said you found something better to do. Was it better or was it a decision you made out of the fear of being foolish?" He inquires, eyes like darts piercing through her. Emma struggles to answer, mouth opening and closing, mind silent. Suddenly, the fluffy robe is ridiculous and she feels like a fool standing before this grown man despite being a grown woman. The inadequacy doubling when he faces her.

"I-I do not know how to answer that question."

"Are you single?" She pauses again, struggling to respond. He clears his throat, lips quirking with silent amusement. A smile, she can work with that. "We need to know if someone else has a key."

"It's just me," Emma answers, pulling a strand of hair out of her mouth. Moving away from the steaming mugs, she opens the fridge and searches for something to feed them. A slightly old block of cheese and deli meats—the feast of kings.

She may not have crackers but cut up blocks of ramen could have the same effect.

"And the girl? Is she your sister?"

"Do I look like I could have a daughter her age?"

Emma laughs but it's his turn to flush. She enjoys watching his cheeks change colour. For his sake, she stops gawking. Even as he begins to choke over his response. Pulling out a cutting board, she grabs a knife, conscious of his eyes following her. They burn worse than Moe's.

The agent does not try to take the small weapon out of her hand. Probably because he sees through her. Even if they went after Avery… Emma's not sure she could kill someone. Her protectiveness may be fierce like her mother's, but it is not filled with the same intense fire. More like a subtle smolder. Psycho killers do not blush in embarrassment, right?

"You do not need to do that," he states, watching her organize a plate of cheese and meat. She ignores him, reaching for the cabinet filled with mugs. Mugs are not one of the things she lacks. Collecting them is not a hobby… it's an addiction. She cannot remember when she started accumulating enough mugs to water a county. At this point, the spread cannot be contained. In fact, it is so problematic she started searching online for a new cabinet two months ago. An entire cabinet dedicated to her favourite dish.

Moe would stage an intervention. She shares her concern about Emma's spending habits as frequently as the ones about her marital status. Even though she arguably saves more than anyone else in the family. Moses owns entire collections of fantasy memorabilia, complete with a *Mandalorian* helmet from the set of the original. He bids on thousand-dollar guns from the real movie sets and puts them in glass cases. At least mugs serve a purpose.

"Do what?" Emma asks, ignoring the insistence in his tone. She throws a tea bag into his mug and hers. The other agents want coffee. She can already tell. Iceman is the only one who said anything but their thirsty eyes spoke loudly enough. Filling his mug, she searches for sugar. No sugar. Half a container of milk and an expired creamer bottle.

She did not prepare for guests.

A genius idea rapidly forms as she opens her freezer. Removing the tub of butterscotch swirl ice cream, she sticks a spoon into it. She will ask them how they want their drinks doctored. While tea with butterscotch ice cream sounds disgusting, it is delicious in coffee.

The man clears his throat quietly, staring at her hands. She wonders at first if she too has blood on them, even though the thought is illogical. Glancing at them, she finally notices they are shaking. Practically vibrating. Forcing them around her mug, she takes a sip and considers asking to go to the bathroom. She does not need permission. Emma pays for this apartment.

"We are not going to hurt you... or your sister," he

whispers, voice softer than anticipated. When did he get closer? She slides away from him, praying for distance and clarity. The cotton balls in her head return in full and thoughts cannot slither through them. Due to the proximity, but more so the idea of Avery being in danger. It incapacitates her.

Relief comes… but how could she trust his word? They do not know one another. He might be lying. She does not know why they are here. Why he is asking all these invasive questions. "We need your view. For a few days. I swear."

Swear? Wait… a *few* days. Few is ambiguous. It holds no actual promise of time. Two, four, six, probably less than a full week but a week? Her boss may forgive her for missing one shift. One is a far cry from three. She needs these shifts to graduate.

Besides, Carter's natural suspicion fed by Dr. Pepper's insistence? Someone could get hurt. Even if they protect her and Avery, no such promise stands for those who come to save them.

"Okay."

Emma hides with the mugs, ignoring the goosebumps elicited by his gaze. None of the other agents are in here asking weird personal questions and making promises they may not keep. Iceman plays the camera by the window. Golden eyes disappears into the hall and returns a moment later with a new laptop bag.

Emma pauses as she watches them, noticing the

computers they use to see the camera feed on expanded screens. The other side of the street appears from a dozen angles. For agents without a badge, this sure looks like a stakeout. The Asian woman removes her gun, leaning it against the wall. She meets Emma's curious eyes, raising an eyebrow.

Emma looks away, gripping her mug tightly. Her breath comes out in quiet huffs.

She cannot forget the danger they pose. Not when they put away the guns. Not when they take a seat at their setup and begin in quiet conversation. Her grip on the hot mug centers her, even as it begins to burn her hands. Avery sleeps right there and the tall man… is right *there*.

Emma jumps away as he reaches for her. She cannot stop the involuntary impulse to cower. The smooth cup slips right out of her grip.

Everything slips into slow motion. The choking she does on her own scream. All the liquid beginning to fall out of the turning cup. Stepping away on autopilot. The split-second thought of wondering if the smashing glass will cause them to shoot. Her apology already begins by the time the man catches the mug.

Her eyes widen as he catches it easily. One blink, and he holds the full cup in one large hand.

"How did you—" She stops herself as he straightens out. The agent slides it delicately back onto the counter.

Emma rears at the hurt written in his expression. *Hurt? What does he have to be hurt about?* She doesn't even know his name. What could he possibly be hurt about? Emma opens her mouth and then shuts it, uncertain what to say. The awful thing is she cannot tell whether she is unsure because of the danger, or if she is concerned about hurting him further.

He *caught* the mug.

She stares at it and then at him. He's not concerned about it. Within the second it took her to process his hurt feelings, he retraced his steps behind the stone wall of his neutrality. Emotionless. Detached. Scary. "You should not have been able to catch that."

"You dropped it—"

"I know that" Emma responds, eyebrows drawing together. How could he be acting hurt when she watched him kill someone? There were others dead. Pools of blood. Bodies all over the place. Red and blue lights swim on the ceiling of her apartment in shards. The sirens ceased but police are down the street. Escorting bodies in ambulances. Assigning the city coroner to see if they can find out how many shooters there were. He killed them. Blood stains his hands. "This is my favourite mug… thank you for saving it."

Thank you? Thank you?! You are thanking the man who broke into your apartment and is holding you hostage.

Technically, no one mentioned leaving. Not her about him or him about her and Avery. He made it quite clear though.

Taking her phone. Implying the duration of their stay. Focusing on the mug keeps her from saying something she shouldn't or looking into his eyes until she loses herself.

Temptation swells, goading her to poke it, just to make sure it is really her mug. None of this feels real. Not like a dream but a delusion. Some kind of sick, contorted version of reality. Could she be at the dentist? Or maybe she got into an accident and the morphine overwhelmed her system?

"I will not hurt you," he repeats quietly, taking his mug gratefully. Thirty bodies. At least. Able to see her across an entire city block. How did he know about her nearly calling the police? Or watching them? Then he got here in less than a minute. Somehow, he knew the exact number of her apartment though he saw it from the *outside,* a city block away. What if he heard her? Knew it must be her. After all, he caught a mug.

A mug she dropped from her waist height.

He stands half a foot taller than she... at least. It would have been dropped below his midline and yet he caught it. In a split second. Midair. She searches the floor, but not a single drop of the dark tea reflects off her yellowish tile.

"Are you a vampire?"

CHAPTER 8: KICKED PUPPY

It seemed like a reasonable question... at the time. The momentary loss of logic quickly faded away. She realized just how stupid it had been when his surprised expression turned to one of amusement. At least he didn't point out the foolishness or make her feel stupider. Emma considered it the only consolation of the evening. Strange people invaded her house. Held her at gunpoint. Interrogated her *and* she witnessed a massacre.

Emma cannot imagine anyone else being ashamed of asking a murderer about what species they are. Mortification followed her all the way into sleep and consumed her there with dreams of standing naked in class. Somehow, lying in her bed, pretending to be asleep offers no relief to the horror her mind and mouth conjured. She prayed the extra minutes of play-acting would award her with a wise, mature response. A distraction to erase the odd encounter from his mind... when she should be planning an escape.

She escaped... in a way. Hours earlier she simply drained her tea, claimed a headache, and threw herself into bed to escape the handsome spark in his eyes. The soldiers did not bother her... not directly. Except none of them stopped working. A couple would take breaks intermittently. Rifle through the kitchen. Use the bathroom. Slouch against a wall and close their eyes. Three people always remained watching the camera or telescope.

Who would go in for acupuncture at two in the morning?

She watched, occasionally losing the ability to focus. At one point she blacked out. Through it all, Avery slept. At one point, she threw an arm around her sister. Emma enjoyed the unconscious snuggles but she worried about what would happen when the agents ultimately changed their minds. Prayer settled her but not enough to make her forget the prying eyes. Their presence unravels her.

Especially the giant, whom she quickly confirmed as the leader. It made sense the first time he walked into the apartment and they all made a way for him. His presence reinforced the theory multiple times. Every time he switched stations during the night, the agents straightened. Printouts were brought to him first.

Despite his size and at times terrifying appearance, he treats everyone gently. She never heard him raise his voice. Or get annoyed. Even when one of the agents struggled with compiling information in a document. He guided her through the simple process delicately.

Pressing her face into her pillow, she plays with a loose thread and takes a deep breath. Iceman meets her eyes across the room. She has been made. Instead of getting out of bed, she twists around. What will she say to Avery?

She counts every freckle on her sister's nose. Watches the way her eyelids flutter slightly. How will she tell her little sister who is in her apartment when even she does not know? What will Avery say? She is too smart to believe some half-prepared lie. Emma taps the tip of the girl's chin before she pushes herself up.

Running her fingers through her hair, she braids it over her shoulder, refusing to look at any of them. Securing her elastic on the end, she glances down at her satin nightgown. Unfortunately, she felt too hot with the robe on. Her fluffy blanket became the only protection she had from all of them. Reaching down to the floor, she takes the discarded fluff ball off the ground and slides it on, glancing at herself in the mirror between her bed and desk.

They are not staring at her and yet she feels like a pathogen underneath a microscope. Glancing at Avery, she rolls her deodorant on and sprays herself with some perfume.

Her body tenses at the cool mist and its perceived attack. Despite feeling somewhat safe, the fact she stands a prisoner in her own home cannot be avoided. Every nerve in her body fires off warning at the slightest stimuli. She is painfully aware of their every movement. Their eyes feel like a match against her skin.

Emma briefly considers returning to bed. What point is there in being awake if she cannot go anywhere or do anything? Not that she slept. Sleep evaded her control until her body went into the dark without giving her rest.

"Good morning," the agent in charge greets, his breath

curling around her bare ear. She jumps at his warm voice, especially when she realizes just how close he is. Wrapping her arms around herself, she faces him, schooling her expression into neutrality. Her siblings, especially Cody, can see through her poker face. A stranger should not be able to. "I hope we did not keep you up?"

Why is he acting like this is a slumber party? She stares at him, her eyes dragging over his face gingerly. Between the warmth in his voice and her lack of sleep, she begins to wonder if she is truly delusional. Abundantly so. Between the accent, the body, and the manners he acts like every honourable love interest in her fantasy worlds— "Do you need food? I don't have a lot to offer but I have eggs...."

"No, we have it handled," he promises, clasping his hands behind his back. Her eyes narrow slightly as she looks past him. There is no other food in the room. Handled?

Refusing to meet his eyes now and unsure what else to do or say, she digs her toes into the furry rug underneath her bed. She could clean. Although what is there to clean with people crawling all over her apartment? The last thing she wants is to get in the way of the wrong person.

"Are your eyes naturally that colour?"

Her eyebrows draw together as she peers into his dark ones. Of all the questions in his arsenal, she did not consider eye colour to be one of them. Her eyes are green. Bright enough to confuse most people. The same colour as her mom's. Dad loved the way Moe's eyes grounded him. Like the forests he remembered playing in with his cousins. Pretending to be knights in enchanted forests, saving princesses. "Yes, they are."

"Have you had surgery done to you before?"

Blinking rapidly, she presses her hand to face. *Is he implying something?* Insecurity smacks against old stone walls. Old wounds threatening to open up again. She knows she looks enough like Moe, a widely hailed beauty, to understand her own physical appeal. However, his question and unnerving eyes instantly force her to wonder whether she *should* have surgery done. "Uh… dental surgery. I had my wisdom teeth and a couple others removed."

"Never a face lift or reconstructive surgery?"

"No, of course not," Emma answers cocking her head to the side. *Am I supposed to be offended or flattered?* She toys with her golden earring, tempted to finally ask him a question. He beats her to it.

"Have you ever gone by a different name?"

"I've been in school plays before." Mouth opening as he scans her over. This question makes sense. Mostly…. "But no alias'."

"And you were born twenty twenty-nine?"

"Yes," she confirms, hearing the snark in her tone before he reacts to it. She almost presses her hand against her mouth. Almost. Avery shifts in the bed, reminding her just how dangerous this is. Just how much she has to lose by stepping a toe out of line.

"And that makes you twenty years old?"

She begins to consider the possible reality where he is either half-deaf or slow. Then again, English may be his second language and he may not have understood her the first time. Guilt stares her in the face with disappointed eyes. She stands up properly, enunciating her word. "Yes."

"How long have you been twenty years old?"

Pausing, she inhales rapidly and moves over to her desk. He follows her closely, stopping when she drains her cup of water. The questions are hurting her head. Lack of sleep. No food. Epinephrine from last night having no outlet, left to wreak havoc on her nervous system. "It is March, I turned twenty in December. It has been technically three months. I turn twenty-one this year."

"And that will be your first time turning twenty-one?"

"I do not understand the question," Emma sighs, slipping away from him and those eyes. She brushes past a small group of agents, breaking into her kitchen with some relief. None of them are in the smaller room. While she enjoys seeing her apartment filled with people, she also enjoys being able to spread her arms out without hitting someone. Particularly those she is terrified to touch. "You cannot be the same age more than once."

"You said you were single?"

"No one else has a key," she corrects under her breath, filling up her glass water bottle. He watches as she drinks it. After the first gulp, she cannot take anymore. Not of the water... but of him watching her drink it. A blush begins to rise, burning her face as she turns her back to him. Emma spent the better part of her life being invisible. It upset her when she was in junior high. Every girl wanted to be noticed. When people made fun of her for being unremarkable, she struggled. Now, she's learned better but he watches her with the eyes of an eagle. "Yes, I am single."

"When were you born? The time. Date. Place."

"You already know," Emma reminds, disturbing her braid as she runs a hand over her scalp. She flips on the heat for a pan and grabs a handful of salt packets. "I do not know the exact time. You could text Moe."

"And do you think they would have a newspaper from the day you were born?"

Emma's eyebrows draw together as she crosses her arms. "Do your parents have a newspaper from the day you were born? I have never heard of someone doing that."

"Do you enjoy reading?"

He holds up the copy of the Shakespeare copycat, eyebrows raised. Emma grabs the half-filled egg carton from her fridge, counting the agents outside. Shaking her head, she begins breaking the eggs into a small bowl. They may have their own solution for food but she did not see any of them eating. If they will not eat it, she and Avery will. "I do."

"And you enjoy Shakespeare?"

"For the most part," Emma answers carefully, glancing at him. He shoots off other questions but she refuses to hear them. Every question he asks becomes more and more invasive. She doesn't even know his name yet. "Are you going to let me ask some questions?"

Interrupted, his mouth hangs open purposelessly. Emma delights in the momentary confusion breaking through his serious mask. She tries to guess his age. It escapes her but trying to figure out anything about him besides the obvious is impossible. The man has a strange agelessness to him. His skin practically glows. It is too smooth. Like someone stretched plastic wrap over his face to preserve it.

Turning back to the pan, she frantically scrambles the eggs. He is a fire hazard. Avery may wake up when she begins to smell food. Still, for now silence prevails and the soldier stands openly towards her. Emma laughs a little to dispel the tension, pulling at a free curl around her face. "Because you are the one who broke into *my* apartment. Not the other way around."

"It required no breaking," he counters, crossing his arms. As he does, his fists push up his biceps. The perfect reminder of how dangerous he is. One punch and he could dent her skull. She has no intention of giving him a reason to punch her. Or Avery. "The door was unlocked."

Her hand stills on the spatula as she stares at the time flashing on her oven. Unlocked? It most certainly was *not*.

In fact, it had three locks on it. One of which he could have picked easily but the other two were installed as reassurance. One cannot simply look at a reinforced metal bar over a door and label it 'unlocked'. Begging the question of how they entered in the first place. She ponders asking the question she should have last night, but his face closes back down. Try as she might, she cannot peer past the invisible veil.

"I need to go to work," Emma remarks instead, staring at him through her lashes. He should not be able to tell she is lying, and yet the way he looks at her causes a confession to come welling up. Her next shift is Wednesday. They said a few days. A few. The ambiguity does not sit well with her.

Especially not with Avery sleeping in the other room. The agent does not respond to her, reaching up to grab the special seasoning she cannot reach. She immediately steps away, refusing to take it from his hand. He puts it down with a quiet sigh.

"I have bills to pay. I need to work."

"We will call in sick for you," he counters, voice low and quiet. Pouring some of the seasoning onto the lump of eggs, she pushes them around, searching for a way out of the offer. She begins to argue but he brushes his hand perfectly over the butt of his gun. Not the long one secured on his back. The pistol snug in the holster on his hip.

Promises no threat to her or her sister, and then flashes a gun at the first hint of trouble. She refuses to feel upset by it. Despite the flare of betrayal burning her ears.

Emma focuses on the eggs, her jaw locking. The protectiveness inside of her rears its powerful head. If he even *thinks* to threaten Avery, he will find out just how unapologetically she can break something too.

Emma glances over her shoulder at the other agents milling about in the living room. She cannot afford to get comfortable. For her sake and Avery's. Not with him. Not with the iceman or golden eyes. She considers a way to set up a message on the windows or the bathroom. Her and Avery found special chalk to draw on glass and spent a day decorating for Christmas. She could find it somewhere and write 'help, call the police'… and then the dangerous soldiers would find it.

Her frustration mounts. As her mind begins to spiral, he draws closer. What does he expect? She will stop being afraid when he puts the guns away? Does he think she will trust his word? The word of a man who killed someone in front of her. A man she does not know. Whom she fights *not* to know. Emma steps away from him, gripping the spatula tightly.

Until she hears Avery's voice.

The second Emma hears her little sister, she throws the utensil down and rushes out of the kitchen. Avery sits on the edge of the bed, cross-legged as she stares at the iceman. "I have never seen a camera so big."

"Good morning Riri," Emma greets loudly, cutting off their line of sight to her little sister. She crouches in front of her, properly protecting her from them. "How was your sleep?"

Avery looks down at her, grogginess trapped within squinted eyes. She stretches her neck, intrigue replacing sleep as she catches a glimpse of stakeout equipment. Emma attempts to block her from seeing anything or anyone else, forcing a grin onto her face. The entire time her heart pounds like a drum. Sweat builds up behind her knees. Naturally, Avery takes one look at her face and frowns. "Em? Are you okay?"

"Yeah, I just had to get up early to let my friends in," Emma answers, almost sick from lying to her. Has she ever lied to her family before? The tattoos are different. What she puts on her skin does not pose any danger to her family. Lying to her, making Avery believe she knows these people, it perpetuates the threat. It may lead her to trust them. Befriend them. Avery makes friends out of any and every person. "I forgot they were coming. We can still have fun though. We'll leave them to their work."

Avery's eyebrows draw together as she peers over Emma's shoulder. This time she does not move. She should. Keep Avery from seeing anything that could put her in danger. No matter what steps Emma takes to protect Riri, they are stuck here for an indefinite period of time. She cannot pray temporary blindness over her... or can she? "Working?"

"They are building photographers."

Even golden eyes scoffs at the stupidity of her excuse. Avery's scrunches her nose as she stands. Looking at the technology set up between the curtains, she puts her hands on her hips. "I didn't know you could be a building photographer. I thought they were astronomers or something."

A much better excuse. Emma sighs to herself, already annoyed for temporarily letting her guard down. She considers reverting to a different lie but forces herself to act nonplussed. Avery cannot see through everything. Not if Emma makes herself believe in the simplicity of this circumstance. "It is a really boring, *stupid* job. Only the bad photographers get the job because they cannot catch moving objects... are you all better now?"

"I still don't want to go home," Avery whispers, grabbing Emma's hands in a vise grip. Her eyes bore into Emma's as if she can strong arm her older sister into submission. Little does she know the danger they are facing. What Riri wants is, for once, the least of Emma's concerns. They need to get out of this building. Out of the city. "Moe doesn't need me back. I am off for a week. Please."

"Ri, you *need* to go home," Emma counters, pulling on the end of her long braids. She prays her desperation comes across clearly. Avery pays no heed. Not about her desperation or about the fact her 'friends' have guns. "Moe barely let you come over."

Tears burn the back of her eyes for the first time. A knot of emotion clogs the back of her throat. She takes a deep breath shakily, peering into her little sister's eyes. Siblings are supposed to have telepathy. From a single look Moses and Emma would have a distraction and escape route planned. Avery is young but not young enough to be wholly ignorant to danger.

"No one is leaving," Mr. Tall, Dark and Handsome states, arms crossed as he leans against the doorway into the living room.

"Obviously, лапочка needs a safe place to heal Emma," the Russian man remarks, smirking. Emma's fist tightens against her side as Avery nods in agreement. "Come look at the camera. I will show you how to take interesting pictures of the buildings."

Emma catches Avery's arm, holding her back. The other agents pause, shifting uncertainly as they glance between her and their leader. His fists clench as Emma sets her jaw. Anger reaches its tipping point, the smell of smoke curling around Emma's nose. "She needs breakfast—"

"I don't want to leave *sis*," Avery remarks, ripping her arm away. She crosses her arms, her smirk stolen from the Russian's face. Emma considers exploding, but then she realizes the smoke is not coming from her anger.

Mr. Tall, Dark, and Handsome pushes off the wall and runs. The others turn towards the kitchen as Emma follows him. She slides to a stop a step outside the kitchen, her arm shooting out to stop Avery from entering the smoke-filled room. Together they watch the giant remove burning eggs from the stove. He sighs loudly as he turns off the burner and waves a towel around.

Emma flips on the vent above the stove and rushes to the bathroom, opening the window there. The smoke clings to the ceiling, drifting through the rest of the apartment to form clouds.

"You need to be more responsible," the leader snaps, putting the pan onto the counter. He pauses in his lecture to stare at her smoke alarm. Not where it should be attached to the ceiling... but on top of her fridge without batteries. She meant to replace them. Honestly, she rarely cooks anyway. "You could have burned this whole building down."

Her jaw drops. Avery returns to the iceman, asking about the camera. A blessing in disguise. No younger sibling should have to watch their older sister have a meltdown. The man crosses his arms in response, completely unaware of the bombs exploding across her brain. Fragments steal her ability to speak. A small squeak escapes her parted lips. Maybe it is the smoke inhalation but her brain will not work.

Is he lecturing her on responsibility? *Her*. This stranger who broke into her house less than twenty-four hours ago? The audacity. More than the audacity, the complete *nerve* to actively lecture someone whose home you broke into.

When he gets uncomfortable with her staring at him like he sprouted a third head, the pan becomes a distant memory. As he approaches her, her eyes follow his progression. The smoke begins to dispel as the vent kicks into full speed. Or her eyes are adjusting to the burn because she no longer feels like she needs to blink.

"Are you okay?"

She flinches away from him, crashing back into reality. He drops his head, sighing quietly as she shoots past her breaking point. Emma can almost feel her patience shatter like glass around her. "Do not look at me like a kicked puppy. I watched you *shoot* someone in there. He was unarmed and surrendering and you *killed* him."

Her voice is too low for Avery to hear. Not that it matters. Her little sister is enamoured with the iceman. One of the agents helps her onto a stool so she can see through the lens he lowered to accommodate her height.

The man in front of her drops any pretense of friendliness. Just like when he flashed his gun, his eyes darken. The shadow that passes over his face settles into place, leaving Emma to stare into a midnight sky hiding a tornado within it.

When he steps closer, she backs away. Fear bubbles from her chest but she forces it to remain in place. She cannot let it show. Even if she can barely breathe. "You do not know what you saw. Do not pretend you understand anything."

"Then explain it to me."

She almost passes out. Emma has never been prouder of herself. Her voice does not waver. Even the agent seems impressed with her lack of fear. If only he could read her well enough to notice the bravery melting behind her eyes. Already leaning in to whisper to him, she feels herself beginning to fall forward. With the worry of falling over, comes the brief curiosity she has of whether he would feel like man or like marble.

The thought sets fire to her face and she suddenly wishes he were not staring directly at her face. Emma forces her head and body back, refusing to entertain ideas of fainting to see how he would react.

Avery walks into the kitchen, humming. She bypasses both of them to grab ice cream from the freezer. Except when she turns around, her little smirk directs itself at Emma. Her eyebrows wiggle at her older sister as she attempts a wink. It is poorly executed.

"Stop," Emma mouths, hoping the agent will not see. Of course, he does. He has not taken his eyes off her since the beginning of his lecture. It would be the *responsible* thing to step away from him. Except her feet are practically frozen to the ground. He smells incredible. Between the assault of the smoke and the awful smell of burnt eggs, his cologne is a precious reprieve.

"Is this your boyfriend?"

Emma chokes on her own spit. "Absolutely not."

The agent laughs. Emma flushes in embarrassment. The blush melts away as she rests in his laugh. All the warmth he sent away is back and doubled in his laugh. It does something to her stomach. There is nothing derogatory or dismissive in the sound. "I am too old for her."

Too old? She narrows her eyes at him as he turns away. The agent could not be more than five years older than she. Give or take a year or two. She is finishing school in a year with an already established career. Emma knows who she is. She always has. Age, to an extent, is a silly number. Then again, she began to flirt with someone at church thinking he was twenty-six. A friend informed her of his actual age, thirty-one. This was a year ago already. She learned to start asking ages sooner. The early twenties dating pool ranges from teenagers to fully established adults. Better safer than sorry.

She should not care. Why would she want to date someone she does not know anyway? The guy could be a thirty-year-old again… and there is the little matter of him murdering someone before her eyes. After which he 'broke' into her house. Threatened to shoot her. And she still does not know anything about him. Age does not matter as much as his name. Or actual occupation.

"How old are you?" Avery sings excitedly, hands clasped behind her back as she swings from side to side. The agent looks down at her, the smile returning to his face. Giant man can go from The Friendly Giant to Hulk in three seconds flat. How does he morph in front of her eyes so flawlessly?

He taps a finger against Avery's nose. "Too."

"Too old," Emma states at Avery's confusion. Riri watches Mr. Tall Dark and Handsome saunter away, practically melting as she twirls towards her older sister. Emma accepts her little sister into her arms. Pressing a kiss against her head, she takes a deep relieved drag from the clearing air.

"Hate to see him go, but love to watch him walk away," Avery whispers, shaking her head against Emma's stomach. Shaking her head with a scandalized gasp, Emma gazes down into her younger sister's sparkling eyes. The two make funny faces at one another until Avery's expression turns deadly serious. "Don't let him slip through your fingers."

"Because I am going to take dating advice from a twelve-year-old," Emma snorts, keeping a playful smile on her face. She taps her fingers against the egg pan's handle, tempted to toss the entire thing away. Cleaning it will be worse than burning the eggs in the first place.

"I've had more action than you and I am half your age."

Emma gapes at her sister as Avery takes a spoon out of a drawer. She sucks on the spoon with her eyebrows wiggling and sashays away. *Where did she get the attitude from?* Refusing to answer her own question, she scrapes the eggs into the compost bin. With all the crust scraped away, she tosses the pan into her sink and soaks it with soap. Her expression of disgust grows when she watches Avery fawning over the agents. This is all going to blow up and the results are going to be ten times worse than simple burnt eggs.

CHAPTER 9: TIED UP WITH STRINGS

Phone? Unacceptable. Schoolwork on her laptop? Mandatory for the strange agents. The Tall, Dark, and Handsome one practically threw Emma's laptop at her when he saw her colour coordinated school calendar. Avery decoded it for him, explicitly breaking sister code. One minute after finding out she was three weeks behind on work, he sat her down at her desk and created a barricade of books to keep her trapped.

Even now, they watch her.

She tried to find a way to open a messenger portal with Carter. He may be the only one to believe her about this ridiculous situation. Knowing Carter, his crazy theories about why she hasn't responded to his texts are slathered over the internet.

Tapping the end of her pen against her teeth, she pulls her legs into her chest. Doing school is painful enough as is. Being forced to do it? Torture. Avery is having the time of her life. She sits at the iceman's side, listening to his instructions as she types on one of the laptops. Her years of gaming have given her fire fingers. Not that Emma wants her little sister to be utilized by... whatever they are.

She still does not know. Avery hasn't asked their names. If she asks Emma, she's going to have to lie again. Make up silly names for these strangers out of pettiness. Call iceman

Igorbigmanich. Name Mr. Tall, Dark, and Handsome Jim. Golden eyes… well she scares Emma so maybe she will let the agent supply her own name.

Carter would know. He'd find tap his phone screen twice and find birth certificates. Somehow Emma just knows he'd already be out of this apartment and *that* kills her more than anything.

The one person able to name exactly what secret organization they come from is waiting on the other side of a screen. All she needs to do is find a way to contact him.

"Em!" Avery calls, turning around from her little seat. "Come look at this adorable dog we just took a picture of."

"Are you… taking pictures of other people in their apartments?" Emma questions, staring at the iceman, not Avery. Her little sister doesn't care. To a twelve-year-old the idea may not be creepy. Especially when the 'cool' adults act like it's okay. The iceman shrugs nonchalantly, turning his camera for her to see. "You are."

"We are building photographers," the wise guy cracks, smirking at his own cleverness. She takes a slow, deep breath and leans over to see through the camera. The dog is cute. A tiny little white thing covered in fluff.

This is the first time she has been allowed to see outside of her apartment. Taking full advantage, she shifts the camera to look at the museum. Russian man must know what she is doing but he makes no attempt to stop her.

VACANCIES IN TIME

The glass museum is crawling with police. Red and blue lights swirl in competition with the morning sun. Yellow tape surrounds the front gates. While there are no bodies left, Emma zooms in to see the blood and tags where the police are marking the separate murder sites. Underneath her breath she begins to count. *1, 2, 3... 37.* Thirty-seven bodies.

Her breath catches as she returns the camera to its place and steps away. The Russian watches her with piercing eyes, waiting to see what she will say. He does not yet understand she would never let them find a reason to hurt her and in turn Avery.

"Agent Bingley takes the best pictures," Avery declares, smiling at her sister playfully. She glances at the iceman who smiles proudly in turn.

"Bingley?" Emma inquires, careful to keep her face blank. He nods, refusing to meet her eyes now. Avery claims his attention as his small proud smile turns into a radiant beam. "What an interesting name you have."

"Is this the little red person?" Agent Bingley inquires, eyebrows drawing together. She narrows her eyes on him but stops when the team leader walks in. One glance between them and the window is enough to make his fists clench. Veins bunch underneath his dark skin.

She quickly retreats from their little hangout and returns to her desk. He may decide to lecture her for her lack of responsibility all over again. While his accent makes the form of punishment almost a treat, she would prefer to abstain from all forms of yelling. She hates yelling. Hates disappointing anyone... even strangers apparently.

Why I should care is beyond me—

The internal monologue breaks when something in a white bag drops in front of her. She blinks at it as she taps the pen against her lip. Dragging her eyes up from where they focused on the page, she stares at him. "What is this?"

"Breakfast," he answers, glancing at the clock above her head. "More like an early lunch. You need to eat."

If Avery were not sitting beside Agent Bingley, she would be tempted to throw the bag at his head. Instead, she leisurely unwraps the bagel inside and sighs. Unfortunately, it looks and smells delicious. Bagels are a notch below ramen. Not in her obsession but in taste and quality.

She fights with the manners she was raised with and the stubborn anger his former actions warrant. His gun shines from his hip, so maybe it is better to be polite and say 'thank you'. To the nameless man who broke into her apartment at gunpoint. Why is he trying to get her to eat and do schoolwork as if he hasn't interrupted her life?

They are going to get caught. She already knows it. Police swarm the museum. Hundreds of people pass by the scene every hour. Someone else must have seen the agents. Someone who is not being held captive at gunpoint.

They are so obvious too. The owner of the white fluff

across the road will see the cameras eventually. Even if her glass is reflective. Neighbourhood watch is active in this area. Creeps with cameras pointed at buildings? Definitely enough to garner police attention.

Had Avery not been sleeping over, she would have already tried to make her escape. Thrown her laptop at their heads and sprinted. Years of walking around the city and biking powers her legs. She only uses the motorcycle to get to her parents' house. Work, library, groceries, she walks. Even jogs occasionally, though she prefers not to sweat. The humidity in the city is killer enough without the added layer of moisture and heat.

"You need to eat," he repeats, dragging a chair over. Where did he find a chair? In fact, where did he get the bagel? She did not hear the door open or close. No one knocked on it. Maybe they got someone to bring a bagel in through the window. Or magically found a way to open the walls. After all, he claimed not to 'break' in.

"You could have poisoned this," she counters in quiet rebellion, turning her shoulder towards him. Trying to focus on the textbook in front of her, Emma feels her mind floating away. She needs to memorize these compounds. It should be easy. For goodness sakes, she started at the clinic over a year ago! While she is not allowed to fill prescriptions by herself or measure out pills, powders, liquids or the likes, Carter and Dr. Pepper let her do it under their watchful eyes. "I am not hungry for your guilt bagel."

He sighs. Loud and out of his nose. "You cannot think on an empty stomach. You need to eat."

Picking the bagel back up, he thrusts it in front of her face. This time she does not flinch. She stares at it. The cream cheese seeps out, threatening to assault the diagram of milligrams versus micrograms on the page beneath it. "You're wrong. I am quite affluent in studying on an empty stomach."

The agent refuses to move his hand. She stares at it and then the bagel before trying to shift away. When she does, he stands up, so he can hold it further out. His forearm covers half the textbook with its girth. Enough to make it impossible to read. She could try to unearth her cue cards but he'd probably drop cream cheese onto them.

"Fine," she sighs, taking it out of his hand. Emma fancies thinking she ripped it away, except being rude and impolite goes against her character. Even towards someone who broke into her apartment. Well... in his mind he 'entered'. Semantics. "I will accept your guilt bagel but I am not going to enjoy it."

She twists her back on him further, ready for his lecture about her posture next. Before he can, her shoulders begin to hurt and she forces herself to straighten up.

"What are you studying?" He inquires, unwrapping his own bacon and egg bagel. Emma dutifully ignores him, running her hand over the cream cheese and sucking some away. How is it he knows her favourite kind of bagel? Her eyes narrow as she searches for Avery. The little girl disappears down the hall, her exit emphasized by the slam of the bathroom door.

"I am not going to answer any more of your questions until I get to ask some myself," Emma hisses, pointing at him with the bagel in hand. She bites into the end for emphasis and fights her immediate reaction to do a happy dance. Maybe the delusion caused by her imprisonment tricks her senses, but this is the best bagel in the world. "I am trying to focus on my studies. Go bother someone else."

Instead of leaving, he leans forward and points to the name of the textbook at the top of the page. **Pharmacology**; right there in the textbook title. She glances over at him, inches from her face with a covert smile revealing bright straight teeth. "I was asking to be polite."

"You are nothing if not polite," she agrees, brushing a rebellious curl behind her ear. He blinks, eyes trained on her face. They temporarily move to the cuffs around her ears and the mutinous pieces of hair curling at the nape of her neck. Emma did not bother to do anything more than put on a matching lounge set and socks this morning. Making drinks and food for her 'guests' confused everyone, no need to dress up for them too.

Emma clears her throat quietly, trying to make her intentions clear with the way she swivels her office chair. He continues to lean read, shoulder brushing against her back as his lips murmur the textbooks words. A shiver shuffles down her spine as every breath caresses the shell of her ear. Spinning to lecture him for his utter lack of regard for personal space, she finds herself nose to nose with the gorgeous agent. Neither of them moves back immediately, although he does look surprised to see her so close.

"I would like some privacy please."

"You do not get that in such a small apartment," he remarks, though he does shift back. She spins her chair, kicking her feet off the ground to get some space between them. Without his incredible cologne and beautiful eyes clouding her mind, she can actually think.

"I work at a pharmacy as an assistant, well legally a secretary, and go to school in my 'free time'. You have probably searched my garbage and seen the food I eat. House prices have always been ridiculously high in this city. You could pay hundreds of thousands to live in a cardboard box on a hill." Emma describes lowly, bringing her head down. In her mind, the closer she gets to the textbook, the less he will talk to her. Maybe the pages will absorb her. "It is all I can afford. And I am not ashamed about it either. My 'small' apartment fits me... like it is supposed to."

She stares at him and then the other agents for emphasis. The most people in the apartment at one time was her family, sans Cody. Nine people. Even then it felt too small. Suffocating, but that was probably because Moe had shared her displeasure with every detail about the two-room apartment and it made Emma feel... small. Inadequate.

Like he is now.

"Your parents must be well off." Emma glares at him. She underestimates the magnitude until he stumbles back. Anger is not something she employs or feels often, but the mention of her parents' wealth crawls under her skin and grates on an old, frayed her nerve. "Avery was talking about her gaming equipment at home and her soccer games. It costs to have a kid in sports. Especially when they are talented."

"My *parents* are well off. Dad started working at fourteen. We would go weeks without seeing him as little kids. He's spent his life building his company, building a home, building their life... but it is their life. Not mine. Their money, not my own."

"Why build wealth if not to share with your children?"

He stares at her expectantly, refusing to allow her the peace to study. Sighing, she faces him and taps the end of her pen against her finger. "My parents want to share everything with their children. They are endlessly generous. But with money comes strings and I cannot afford the strings attached."

The agent leans his elbow against the desk, closing her laptop when she tries to look at it. She should throw an eraser in the hall to test his reaction. Emma's desire to talk about this with a complete stranger is little to none. Who would be better though? He does not know her parents. Maybe Mr. Tall, Dark and Handsome holds the answer she never thought of.

His eyes are so kind when he is not threatening her life. Warm and inviting like a furry blanket in front of a cozy fire. For some reason they remind her of Christmas. Maybe sipping hot chocolate beside Moses as they watched the clear night sky. She does not entirely know why but she would prefer to think about the beauty of his eyes than the uncomfortable reasoning behind refusing financial support.

"You think they are bribing you?"

"No, I think I put the expectations on myself," Emma admits, mind in a different time. He opens his body to her, eyes gentler than ever, and she begins to get upset. Not with him but at herself. Less than a day since meeting him and she feels like she owes him answers. Except he gives nothing in return. "I love my parents. They love me more than I think I deserve at times. I never struggled accepting the love of Jesus because I saw the unconditional, sacrificial love every day when my Dad would go to work and still come home after ten-hour days with energy to play with us. But if I took their money, I would feel like I owed them something. Moe does not blatantly rub it in my face but she smothers me when she has the chance. If she had her way, I would live in a penthouse with a security guard and concierge who reported to her my every move. My feet would never touch puddles—what could I learn living from my parents' cheque book? What kind of care can I provide for someone being so out of touch with reality?"

"I do not think you struggle with independence. Or empathy." The agent assures, standing. His lips quirk at the sides as he pointedly opens her laptop back up. "There was a saying once that 'a fruit hand-picked will always be sweeter than that which is given'."

"And who said that?"

"My moe," the agent answers, tapping his index finger on the desk as his face takes on a hint of gloom. "About a man who had plenty when I complained about our little. Entitlement makes lazy, gluttonous fools out of men. Proverbs shares many things about sloth which I am sure you know."

"I could be one of those 'Christians'," Emma murmurs, for no reason other than to argue with him. To stop the softening in his heart. The man speaks about his mother once, with love in his eyes, and she splits apart. "Maybe I do not know what Proverbs is."

"With a sister like that?" He inquires, smiling at her as Avery wanders back into the room. She throws herself onto the seat beside Agent Bingley with a bright grin on her face. "I assumed a young girl so on fire for the Lord must come from a believing family."

She subconsciously brings her thumb up, running her nail under the ridge of her bottom lip as the cross brushes her chin. Her first tattoo. Emma reasoned Moe would have no reason to be angry if her first tattoo came from a place of faith. It serves as a constant reminder of sacrifice, love, and steadfastness.

After getting the tattoo she realized fear of your parents' opinions should end at eighteen. 'Perfect love casts out fear'. It took her almost nineteen years to realize her mother's love is not conditional. She never questioned her Father because he was never as severe. Years of expecting the worst created a complex. Even now she fails to understand how unfairly she painted those she loves. Her parents will not reject her or withdraw their love, even if she gets a face tattoo… though Moe might have a heart attack.

"Agent Darcy!" Avery calls, grinning from ear to ear. She holds a camera in her hand now and waves at the Tall, Dark, and Handsome one. Emma chokes back a laugh. Darcy and Bingley… those are certainly not their real names. She did not believe it in the first place.

One name from a classic could be coincidental, but the name of a famous love interest and his best friend? Absolutely not. Jane Austen would be proud though. Agent Darcy does his predecessor proud with his demeanor… Agent Bingley could use some help in being openly inviting.

CHAPTER 10: LITTLE SHARK

By the second day, the 'exciting' appeal of the building photographers wears off for Avery. For Emma, the party has just begun. Confined to the house with no phone, no social media, and unwilling to speak to any of the agents unless forced, she reaches a new standard of productivity. While she only left the simple assignments behind, her schoolwork lagged. Now her colour coordinated calendar is covered in green checks and gold stars.

There is the irritating fact too that Agent Darcy refused to return her books until she finished her overdue assignments. Except, she finished everything overdue this morning and now moves on to finishing some of her assignments early. Bingley keeps Avery distracted with little games or tasks. She drags her feet to and fro, occasionally requesting an adventure outside but he manages to distract her every time. Agent Darcy spends most of his time telling the agents what to do and whispering into a little communication device on his wrist.

Emma imagines what texts she's missing and how her family and friends are panicking, but the thoughts come less and less. Without her phone easily accessible, time slips away.

Yesterday passed so quickly she was surprised to see midnight flash on her laptop. After ten o'clock Agent Darcy started giving her a look. The same look he gave the agents who covered the long day shift. Not that she knows why they need different shifts when they cannot find anything in the first place. He shut down her laptop after 12 and rushed her with the intensity of her eyes as she got ready for bed. By the time she got underneath her blanket, sweat clung to the soft fabric of her pajamas.

"When are you guys going to be done?" Avery drones, hanging over the side of the chair. Agent Bingley carefully moves her head to grab a print-out. He slides it through a scanner before either of the deVries sisters can see it. "What are you looking for anyway?"

Emma's head jerks away from the textbook she studies, glancing at Avery. The pulsing cursor on her computer document reclaims her attention momentarily. Her blank essay taunts her. The document supposed to be filled with the details of her case study. Except she spent the last hour debating her choices with no progress in either direction.

Her attention splits between the mind-numbing paper and Avery. Will they punish Riri for innocent curiosity? Avery's bravery shocks everyone they meet, and it outweighs Emma's every time. Of course, she is the first one to ask the real questions. Her little sister does not know the danger they are in right now... this one thought offers little comfort.

"The perfect angle on the buildings," Agent Bingley answers with a sweet smile. He runs his hand through inky black curls and points at the pictures they taped to Emma's walls. They are putting the photos up for Avery's benefit. Bingley brought a printer at her request. She wanted to see the different perspectives taken by different people. Admittedly, all the photos are different despite being the same building. "Building photography is all about patience, Avery."

"I am not very patient," she confesses, yawning. He nods in silent agreement, sipping his beer as if it isn't one o'clock. Emma still does not understand how they are getting in and out. The front door remains triple-locked. "Taking photos of a bunch of buildings isn't very interesting."

"No one said the job was interesting," Agent Bingley counters, smiling into the neck of his drink. He swirls it and takes another swig, handing her a puzzle cube. She stares at the wooden block with piqued curiosity. Within seconds, she is twisting the different pieces into place.

Emma melts into her seat. She takes a deep breath, thanking the Lord internally. Avery needs to be safe. Agent Darcy made a promise of no harm... but then he flashed his gun with malice in his eyes.

He sits against the glass across from Emma. Holding an earmarked book in his hand, he glows in the sun. What an attractive man. His skin becomes gold under the afternoon light, his eyes melted bronze. Agent Darcy perfectly sculpts his facial hair, displaying along with his muscles and smile how well-kept he is. Holding a book in one arm, with one leg stretched out in front of him, he makes the perfect muse. If only Emma had the skin to immortalize this moment.

It is oddly wonderful having the agents here. If she ignores the danger they pose and the blood they spilled, she could even be happy.

Agent Darcy remarked she had no trouble being independent, but independence feels more like loneliness sometimes. Emma spent the last year basically alone. Every night listening to her heartbeat to fill the silence. She is comfortable being alone.

Knowing how to be alone and wanting to be alone are two different things though. No one is as extroverted as she is. Even Avery, one of the most charming people in the world, is an extroverted introvert.

Not that this has anything to do with the agents, but she's been single her entire life. No boyfriends. Not officially. A couple dates. Flings. Been part of an item—situationtionships which carried the burden of a relationship sometimes.

Never has a man looked her in the eyes and asked her to be his girlfriend. Three dates stand as the record, and somehow the man expected her to undress and give herself to him. When she made it clear clothes stay on until vows are exchanged with the witness of the Lord and man, he fled.

It might be nice to have someone to go to the library with. Check out the museum, have his hand slip into hers as they look at a painting done by lover of lover... although the museum will be closed for a bit. Avery and Moses are her friends but they are her siblings first. Her older brother tries to avoid leaving the house if he can… and to an extent it is kind of pathetic to have a twelve-year-old best friend as a twenty-year-old. Carter detests museums because of the way they 'manipulate history and perpetuate lies'.

And do you anticipate being best friends with Agent Darcy? Or Agent Bingley?

No. She is not sure she likes either of them. Stockholm Syndrome exists…

Agent Bingley treats her little sister with perfect kindness and remarkable consideration. He has yet to make her feel threatened. Darcy asks too many questions. When he is not asking questions, he is reading and blocking out the world. An increasingly frustrating thing considering he looks too good reading a book. Like they should be taking pictures of *him*, not the buildings across from her.

Emma hides behind a curtain of her hair to admire him. The Chinese woman notices everything, but she feels no shame for admiring a handsome man. At least until he catches her. If Agent Darcy figures it out, and calls her on it, she will probably be humiliated into speechlessness. This is her home though. She should not feel mortified in her own house for admiring the attractiveness of a man who broke into it.

Right?

Moe would be scarred. To think she finds an armed intruder attractive.

Emma begins to wonder about her own sanity. She blames it on the smoke clinging to the walls and her lack of sunlight and fresh air. Despite her somewhat unhealthy living standards, she spends two hours a day walking. Whether to the library or the ocean or parks. Most of the time she listens to audiobooks or music and one work days, she walks twice the typical amount.

"But why is the acupuncturist clinic so special? Most of the pictures are of them."

Agent Bingley glances at Darcy on the ground. He looks up once from his book but it is clear enough. Emma's fear shoots right back up her spine as she straightens. Her little sister's first questions were not worrisome for the agents, but apparently this one is.

"The clinic has the coolest lights. Look at this photo." Agent Bingley states, grabbing a picture from where it is taped on the wall. He hands it to Avery for her to admire. It captures the unique colours and shines from the glass. One of few pictures where it looks like it was taken for the purposes of the aesthetic... and not for the people inside. "When the other buildings get cool, we will take photos of them."

Avery smiles and tries to mimic his accent. Snorting, Bingley puts the photo into place. Tension dispels as the two begin to whisper secretively. Agent Darcy returns to his book, not even glancing at Emma. She cannot relax. Not until she knows Avery will stop asking dangerous questions. "What does *лапочка* mean?"

"It will not make sense in English," Agent Bingley assures, poking her nose. She tries to bite his hand and that sends him into a laughing fit. Muttering in a string of fast Russian, he puts a chair between the two of them. "It means adorable, but maybe I should have said *маленькая акула*. If you bit my finger, I would have needed to bite your entire hand off and I do not enjoy the taste of blood."

Avery tries to say the word back and stops when she stumbles on it. "What does that mean?"

"Little shark," Agent Bingley answers, using a pencil to smack her hand away as she tries to shove him. He twists it over his fingers and smacks her other hand when she tries again. "That's how you stop sharks. Except you hit them on the nose."

He tries but she manages to dodge and throws a crumpled paper at his head. It grazes his curls and ends up landing in the wild curls of a young woman. Agent Bingley guffaws, using the pencil as a bat against Avery's paper ball volley.

Laughter is a good sound to hear in the apartment. It means safety. Hearing Avery's laugh works faster than any anxiety medication. She runs over to Emma, throwing her arms around her sister's neck. "What are you doing?"

"Writing a paper, trust me it is even less exciting," Emma assures, although she is not the judge of what is interesting. Some days she would lie upside down with her legs against the glass and throw sticky balls at the ceiling to catch them when they fell. Interesting is not the way she describes her daily activities. With or without the agents. "Do you want my laptop? I'm sure it could handle a game download or two."

"You need it to write," Avery argues, sitting on her desk. She fights to stand up, using the shelves to balance. The desk is not some cheap, plywood thing. Her Dad gave it to her as an acceptance gift when she got into college. Solid oak. Made to last through wars. "The sooner you finish the boring paper, the sooner we can do something fun together. We could go to the arcade or something!"

Emma meets her eyes and then Agent Darcy's. He stares at her with open curiosity. What lie can she come up with next? Lies rarely come from Emma's tongue. It's wrong to lie. Hurtful and a sin among other things. "Maybe… what if we set up an arcade ourselves? I have a key to Trevor's apartment and he gave me full permission to borrow movies or consoles whenever I want."

They may not let her outside, but they are finding ways to leave the controlled environment. She raises her eyebrows at Agent Darcy, asking the silent question. He nods slowly, hiding it in his book when Avery looks over. If Avery suspects anything about the agents, she keeps it to herself. Acting is another weakness of Emma's and she refuses to show extra warmth to these people. Deceiving Avery and convincing her to trust the agents are two different things.

She has not called her sister out for the odd behaviour, but she will eventually. When the excitement fully wears off. Being with her older sister in her 'luxurious' apartment will only last so long. Moe will want answers too. She may accept a day without response, if Emma tells her they were just having too much fun, but there are no guarantees after that.

"Have you ever gotten acupuncture?" Avery inquires, taking a seat on the desk with an old comic book. Moses gave it to her among a dozen others. "Don't they stab you with needles?"

"Something like that. It's used to stimulate different parts of the neuromuscular structure, like your nervous system." Emma explains, smiling at her sister's confusion. "The brain and spine. It kind of resets your body. Loosens it up and helps with pain. From a medical perspective. I don't know anything about the spiritual aspects some people claim about it."

"Like yoga, right?"

"Maybe," Emma replies, smiling at the laminated comic book. Moses would be appalled to know anyone other than her touches them. Especially a kid. He is not high-strung except when it comes to his nerdy treasures. It is one of her favourite things about her older brother. "Why? Are you hoping to get stabbed?"

"No, I just wanted to know if you've gone to the acupuncture clinic," Avery yawns, crossing her ankles. She pushes her hair, now curled from her braids, over her shoulder and smiles at the pictures. "When are we going to get the console from Trevor?"

"After Emma finishes her paper."

Emma glares at Agent Darcy over her shoulder. She should be grateful. Part of her is. However, it is easier to keep her guard up and be angry, than allow him to see how appreciative she is of their presence. "I am going to get this done for you kiddo. I just need to focus."

Avery jumps off the desk and throws herself into Emma's bed. Curling around a long pillow, she refocuses on the comic and flips through it.

What do special agents and an acupuncturist clinic have in common?

Emma glances at her blank document and does nothing to fill it. Not while her brain is focused on figuring out a more interesting case study. The case of non-government agents and an acupuncture clinic.

Mob bosses use medical clinics as drug fronts all the time. For human trafficking rings or equally as illegal and awful things. The list is endless. However, she has seen people going into and out of the acupuncturist clinic. Watched the doctors inside. Even witnessed the half-dressed patients... Always by mistake. She ended up hiding in her bathroom every time, asking God for guidance on whether she should cross the street, find the person, and apologize. She decided every time it is better to suffer alone.

VACANCIES IN TIME

How many times has she walked down the street? Right past the acupuncturist clinic. Greeted the guards inside when they come to grab the mail. Spoken with the doctors when they go to get lunch from the kiosks or gas stations.

When she started looking for a new apartment in the city, she was thorough. Endlessly. By then she already worked at the pharmacy and Carter helped her. He used his sources on the dark side of the web where Emma cannot venture to find out about crime rates the police fail to report. She checked every forum and neighborhood group.

Finally, she found one with barely a theft in the area. When they scouted the different apartments in the building, she met Trevor for the first time. Fell in love with Chewy and the neighbours on this floor. What better neighbour to have across the hall than a paramedic?

One of her other neighbours on the floor works in the navy and another works as a dentist. All jobs which could be helpful to her. She considered everything.

Now her mind wanders to places it should not. Wondering if murderers hide within the clinic. Of course, in this spiral she makes the fatal mistake of assuming the agents are good guys. Working for a better cause. Trying to stop a great evil in the world. When in fact they may be thieves casing the next place to rob.

Moe begged her to get an apartment in a different area. Chinatown was and still is cheaper than the newer high-rises.

They offered to pay for the apartment but she meant what she said to Agent Darcy.

How can she call herself an adult while depending on someone else's income to live?

After they leave, and they must leave eventually (sometimes she needs to remind herself), she will need to look into getting a new place. Somewhere far from the museum. Her lease expires in a year (enough time to finish school and see if the pharmacy plans to follow through with hiring her as promised) but the apartment really is a steal. Anyone would be overjoyed to find something of so much worth for so little money.

Maybe she should have questioned why it was so cheap. Her mother made comments when Moses suggested she be more selective but it never occurred to her the magnitude of possible danger. Agent Darcy would probably tell her if this is a dangerous place to live. She considers asking him now but decides better of it. After all, why purposefully ask risky questions that already got her little sister in trouble?

CHAPTER 11: STEP OFF BRO

Agent Darcy must pity her. Only the third day after meeting him and he's already taken it upon himself to feed not only his troops but Emma and Avery. Despite her plea for independence, she cannot force herself to resist his attempts at bribing her. Especially because he brought cereal. Not the plain wheat kind of cereal that gets overly soggy... but the GOOD stuff. He knows it too. Avery could not contain her squeal of excitement when she woke up to the sugary cereals and the second she showed her excitement, Emma could not contain hers.

Now on her third bowl of cereal, Avery slows down. With the lack of slurping and excited, if not slightly obnoxious, grunting, Agent Bingley begins the interrogation.

"'Chewyman' texted 'completely spaced. My succulents will need water on Sunday, would you be willing to water them?'." Agent Bingley reads, eyebrows winding tighter together with every word. He scratches the mess of inky curls on his head, scanning her over. "Why do you chew men?"

Avery giggles into her hand, not seeing how seriously disturbed the man is. He glances back at Emma's phone in obvious confusion while Emma smiles into her cereal. At times the group of agents are so scary, she considers hiding underneath her bed to escape their eyes. More often than not, they act so adorably confused at normal things, like funny phone nicknames, and it convinces Emma they can be trusted and even liked.

"His dog's name is Chewy. He is Chewy's man." Emma explains softly, biting her lip to keep a full-fledged smile from breaking out at his disgust. He stares at her phone with the same confused look every time she explains the different names. Cody Coyote (Cody), Basket Boy (Moses), Freckles (Avery), Electric Man (Dad), and many others. She waits with bated breath for Dr. Racecar, otherwise known as Carter.

"What is *his* name?"

"Trevor."

"Why not make name Trevor? Why complicate it?"

"It is not complicated because I know whom the name belongs to," Emma counters with her eyebrows raised. He shakes his head in complete disagreement. Agent Bingley is the friendliest Agent by far, but he is also the most outspoken. Emma enjoys his unwavering stance on his slew of beliefs. Specifically when things do not make sense to him.

"But that is thing… 'Chewyman' is not his name. He does not belong to 'Chewyman'. He is Trevor." Agent Bingley argues, his accent deepening with every drop of frustration. He swipes a hand through his hair, ends of his lips pulling down into a comical frown. Avery giggles into her hand, glancing at Emma no longer tries to contain her amusement. The agent is not impressed. "*Я сыт этим по горло,* can you water his plants or not?"

"I don't know, can I?" Emma inquires, twisting around him. She seeks Agent Darcy in the crowd of agents. As their leader, he determines when they will leave. While she will be sorry to see them go, she cannot be more excited to get rid of her 'guests'. "Four days from now?"

"If not you, one of us," Agent Darcy consents, nodding from where he crouches by a camera.

It is not the answer she hoped for but what more can she expect? He rarely gives a straight answer, preferring vague and even obscure suggestions on time, date, and place. Coated in strange poetry and mysticism.

Avery jokes about the mystery but Emma lost interest in the 'mystery' when her little sister's safety came into question. Especially considering her mother knows her work schedule and knows she is supposed to be at work today. They have not reached Moe on the order of texts/messages to respond to. She cannot touch her phone but Darcy commanded her to respond through a mediator to maintain some normalcy. Maybe he suspects Moe will kick down the doors. The girls already know how their mother is going to react. Avery was supposed to go back home on Monday… now it is Wednesday.

Moe knows about Avery's 'plan' to run away. It is the only reason she allowed Emma to take her little sister into the city. Emma may be able to play the sympathy card for a little while longer but Moe is like a bloodhound. At the first sign of trouble, her radar starts chiming like a fire alarm. Her response time is faster than any emergency vehicle. Unlike first responder, she is not going to announce her entrance, the door will go flying off the hinges with an axe stuck in it.

How is she going to react to the so-called 'building photographers'?

"Text him 'yep', with an e, 'I can do that for you. Hope you're enjoying the mountains with my man! Bring him back in one piece'. Make sure to add an exclamation mark and a big bright smiling emoji... yes, that one."

Emma watches Agent Bingley's eyes narrow on her phone as he taps away. He has not gotten faster since they began responding to texts and messages this morning. Emma is not the most popular woman in the world but she holds many responsibilities. Volunteering at church, sitting on the board of women's ministry there, working at the pharmacy, study groups, her family, and her friends. Carter sends her a minimum of five articles a week with possible 'missions' attached to them. Even the library sent her an email regarding the books she borrowed and other ones she might be interested in.

Does he find this degrading? Of all the agents, he ended up sitting here scrolling through the phone with her. They probably drew sticks and he pulled the shortest one. No one can find enjoyment in this. Certainly not a highly trained agent who speaks broken English when he gets confused or frustrated and barely knows how to work a phone.

It would be simpler to let Emma respond, but no. Agent Darcy does not trust her. Bingley made up an excuse to Avery about wanting to practice his 'pop culture English'. He choked on his own tongue when he realized what an emoji was and how often Emma used them. Luckily her favourites pop up with keywords... but even then, every time one shows up, he whispers 'колдовство'.

Emma pondered giving him mercy but she needs to make her texts sound like nothing is wrong. Besides, a tiny part of her stomps its foot every time they steal away her freedom and force her to be a silent prisoner. Not enough to make her fight them... yet. Once Moe comes to steal Avery, her escape plan goes to a code red and it does involve screaming like a turkey.

"Who is this 'Dr. Racecar'? Why does he text you so much?" Agent Bingley questions, shaking his head as he presses on the newest message from Carter. An entire stream of dark texts fills the screen. Most of the texts are about different things he found surfing the web. Especially a ship spotted on the ocean that looks exactly like the Titanic, wreck and all. "Is this man in love with you, Emma?"

"No," she laughs, her eyes narrowing when Avery nods with a smirk. She grabs a grape from the fruit bowl in front of them and launches it at her little sister's head. Avery catches it in her mouth instead, wiggling her eyebrows.

"He texted you twenty-three times since you told him you

cannot come in for the rest of the week," Agent Bingley remarks, scratching his chin. "He loves you."

"Like a puppy loves another puppy," Emma assures, leaning forward to read the texts. Agent Bingley allows her to see as he scrolls through them. Her heart clenches painfully. Normally she would be in the clinic by now, listening to his crazy stories about his dark web friends or even going on strange geocaching journeys that deal with weird secret societies. If she possessed a sharper mind, she'd find a way to send a coded message but she cannot find a wording subtle enough to pass under the agent's radar. "I miss him."

"He misses you too," Agent Bingley comments in a mixture of disgust and amusement. He analyzes Emma with eyes as sharp as tweezers, reducing her to a bug under a microscope. She withdraws into her chair, stirring her cinnamon filled milk with silent distress. Miss you… **miss u xoxo**! "I do not know how to respond to so many texts."

"I do," Emma offers, almost snatching the phone out of his hand. She and Carter set up that codeword a long time ago! He worried aliens or government agents would snatch him up for his knowledge… and needed someone to call for backup. Redpanda69 could probably do a better job of saving him but she refused to disappoint him. *Lord thank you for Carter's paranoia—*

Bingley shoots back, holding the phone close to his chest. "No."

"If you just let me see the phone, I can respond—"

"You can *see* the phone right now."

Her fists clench for the first time. Anger, a somewhat foreign emotion, bubbles underneath a cool crust of nonchalance. Emma rarely lets the steam out but it's coming. She gets it. They do not know her. How can they trust her? Despite Agent Darcy's best attempts, she does not trust them either. However, an understanding exists, which began the moment they broke into her apartment:

She will not do anything to endanger her little sister.

"Step off bro," Avery demands, swinging her spoon at Agent Bingley. A drop of milk catches his shoulder. He looks at her in surprise, not used to a sharp edge attached to her soft voice. "Women deserve phone privacy as much as a guy does. Emma is letting you practice your English but that doesn't give you a right to her stuff. Stop being weird."

Agent Bingley blanks as Emma stares at him expectantly. Putting out her hand, she waits, but he only shakes his head. If anyone could change his mind, it is Avery. With her little sister's greatest efforts ignored, nothing else can move him.

"Fine, tell him 'wish I could adventure with you this week but Riri', capital r-i-r-i, 'really needs me. Miss u'—just 'u' the letter—'XO'."

"I am not familiar with this 'XO'."

"Kisses and hugs," Avery points out, brows dropping over her eyes. She looks to Emma this time, huffing loudly. "Just take the phone."

"Learning is important."

Emma watches him type the message with greedy eyes. She tries to hide it but when he sends the message, her shoulders drop. Carter may not assume she is in an entirely dangerous situation, but at least he will know something is wrong. If she texts it a second time, he'll show up at her apartment with a two-by-four and his cat, Smuckers.

She taps her finger on the measly kitchen table, glancing around the arch of her kitchen to see Agent Darcy and Agent Rosalind, IE golden eyes, murmuring hastily to one another. When she first heard Agent Rosalind referred to as such, she nearly laughed. Not because the name is ill-fitting... although Shakespeare's character held a lighter amusement and dry humour than the agent demonstrates.

Agent Rosalind is every bit the strong, protective leader Shakespeare wrote and his crowds adored. Her fellow agents practically shudder when she enters the room. Yesterday evening Agent Bingley attempted to scale Emma's curtains like a monkey. He dropped like an anvil when he heard Agent Rosalind's voice. Emma worried about his ankles all night.

Now, the same woman hisses fiercely with Agent Darcy as they stare out the glass windows. Their twin expressions of displeasure push Emma towards the edge. She glances at Avery, who is scolding Agent Bingley, and fights the urge to hold her close. This happens every time one of the agents display a semblance of upset. Every maternal instinct in her body prepares for war. Her best plan so far consists of throwing her sister into the tub and stealing a gun on the way there.

Emma's got no idea what she would do with the gun afterwards but hopefully it would make her too intimidating for reproach. Shooting it is self-explanatory right? Her experience begins and ends with Moses' video games. Her family wanted to go paintballing once but Moe worried it would be too much for Avery and none of them wanted to go without her.

"And another text from Moe," Bingley reports, tapping with extra emphasis against the screen. Avery makes him nervous. All her amusement about it fades with her concern about things happening outside of the apartment. Perhaps powerful women in general make him nervous. Agent Rosalind looks at Agent Bingley a certain way and he reduces himself to an innocent puppy. Admittedly, no agent contains a heart softer than his. His fellow soldiers, save for Rosalind, brighten when he enters the room. "She wants to know if you are dropping Avery off tonight or tomorrow morning. Her other offer is that she will come pick up Avery tomorrow afternoon herself."

"Tell her 'IDK. Probably tomorrow morning.'"

He blinks at Emma, languidly like he is having difficulty keeping his eyes open. She really does not enjoy it when he gets that expression on his face. It plays on old insecurities about her intelligence or lack thereof. "You will not be leaving."

"I am aware," Emma assures, shaking her head. Avery brings her dishes to the sink and bursts into the living room to share her tips with a couple agents on how to properly conquer the rainbow map in her favourite racing game. "The longer we can lead Moe on, the better. Let her believe Avery will be home tomorrow morning and then I can make up an excuse like a new exhibit at the museum she simply *must* see. My mother does not want Avery to stay a week. She barely wanted to let her stay the night."

"I cannot imagine why," Agent Bingley drawls, typing the text. Emma grabs a grape and throws it at his head, oddly relieved when it bounces through his curls. He rips it out of his hair and tosses it into his mouth without a care in the world. "You have so much to offer. Noodles and instant coffee."

"That's what I tell her but somehow it does not appeal to her," Emma sighs dramatically, tutting her tongue as she drinks her milk. Agent Darcy walks into the room with a quiet huff, grabbing a water bottle from the fridge. When he closes the fridge, he does not move. Instead, he stares at the large metal thing as if it could answer all his questions about the universe. "She barely thinks I am capable of feeding myself, nevertheless Avery. The lack of a proper bedroom and the placement of this apartment offends her."

"Is your Mom protective like this for all of you?" Agent Darcy inquires, leaning onto the back two legs of the chair. Beneath the tight-fitting black shirt, his abdominal muscles flex. Enough to make Emma's throat dry up. He crosses his arms, distracting her, and forcing their eyes to meet. "Or is it just her youngest? Were you allowed 'slumber parties'?"

Emma stops staring at him and instead watches the swirling cinnamon in her bowl of milk. Avery is a special case. Only one deVries child stepped onto death's doorstep and managed to live.

They never thought they'd be the family to lose a child, or come close to true grief. How can tragedy strike a family constantly praying to the Almighty God for protection, health, and safety? Except it did.

Avery was healthy one day. Laughing, playing, running around with her older siblings.

Overnight she started getting sick. Fevers. Infections. Constant trips to the doctor and a never-ending stream of antibiotics. The fun-loving five-year-old wilted into something frail, constantly cold, and never able to do much more than get out of bed. The deVries started getting scared when the infections stopped getting better... but the first seizure is what sent them over the edge.

Henny deVries dug her heels in when they told her it was a side effect of the ear infection she suffered and told them they needed to find a better diagnosis, or she would search out someone who could. Within hours they had a real, informed diagnosis... one which turned their blood to ice and threatened to stop their hearts.

Leukemia.

Even the word is enough to rip one's heart out. Render the chest an empty chasm, sucking out all joy, all light.

Cancer. The monster hidden in the shadows. Always spoken about in hushed tones with tearful eyes. Her family ranted about the horrible illness. One year someone from church announced their diagnoses and the entire congregation prayed together. Emma never heard of someone who managed to survive the beast. She believed, prayed, and knew God could heal anyone He wanted... and yet so many were not lucky like Avery.

She got treatment. Chemo. She possessed the strength to fight.

Moe declared her strength came directly from God. When He created the little girl, He gave her a double portion. Emma grew up thinking her little sister could raze mountains by sheer force of will. The deVries siblings became intimately aware of the youngest's strength and fight and stubbornness by the time Avery turned one. Emma gave up trying to tell the girl what she was and was not allowed to do when she hit her terrible twos.

... Only to find out Avery needed every bit of it to survive.

The doctors claimed she would not be able to read, write, run, or dance. She never ate as much as she should have because she felt sick, and what she did eat, she threw up. In the span of a few months, her hair disappeared, first in strands and then in chunks.

Of all the bald people Emma knows, Avery was and will always be the cutest one. Somehow, she managed to look equally adorable and terrifyingly frail at the same time. Moses and Cody refused to hug her for almost five months after she left the hospital because they thought one wrong squeeze would shatter her.

It took two years for her to be in full remission.

Emma snaps back to reality. To her dingy kitchen, sitting with Agent Bingley in front of her, Avery strong and healthy cheering on two of the agents as they race in the other room. He is not expecting or waiting for an answer, typing away at her phone instead. She catches herself pulling at her newest piercing and forces her hands to stop. "Moe is protective of all her children. Avery is the youngest though, it makes sense she would be a special case."

"If you say so," Agent Bingley remarks, shifting in the chair. "The chewy man said 'thank you, I owe you one'."

"Trevor will be coming home on Sunday," Emma announces lightly, watching Avery throw herself at one of the agents. She laughs wildly, claiming their game victory as her own. None of them try to stop her from jumping on the bed, even when it sends them sprawling. "And I watch Chewy when he works the night shift."

She pins Agent Darcy into place as she says it. He and Rosalind may continue their plotting after he has answered some questions. Well perhaps not questions, but at least he needs to respond to this observation. If he simply tells her when they are leaving, she will stop asking and fighting. Until such time, she needs to find some way to extract the information out of him.

Maybe he is making it difficult because he wants her to talk to him. She has no other reason to do so otherwise. Agent Darcy stopped with the strange personal questions for the most part. He comes at strange times to sit at her side and inquire after her book or schoolwork. Darcy brought her dinner at her desk last night. Not ramen noodles. Freshly made alfredo with shrimp and steamed vegetables.

"You water his plants and take care of his dog?" Agent Bingley questions as Agent Darcy smirks at her. Smirking because he knows why she is asking what she is and what she hopes to get out of it. He must enjoy annoying her, if he continues to insist on it. "You are a wife with no ring."

"Thank you, Agent Bingley," Emma murmurs, fighting the urge to roll her eyes. They are bad influences. "His first night shift should be on Wednesday or Thursday. Will I be able to take Chewy?"

"I am a fan of dogs," Agent Darcy answers, gazing at his

best friend, Bingley. "We all are."

"Not the rat kind. No one wants the rat kind." Agent Bingley agrees, smiling proudly. He slides her phone to the table mirroring her leaning body over the uncomfortable kitchen chairs. "This 'Chewy' dog is not a rat."

"He is my screensaver," Emma points out with a soft smile, aptly distracted. Her eyes narrow on Agent Darcy the moment she realizes his scheme. He barely hides his smugness with a large, genuine smile. "Avery has school again on Monday."

"I could quit school and join the *exciting* career of building photography," Avery drawls sarcastically, grinning when the agents shake their heads. Especially Agent Bingley who grins so widely his cheeks almost splinter.

"Not while you're with me," Emma gawks, imagining Moe's reaction. While their parents do not expect them to be ivy league honour roll students, they do expect them to contribute to society. Contributing to society means a stable job earned after getting a diploma. While they do not command their children to attend post-secondary... it is highly *suggested*. "You cannot drop out before you are eighteen Ri. The government and our parents will not allow it."

Avery only laughs maniacally. "Then I will get eight tattoos and dye my hair pink."

"I support that... while you attend school as you should." Emma remarks, standing. Despite knowing Avery is joking, a very real part of her grows concerned. A flash of stubbornness hides behind those sparkling green eyes. Emma is no mountain and even Everest would move at that look. "Tattoos and dying your hair will not change the tide of your future; dropping out of school would."

"Don't worry. I won't turn Moe and Dad on you."

Avery turns back to the gaming console, elbowing one of the agents as she turns back to the screen. The one nameless agent. She is shyer than the others. Practically hiding away in the corners of the apartment. None of the agents try to speak with her. At least from what Emma witnesses in the corners herself.

Normally she feels so awful at the exclusion of others that she jumps to fix it, but the girl seems to disappear at the slightest thought towards her. Naturally, Avery managed to make a quick friend of her. Coming as no surprise to anyone who knows the young girl. She is, after all, a drop of golden sun in a world that is at times bleak and cold.

"You did not want to travel on your break?" Agent Darcy inquires as Emma watches them interact.

"Some colleges have a different break time," Emma answers, smiling to herself. She changed nothing for her break. Reading, working, watching TV when she got really bored, and adventuring with Carter. He made it her favourite spring break so far, rivalling even her family trip to Hawai'i and the one to Holland. "I already had mine. Carter and I went geocaching on the islands and took a trip out to the mountains to follow an online scavenger hunt. We won a gift card to a local diner."

"And you are sure you are not romantically involved?"

Emma raises her eyebrows at him, pushing away her smile. The last thing she needs is to lighten the seriousness of her answer. "Absolutely. Carter and I are fantastic friends but we are too different. In values and personality. He is not the kind of man I need and I am not the kind of woman he needs either."

"And what kind of man do you need?"

Emma opens her mouth and instantly shuts it. How is she supposed to know? The one 'relationship' she had ended because they were more friends than anything else. Every date since ends in the same consensus. Perhaps a man is not supposed to excite her... but then again, why do people write about butterflies if they do not exist?

She knows what she does not need, and certainly what Carter does not. They are both too relaxed, but in their own different ways. Carter is more introverted where she is not. Spending hours in a dark basement researching theories and then running the streets raw in the dead of night is not a lifestyle she wants to lead. As rare as the sun is, she loves it. Emma loves chasing ideas, chasing adventure, searching for the fantastical. Surrounded by light but most importantly, a lot of laughter.

Her first love remains people. Most people scare Carter despite his charm and charisma. He would run away from them while she'd try to drag him closer. As friends they laugh about it; as partners? It would make them both miserable.

Besides, Carter does not love the Lord. Raised Catholic, he considers himself agnostic more than anything else. He never possessed the heart knowledge. Unfortunately, he had the typical upbringing of an overly religious home where doctrine was thrown at him and the Holy Spirit came up in one conversation and never again. The poor boy did not stand a chance.

"I am not sure," Emma confesses, playing with the end of her hair as she stares at the tall man. She withholds the urge to run her eyes over his entire body. Agent Darcy is numbingly attractive. He knows it, she knows it, everyone in the room must know it. Physically the appeal is there but it is more than that.

The wit. Sarcasm. Ability to easily converse. Just as she knows he is attractive, she also knows she should not think so. Especially knowing what he is capable of, but he reads. It's a strange stipulation but one she holds dearly to. He reads. Classical literature like she does, and likes it enough to name himself and the other agents after these characters she has always loved so deeply.

His presence is magnetic. People find their eyes following him. She knows when he enters a room before he does (not that there are many to enter in this apartment). Every agent he talks to perks up when he does. Not out of duty, but because they like him. A leader who's people *like* him is high praise. Emma's father said as much to Moses about the company.

If someone, not the man in front of her, asked that question, she'd list characteristics off the top of her head. Put together and given a face, they'd resemble Agent Darcy exactly.

Forcing away the thought so he cannot see it in her eyes, she leaves his side to grab a remote. "Add me to the game, Riri."

CHAPTER 12: PERPETUALLY 24

"*Маленькая акула* cheats!" Agent Bingley declares with feigned exasperation, shaking his head in bemusement. He slaps his cards down with extra force when Avery begins to laugh maniacally. Emma glances at Agent Rosalind for support but her expression sours with his shout. "Roll up your sleeves. You are hiding something."

"We should be playing for real money," Avery argues, collecting the poker chips and the candy that comes with it. Rosalind mutters something in Mandarin, tossing her cards into the pile. "I could start saving for a new webcam."

"How is it the older is nicer than the younger?" Agent Bingley jokes, slapping Avery's hand away when she tries to hit his arm. They stick their tongues out at one another.

"I don't think you deserve Bingley, you're too mean."

Agent Bingley's jaw drops in open hurt. It takes Emma a moment to realize he is joking. His expression would trick even a master. "You would be... what is the man with the *невежливый*, Z?"

He casts his eyes at Agent Darcy, planted firmly by the glass walls with a book in his hand. Z. Emma stares at the agent as he lazily peels his eyes from the books and looks up at their makeshift poker table. What could Z be short for? Ezekiel. Zeke off that. Zander. Zechariah. Zachary. Ezekiel.

She watches him run the pad of his finger over the tip of the paper and decides it must be. Any other name does not suit him properly.

"Wickham? You cannot compare a little girl to the wicked man." Agent Darcy states with a mixture of amusement and disapproval. He stares at Emma knowingly, dropping his eyes back to the pages of his book. Not a word about being called 'Z'. "Little shark is good. Clever, fast, sharp, resolute but light. You should be the picture beside the description."

Avery grins proudly, snapping her teeth at Agent Bingley when he tries to poke her nose. He does it back, sending them both into a giggling fit.

Emma deals out the cards, peeking at her own when she can. Jack and a ten. Not too bad. Then again, Avery always seems to know exactly when to bet and when not to. Hence Agent Bingley's playful accusations.

Agent Rosalind runs a finger over her hand, slicking her ponytail in the same move. It reaches all the way down to her waist, the ends almost tucked underneath her body as she sits. She carefully adjusts it as she shifts and mutters to herself in her own language again. Golden eyes intimidates anyone she sees, but her tells are obvious enough in games that *Emma* knows when she's got a bad hand.

"No speaking languages everyone cannot understand," Agent Darcy calls, not even looking up from his book. The fierce soldier glares at the back of his head, adjusting her cards as she twists to face the river again. "You know the rules."

"Everyone used to speak it," she argues, her voice conversational but her expression frozen in disapproval. Agent Bingley scoffs at her, earning a glower. Her sunlight eyes burn Emma's side, and the pits of fire are not even directed near her. She glances at the Russian man nervously but he does not react at all. The man murmurs to his cards and begins to pick apart his chips. "Do you have something to say Russki?"

Agent Bingley sucks his teeth, meeting her eyes with a half-smirk on his face. "You people like to think you started everything."

"We did. Longest recorded history and succession of dynasties. Do not get offended that your little country shrinks in comparison."

Agent Darcy sighs from his spot, dropping his head as Agent Bingley adjusts in his seat. Every agent in the vicinity is quick to sigh or distance themselves from the two of them. They must have this argument a lot. Often enough to have them both already so upset with little said between the two.

"Our 'little' country is bigger than yours," Agent Bingley counters, slamming a finger into the table. His accent thickens as he sneers. "Our forces are three times as strong."

"Where does that number come? From your noses?" Agent Rosalind questions, refusing to raise her voice. It remains devoid of emotion, but the slow raise of her eyebrow is enough to vex him. "China came first. Our language came first."

Suddenly the entire apartment explodes with conversation. Emma and Avery stare at each other in shock as a slew of different languages join in a dissonance of anger. Agent Darcy calmly slides his bookmark into place, setting his book on the desk. For the first time the equipment is left alone as he adjusts his military jacket and slides into the kitchen.

Relieved by his calm presence, Emma drops against her chair, but then his voice enters the mix. She understands some of what he says in Afrikaans but most goes over her head. Especially with the mix of Russian, Mandarin, Spanish, Hebrew and all the ones she cannot name.

Avery watches wide-eyed as an agent in the back starts vehemently wagging her finger at another agent. Two stand toe-to-toe as their shouting match produces enough spit to be considered rain.

Meanwhile, Agent Rosalind delicately slides her wager forward and meets Emma's eyes with quiet amusement. She crosses one leg over the other, holding her cards close to her chest. Agent Bingley starts waving his hand dismissively as Darcy lectures two agents in English.

"Russian was the first language. Eden used to be in our land before you *грязные воры* came to steal it."

"You are all wrong," Agent Darcy shouts, his voice silencing them. Rosalind drops her nonchalance at the authority in his tone. The Russian takes a seat, clearing his throat apologetically as the room returns to a calm. Their team leader glares at each one slowly, and then a smile breaks out. "Israel is the first nation as recorded in the Biblical texts... that is in Africa. My people were the first ones. Everyone knows Adam and Eve were black."

Discourse explodes like a volcano, except from Bingley who laughs obnoxiously as his best friend shrugs. It is Rosalind who challenges him first, flicking her hair out behind her. "First people maybe, not first language."

"African isn't a language. Your people are so broken up you cannot agree on one language—"

"Africa is a continent, not a country," Avery argues, her nose scrunching in disapproval as she stares at the iceman. He feigns ignorance with a wave and muttered dismissal. "You do not have a national language for a continent."

Agent Darcy puts his fist out for her and she swiftly smacks hers against his. "Besides, that is not our fault. We did not ask for new languages and culture to be forcibly injected into our land's lifeblood. Who knows who Africa would be if she was given a chance?"

"That is not my people's fault," Agent Rosalind scoffs, crossing her arms. Her eyes freeze two agents in place as they snort. "More people speak Mandarin than any other language and do not say English. Colonizers get no credit for imposing their language on another."

"More people speak Mandarin because your people reproduce like rabbits," Agent Bingley remarks, rolling his eyes. He slams his fist against the table, catching the chip that goes flying, and twists it between his fingers. "You do not get points for reproduction; you get points for landmass."

"And yet Russian is a dying language," Agent Rosalind counters, waving her hand. "The first language divided at Babel was Mandarin."

The entire room groans. Bingley rolls his eyes as the chair beside Emma groans. She keeps her eyes on the Chinese woman as Darcy slides into the chair beside her. He stretches out his legs, brushing against hers underneath the table. The fabric tickles her bare skin as he leans back. "You already know that is not true. Thousands of languages exist and none can be traced back to Mandarin other than your 'dialects'—Dialects are not languages!"

Her eyes narrow as he interrupts her. The two lean forward to glare at one another as the room silences. Instead of arguing now, they wait for her response. "Russian was not the first. If I must concede I will only do so to Aramaic, Eyre is the only one who would have any ground to stand on."

"Are they forgetting about Latin?" Avery whispers to Emma, pressing her lips together when Darcy begins to shake his head warningly. "I think Latin was first."

"Russian is closer to Aramaic than Mandarin."

Agent Darcy rolls his eyes, leaning his elbow on the back

of his seat. "And I am closer to that language and those people than either of you or anyone else in this room... even Eyre."

His eyes meet with those of the shy, wordless agent. She flushes as so many agents swing towards her and spins on her heel, scampering towards the window. Agent Darcy opens his arms for argument but no one opens their mouth.

Mentally, Emma awards herself. Afrikaans and from Africa puts him in South Africa, like she guessed when he first spoke. This seems like a silly conversation to be having though. No one can substantiate their claims. Guessing will only get them tangled up in politics and subjective opinions. Obviously, this is not the first argument on this topic and it still remains unsettled. How often do they come back to the exact same discussion?

"What proof do you have of that?" Agent Rosalind questions, matching his tone and posture. "Your people have not kept the same meticulous records—"

"The first texts of African history date back to four thousand BC," Agent Darcy calmly counters, cocking his head to the side. His hand, over the back of his chair, brushes the ends of Emma's hair. Goosebumps erupt over her skin, doubled by the confidence in his voice. "And yours date back to... twelve hundred BC? If I am not mistaken.'

"I am eons older than you, what do you know?" She waves her hand dismissively, adjusting the cards in her hand. His eyebrows raise as a triumphant smile breaks his cool mask.

"You read it. I *lived* it."

"You are the same age," Emma states in genuine confusion, her eyebrows drawn together. "At least you look it."

The victorious smile drops. Agent Darcy's shoulders bunch as the Russian laughs maniacally. What is so funny about that? She watches Rosalind's cool composure breaks for a second as golden eyes drop to the table. Laughter stops in time for them to hear her mutter something in Mandarin. Her glare pins Bingley to his seat. "It was a metaphor."

"You look like the oldest one here," Avery declares. Not to Agent Rosalind, but to Darcy whose expression drops slightly. Rosalind begins to laugh, for the first time Emma can remember. The sound is dry and low-pitched, lacking any warmth one expects from laughter. Iceman sticks his finger out at his friend, his amusement pouring off him. Even the normally silent agents begin to snicker to one another. "What's so funny?"

"They age me," Agent Darcy comments, glowering at his best friend and then Agent Rosalind. "An eon a day."

"It's because of that expression," Agent Bingley assures with a toothy grin, leaning forward to poke Darcy's face. He gets a resentment-filled snarl for his efforts. "It gives you wrinkles Darcy boy."

"*You* give me wrinkles."

"How old are you?" Emma asks, fully aware of the rare

opportunity to catch them off guard. This is her chance! They are relaxed and by Agent Darcy's reaction, they are already saying more than they should. Why not press the advantage? "You look younger than me Rosalind, but obviously you're older than everyone else."

She meets Emma's eyes, devoid of emotion or amusement. With her mouth a line and her face lacking influence, she could pass as a sixteen-year-old. They all look timeless in a way. Like their expressions are partially frozen. The Swedish agent is the only one without a plastic quality to his skin. Those features paired with Rosalind's slight stature make her appear to be younger than Emma. She considers asking them every night what products they use to make their skin so clear and shiny. Agent Eyre as they called her has a silky quality to her mane of curls. The kind of appearance every curly girl secretly envies.

Emma thought Agent Darcy must be the oldest simply because he gives the commands, but it could be possible Rosalind is older than the rest. It certainly does not seem like it though. Her eyes are filled with ancient wisdom. They all share that trait. Sometimes looking into their eyes makes Emma feel like she is being transported. Or trapped in an aquarium on the inside looking out. She thought it would fade over time as she got to know them... but it has almost been three full days and she knows so little about them.

"I am perpetually twenty-four," Agent Rosalind answers

with a forced smile, cocking her head to the side to appear younger.

The other agents laugh. So much so that one begins to gasp and clutch his stomach. Both sisters are equally confused and try to find answers in one another. Perhaps the joke is funny because there is something they do not know. While she is ignorant about many things, she prefers to be on the inside of a joke. No one wants to be on the outside looking in. Especially not when surrounded with so many intimidating and powerful people.

"Here, here," Agent Bingley responds, slapping his hand on the table. He grins at Emma and grabs his cards from where he discarded them on the table. "Now, back to the game—"

"I am going to fold," Emma states, glancing at Agent Darcy. He did not laugh. No subtle twitch to his full lips. While the man is a studious leader, he is not shy about with laughing at their jokes and encouraging the 'fun'. Unless he does not think what they said is funny.

She wants to know everything. Everything about him. About *them*. Are they a government agency? What does their symbol mean? Once she has answers about the group, she wants to sit in front of him and absorb everything. His favourite colour, family, anything, and everything. Maybe the fascination grows because he is a mystery, or maybe he seems like the kind of man everyone wishes to know. The kind of man she wants to know.

Instead, she gets secrets and dismissals.

Emma pushes herself away from the table, careful to watch Avery in case her little sister wants her to stay. Agents dote on her, encouraging her in hidden whispers and with secrets about her opponents. Her grin spreads wider with every word they say.

The shy agent, Eyre, greets her with a forced smile, spinning back to the monitor as she pulls her legs up. If Emma didn't worry about scaring the girl, she might say hi. Where most agents are intimidating or boisterous, Agent Eyre acts like the shadows will consume her. Like she enjoys being invisible. Another mystery to add to the list as Emma wanders to the edge of the last glass window and pulls the curtain away.

Leaning her head against the wall beside it, she draws a heart in the fog her breath creates. Rain rolls down the other side of the glass, following her finger. Taking a seat hesitantly, she crosses her arms and smiles at the outside world. Three days inside is too long. She misses the library, and Carter.

"We should go to the museum tomorrow," Avery declares, dropping at her side. She snuggles up to Emma's chest, yawning as her older sister affectionately plays with her hair. "Or go to the beach!"

"That sounds lovely," Emma agrees, glancing over her sister's head to the table filled with agents. Two of them are arguing over something as Rosalind and Bingley face each other fully. Before competition made them enemies. Now the intensity in their shared gaze is anything but resentful. Try as she might, she cannot guess what they communicate without words.

How long will it take Avery to realize they are trapped here? She must be feeling the effects already. "And we should go see Carter and Smuckers. He has the cutest cat."

"She is the cutest," Emma laughs, her lips quivering. The emotions of this whole situation have held off until now. Thinking about the fluffy grey cat is enough to have Emma choking. Careful to keep her breathing steady, she fights the tears threatening to escape. Avery will start to worry, and the last thing Emma wants is for her little sister to be scared for her life again. Once in a lifetime is enough. "I should talk Trevor into convincing the landlord to let me have a cat."

"Can I name it!?" Avery asks excitedly, sitting up as she twirls to face her older sister. Her eyes widen as she taps her hands against her legs. "Please?"

"*If* I get a cat, I will let you discuss a few options with me," Emma remarks, smiling as Avery celebrates by jumping on her bed. Avery named her ferret, Chocolate. Her parents wanted to give her a reason to stay motivated and get out of bed after coming home from the hospital. The doctors said that's the hardest part... but Avery was the first one up every day.

Emma watches her sister jump on her bed, tempted to tell her to stop, but too proud to. Avery jumping, laughing, having fun means she is healthy. Almost five years after ringing the bell, and they still watch. Waiting to see if infections return or another seizure strikes.

Avery drops off the bed, running up to Bingley with a grin on her face. They never thought she would have the energy to run and play. Not with the stomach issues caused by the chemo and cancer combination. She was so malnourished; it took her a few months to bounce back from hospital condition and be able to enjoy playing again.

Her five-year checkup should be coming up soon. With confirmation of being cancer free, they should never have to worry about her relapsing. Emma's chest almost seems to fall at the idea as a weight lifts. She never meant to worry… she is not a worrier. Not by nature. Except for Avery and her family.

"What's wrong?" Avery inquires, eyebrows knitting together as she flops onto the bed. Emma comes back to Earth, watching her sister kneel on the bed.

"I was thinking how glad I am that you're alive," Emma answers, pressing a hand into her chest to massage away the weight there. She blinks away the emotion, laughing when Avery launches into her arms. Hugging her little sister tightly, Emma presses a kiss to her head and takes a deep breath. "*Ik hou van jou, mijn schatje.*"

"I love you too."

"Now you should sleep," Emma points out, glancing at the clock as she slowly shakes her head. "Moe will never forgive me for letting you stay up so late."

"I won't tell her," Avery whispers back, grabbing her things from Emma's bedside table. Rushing down the hall towards the bathroom, she stops for a moment to watch the poker match.

Emma laughs quietly to herself, gazing out the window again forlornly. She wanted more people in her apartment. Now there are people inside and she is still sitting alone by the window.

Admittedly, she did not mean she wanted people to force their way inside her apartment. God has a funny way of answering prayers sometimes.

They could still kill her. Would anyone notice?

Pulling at her ear, she glances at Agent Darcy and tells herself to calm down. He could kill her and disappear without a trace. Just look at the museum. Police tape wiggle in the evening breeze, wrapped tightly around makeshift fencing. Cops go inside every single day. Emma caught ghost cars parked in the alleyways during one of her moments behind the camera. Do they think the criminals will return? Of course, they are not searching the buildings nearby to see if they are hiding away. After committing mass murder and getting away with it, most criminals stay far away.

She would like to trust Agent Darcy. Mostly because he is attractive. A silly, foolish reason but it does help. He possesses a beautiful smile and a charming laugh. If he had not broken into her apartment and flashed a gun at her, she would even pursue him. Wear her nicer clothes, locked in her apartment, to catch his eye.

Any effort Emma employs is shut down. She asks him questions whenever possible. Yes, she asked them in hopes he would give her clarification on his reason for breaking into her place, but she does want to know him. She wants to know all of them. Yet they meet her every attempt with half-answers and redirection.

Is that...? No, it couldn't be. Emma snickers as she presses her hand against the glass and leans forward. It must be the man from before! The unfortunate one who looks identical to Hitler. She laughs at herself, pressing a hand against her mouth. It's rude to laugh but he shares an unfortunate likeness. Or the cabin fever is settling in…

Even standing underneath a streetlight below her, she can see the lines of his moustache and the receding hairline.

"What are you laughing about?" Agent Bingley asks from the table, throwing down his cards as Rosalind collects the chips with a victorious laugh. "Not you—Emma."

Emma's head shoots over to him as she giggles to herself. "Nothing."

"It's rude to lie," Agent Darcy counters, meeting her eyes with quiet challenge. She narrows her eyes on him, tempted for the first time to yell at him. He infuriates her now more than anything else. Especially because he knows so much about her and she cannot demand answers from him like he can from her.

"I do not enjoy being a bad person."

"You are not a bad person and there is nothing you could say to convince me otherwise," Agent Darcy challenges, stretching to his full height as he stands. Bingley agrees with a nod, shuffling the cards with a quiet swagger. He makes a face, twirling his finger in the air. Three different agents, Rosalind included, stand up and face the wall as he deals. "What is it?"

"I was thinking one of the regulars at the clinic looks like Hitler."

Emma brushes a strand of hair behind her ear, prepared for them to call her ridiculous or rude. Instead, she sees the colour drain from Darcy's face. Unsure what she said wrong, she opens her mouth to reassure them the man is probably innocent of his doppelgänger's crimes, but they do not care.

Agent Darcy rushes toward the window, sending the other agents into motion. Emma scrambles away from the glass, watching as they grab equipment. She anxiously draws herself onto her bed, sucking her lips in as she picks at the bottom of her jeans.

"Why is everyone looking outside?" Avery questions, throwing her old clothes onto the floor beside Emma's bed. She would tell her to put them away properly, but the group's reactions intrigue her.

"I don't know," Emma confesses, scanning them over.

She cannot understand what they whisper to one another, but they are getting as agitated as Rosalind and Darcy were earlier in the day. What about a Hitler lookalike could intrigue a group of highly trained agents?

CHAPTER 13: HE DOESN'T BELIEVE IN FAIRIES

Who knew it takes a group of secret agents breaking into someone's home to make them do school? Emma giggles to herself as she closes the browser tab. Another paper done. She already finished every assignment for this month and the next, including her readings for the next few months. Splitting her time equally between making cue cards and doing assignments to be submitted, she memorized half her course material in four days.

She glances at Avery working through some math homework with Agent Rosalind. While she did not bring her assignments physically with her, there were a few things her teachers asked her to complete before returning to school. Avery barely mentioned the problem before Agent Rosalind thrust a laptop at her with an internet connection to reach her school portal.

Emma joked about her climbing boredom but Avery surprised her. After watching Emma finish so much schoolwork and build towards a successful end to the term, she decided she wanted to get some things done as well.

Emma smiles to herself, tapping the end of her pen against her notebook. Agent Rosalind is not the friendliest agent but she practically shoved Agent Bingley out of the chair when Avery asked for help. The Russian man's solution consisted of strange metaphors about farm animals and potatoes. While it may have been helpful for some children, Avery ended up laughing when he began to make the animal noises and describe them in a mixture of English and Russian.

The two of them make a silly pair, barely able to contain their giggles. With the strict agent, Avery sits tall and asks important questions. Her tongue pokes out from her lips as she nods, listening intently, and applies to the best of her ability. It gives Emma the chance to see some of the warmth Rosalind gives out sparingly. One approving nod and Avery breaks into full-out grins. The endless praise Bingley gives cannot compare.

Now he is upside down on Emma's bed, throwing a ball at the ceiling like she used to in the depths of boredom. He sings an unfamiliar song in Russian, swinging his legs as he hums the ending. She glances from him to Agent Darcy, hiding her gaze behind a curtain of hair. His focus locked on the acupuncturist clinic last night and remains now. The red light from outside adds a handsome hue to his dark skin. At this point, Emma concedes any light adds to his attractiveness because it gives her the ability to see more of it.

A muscle ticks in his jaw as his eyes scan the streets. With his hands clasped behind his back, and feet shoulder width apart, he makes every military commander proud. Over a dozen hours later and he does not move from the position. Every agent, save for Bingley and Rosalind, works double-time with their surveillance.

"Carter would know," Avery sighs, glancing at Agent Rosalind. For the first time, the agent looks confused. Emma's siblings love Carter; Avery most of all. No one else could be as fun or smart. Kids freak Carter out and yet even babies adore him. Emma blames it on the fact he sort of looks like a surfer and a cloud combined. People sense the inner zen he carries everywhere, despite his firecracker energy. He carries extra smiles with him, ready to supply them for anyone who needs one. Moe said he reminded her of a cherub once. It is the long blonde hair paired with bright, doe eyes. "I miss him. We should invite him over."

"We should," Emma agrees, too tired to try and fix the agent's problems for them. Oddly, Agent Darcy does not respond. Something must be wrong. Her eyebrows draw together as she glances at her sister. "He is covering my shift today. He doesn't have the time to come over."

"We have been staying up until midnight almost every day," Avery counters, stretching her hand to Emma in a hope to make her consider the point. Knowing just how clever her little sister is, Emma smiles. "So, it's not really *that* late, right? Carter stays up until five AM sometimes."

"And how would you know that?"

"We have a server together. I wake up at seven, log-on, and he's finished an entire castle," Avery answers, shaking her head. Emma presses her lips together, snickering quietly. Yet, he refuses to show up on time to work most days. "Do you think Summer and him could get married?"

Emma chokes on the air, blinking rapidly to force her mind to process what Avery said. "Pardon me?"

"Well, she calls him Dr. Yummy. I heard her telling Winter how hot he is." Avery replies, twirling a strand of hair as she doodles on the paper she used to show her work. Agent Rosalind tries to stop her but Avery is long gone into the fantastical daydream. "I don't know if he's hot... he kind of looks like bum. At least that's what Moe says."

"Summer is sixteen Ri. Carter's going to be twenty-three soon." Emma remarks, shaking her head to dismiss the idea. Carter would never think about her little sisters' that way. She's not even sure he has thought of a girl that way. He shares the celebrities he finds 'appealing' but never mentions real women. Two years of friendship and not one girlfriend. Not one situationship. They made jokes about dating apps once but neither confirmed nor denied the use of one. "She calls him Dr. Yummy because she knows it makes him uncomfortable."

"That's rude," Avery states, her lip curling up. "Why would she do that?"

Emma shrugs, tapping her pen against the side of her head as she looks at Agent Darcy. Making a fool out of yourself or teasing someone to draw attention is an immature way to handle a crush. It shows a complete lack of better character and common sense. Yet, coming from a woman with copious amounts of self-respect, Emma understands her sister's side of things. Men can be obtuse. Specifically in circumstances where their brains do not recognize a woman as a possible candidate for a future partner.

Throwing Agent Darcy off his game is the only way to get answers from him. The old saying goes there is no such thing as bad publicity. If you want attention, any attention will do.

"Because she enjoys getting a reaction from him. It means he's looking at her." Emma answers, careful not to say it with too much disapproval. Summer knows it bothers her as well but she also does not care enough to stop. Avery does not need to be poisoned against their sister though. "Don't do that Riri. If you need to fight for a guy's attention, he's not worth it. A real man would fight for you and hang on your every word just as you would for him."

"I know," she sings, closing the laptop. "Do you still have those colouring books?"

"If I do, they are in the cabinet," Emma answers, nodding towards the hall. A smile curls over her face as she presses the end of the pen against her lips. She struggled for a little bit as a young girl, seeing every other girl around her desperately seeking the approval of people. Especially men. Moses taught her differently. He is a good brother like that. Joseph and Oliver are less close with Avery than her and Moses, so it's important to set an example and share wisdom. Knowing

Avery will never question her own worth changes a generation.

Agent Rosalind, devoid of a task, returns to the window and equipment. She nods her head as Agent Darcy speaks to her, arms crossed and eyes focused on the streets below. A pair of binoculars are handed to her and then she begins speaking rapidly to Agent Eyre who sits behind the biggest laptop. With every word, the *clacking* of the keyboard sounds. Everything comes to a halt when her words stop. The room goes still.

Emma does not know what they are saying, but it must be important. She realizes just how much when Agent Bingley lets the balls roll over the ground as he twists on the bed. He saunters to the window and leans up against it, watching something below them. The silence becomes tense as the agents stand at the ready. One even reaches towards their gun.

Then a cellphone goes off.

Emma jumps before they do. Normally 'cool as a cucumber' expresses her natural state, but it's impossible to relax when they are so tightly wound. Her panic increases when she realizes the phone ringing is her own.

Shutting her laptop, she jumps to her feet and sprints to the kitchen where it is hidden above the fridge. Agent Darcy intercepts, sliding into place between her and the kitchen. Six and a half feet of pure muscle, she could not conquer him if she tried. She and Moses refused to wrestle when Cody tried to convince them to. The two watched as he tackled Oliver or even fought the twins.

Her only advantage normally would be her height and surprisingly strong legs. Being 5'9 is nothing compared to the towering giant in front of her. Especially with his arms crossed and a single brow raised.

"That is Moe's ringtone," Emma says breathlessly, trying to make him understand. He stares into her eyes with blatant disinterest. Unused to needing to fight so hard for herself, she clenches her fists. "If I do not answer that phone my mom *will* drive all the way here. She will march right through that door and when she sees strangers in my house, she will ask questions. I would rather you did not shoot my mother. Which means for her safety and yours, I *need* to answer that call."

"*If* she shows up here, we can handle it—"

"Not if. WHEN." Emma corrects, unable to process the sheer stress pounding through her body. Exams and tests worry her but not like this. Even Avery's sickness did not cause her such deep-seated terror. In that case, she understood her powerlessness. No matter what she did, nothing would change the outcome except for prayer. Agent Darcy stands in the way of her doing the one thing she can control—convincing her moe not to march into her apartment and get gunned down. "She will show up with an entire army. Please."

The phone stops ringing and silence reigns in the apartment. Emma's jaw locks painfully as she looks at Avery. Luckily, her little sister is in her own world, gathering art supplies from the small cabinet with all of Emma's extra things. She cannot see her older sister's desperation or her fear. Agent Darcy can and he is unmoved.

The phone begins again. Moe's ringtone bounces off the small apartment walls and into the glass. Normally the violin soothes her but with every passing second the symphony gets darker, more frantic. Emma can feel the other agents watching them as she stares into Agent Darcy's eyes. She does not consider herself the most stubborn person on Earth, but that means when she digs her heels in, she is willing to lay her weapons down on the hill and fall onto them. Now is one of those times.

"You will either move, or I will get past you," Emma whispers, meeting his eyes unwaveringly. "You are not going to ruin my life for some mission."

Agent Darcy steps away from her. Instead of moving out of the way, he strides towards the fridge and opens the cupboard above it. Removing her phone, he accepts the call and extends his hand towards her. His expression leaves little room for misunderstanding. She is not to say anything that will give them away.

"*Goedemorgen* Moe," Emma greets, pressing a hand against her stomach.

"Emma Marie deVries!" Moe shouts, shrill and angry. Emma holds the phone slightly away from her ear, closing her eyes. "When I call, you answer the phone. I thought you were dead. I thought Avery was dead—"

"We are not dead," Emma assures, glancing at Agent Darcy. He pushes his military jacket back, resting his hand on the pistol. Moving away from the fridge, he blocks the doorway to the hallway. Avery's quiet hums silence behind his large frame. Emma's pulse triples, the sound of blood rushing through her head clears away every other thought. *He is separating us.* She wets her lips, praying the panic away, and leans back against the counter. "We were running down to the little ice cream shop by that busker you liked. I forgot my phone on the charger."

"You cannot leave your house without your phone," Moe breathes, maternal concern taking over her panic. Emma hears her sigh and shift on the other side of the phone. She nearly laughs when she hears the sound of her mother cutting something. Presumably vegetables. Such a normal sound brings a world of comfort. The familiarity of the woman needing to do something productive at all times soothes the voices screaming in her mind. "What if you got into trouble? Who would call the police?"

"Everyone has a phone, Mama."

"Not you obviously."

Emma laughs mirthlessly, picking at paint chips on her metal sink. She stops when she realizes there are no dishes to clean. Normally Moe calls to speak at her more than with her. Her phone calls are always a good opportunity to get chores done. Confused, she glances at Agent Darcy. The intensity in his eyes forces her back around. Have his legs been *that* muscular this entire time? "Touché."

"Are you stealing my child?"

"Moe, I can barely afford myself—"

"Will she ever come home?" Moe demands, and then she hears her mother sniffling. Emma presses a hand to her heart, practically feeling their mother's tears through the phone. Unable to hold her emotions back when her mother begins to cry, Emma's vision blurs. "I know we are not perfect parents. God knows I have so much to work on but Avery is our little girl. We want the world for her—"

"She's not upset anymore Moe… she's just having fun," Emma sighs, pressing the back of her hand against her face. She lowers herself into a kitchen chair with her back to Agent Darcy. Looking at him right now will make her angry. She can feel it stirring. Two decades of living and she cannot remember ever being so mad. In four days, Agent Darcy shattered the ground underneath her and left her kneeling on the shards. *He did this. He caused Henny deVries to cry again.* "She is not angry with you or Dad anymore."

"Are you sure?" Moe inquires with a watery tone. "If she needs to stay for a few more days, she can… I want to make sure she knows she is loved and missed. Dad didn't think it would upset her so much when he said that."

"She's a sensitive kid. When you're twelve your dreams

seem like they are the entire world." Emma admits, crossing her arms. She fondly recalls hiding from her parents and siblings in the months of wanting to be a spy. "You feel misunderstood all the time because people never seem to understand just how seriously you take everything."

"You kids are *my* world."

Emma nods silently, wiping away her tears. She no longer knows whether it is from her Mom or herself. Is it the fear trying to come to the surface and escape? Or the anger still swirling in the pit of her stomach? Moe and her disagree often but no one brings comfort quicker. No one in the world loves like Moe. She'd blaze a trail across the globe if it meant protecting her kids.

The walls are caving in. Her breath fights to leave her body. Emma's toes are going numb. Instead of wanting to run outside in the sun, she considers curling in a corner and asking Moe to sing her one of their old songs. Being brave is exhausting.

"I know. The novelty of my 'luxurious' life will wear off soon enough. She just likes feeling seen."

"I try to make her feel seen," Moe whispers, grief filling her soft voice. The cutting pauses as she sniffs. "I have never been good at the 'dreams' and 'passions'. I am boring."

"You are practical, not boring."

"Those are the same things sometimes *liefje*."

"And kids never feel seen at this age by other adults.

Everyone seems to be the enemy of their imagination and growth... *especially* parents."

"You are an adult."

"Not really," Emma laughs, glancing at her garbage, filled with ramen boxes and burned eggs. The agents must be using a different garbage bag for all of their trash. How odd. "I do not count. I live what I am sure Avery thinks is a very exciting life. I ride a motorcycle and live in an apartment in the heart of the city."

"Was I a bad mother to you?"

"No! Of course not!" Emma assures in surprise, her eyebrows shooting up. Her Mother rarely displays emotion. When Avery got sick, it was their Dad who cried and worried. He lost hair. Moe internalized everything and stood as the voice of reason and strength. She practically marched the family out of the dark and into the light with Jesus at her side. "Moe, is everything okay?"

"Yes, yes! I am just being silly. A mother's worst fear is that her children want nothing to do with her and hate her."

"I do not hate you. Ik hou van u." Emma whispers, pressing the back of her hand to her eyes. She hates lying. Now her mother thinks she is a bad mom because she and Avery are trapped in her apartment. Worse yet, Emma must maintain the lie. Her heart clenches as her teeth grind. "You are the best Moe in the world. When Avery got sick you kept the family together at home while Dad worked to pay for everything. You held me when I cried even though I know you wanted to be crying in your bed too. I know how hard you two worked to provide this life for us. No one who loves their children as much as you do could be a bad parent."

"I blame menopause," Moe announces, half-laughing as Emma sniggers. She sighs shakily, like the world rests on her shoulders. "Do not get old *liefje*. You stop recognizing yourself."

I barely recognize myself right now. She never thought she would be the kind of person to keep secrets from her parents. Or lie to them. Conviction fills her as she stares at her new tattoo on her wrist. Now is not the time to tell Moe. She needs to leave this call feeling supported and absolved. It is the only way she will not worry about Avery and come get her.

Emma fights the sudden nausea twisting her stomach. Knowing exactly how to manipulate her mother to do and think what she wants is not something to be proud of. When this is all over, she will have to tell her about the newest addition to her collection. Maybe she can convince Moses to tell their parents about his tattoo as well. God knows they have both felt guilty about it.

"You're not old Moe, you are seasoned."

"I am not a potato," she responds harshly, sending Emma into hidden laughter. She can almost hear her mother's face curling into a loving smile. "Can… may I speak with Avery?"

"You want to speak with Avery?" Emma looks at Agent

Darcy for the first time. He shakes his head, hands now toying with the pistol as he examines it. He won't even meet her eyes. She takes a deep breath and presses her hand against her forehead. "Riri just jumped into the bath actually. You know how she gets with those bubbles. She may not come up for air for a couple hours."

"Tell her to call me when she gets out... please," Moe asks, clearing her throat. She shuffles uncomfortably on the other side of the phone as Emma bites down on her lip. If only her teeth could have trapped the lie inside. She and her mother should have set up a code word like Carter and her. "I would like to hear her voice and apologize."

"I will, but if we forget, I will text you a voice memo or something," Emma offers, trying to steady her voice against the anger and guilt. Heat bursts up her neck, gathering underneath her ears. "I should go. Work gave me the week off to catch up on schoolwork."

"Catch up? You were behind?"

"A little bit," Emma answers, knowing her mom would have asked about the lack of work if she didn't. Now she will need to perpetuate the lie. Would any of her family members believe her about the agents? When they leave, she will be left with the knowledge they exist... and the inability to prove it to anyone other than the picture she saved on her phone of their logo. "Books and I have a complicated relationship."

"You need to focus. I would hate to see all your hard

work go to waste... I know how much you pride yourself on your grades."

"Trust me Moe, I intend to be delivering the valedictorian speech. Make sure Cody is there."

"I will drag him back myself," Moe assures as Emma smiles. Her mother would scare the scales off an alligator. The drop in her voice alone is enough to send a chill down Emma's back. "Make sure you are feeding her well, and yourself. Every food on the pyramid. Have you been eating your vegetables?"

"Broccoli, carrots, peas, spinach," Emma lists off, grinning. "*Ik hou van u.*"

"*Tot ziens.*"

"*Tot gauw.*"

Emma hangs up, staring at the bare wall of her kitchen. A shadow falls over her as Agent Darcy reaches for the phone. Slowly lifting it, she drops the metal box into his hand with extra force, retracting her hand like he burned it.

"She did not sound angry," he points out softly. She ignores him, closing her eyes when the number of thoughts and emotions consume her busy brain. Moses would tell her to chill. He'd settle at her side, drink in hand, and sing something to distract her. Except she is not watching the scenic land stretching away from her parent's house in the great outdoors, safe beside her best friend. No, she sits, trapped in her kitchen by a mountain of a man being held at gunpoint. "You sounded happy with her—"

"She is not the one I am unhappy with."

Rising furiously, Emma pushes her chair back into place, glaring up at him when she realizes he stands in her way. Unused to such a strong reaction from her, he steps aside.

Blinking, he turns on his heel and marches towards the fridge. She squints at her socks, trying to force oxygen to her brain. Darcy puts the phone into place, locking it away, before he spins to watch her fight for composure.

Shaking out her hands, Emma runs them through her hair. When it tangles at the end, she takes the elastic right out and brushes her fingers through the curls. Stands catch underneath her nails but the ache helps to settle her nerves. She tames the mess into a new ponytail, watching the agents milling about in front of her glass walls the entire time. Avery walks past them into the living/bed room and takes a seat at the desk. The girl is not shy in pushing away Emma's school supplies to make room for her art.

"This is a temporary—"

"It may be temporary to you. You may be used to invading people's homes and stealing their lives, but that does not make it okay or *temporary*." Emma snaps, twisting to face him. Vibrating with pride for herself, she steps towards him and presses a finger against his bulletproof vest. "I do not have the liberty of forgetting this. *This* is going to have a permanent impact on my mother whom I just lied to multiple times. Avery will not forget Agent Bingley and will speak about him to my parents, wherein I will be forced to make another lie because they would not understand. I do not understand!"

"You—"

"No, shush," Emma demands, pressing her hands together to mimic what his mouth should be doing. Eyebrows shooting up, he clamps his lips together. "You made me lie to my Mother. That is a sin and it is disrespectful. I am *not* a liar."

"You have never lied to your parents before?"

"You do not get to ask me any more questions. Not without opening up and explaining a couple things about you." Emma states, wagging her finger. She takes a deep breath, forcing relaxation into her body and face. "Find someone else to question."

"Are you being serious?"

"I said, I am not answering any more questions until you answer some of mine," Emma answers cheerily, walking past him as she swishes her ponytail. Avery glances up from her colouring book with a crooked smile. "I see you found them."

"I chose the fairy kingdom," Avery announces, gesturing to the half-finished fae underneath her purple pencil crayon. She glances up at Agent Darcy who marches into the room, all pretenses dropped. Jaw locked, fists clenching, teeth flashing as he stops beside Bingley. The other agent steps back in surprise when he sees the easygoing man so wound. "What happened?"

"Darcy said he doesn't think fairies are real," Emma

scoffs, rolling her eyes as Avery smiles. "It was just a disagreement. We'll be okay."

Avery nods slowly and offers the case of pencil crayons. "As long as you promise to colour nicely, you can help me."

Emma smiles, grabbing the green one and starts on the flower stems at the bottom of the page.

CHAPTER 14: THE TRAP

Pride and Prejudice alone provides an escape from the claustrophobia and frustration suffocating Emma. She watches Agent Bingley and Darcy over the edge of the book, half-expecting them to morph into their counterparts. After their argument this morning, she cannot think about the giant without feeling angry. Therefore, she tries her best to avoid any thought or notion of him. It is impossible in such a small space and stewing in anger makes her sick to her stomach. This new attitude alienates her from herself.

Four days now they've held her hostage in her own home. Without a breath of fresh air, her mind turns on itself. They make her the stranger in her own home, ruining the safe haven she created. Poor Avery, it took four days but she finally realized the strange circumstances of this place. Emma can't explain, she can't save her, and she can't reason with the agents. It adds to her cacophony of anger, helplessness, and grates her to the bone.

Avery sleeps at her side, catching up on what she missed over the last few days. With nothing to hold her interest, she either sleeps or complains. Emma runs her fingers through her sister's thick hair, deciding the little girl needs to shower when she wakes up. In all the excitement, Emma cannot remember the last time she bathed. After she gets out, Emma can brush and braid her hair. For the first time ever. Avery's hair never grew this long or thick before chemo. It took five years, but her hair is long and healthy enough to be styled!

Pulling her hand away from Avery's head, she flips her page and returns to her little sister's hair. Riri shifts against Emma's side and throws her arms around her waist. Her nose scrunches, covered in tiny freckles, as she readjusts again. Smiling to herself, Emma begins to read the next page and scratches the back of Avery's neck. She stiffens at the feeling of being watched. Lifting her eyes off the page, she meets Bingley's stare. Smiling warmly, he opens his mouth, and promptly shuts it when she closes her eyes and curls around the book.

She doesn't consider herself a particularly petty person and yet she ponders locking herself in the bathroom to escape them. Avery could come with her. They have colouring books now. Bathtub colouring? It would be fun. Bring her pillows and blankets. A little bathtub/couch/bed thing. Lock the door and keep them all out… they managed to get into the apartment with the door locked. Emma no longer sees a point, save for clearing her head.

The microwave beeps and with it a familiar smell wafts through the air. Emma's eyes pause on the page as she licks her lips. Guests have every right to her food.

They are not 'guests' and they should not be touching her ramen. She buys her favourite brand and hides it from herself so she does not eat it too quickly.

Are you going to say something or just sit in your bed sulking?

Emma takes a deep breath, staring at the worn page of her antique book. Neither. There is no point saying anything. Between the scare tactics and downright threats, they've made it clear Emma's safety and opinion means little. At every chance they have, the agents assert themselves as the brutalists they are. Sulking is not helping either. She's more miserable than ever while they live complete unaware, or apathetic, to the damage they continually cause.

"You should eat." She jumps, closing her book with a snap as she peeks at Agent Darcy over her shoulder. He comes around the foot of her bed, walking to the bedside table closest to her. Moving some of her books and the alarm clock away, he sets a bowl down and pulls out chopsticks from one of his vest pockets. "You have not eaten all day."

"I've lost my appetite," Emma answers, though she feels her face heating. She should say thank you. Every polite fiber in her being shouts at her to fix her attitude. Her body does not seem to understand these people are not her friends. They are not honoured guests or even strangers. Agent Darcy is an active threat to her. He weasels through every block she sets up. Disarmingly charming and yet cold the next moment.

If he thinks bringing her a bowl of food will solve their problems... well it may because she is too forgiving for her own good.

And hungry.

Seeing him cradle the bowl of ramen threatens her shaky resolve. Careful not to let anything spill from the sides, he shuffles closer, and gently lowers some of her books to the ground. When he straightens, her bravado returns. Agent Darcy does not belong here. Maybe because of his size. The old-fashioned demeanour. How he handles himself. There is something wrong with him and he does not fit in this apartment.

Every mannerism, every word, every action, and every appearance convinces her there is something strange about him. Partially because of his timeless appearance. It is impossible to guess his exact age, or any of theirs, because they all equally look like teenagers and middle-aged adults.

For the tenth time she wonders just how old he is? Where he grew up in South Africa? Who his parents are? What he was taught? She might act like the perfect captive if he opens up and shows a little bit of humanity. Maybe because it would afford her some comfort. At least if she knew his name, it would not feel so strange having him holding her hostage.

Or maybe she thinks in getting to know him, she will be able to reason with him.

"You cannot refuse to eat because you are angry," Agent Darcy sighs, kneeling at her bedside. He adjusts her bowl and places the chopsticks on top of it with gentle hands. Emma watches him, already losing her anger at how he delicately cleans off the scraps and garbage from her end table. "Your body needs food to function."

"I believe you were the one who said 'cardboard noodles' are not proper nutrition," Emma argues quietly, reopening her book. Her eyes refuse to take in the words or allow her to read. Not when he is looking at her and she knows how rude it is to ignore someone. The back of her neck burns as she finally closes the book, surrendering to her own impracticality. "I am not one to waste food."

He carefully lifts the bowl, handing it to Emma with one hand as he uses the other to cover Avery's head. Sliding the ramen against her chest, Emma uses her arm to separate her sister from the man. Once again, hurt flashes in the depth of those warm eyes. Warm eyes which become cold as ice the moment Emma shows a symptom of autonomy. Accepting the chopsticks with a quiet thank you, she watches the owner of those chameleon eyes settle on the edge of her bed.

He scratches the back of his head, staring at his open hands wordlessly. Instead of his awkwardness making her feel better, it exacerbates her guilt. Suddenly she searches for something to say in the silence. Except she has nothing to say outside of absolving him: *Just acknowledge it, I'll let you off the hook.*

"I like to draw maps."

Thrown off guard and barely able to process his words, Emma stops twirling her noodles and stares at him with furrowed eyebrows. "Pardon me?"

Agent Darcy stands up and walks over to the equipment, rifling through a bag. Curiosity removes every other feeling, forcing her to lean forward to see what is hiding in there. She is not the only one.

Bingley watches him from beside the window, a smile beginning to curl up his face. He meets Emma's eyes with the same knowing expression and nods once. The second his nod is over, he returns to his surveillance, leaving her even more confused than before.

When the leader returns, he comes to the other side of the bed, careful to maintain his distance as he sits at her side. He looks from his boots to her patterned blanket splattered in white. "May… may I sit on your bed with my shoes off?"

Intrigued beyond belief, Emma nods. "Please."

He puts a binder down on the bed as he leans forward to remove his boots. After a few moments of undoing the ties, he gingerly brings his sock-clad feet onto her bed. Crossing his legs, he opens the binder and slides it towards Emma.

She carefully redistributes her sister, making sure the ramen does not slosh as she moves. Unfolding her legs, she crosses one ankle over the other. leaning towards the papers he removes gently. Agent Darcy surprises her by practically shoving the binder into her lap. He takes the bowl when she struggles to balance the two, sliding it safely onto the opposite nightstand.

"Growing up I worked as an... assistant to a privateer with a trading company," Agent Darcy explains, voice becoming nostalgic as Emma delicately moves the maps aside. Some of the ink rubs off on her fingers and though she goes to apologize, he waves a hand. Her head brushes against his chest as she pulls one out after another to make a spread of old, musty parchment on top of her linens. "We are not supposed to interact with the captains or leaders, but one of the boys lost control of his master's horse and it would have kicked a couple crates into the ocean if I had not intercepted it. I managed to tame the animal and the shouting sailors. The privateer decided I was worth something then."

"He taught you cartography?" Emma inquires, her eyebrows drawing together. Moe collected old world maps for her history classroom. The family spent a Saturday trying their hand at cartography based on a hike they did. When they ate dinner afterwards, Moe spoke about how every expedition group needed a cartographer. 'You know where you are going based off where you have been'. None of their maps were good enough to show anyone where they went, but the day brought many good memories. "You sailed with him?"

"He taught me about the world but I did not see a lot of it with my own eyes." Agent Darcy responds, warmth pouring off his voice as he glances at Emma. She meets his eyes, glancing away shyly when the moment stretches. "For a boy who grew up in a little village and only knew the path I took from our home to the port… hearing about distant lands felt like a storybook. He told me about France and how they were trying to make plans for a large metal tower, and the Americas and their Civil War and how he got land before their Declarations were made. He bought maps for me to see. I dreamt of sailing with him to the grand worlds beyond our tiny country and about all the adventures we could have. My Moe caught me pretending to be a sailor once when I should have been doing chores but she laughed and made herself my secondhand."

He sucks his bottom lip in as her hands pause on the illustrations. Grief's distinctive effect is recognizable across every distinction. Race, sex, age, nationality…. Emma rests her hand over his involuntarily. "It made a labourious, at times deadly, life seem special."

In the silence her mind wanders past the grief. The Americas? Civil War? Metal tower? The Civil War took place in the 1800s… if not earlier. Emma stares at his face as he recounts the path a ship would need to take to get from Cape Town to present-day New York. His maps depict cities no longer called by these names. She must assume they are heirlooms… and yet he is talking about his own experiences.

Maybe these are old maps the privateer inherited. Or perhaps they spoke about old trading routes and how they changed through the years. Moe used to. She searches for an updated map and finds it. It does not have the same ink or style as the other maps. Agent Darcy's. She notices every change in the strokes of his pen and curve of his writing.

Agent Darcy depicts trees, waves, and places where the weather may cause trouble. Great sea beasts curl through his oceans. A woman's face takes up the corner where the compass is, her eyes the true North. She carefully runs her finger over the woman. His drawing abilities are not perfect but even the rough edges of the art reveal something about him.

"How young were you?"

"I stopped working with him when I was seventeen," Agent Darcy answers, his expression darkening. Gloom claims his eyes as his shoulders tense against her. She notices but instead of drawing away, she squeezes the hand over his. Refusing to berate herself for it, she openly meets his eyes. "I viewed him as a friend, I should have realized he could not see me as anything more than a pet."

She chokes on her breath, her mouth opening and then closing. "Because you were young? Or because...?"

He smiles slightly at her silent question. "I am black, he was white."

"I am sorry. I have never understood why people think they are better than anyone else because of their genetics. No one gets to choose... we were all made by the same Creator."

Emma watches him nod passively as he gingerly brings his other hand over hers. One rough finger brushes against her knuckles as he stares at her slender fingers. She leans towards him despite herself, tucking her head against his shoulder. It does not take a psychic to see the pain he holds. His pulse slows underneath her finger as she runs it from his wrist up his bicep, following a thick vein to where it disappears into his underarm.

"He gave me a love for adventure. I learned I would not see the world with him, but the maps brought me there. I imagined the shores of America and dreamed of a wall made from stone in China. My days were filled with the tulip fields and windmills of Holland," Agent Darcy confesses. He glances at the agents and then at her. "Would you like to see something?"

Her eyebrows draw together as she glances back at Avery. She does not want to leave her sister. While she loves the idea of being let out of her apartment, she cannot go without Avery at her side. "What is it?"

"A tattoo," Agent Darcy answers, standing. He removes his vest, putting it down beside the nightstand as the others pause. The temperature in the apartment raises when he grabs the hem of his shirt. Agent Rosalind cocks an eyebrow as he removes his shirt in a fluid motion. Four different muscles tense in his arms, emphasizing the veins protruding from his skin. The women's eyes meet, one begins muttering to herself in an indecipherable language while the other plays with an earring. Agent Bingley whistles and for the first time, Agent

Darcy's mask breaks. A smirk curls over his face, the kind saved for your best friend.

Emma turns towards him, trying not to flush or react. It is not her first time seeing a shirtless man, but this is not just a man. She knows very little about Agent Darcy, but there is an undeniable chemistry between them. His story successfully settled her and dispelled any leftover resentment. Being shown his art? Listening to the warmth in his voice as he spoke about his mother? The grief? It fed a little hunger growing inside of Emma to know him.

He removes the white undershirt and holds it in his hands as he turns his back to her. On her knees to be in line with his shoulders, she follows the intricate lines of the tattoo. It starts with a boat docked in Cape Town on his left shoulder. The world explodes from it, complete with a compass and the names of the seas and oceans. A windmill stands in the Netherlands, followed by the famous arch in France, and a clover over Ireland. His skin is smooth underneath the explorative pad of her finger. When she reaches the small of his back, he shivers, goosebumps breaking out.

"The privateer wanted me to have an accurate map in case he ever lost everything in a shipwreck. We both drank too much rum and I woke up with this." Agent Darcy rasps, half-ashamed but he does not sound remorseful. Laughing quietly, he looks at her over his muscular shoulder. "They used a couple needles and octopus ink. My mama slapped me over the head with a bushel."

"This entire thing?" She gapes, staring at the way it crosses his back and onto his arm slightly. Her hand unconsciously moves towards his heart, resting against the bulge of his shoulder blade. "You must have been in a lot of pain."

"I barely remember it." His voice fills with a distant fondness as he begins to slide his tank top back into place. When he twists to face her, she fights the urge to avert her eyes. His muscles have muscles. Did he have another tattoo on his pecs? "He never worried about losing his maps after this."

It was not enough to consider him a pet. The man had to dehumanize him and make him into an object.

A protective anger flares in Emma. She watches him suit back up, following his hands as they buckle his vest back into place. "I am slightly less upset."

He smiles up at her, leaving the maps sprawled around her bed. "Eat. Mama always said man becomes beast with an empty stomach."

Emma watches him return to the other agents, relaxed now as he speaks with them. She grabs her bowl and carefully shifts towards the maps, scanning over them. Part of her hopes to find something with a date on it. What would she do it if said something unreasonable like 1755? Laughing to herself, she glances at the kitchen. Carter must be getting to her.

Racism is a timeless disease unfortunately.

Her heart clenches at the thought, watching Bingley and Darcy speaking. Bingley must say something sneaky because he glances back at Emma. A smirk crosses his face and moments later Darcy is elbowing him. The best friends laugh together and then Agent Rosalind calls from the kitchen.

Emma watches up to the point Darcy disappears behind a wall and quickly scoops food into her mouth as she organizes the maps back into place. She always loved geography, but her interest leaned more towards pictures. These maps show places and distances. Times. Pictures show the world.

Immediately she wonders what he would think of her collection of photos. He would probably love to look through them. How many countries has he visited so far? Did he get to France? Or the Netherlands? Has he seen the tulip fields and windmills for himself? Watched the 'big metal tower' in all its glory?

She opens her mouth to ask him as he returns but stops when she sees his gloomy expression. Agent Rosalind stands at his side, holding Emma's phone in one fisted hand. Maps forgotten, Emma shifts towards her sister. The tension is creeping back in. A sad story and she let her walls down. Foolish. Agent Bingley rushes to their side, lowering his voice so she cannot hear, and blocks her view of the other two with his broad back.

Her eyes seek Avery's sleeping form as her heartbeat picks up. Finishing her food, she slides the bowl away and puts the maps gingerly into their sleeves. As the binder closes, she hears Agent Darcy's voice raise. "I knew it was too convenient."

"It is a set up," Agent Rosalind agrees, shaking her head. "We walked into a trap."

Agent Bingley hushes them when he realizes she can hear. They do not look happy. Emma turns away from the trio, pushing the binder onto her nightstand, a safe distance from the now empty bowl. Avery's eyes flutter open, as if she can sense the tension rising in the room.

"What time is it?" Avery groans, rubbing her eyes as she stretches out. She grabs Emma's thigh, bringing her head down on it. Emma forces herself to remain calm, brushing her fingers through Avery's hair again. Meanwhile, the agents' heated argument worsens as Agent Rosalind's eyes fill with liquid fire. She practically melts Emma where she sits when their eyes meet. Bingley steps away, removing her wall of protection, with a loud sigh. "Emma?"

"Uh I don't know," Emma replies, about to tell her to shower when they finally stop. Agent Darcy takes a deep breath, closes his eyes, and then marches to her bedside.

"We need to talk about Dr. Racecar."

CHAPTER 15: DR. RACECAR

"Hey Ri, you need to shower," Emma whispers hastily, brushing her sister's hair away from her ear. She pushes herself off the bed, her shoulder rubbing against Agent Darcy as she slides to the floor. He follows her movements as she collects Avery's clothes. "Come on kiddo. Up and at 'em. No supper until you stop being so smelly."

Avery grunts into the bed, but eventually pulls herself off it. She slouches against Emma, allowing herself to be herded into the bathroom. Emma starts the water for her, knowing the exact way to start the water and get the proper temperature. When hot water sputters out, she twists the cold and hits the wall. It gurgles in response and evens out.

"Can we have takeout tonight? From that burger joint?" Avery inquires, watching Emma pull out the shower supplies from the closet built into the walls. Avery's hair is different enough from hers. Especially because it needs twice the moisture and not the curl-friendly formulas. "You're acting weird."

"Sorry, I am thinking about everything I need to get done before graduating," Emma lies, catching herself with a grimace. Lying to Moe, and now to Avery. Four days of deceiving her sister and now to straight-up lie? The very thought sickens her. *What kind of sister... daughter... woman of God am I?* "Do you prefer to smell like apples or the ocean?"

Avery jumps up from where she sits on the counter and grabs the two bottles. She takes a drag from both, grinning happily as she picks the red bottle. "You're the smartest person I know, Em. You are awesome. You've got this."

Emma catches her emotions before they well up. She grabs Avery's head and presses a kiss to her forehead. "Call me if you need me."

"I have showered before," Avery jokes, tapping the towels Emma laid out. She watches her older sister leave and locks the door behind her.

"What about Carter?" Emma inquires, walking into the kitchen instead of the living room. She fills up a big glass with water and practically drains it in a single gulp. Drinking water does little to calm her but it gives her something else to do than worry.

"Where did you meet him?"

She stares at Agent Darcy's crossed arms and forces her defensiveness down. There is no point getting upset at the accusatory tone in his voice. Everything about this situation is complicated. Adding more emotions adds another layer to the complexity and it might be the final domino to fall before death. They obviously misunderstood something he said. She cannot guess what text or article Carter sent her. Maybe he jumped the bandwagon again and believes mutant alligator men live in the sewer system below the city.

"At work. I took over his job when he finished school and officially became a licensed pharmacist."

"Where is 'work' exactly?" Agent Rosalind questions, hands on her hips. Another sigh comes from Bingley. While his leader and partner radiate fury, he appears bored. Tired. He offers her a bag of chocolate covered raisins, undermining their entire attempt to intimidate her. When no one accepts, he flops into the chair beside Emma, and tosses the bag onto the table.

"Remedy Pharmaceuticals," Emma answers, meeting her eyes easily. "Do you want an exact address? I do not know it off the top of my head but it is saved in the maps app on my phone."

"You expect us to believe you are a measly student?" Agent Rosalind demands, scoffing angrily. Emma's eyebrows raise at her fury. She glances at Agent Darcy for an explanation but he stares at her wordlessly. "And he is nothing but a doctor? He is not a doctor. What is he looking for? In what capacity are you assisting him?"

"I assist him at the clinic by answering phones, organizing orders, occasionally helping him fulfill prescriptions and selling over the counter meds." Emma glances between them, confused by the dynamic of their interrogation. "I do not understand why you are asking me any of this. I assume Carter said something?"

"We should have checked your correspondence with him previously," Agent Rosalind snaps, glowering at Agent Bingley this time. He chews innocently on his chocolates, shrugging when she bares her teeth at him. "That mistake will not be repeated."

"If you show me my phone I can probably explain," Emma offers, raising her hands in surrender when Agent Rosalind pins her with a deadly look. Bingley shakes his head, side-eyeing her. Instead of looking at either of them, she turns to face Agent Darcy. The team leader meets her eyes unwaveringly but conflict swirls underneath the impassive mask. "I don't understand… I have not been allowed to see my phone for four days. I know the texts Agent Bingley read to me—"

"Some of them were before."

"Carter sends me so many things I rarely even catch up to the last message before he sends a new one," Emma pleads, choking back desperation. The shower sprays loudly, Avery's offkey voice drifting down the hall to block out their conversation. As long as she is safe and far from the angry agents, Emma focuses on remaining calm. She presses her lips together in an attempt to keep herself centered. *Lord, give me patience and wisdom.* "I don't think it is fair for you to be angry at me. You're accusing me but won't tell me what I'm being accused of. I have no clue what I am supposed to be explaining. I don't know how to defend myself."

Did he send the code back? Or ask if she was okay?

She sent the XO code, but he is only supposed to acknowledge the code with his own repeat back. It should not have been out of place... unless they read every single conversation they had and noticed the lack of the signature. Carter would not have done anything to put her in danger or acknowledged that there was a problem unless he got worried. It is completely normal for Emma to drop off the map for some time around exam season. Although she normally does a better job of communicating her sudden disappearance. Maybe he sent the code back and without a response he assumed something is wrong and threatened to call the police.

Wait... what if Carter figured out who they are? She never sent the picture of their logo, but his friends are watching everything. They love secret societies and government organizations with no names. Carter believes there is a small group of people controlling the entirety of the world's trade and government. He thinks they spend their days in a tower located in the Bermuda Triangle, and that is why so many ships go missing—because they need to stay hidden.

If Carter figured out what they are, it means their entire operation could be exposed. Emma does not know the repercussions of that, but if they are supposed to be a secret, being discovered is not a good thing. Especially if they do not have the authority to forcibly enter a Canadian citizen's house. She doubts anyone is given permission to hold innocent people hostage at gunpoint... even for the government.

"Your friend is involved in dangerous business," Agent Darcy answers carefully, his jaw locked. "We need to know if you are involved."

"Involved in what?" Emma gawks, eyes bulging. She rubs her hand against the stem of her thumb, trying to decide whether they are threatening Carter or if he did something stupid again. He got too far onto the dark side once and ended up discovering an entire human trafficking ring through conspiracies about CEO's. Luckily, he managed to turn all the evidence over but he was eighteen at the time. Practically a baby. How much trouble could he get into four years later? "Carter is—harmless."

Carter spends most of his time in his basement with Smuckers, chortling over silly conspiracy memes. Half the time, he is the one who made the memes in the first place and he circulates them until his online friends start a new thread in the group chats about their own theories.

Carter once lost eight hours because he got tunnel vision about a conspiracy around beans never existing. Emma thought he died and broke into his house (using the key he keeps inside his trash can) to find him with four empty bags of chips around him and eight crushed energy drinks. Smuckers looked concerned for him... and she's a cat.

"Is he?"

She glances at Agent Rosalind and laughs despite herself.

"Car is a conspiracy theorist. He still questions whether the Earth is flat. He is one of the guys who will argue with you about it if you give him the chance and bring up some obscure Bible verse and ancient text found in the indigenous histories."

"You can never be quite sure," Agent Bingley comments, earning the third degree from the only female agent in the room. He snickers to himself, winking at Emma. Oddly, his support is exactly what she needs to stop cowering. "None of us have been to space."

"Carter seriously—*seriously*—does not believe the moon landing happened. He thinks it was a scam and that we have never gotten close to stepping foot onto the planet because of its different atmosphere. The poor guy believes NASA is a cover for a military organization focused on setting weapons up through satellites. He thinks they are trying to build a fortress on the moon… and he believes in aliens!"

"So, you spend time with a fool?"

Emma's jaw drops in offense for her best friend. Defensiveness wells up and while she keeps the edge from her tone, she feels her voice strengthen. "Carter is curious. He refuses to see the world as black and white and to put it into a box simply because people tell him he should. I have never met someone so smart, considerate, and thoughtful. I look at a car and I think 'wow, that's incredible. We can transport ourselves in an electric powered metal box.' Carter sees a car and he wants to know why it works how it does. He wants blueprints and history lessons. He wants to know why we drive forwards, not backwards. How we decided to drive on the ground before flying everywhere first if it is safer."

Agent Rosalind blinks at Emma blankly. Neither of the men jump to rebut or challenge the statement. Emma crosses her arms softly as she pulls her knees up. "Carter is not a fool. He is brilliant. A brilliant, somewhat unorthodox weirdo. I can assure you; if you think he has planned some elaborate trap for you, you are the fools, not him."

"And what do you believe?" Agent Rosalind questions, arms crossing dangerously. She raises a single thick black eyebrow, waiting for a response.

"I believe in what can be seen, known, and tangible. Carter argued my belief in God makes no sense, but the evidence supports Him more than any other theory. The Bible. Extra-Biblical texts. Sedimentary layers. Time. Genetics. Even medicinal compounds. Everything points to an intelligent Creator and the Christian God is the one with the most research, the most explanation, and the most reasonable basis. I believe in what is simple. What is probably." Emma explains, tired now. She is not used to confrontation or defending herself and others. For the most part, life is simple for her. People rarely ask her deep questions about her beliefs or life. Most of the time they laugh and she asks about them. She focuses the microscope on others. "I hardly believe what comes from Reddit or the dark web because people like to make stories that fit their narratives. While you cannot argue the validity of someone's testimony if they did experience it, you can understand subjectivity and objectivity are different and sometimes incomparable."

"You should give those dark web nerds like your Dr. Racecar more credit."

Agent Bingley's mutter disappears under the sound of the quick slap Agent Darcy exacts on him. His hand collides with the pocket of Agent Bingley's vest but the message is clear: **stop.** They share a look, which drains Bingley of his nonchalance, and infuses their leader with exasperation.

Darcy puts out his hand expectantly, nodding when Agent Rosalind produces the phone. He removes her SIM again and removes the battery along with it. Standing, he tosses the phone back into the cabinet and slides the two extra pieces into his pocket. "You are not to be in contact with him again."

"You cannot stop me from speaking with him after you are gone," Emma remarks, her breath catching at his expression. "You will leave... eventually?"

"No one will be able to reach you. If your mother comes with an army, she will be safe. Avery can go home with her so long as she can promise to keep us a secret," Agent Darcy declares, crossing his arms. Emma does not tell him the obvious. Twelve-year-old girls do not keep secrets. At least not ones like Avery. Especially not from Moe. "Do you understand?"

"Is this interrogation over?" Emma asks instead, staring at Agent Rosalind. When she nods, Emma pushes herself away from the table and walks right past them. Tears scratch the back of her throat. *Not now, please Lord, not now.*

She settles herself against the wall outside of the bathroom, lowering herself to the ground. Her legs come up against her chest, providing her a shield against the curious eyes of prying agents.

He said Moe and Avery are safe… what happens if Carter shows up with RedPanda69?

CHAPTER 16: I AM NOT A RACIST

Dr. Carter Finnegan Friesen was born an odd cookie, but Emma finally understands another piece of his complex puzzle. His addiction to caffeine. She drinks a cup of coffee if church friends want to meet up at a cafe, or if Carter wants to treat her as he feeds his addiction. For a short period of time, she wanted to get a French press to offer curated drinks for guests.

Now, she consumed four cups of coffee in less than six hours. Her restlessness settled in before she began drinking, now it's here to stay. Caffeine powers her resolve to stay awake and work. Admittedly, after the third coffee she should have stopped drinking. Her mind began to wander during the second and is now lost because of the fourth.

Avery is asleep. Settled in long before the stroke of midnight and fast asleep as Emma's mind slips further and further into a caffeine delusion. Right before dinner most of the agents left. It was the first time she got to see outside of her apartment in four days. The glimpse of the ugly wallpaper and random signs with little valuable information made her emotional. It felt cooler too when the door opened.

It is the first time she witnessed them using the door, although she knows they find ways to leave. Honestly, she is concerned about the full tactical gear they donned before leaving though. They removed their helmets after breaking in and didn't put them back on. Until now. They were helping each other with equipment checks, including loading their guns with ammunition. She did not have the energy or patience to ask them where they were going, although now she wishes she took a moment.

Agent Darcy should have gone with them. Both as the leader and arguably their most capable soldier. Instead, he remains seated in front of the glass walls. Occasionally he gets up, checks each of the cameras, and if he sees something he likes, he takes a shot or two. Afterwards, he takes a seat back at the desk they made out of her old IKEA table and opens up his book.

He manages to look blissful during it all. Never bored.

Emma has never been *so* bored.

She requested an advance on every single assignment possible. Short of completing a couple of in-person essays, she has practically completed her year of school. If they plan to keep her in captivity for much longer, she could very well graduate and become a licensed pharmacist before the month is up.

One essay. The last assignment she could get from her professors. Capitalizing on this time left to her own devices is her ticket to valedictorian. However, with the crash of the coffee high, she can barely look at the online document filled with her own words. She should be editing it but she cannot string two words together in her head.

Using sugar cubes and toothpicks, she organizes the squares into their chemical compounds. The amount of joy she gets from the shapes makes up for this afternoon's—or yesterday afternoon's—interrogation.

Holding back her grin, she pulls apart the cubes and begins a new one. She dips the end of the toothpicks into her coffee so the sugar cube will not crack. The stack of broken toothpicks is a testament to her past failures in her journey to this discovery.

She snickers to herself, half-mad, by the time she finishes the chemical formula for caffeine. Using the tips of a coffee covered toothpick, she draws the letter values onto the blocks. Her glee is never ending as she pushes the little craft against her coffee cup and chuckles to herself.

The smile falters when she realizes her phone is gone. Carter would hail her a comedic genius. He'd wait two hours, until the crisp time of 4 am, to send a video of him laughing maniacally. Moses lacks the same enthusiasm but his thumbs up would be enough to make Emma smile. She misses her friends.

Neither of them will get to enjoy her sugar cube adventures because her batteryless phone is locked above her fridge, the SIM carefully placed on Agent Darcy's body where she dares not go. Even if he were asleep, which he never seems to be, she would not try to sneak up to him. He strikes her as the kind of person who sleeps with his eyes open and strikes like a cobra when he is ripped out of his dreams.

Disassembling her little display, she collects the sugar cubes and brings her half empty coffee with her into the kitchen. She knows better than to grab another cup, and yet that is exactly what she does. Pouring herself a small mug, she tops it with cream and four cubes of sugar. The sugar and cream are the concerning part but she would rather have it tasting like iced cream than bitter beans.

"If you keep that up you are never going to sleep tonight," Agent Darcy remarks from behind her, leaning against the doorway into the kitchen. She glances at him over her shoulder and shrugs, watching the swirl of the cream as it mixes with the coffee. "Or have a cardiac arrest. Is that your plan? Have us transport you to the hospital?"

He smiles but she does not. The idea would be worth its weight in gold... if she was willing to hurt herself to get out of the apartment. Unfortunately, Emma lacks a fondness of pain and does not intend to start causing it unduly to herself. Them on the other hand? She could see herself running 'interference' after a long day and a pot of coffee. People have psychotic breaks when held captive, why should she be any different?

"If I am being forced to stay here, I may as well take advantage of having no plans and get schoolwork done. I need to edit my essay and then I am ahead of anyone in class and can spend the next two months after this making up for lost time." Emma answers, grabbing a new mug from the cupboard above her head. She puts it down in front of the pot and fills it to the brim, finishing off the pot. If she really wanted to go wild, she would make another pot, but there is still some sanity to be found in her jumbled mind. "I don't exactly feel safe enough to sleep anyway. No point lying in bed for hours staring at the ceiling when I could be productive."

"You are surrounded by people who will guard you with their lives. After living alone for so long it should be relieving to know you are not isolated and defenseless." Agent Darcy argues softly, arms crossed. The coffee must break her propriety down because she snorts at him. Derisively. Loudly. Neither of them expected the noise from her. "You have never been safer Emma. I am a trained soldier—"

"We both know this has nothing to do with people outside my apartment."

She stares at him, waiting for his response. His mouth shuts slowly as a muscle pulses in his jaw. The irritation on his face does not scare her. Especially because she reached the point of no return with her coffee and stress about an hour ago. If they intend to hurt her, she can do nothing but stand in their way. Agent Darcy made that blatantly clear.

She puts a cube of sugar into the coffee as he comes closer. The muscles in her shoulders bunch without meaning to. Alarm bells ring internally as she inches away. Her movement puts a stop to his. In the silence of the apartment, his remorseful swallow is too loud. Silent whispers begin on his lips but end before they reach her.

While she wants to believe his good intentions, he flashed a gun at her when she began to dissent. He is a walking oxymoron. Both sweet and closed off. Warm and cold. It is a constant fight within her own brain to reconcile the man with the map on his shoulder and the one who threatens and interrogates her.

"You must understand we are not the bad guys—"

"According to whose definition?" Emma questions, turning on him completely now. His eyebrows raise at the sudden affront. Their positions on opposite sides of her little kitchen emphasize the battle. "Yours or mine? What am I to understand? I witnessed you murder someone who had no weapon and surrendered to you. I know you broke into my apartment, by the legal definition—not your own. You will not let me see my phone and have completely cut off my communication with the outside world. I know you are holding my sister and me hostage and refuse to give us any indication of when your reign of terror may end. Have I *misunderstood* something Agent Darcy? Would you like to provide clarification?"

A lump of emotion attacks her throat. She tries to swallow around it and hide her face from him. Crying is not a shameful thing for her, but he is a stranger. Emma trusts him as much as she can, possibly even more than she should, but not enough to enjoy being vulnerable in front of him.

She steps towards the counter again, picking up her mug and his. Agent Darcy accepts the cup, half-stunned at both her offering and her words. They make eye contact for a moment too longer. Emma flees past him with her coffee and makes a beeline to her desk. Shoving her earbuds in, she leaves the music off. She needs a barricade, not noise.

In the silence, she stares at her laptop's now dark screen and imagines life after this. Is she going to forget this? Conversations with Agent Darcy about random things. Her space being invaded and taken over. Agent Bingley's constant Russian nicknames or Agent Rosalind's Mandarin monologue? Maybe they will erase her memory. The technology must exist. Fifty years ago, they were making movies where they had people carrying weapons that could do it.

She closes her eyes when she notices him sidling up along her desk. Heat pours off him, which is all too welcome in this cold corner. Along with the heavenly smell of his cologne and she fights not to inch closer.

Hugging herself, she peeks up at him through her lashes. He gestures to his ears in an obvious bid to have her remove her earbuds. If she were more rebellious, she would probably refuse. Except her years of being an immature teenager are gone and part of her hopes he will finally shed some light on why they are here and what they intend to do about it.

"How did you know my coffee order?"

"I saw you make it," she shrugs, confused why he needed her to take her earbuds out for this. Holding them in her hands, she stares at him expectantly. The least he could do for interrupting her thoughts is give her some peace.

Agent Darcy stares at the cup in his hands, leaning against her desk silently. One ankle crosses over the other, elongating his legs. His eyes travel the entire small space of the living room before meeting hers again. "You may ask me a question. It cannot be about who I am, what I do, or why we are here."

"So, nothing important."

He blinks drily at her as she chuffs. The coffee brings out her sass and for once, she feels unapologetic for the snark in her tone. "Does it help you to know it is for your safety? If we explain who we are, your life will be in danger. Avery's too. You do not want to endanger your entire family."

"You are endangering my family by being here then," Emma argues, meeting his eyes with her chin held high. The enthused coffee side of her brain cheers in agreement. Her fingers are moving so quickly now, her rings are beginning to heat up. They tap her cup maniacally until she forces herself to put it down. "Are you not?"

"It is different."

"If you say so. For the record, I think Hitler would have seen himself as the good guy too." Emma remarks, no longer staring at him. An empty coldness grips her heart, warning her to apologize. Perhaps comparing them to a murderous dictator is too much. "I don't mean to say you are like him. I mean that people always think they are in the right, no matter how many people challenge them."

"The question Emma."

"I want to ask you whether you were born in Cape Town or whether you just worked there," Emma states, peering up at him. "But that would be a personal question. I already know you are South African and you worked in the city with a privateer."

"I was not born in the city, but I lived there with my family after my Father was... enlisted by a group of traders." Agent Darcy explains, crossing his arms. Emma's eyebrows draw together at his wording. Were they... slaves? Her mind can barely grasp the concept. It has been thousands of years since the slave trades ended. No one should be born into service to anyone. Especially not because of their skin colour. "What makes you so sure I was born in South Africa? We could have been immigrants."

"I went on a Missions Trip with my church across Africa. Our leader was South African. I remember the accent well. She enjoyed yelling at us and lecturing us about our western habits." Fondly playing with one of her necklaces, Emma releases a soft laugh. At one point the woman stood on their transporter and threatened to run herself over if they continued to be so problematic. The youngest people involved were sixteen and two of them were teenage boys who came within inches of stampeding giraffes. Within the same week they survived a near-miss with an elephant. "When did you leave?"

"A couple months ago."

He watches her twist in her office chair, eyebrow raising when she nods dramatically. A giddy part of her brain, probably released by way of a caffeine overdose, just wants to come right out and ask every question on her mind. Except she realizes she needs to be coy. Somewhat underhanded. Even unassuming. Agent Bingley implied Carter knew something about them and if he does, they are already off their game.

"What brought you here? Adventure?"

His lips twitch, betraying his amusement. Emma would berate herself if she had not assumed he would see right through her thinly veiled ploy. She grabs a sugar cube, popping it right into her mouth as she watches him. "Work."

"There were no jobs at home?" She asks, eyes bulging when she catches herself. Her nonchalance shatters as she sits up straight and sputters. "I meant that in sarcasm, not racism."

Agent Darcy laughs. Not lightly, but with surround sound. Laughter consumes him, gripping him by the shoulders and shaking him and the desk. Her laughter joins his, though it is more of a silent wheeze than a boom. Poor Avery is trying to sleep and will wake to her sister, the caffeine-junkie-hyena.

"I would never think you capable of racism," Agent Darcy assures, meeting her eyes sincerely as she composes herself. Emma sobers at his words, grateful, although a part of her wants to remain furious with him. "You are too considerate and kind."

"Thank you," Emma murmurs, scratching her head. "But I can be naive."

"Yes, but the ignorant can be saved. The hateful are lost."

"But if hateful are willing to change, is it different?... Most bitter, resentful people have never been forced to question themselves and what makes a heart golden. I am sure if they could see the blackness of their own souls, they would want to change. Like Paul the Apostle." Emma catches herself, wetting her lips. She blinks at the swirling of her coffee and pushes it away from her with a half laugh. "It's not my place to say anything about it, my mouth is working faster than my brain... I think I have had enough."

"We can both agree on that," Agent Darcy remarks, taking her mug. He puts it with his own at the end of the desk and hops fully onto the tabletop. It is strange seeing such a large man, folding on her desk. His presence fills up the entire room, though he makes himself small in front of her. "May I ask you a question now?"

"I do not think my three questions equate to the dozens you have asked me."

"You asked me four questions."

"No, I said I wanted to ask you if you were born in Cape Town," Emma corrects, smiling when his eyebrows raise. She sighs quietly, grabbing a sugar cube to play with. "Shoot. It better be a good question because it's the only one you are getting tonight."

"What is wrong with Avery?"

She shoots up, ankle catching on the end of her desk. Refusing to react to the pain, she hurries to look at Avery. "What are you seeing?"

"Not right now… she is paler than you. You can see every one of her veins." Darcy explains, his hand grasping her shoulder. He stopped her from shooting straight into the bed and shaking Avery awake. The thought of her little sister being hurt would push her over the edge. "And you are overprotective. More than any sister I have seen. You try not to smother her but I see you watching her when she is not looking and reaching towards her when she is trying to grab high things. You twist your earrings when she is jumping on the bed and when she was wrestling with Bingley, you kept opening your mouth to tell her to stop but never did."

Emma stops herself from playing with her earring as he speaks. Habits die hard. She laughs humourlessly as she runs her hand through the mess of her braid. Part of her does not want to tell him. Not because of the rebellious streak of no longer wanting to share herself with him, but because she worries what he would do with the information.

She sees the parts of her Avery does not want others to. The times she pauses for a breath between soccer runs, hiding it in a cheer or a 'stretch'. Holding onto something for dear life when she stands because her blood pressure changed with the meds. Sometimes Avery struggles eating full portions. There are foods her medications caused an aversion to and she tries her best to power through, so no one sees the weakness leftover. Her hair is long but there was a time when it grew in patches and she kept it short to avoid looking like 'a ripped broom'.

Avery keeps a brave face for Moe and the rest of the family, but after Emma caught her sobbing to herself in the bathroom at nine years old, she realized how much the little girl needs for others to think she is brave and untouchable. Despite being reassured she did not need to pretend for the family, Avery asked Emma to keep it a secret. It made her happier for the parents not to worry... and they knew Moe would.

Moe lost close to thirty pounds during Avery's hospital stay. Running through the hospital and worry kept her from eating and sleeping properly. Dad gained what she lost and worked fourteen-hour days six days a week. He kept the Sabbath but it became his day of sleeping rest, more than church rest.

Her family went through the wringer. It makes complete sense why she wants to protect them. Emma does not talk about it with people, per Avery's wishes, because giving a voice to the worries makes them real. Then again, Agent Darcy shared something substantial about himself and she has yet to reciprocate.

"Avery had leukemia." Emma's voice cracks on the word, like always. The agent shifts closer, lifting his hand to her cheek to push away a tear she cannot remember forming. "You cannot 'claim' it is cured until five years of clean screens... they think it was undiagnosed for around a year, but her diagnosis and treatment started when she was five. It was two years of torture. We barely saw my Mom because she wanted to stay with Avery at the hospital and my Dad needed to work to pay for all the bills and Moe's travel." Emma explains, trying to blink away the tears. They burn. All the way down her throat and into her jaw. "One day my little sister was at home, forcing me to play with her and her dolls, and the next she was hooked up to a hundred different machines, bald, and practically a skeleton."

Agent Darcy grabs a tissue from his pocket, surprising her so much she laughs. He offers it soberly, crossing his arms when she takes it and presses it underneath her eyes.

"You cannot forget that. I only got to see her in the hospital a few times but seeing your baby sister hooked up to an IV, a shell of herself, and so tired... the image burns itself into your eyelids." Emma describes, picking at the ring on her middle finger. She watches Avery sleeping, her heartbeat louder than the silence. "We lost her for a little while. I saw the brave face she tried to put on. She felt like she needed to fight for us and keep the smile on her face. I didn't realize how alone she felt until after she was out of the hospital."

"She's a good kid. I do not think anyone would guess how much pain she's experienced."

"Her hair has grown out and she's getting healthier every day," Emma agrees, looking back at him. His eyes stay on level with hers. Shifting in the office chair, she pulls one knee up and pushes it down to stretch out. The caffeine high bleeds away with the solemnity of the conversation. "But I feel like I keep waiting for the other shoe to drop. Her sickness came on so suddenly. The doctors think she had it for over a year before she started showing symptoms."

"But you do not?" He inquires softly at her pause. Emma shakes her head, staring at her rings.

"I think she tried to hide them because she did not want to be inconvenient... I keep expecting the infections to return. Any time she even feels slightly unwell, I feel my stomach drop."

"That is no way to live," Agent Darcy remarks softly, his booted foot brushing against her bare one on the floor. She shrugs helplessly, watching Avery. The girl moves in her sleep, a small mercy God provided for the worrywart Emma becomes for her little sister. She would never describe herself as tightly wound. If anything, she characterizes herself as being too relaxed sometimes. At least, that is what Moe says when she is upset and Emma rarely reacts the way she thinks she ought. "Has it been five years?"

"And her five-year checkup is coming up. If the screens come back negative… she shouldn't relapse."

"Did her sickness make it difficult to trust God?"

Emma purses her lips but ultimately, she shakes her head. "No. If anything I got closer to Him. God didn't want this for us. He created a perfect world and we ruined it. We brought death and disease into it. Cancer is a natural consequence for our genetic unravelling, pollution, and wrongful living. I knew God was the only one who could do anything. There was a point where we thought we were preparing to say goodbye… and I wanted to make sure God would take care of her."

"It appears those who deserve it least, suffer the most."

"Because the ones who do not seem to deserve it have supportive, loving families and treat people well. I think more people get sick than we think but not all of them have a family and support system backing them." Emma states, playing with her earring again. She notices Agent Darcy staring at the action and stops herself. With nothing to entertain her hands, she sits in the stillness. Something about the moon draws a confession out. "Avery told me once she asked God at one point to let her die, if it meant the other kids could be in remission."

"That must have been hard to hear."

Emma laughs, pressing away the tears coming back to bother her. She blinks rapidly, surprised by the relief in her chest. "She knew most of them were not Christian and she thought if anyone should die, it should be the one sure of her salvation. She was seven."

"A very noble thing to think," Agent Darcy comments, smiling at Avery. His hand snakes into hers, squeezing her trembling fingers. "What did you say?"

"I told her it was a kind idea and that I was proud of her thoughtfulness and wisdom. I tried to keep out the fear out of my voice." Emma begins, tapping her free fingers against her neck. He nods, as if he understands, emboldening her "And then I told her God wouldn't let her die. In a world filled with so much darkness, He needed her light here... I felt so guilty about it. I had no right making that promise but I didn't know what else to say."

"How soon after did she go into remission?"

"A couple months, I cannot remember exactly how many. Time passed by fast and yet excruciatingly slow. I remember Sundays when Moe and Dad both came home and that's it." Emma confesses, watching Avery shift in her sleep. She murmurs something loudly and punches her pillow. A smile tugs on Emma's face before she faces the agent once again. "I don't think my parents understand why she wants to be a famous streamer. It's not the money or the celebrity status. She wants to spread the love of Jesus and create a place where people feel loved and accepted. She's trying to shine her light."

"Have you mentioned that to them? Or suggested she explain it?"

Emma's eyebrows shoot up in genuine surprise. She hadn't thought of it. "It's not really my place... I honestly never thought about it." She glances down at her lap when his imploring eyes become too much. How does he make her feel so much with a single look? "Avery is independent. She likes fighting her own battles."

"It may be worth bringing to their attention if you do not think they can learn to understand on their own."

Nodding her head, she toys with the earbuds on her desk. Where do they go from here? He will not answer her questions but it is too difficult to break the conversation alone.

"I have a gallon of coffee in my system," Emma begins, drawing her finger over her desk. "Do you want to play a game with me?"

CHAPTER 17: ENDLESSLY HONOURED

"I have eight grilled cheese sandwiches ready!"

"If you want another speak now or forever hold your peace," Emma adds, smiling shyly at Agent Darcy as she chops carrots. How does he make an apron look good? Something about a man cooking... it is hot enough in this kitchen with the poor ventilation, but now blush stains her cheeks.

Darcy moves easily around her, grabbing plates from the cabinet to her side. The smell of grilled cheese and tomatoes fill the air as someone groans appreciatively behind them. Soup and sandwiches cannot be replaced as the superior rainy-day lunch.

"Speak now or forever hold your peace?" Darcy inquires, rolling his tongue to taste the phrase. Emma nods, taking one of the plates from his hand and sliding it onto the counter. Her cheeks ache from the smile he elicits with his whispered repetition. "I am turning the burner off."

"I will take another one," Agent Bingley declares, grinning devilishly when they make eye contact. Darcy shakes his head but unwraps the bread bag and throws two slices onto the counter.

"We are going to be here all day," Emma jokes, portioning some hummus onto Darcy's plate. He shakes his head but smiles to himself as he hands her one of the finished sandwiches. Cutting it in half, she stacks the pieces and slides it past the sink with the others.

"Do you have plans?"

She tosses a carrot butt at his head as he snickers. Hiding her smile from him, she slides plates onto her arms and into her hands, ready to serve the agents. Agent Rosalind makes it easy for her, grabbing two of the plates for her and Agent Eyre. The shy woman thanks Emma with her eyes ducked, holding the grilled cheese sandwich against her chest like she thinks someone will snatch it.

Avery reaches for her own plate when a loud knock interrupts all activity within the apartment. Emma glances at Agent Bingley as if he is the one who lives here and pays the bills. She waits for one of them to do something, but they are equally shell-shocked. Trevor is not home yet. Is Carter here? Or worse... Moe?

The second knock echoes twice as loud. Emma is already rushing towards the front door when Agent Darcy snaps back to reality. Before he can tell her otherwise, she unlocks everything and whips the door open with a greeting, half out of breath.

"Good morning, ma'am," a police officer greets, hands on his utility belt. He removes them when her eyes catch on his gun. Not Carter and his calvary then. Emma pushes down the disappointment, mustering a smile. "My name is Officer

Wright; this is my partner, Officer Cortez." They stare at her and it takes Emma a moment to remember she is a human being. *Nod your head.* She does so, stopping when Officer Cortez raises a skeptical black eyebrow. "We are part of the ongoing investigation happening down the street."

Words cannot leave her mouth. She opens her mouth, soundlessly, standing there like a fool as Officer Cortez adjusts her gun. The partners share a look, silent as Emma. It is too quiet in here.

Office Cortez frowns, crossing her arms. "The murders down the street?"

"Someone was murdered down the street?" Emma inquires, choking on her own spit. The alarm bells in her head are ringing too loudly for her to understand anything else. Options flash clearly through her mind but they get jumbled with panic. She *should* communicate her state of peril. Widen her eyes enough to look crazy. Tap morse code on the door frame... but there is no guarantee they'd understand and she does not know how to do it. Agent Darcy and his soldiers brought automatic weapons. Two pistols, tasers, and batons cannot compare.

"It was a mass shooting," Officer Wright answers, gritting her teeth. Her biceps flex as Office Wright hums sadly. "You may have noticed the increased police presence in your neighbourhood?"

"I don't get out much," Emma confesses, throwing her

head back. Their eyebrows drawn together in joint confusion as she does it again. Her neck begins to hurt by the time Officer Wright clears his throat to speak.

"Are you—?"

A warm hand presses against the small of her back, interrupting the question and the officer's concentration. Darcy sidles up beside her, his chin brushing against her hair as he lounges against the doorframe. Both officers size him up with wide eyes, not expecting the giant with arms wider than an elephant leg. He holds the door for Emma, bicep cushioning her neck, and presses his other shoulder against the frame.

"I thought I heard voices. How can we help you officers?"

"We are investigating the mass shooting that took place at the end of your street earlier this week," Officer Cortez states, hands on her hips. Her eyes narrow as she looks Emma over and then the agent.

"That explains all the police tape," Agent Darcy remarks, laughing at Emma. She meets his eyes with zero amusement. Irritation melts into something warm and fuzzy when his thumb begins to rub her spine gently. Chills race up to her neck, exploding over her scalp. The hairs on Emma's nape stand at attention as she forces herself to remain present. *You are the one he'll use to protect himself from getting shot.* "How many victims?"

"We're still finding more. We broke fifty this morning." Officer Wright answers, watching Emma. She keeps her expression neutral but a tiny part of herself withers and dies in front of them. Of all the things she previously thought about herself, 'stupid' never crossed her mind. One late night playing games and laughing together erased the fact Darcy is a murderer. She enjoys his touch and presence too much. Even now she leans into it subconsciously. As if he is the safe one in this uncomfortable interaction.

"What did they want?" Darcy questions, eyes widening as convincing worry fills his voice. He even shifts to cradle Emma to his side. "They just opened that new exhibit, right? Did they take anything?"

Where did his accent go?

"We have no idea," Officer Wright confesses, running a hand over his bald head. He glances at his partner but Officer Cortez' eyes are locked on her target and refuse to leave. Emma forces herself to stay focused on the other, less intimidating, officer. Her focus crumbles away when Darcy begins to twist her hair around one finger. With every curl, he tugs slightly, hard enough to send tingles down her arms. "That is the complicated bit. Nothing was stolen. The victims have no affiliation to the museum. We cannot ID any of them."

Agent Darcy nods the whole time as if he is not the one who killed over fifty people (technically) six days ago. Emma stalls at the idea. Both because it feels an eternity away, and because it feels like yesterday.

"Seriously? That's ridiculous, could it be gang-related? I

thought I read something about activity increasing in the area...."

"We don't know, which is why we're doing rounds. Visiting the residents. Seeing if anyone saw or heard anything. Looking for another *weird*." Officer Cortez remarks, her voice leaving no room for friendliness. An involuntary tremor snakes down Emma's legs. There are other people walking in the hall. She forces a wave and smile at one of her next-door neighbours. Now they are going to think she did something.

Agent Darcy moves closer, stretching his arm over the doorframe. His presence banishes the insecurity, warmth covering her as she presses her back into his side. Glancing up at him, she smiles gratefully, until she realizes why he moved closer.

He is covering the agents!

The understanding crawls over her face as she pulls away. He is tall and wide enough to cover any sight lines the Officers might have into her apartment. Right now, they can only see her and the large man at her side. The large man who hooks his leg around her ankle, pulling her back. If they attempt to see into the apartment, all they will see is large muscular shoulders and a hint portion of Emma's speckled roof,

She lifts her hand to distance them, palm pressing into his steely torso. The fabric of his sweater is too thin, too soft. When did he remove his bullet proof vest? Pure muscle flexes underneath her touch as she scans him over. Agent Darcy left his gun behind, tucking his sweater to reveal a thin leather belt. The thick, leather combat boots they tromp around in are gone too. His toes wiggle within thick wool socks, brushing the back of her heels. Neither of the officers' voice concern about his all-black outfit.

"You folks didn't see anything?" Officer Cortez inquires, cocking her head to the side. Her teeth grind together as her eyes catch on Darcy's belt. "A couple residents said they saw a group of men wearing military gear leaving the museum. One thought they were our people, but we didn't have any Tactical Units in the area."

"What day was this?" Agent Darcy inquires, gazing at Emma. She shrugs, knowing her and Avery's chance of survival is bettered by compliance. He brushes his hand up her back and for a moment, she wonders whether he conjured a gun. Closing her eyes to focus on the feeling, Emma quickly decides it is not. He is not threatening her.

"Time of death puts the first victim at midnight on Sunday," Officer Wright answers, his arms crossing. "The last victim was shot sometime between twelve thirty-seven and one."

"Over fifty people in an hour-long period? They sound organized... are they mercenaries or something? Was there something valuable in the new exhibit?"

"It must have been a team. They were conducting an op of some kind but we don't know what their purpose was. It wasn't a gang, but we've heard about new gangs hiring hit teams to take out the old." Officer Wright explains, scowling at the thought. Gangs? Emma wraps her arms around herself, refusing to meet Officer Cortez' eyes even when she speaks. She's being misled, through her partner, and based off the sour expression, the female officer knows it. Maybe her suspicions will be enough to come back. With reinforcements.

"I wish we could help but we left Friday for the mountains. Wish we stayed longer with all this happening. Unfortunately, the doctor was needed." Agent Darcy laughs, bringing his hand onto her shoulder. He squeezes gently but the reminder of his strength anchors her.

"You're a doctor?" Officer Cortez questions in disbelief, her eyes dragging over Emma with a mixture of disbelief and curiosity. She loosens her lips, so they stop looking painfully stretched over her teeth. *Nod.* "Of what?"

"Pharmacology."

"You think they would give her some grace with it being our anniversary," Darcy laughs, the sound completely different than normal. It distracts her from what he said, for a moment. Anniversary?!

"How many years?" Officer Wright asks, grinning now. His partner turns her glare on him, trying to blaze through the small talk. Their size difference only makes Emma look younger. She must be five years younger than he. While it does not concern her, it might worry police officers who are searching for dangerous assailants.

"One," Agent Darcy confesses, laughing nervously. He curves towards her, eyes meeting hers warmly. She cannot look away. How many times have their eyes met exactly like this? Except now they embrace her. He smells like grilled cheese and his cologne, which could be unpleasant but only convinces her to lean towards him slightly. Darcy's magnetism brings her closer and closer until she falls into his eyes—a bottomless pit. Is she leaning over the edge or did he take her there?

His hand comes gently underneath her chin as the arm behind her back comes to brush her hair away. Dark short lashes surround those pits. Around the eyes, the skin stretches taunt. Emma tries not to look too hard because she knows she'll see nothing. No sign of life. No sign of laughter. An unnatural elasticity to the skin of an aging person.

Breath on her face brings her back to his eyes. Then his full lips. Her mouth opens slightly, their breath mixing in an invisible cloud. Craning her neck hurts but the pain is worth it to share his gaze. She cannot do anything else. Not with her heartbeat slowing and vision going hazy.

"I never thought I'd be good enough for a woman as incredible as her and yet I managed to earn her heart and keep it safe for an entire year." Agent Darcy murmurs, thumb brushing against her bottom lip. It quivers in response as she rests her hands against his chest. His heartbeat thumps in time with hers, slow but steady. Strong like him. Emma begins to close her eyes, tilting her cheek into his palm. "It has been the greatest year of my life. I am endlessly honoured. She has bewitched me body and soul."

Is she still breathing?

Emma sways backwards, but his strong arms hold her in place. The weightless feeling combined with her heated blood threaten to pull her under a spell. *Breathe,* she commands as Darcy pulls her closer. Feeling his hand against her side threatens to send her spiraling again. Emma loves hugs as much as the next girl but this is different. Intoxicating.

"We will stop bothering you then," Officer Wright sings, a soft expression taking over as he nods at the agent. Their eyes burn her skin but she is too far gone into soul of Darcy. Transported back to evenings on the patio beside Moses sipping hot cocoa all over again. Warm forests travelled with her family as Avery laughs and her Dad tickles her neck with pine needles. They are filled with promise and strength. Promise for what? "And to many more years."

"I hope so."

Officer Cortez is less eager to leave. She watches with half an eye before marching to her partner's side when he knocks on the next door. Emma allows Agent Darcy to pull her back into the apartment and soundly close the door. He drops the hand from her back, lifting one to tap the bottom of her chin. Their expressions mirror one another.

With her mouth now closed, she returns to Earth in a deadly crash and stumbles as she steps away from him.

"Darcy and Emma, sitting in a tree," Avery sings from the doorway, grinning wildly. Bingley stands at her side with a wide, confused smile, wagging his finger. "K-I-S-S-I-N-G."

Emma shakes her head, trying to get out every thought and feeling. She gives her little sister a dirty look, heading quickly past her towards the bathroom. The door is not fully closed before she leans against it, out of breath.

What was that?

She presses a hand to her stomach, praying the pressure will destroy the butterflies. The water bursts out of the faucet when she cranks the handle. It freezes her hands as she runs it over her face. Emma abandoned her makeup routine on the second day... is that enough to feed Office Cortez's skepticism? Do most wives look their Sunday best during the first year of marriage?

Marriage... to Darcy. Constant exposure to the brush of his thumb. His cologne surrounding her. Late night conversations about life. Trips to the library together where they pick books for one another. Post church brunches... does he like brunch? It is a lifestyle.

Stop it. Patting the cool water into her face and neck, she pulls the cold water up into her hair. Fantasizing about a man, a murderer, is not going to help Emma's resolve to get out of this with her life and heart intact. She meets her own eyes, ready to declare it aloud. "No."

She leans forward, blinking rapidly. Her pupils are dilated. Surely because of the low light in the bathroom … not because of him.

CHAPTER 18: CASUAL CANNIBALISM

"I do not need help!" Agent Bingley shouts, ruining Emma's perfect stroke with the red marker. Her little sister gapes at the ruined art but they break out into giggles together and craning their necks to see him in the hall. Bingley appears in a pile of grocery bags, waddling like a penguin in his attempt to haul all the groceries into the kitchen at once.

Red lines run up and down his arms from the plastic bags biting into his skin. Other agents follow behind him, offering to shoulder the load, but he insists on doing it himself. Bingley drops the bags onto the kitchen floor, slapping his palms together. The sound echoes off the walls as he rubs his palms together and faces Avery with a devious smirk.

"And for you my *крошечный* potato," Agent Bingley begins, reaching into one of the bags. He looks up at Avery expectantly when she does not move, and only returns to his search when she plants herself at his side. Revealing the case of markers proudly, he waits for his applause.

"What are they?"

"For the glass," Agent Bingley responds, fervently. He taps the description on the case, sticking his hands on his hips expectantly. Taking the case of markers, Avery holds them up to Emma. She shrugs, looking down at the art supplies covering her bed. "You told me you like drawing."

"These are way cooler than the chalk you got for Christmas, Em," Avery whispers excitedly, running her fingers over the colours lined up. Emma playfully glares at Bingley, lips pressing together when her little sister hugs him. How can she be upset when Riri is grinning so gleefully? "Bingley said he's a better drawer than me. You ready to eat your words B?"

"You are the one to eat words."

Avery runs away from his side, cackling excitedly at the feigned expression of worry. It melts off his face, replaced with a wistfulness as they watch her rip open the curtains. *He looks grieved.* Emma cleans up the colouring books and markers, noting the way Bingley wipes the expression off his face when he feels her eyes on him. Sending Emma a wink, he goes to Avery's side with his trademarked grin back in place.

"The curtains remain sh—"

Agent Rosalind's command goes silent with the clap of Darcy's hand on her shoulder. He shakes his head once, going to Riri's side to help her with the blinds. Warm golden light floods into the apartment, reminding Emma to sweep and dust the entire place when they leave. Bingley and Darcy meet in the middle, pausing when Avery shakes her head.

She is the one who begins moving the surveillance equipment. Without question or permission. Moments later, Bingley takes over, grunting as he picks up unopened, heavy cases. He commands help from the others until they drag the boxes and cameras back to form a wall behind the windows.

Agent Darcy watches the makeshift barricade form, arms crossed. His eyes drift towards her as they stand on opposite ends of this new hall. After the police left this morning, he chose not to put his gun and bulletproof vest back on. Other agents removed their weapons too. It makes them more domestic. Emma likes the look.

Too much.

Bingley and Avery move the wall of equipment aside, making the space for her to enter their domain. Grateful for the distraction, she grabs pillows off her bed. Following her lead, Agent Darcy grabs more cushioning. For the finishing touch, Emma brings an old sheet to protect the floor.

"This needs to be closer," Avery commands, tapping the back of her pen against the boxes. Her lips twist as she shakes one of the markers. "For a back rest."

No one questions the order. Together, they push against the wall of boxes until this little girl can lean back comfortably. She giggles, thanking them, as she glares challengingly at Bingley. He shakes his marker back, quickly removing his bulletproof vest and long sleeve shirt. Ink appears through the white fabric. A tattoo covers the left side of his chest, the details hidden underneath. Another one appears underneath the curls at the nape of his neck. The small paw mark stretches when he rolls his head around.

"Colouring does not require nudity," Agent Rosalind remarks, voice deadpan and face even less emotive. Her blank stare does not break, challenged by the infectious, boyish smile on his face. Bingley kicks off both of his boots and removes his socks, tossing them past her head. She doesn't even flinch.

"It depends on the artist. Live a little." Bingley taunts, likely thinking Emma cannot see the glare he gives her. When he looks back at Avery, the tension is gone. "What you already started!? Cheater."

He crawls over the sheet, grabbing the black pen. Avery's drawing already begins to take shape, multi-coloured green boxes stacked on top of each other. Emma leans on the crates behind her, watching the slow progression of their drawings. Despite Avery's lead, the Russian man makes up on time by not removing his marker from the glass. He sticks his tongue out between his teeth as he tries to hide the forming picture from Avery. When Emma leans forward to see, her shoulder collides with Agent Darcy's.

He smiles down at her, elbows down beside hers on the crates. Whatever composure she possessed ends with the brief contact. The heat of his arm pulsates into hers. Their arms line up perfectly, fingers brushing briefly on top of the cold plastic box.

"I saw this in a movie once," Agent Bingley reveals as Emma reminds herself to function. It becomes increasingly difficult as she feels his eyes trained on her. Moving slightly closer, she focuses on Avery and the effort not to blush. "What is the… *горилла*, hairy arms, hairy back?"

He makes an obscure sound, drawing the two of them out of the haze. Emma's eyebrows draw together as Avery bursts into laughter. It sounded like a lion... if the lion's vocal cords snapped. Agent Bingley clears his throat and tries again, beating his chest as he does.

"Gorilla Al-Bingley," Agent Darcy supplies, trying to clear his throat to cover his mistake. He stares at his hands instead of Emma who watches him. Alex? Allan? Alexei? Her mind runs through every nickname and the name it could belong to. Her experience with Russian names is limited but she knows Alexander is common enough. "It's a gorilla."

"Gorilla," he agrees, tapping the back of his pen to the drawing. Avery laughs excitedly at the drawing, moving back to capture its full essence.

The poorly drawn gorilla clings to the side of the acupuncturist clinic's neon sign. Emma claps her hands encouragingly, smiling widely when Agent Bingley grins back at her. He is no artist, but the effect is cool. Avery snuggles into his shoulder to get a closer look and nods approvingly.

"That's really cool...."

"The girls are too nice to say it looks like a blob," Agent Darcy remarks, grinning when his best friend throws a pillow at his head. He easily dodges it, throwing his arm back to catch it before Agent Eyre becomes collateral damage. Dropping the pillow gently back into place, he smiles at Emma, but she is staring at where he caught it. She forgot how fast his reflexes are. "What?"

"You caught that after it flew past you."

"And?"

"So, it's a counter motion, you should not have been able to do it," she answers, waiting for a reaction. Nothing. The picture of innocence. "Are you sure you are not a vampire?"

"Would you like me to bite you?"

Her expression drops immediately as her brain tries to find words. His voice got deeper, raspier, like the question is a secret... Agent Darcy knows the effect of his words. She can see it in the quirk of his eyebrows and the slight curl to the sides of his mouth. "No."

"Are you sure?" He inquires, a wicked smile causing his white teeth to flash. "You don't seem sure."

"Are you a cannibal?" Emma counters, heat creeping up her neck. She bemoans the decision she made to put a sweater on after the police stopped by this morning. After feeling so light-headed and fuzzy, she wanted something to keep her warm and grounded. Now the heat is returning in full force and she is ready to faint for the second time today. "I got a tattoo recently and I've heard those do not taste good. Do you still want to eat me?"

He mutters something, too low for her to hear. Emma considers the fact he may end her entire existence with what he said. Her stomach cannot hold anymore butterflies. They cram together, twisting it into a knot. How much can a heart take in one day?

"Moe says it's rude to mutter."

"I said 'a little nibble never hurt anybody'."

Emma blinks at him and says the first thing that comes to mind. "Tell that to the thousands of dogs that get put down every year."

Her mind goes blank, offering her no rescue or support. Luckily, Agent Darcy's laughter saves her from embarrassment. The sound warms her *toes*. A sheepish smile breaks out as he comes back to her side. His knuckles brush against the back of her hand. When her hand mimics the touch back, he draws the infinity symbol on the back of her hand with his pinky.

"What is it?" Agent Bingley questions as Avery stands to proudly present her drawing. His eyebrows shoot up at her dismay. "Celery! No asparagus. Uh… broccoli."

"It's a monster!" Avery gapes, arms crossing when his expression freezes in confusion. She looks around the room expectantly, waiting for one of the agents to agree. They study her rendition with equal expressions of bewilderment. It is a good likeness. Avery outlined the creature perfectly (but Emma suspects the agents know very little about the world). "From my favourite game?!"

"What game?"

"I told you about it yesterday… come on you've never heard about it? It's been one of the most downloaded games since its release in the early two thousand's?" She blanches, sputtering when he only shakes his head. "What century are you living in? It was voted twenty-fiftie's most retro game last month!"

She repeats the game name, lips pursing when their confusion does not move. Bingley scratches the back of his head, pinching the skin of his neck tattoo. "It sounds like a smithing specialty."

"You really don't know?" Emma questions after her sister descends into silence. She watches Agent Bingley look at Darcy and Darcy at her sister. No one answers the question. "It is kind of an old game, Riri. It may have skipped a generation or two."

"We did not grow up with video games," Agent Rosalind assures, chuffing. "You might call us 'retro'."

The other agents begin laughing. Quietly at first but Bingley soon reaches hysteria. Once again, Emma and Avery are left on the outside looking in. She tries her best not to show it but Darcy's right beside her. Shaking his head warily at them as though she cannot see it.

"Then again, you guys don't seem to understand a lot of pop culture," Emma counters, crossing her arms as she withdraws from the crates. She leans her hip against them admiring Darcy. He gazes at her, resting his chin on his shoulder. "Or how to work a phone."

"I know how to work a phone," Bingley retorts, tapping

the end of his pen against the glass. "This…how do you say—creepy thing I do not know."

"Creep-*er*," Avery corrects, shaking her head as she settles down. She ignores his dismissive shrug, beginning a long black line up the glass.

"Creepy, creep-*er*, all same thing," Bingley mutters, his accent thickening as he waves his hand. Bingley grabs a purple pen, beginning to draw swirls until he glances back at Emma. "See, I am all about the culture. I am cool with the kids."

"I am one kid," Avery points out, smirking when he rolls his baby blues at her. She scribbles something onto the slender thing's hand and sideway glances at him. "And not that hard to impress."

Bingley narrows his eyes on her as Darcy and Emma laugh. He reaches one long arm, shoving Avery into the crates. She turns hysterical as the pillows cave in on her. When she comes up guffawing, Bingley uncaps his pen and slashes it through the drawing with a huge grin on his face.

Her jaw drops. The picture she began now abstract. Bingley sticks his tongue out playfully, returning to his new drawing.

Sniffles begin. Loud enough to break his focus on the purple cloud. Avery's face falls as her shoulders shake. The look of panic on Agent Bingley's face is immediate. Emma presses the back of her hand against Darcy's chest when he surges forward. A small smile curls over her face as she watches Avery fish the pillow out from underneath her.

"No do not cry, *лапочка*. I did not mean to hurt you; I will fix it—"

He cannot finish his sentence before a pillow collides with his face. The resounding *thud* is followed shortly by a laugh.

"Fix this!" Avery suggests, smacking him again before she runs away chortling. War breaks out in the apartment. Emma takes protection against the wall when pillows go flying. She watches with a soaring heart as Avery laughs and jumps onto the bed as a dozen agents pick her side or Bingley's.

"And in the span of a few seconds, they turn into children again," Agent Rosalind states, slinking to her side in the tv corner. Darcy is there in the midst of them, defending Avery and her territory with his dying breath. Bingley tackles him at one point and begins to hammer the pillow into his back. He pins his leader with a knee in between the shoulder blades, singing a victory song in Russian. It quickly ends when Agent Eyre slams a body pillow into his head and sends him to the ground… not without her fair share of blushing.

"It's what keeps you young," Emma remarks, smiling to herself. Moses says that all the time to justify his silly antics. Acting like a child reminds you what it was like to be carefree and fun. It takes the years off your life. She removes her rings, one at a time, sliding them onto the desk at her side. "Will you join in?"

"When I find an opening," Agent Rosalind agrees, smirking at Emma's slight surprise. She did not expect the responsible one to take part. "I only join games I will win."

"Good luck," Emma laughs, rolling one of her blankets into the shape of a pillow. She rushes forward with it and jumps onto her bed at her sister's side.

CHAPTER 19: YOU MAKE ME FEEL SO YOUNG

"No, you are off count," Agent Estella sighs, running a hand over her long ponytail. She places her hands on her hips, moving her feet into first position. Her fingers snap in time with the song as she sways her hips slightly. The severity of her expression intensifies when Agent Darcy steps out of time again. "*Ma dai*, an elephant is more graceful. Look at me—are you looking? Like *this*."

"An elephant has dainty ears," Agent Darcy counters, smirking at her as he dances past her perfect example. Winking over his shoulder, he spins a grinning Avery smoothly, before dipping her. She throws out her skirt like Agent Estella suggested, finally earning a smile out of the severe Italian woman.

"Careful Estella, they may see you have a soul," Agent Bingley warns, tapping the drum he creates from a kitchen bowl. She swipes at him but he dodges the hand, keeping the beat of Frank Sinatra's song. It switches to Dean Martin. "Don't punish me for our *natural* talent and flare."

Emma smiles to herself, staring at the unedited essay with a degree of dread. She turned her music off the moment she noticed them toying with an old record player. Now the earbuds sit uselessly in her ears to make her look busy. Except she watches Darcy teaching her little sister to dance like she cannot afford to take her eyes off them. He lifts Avery onto his toes, bending slightly to accommodate the difference, and grins as she does. Agent Estella's shouting partially taints the experience but Darcy and Avery laugh together at her commands.

He began to dance alone, humming quietly to the music, and then Avery asked him about the steps. One thing led to another and they turned the living room into a ballroom. Agent Estella inserted herself, criticisms pouring off her tongue about his form. More with the waltz than their rendition of a swing dance. An hour later and she provides every barb with the tut of her tongue. When she is not shooting people, Estella must be a dancer. A talented one based off the perfect pirouette she displayed for Avery and the way her toes hold her entire weight without difficulty.

She boasted about her toes. Emma knows a couple dancers and every one of them obsess over their toes. When she was younger it concerned her but she learned the importance of foot health on posture and form. Form is everything to the Italian agent.

"Now a spin," Agent Estella suggests, swirling a finger. Darcy steps back to give Avery the room to spin, arching his arm above her. He picks her up, placing her back on his toes, but Emma can see it wearing on his back. Even with a pair of her heels on, Avery is a head shorter. Emma does not own stilettos. She towers over most of her dates as is. "You can do better. That was sloppy."

"She's a child wearing heels," Agent Bingley comments, nodding his head in time with the beat. He raises his spoon when she tries to swipe at him again. "I will start a fight you will lose, agent. Darcy is making it harder on her—"

"*Zitto!*" Agent Estella shouts, twisting. The long sleeve shirt bunched around her waist hits his shoulder. She waves her hands at him, closing them together. "You cannot do better; you should not speak."

"I spent time at a *Russian* dance academy. Do you really think your half-grade waltz style compares to the Motherland?"

Emma presses a hand against her mouth, glancing at him from her laptop. His disgruntled expression matches the revulsion dripping from his words. All thoughts about actually finishing the paper vanish when Bingley stands up.

Clearing his throat, the iceman removes his vest and throws it onto the floor. Bingley straightens his shirt, rolling his sleeves up to the elbow. His Adam's apple bobs as he steps up to Agent Darcy. His best friend looks as shell-shocked as the others but gives away Avery's hand. Stepping off the makeshift dance floor, Agent Darcy takes his place beside Rosalind, one arm crossed over his body and the other holding his chin.

"This music is not preferable for a waltz in the first place. Sinatra was made for swinging or the foxtrot," Agent Bingley declares with a put-off sigh. He surprises everyone in the room by picking Avery up with little effort. One arm stretches underneath hers to press against her back. Emma watches the muscles in his arms ripple but they remain steady, like iron. Avery is light but he makes it seem like she is a feather. "I will accept the defeat on your face as payment when I prove you wrong."

He meets Agent Estella's eyes with no fear and then the dance begins. Emma's eyebrows disappear into her hair as they twirl. The prowess and sophistication of his movements entrance her. Avery does little but point her toes when the Italian woman glares. Her beam grows twice in size, marveling her previous grin.

Emma presses the end of her pen against her lips, gratitude overwhelming her for a moment. This week though stressful has been full of laughter and joy. Most because of Bingley. His ability to make Avery laugh is uncanny. Maybe she should stop him before Avery's attachment grows anymore. She will never see him again after this little 'slumber party' ends.

The thought leaves a pit in her stomach.

"Come, dance," Agent Estella demands, taking one of the agents. He moves smoothly to her side, holding her perfectly in frame. When they begin to dance, she overtakes him with her flair. The agent stumbles, apologizing before she scolds him. Bingley's lips turn up but he no longer pays attention to her. Every turn he makes, and dip he attempts, causes a burst of laughter from Avery.

"Em! Em! Come dance!"

Emma pretends not to hear. She needs to focus on this paper. Besides, most of the other agents are dancing now and her living room is not large enough to host a dozen dancing couples. She taps the pen against the side of her head and facing the blinking cursor with a pouty lip. This should not be so difficult.

"May I have this dance?"

The richness of his voice trickles down her curls, caressing her face with phantom fingers. Little goosebumps spread over the nape of her neck. His hand hovers over her shoulder, one finger running on the underside of her hoop earring. Does he know she has no music in? He probably caught her looking. A giddy excitement wells up at the prospect of dancing but the responsible part of herself yells. She should get this done.

This is an advanced assignment… it is not due for another month and a half.

"Some might say it is a sin not to dance when Frank Sinatra comes on," Agent Darcy remarks when the song changes. The familiar song floods her apartment and twists her stomach. It is fitting—he makes her feel like a kid again sometimes.

She bashfully removes her earbuds and stares up at his

extended hand. Darcy keeps her a hostage in her own home yet her heart explodes at the soft humour in his lovely voice. If she allowed it, her brain would reminisce on how his shoulder brushed hers in the doorway. Every twirl of his finger in her hair as they spoke to the police. Oddly, the man behind her made her feel safer than them in the end.

He no longer wears his vest, or his gun. Every weapon lays to the side of the long room, untouched by the agents. He changed his sweater for the first time. This one has a collar, unbuttoned to display some of his chest and collarbone. Everything about him shows how relaxed he is here. Unfortunately, he shoots from at-ease to dutiful leader in a split second.

"One song," she consents, standing. Her hand slides into his like they were made for one another. When he glides into place and wraps his other arm around her, she falls against his chest.

Mimicking Avery and Bingley, she slides her hand to his shoulder, sure he is hiding rocks underneath the light green shirt. She stands close enough now to smell his cologne again. It reminds her of her favourite tea. Emma leans in closer, nose brushing the skin of his collarbone. A line divides the two plains of his chest, chest hair parting for it. She decides this is her favourite place. His heartbeat calmly beats against her cheek.

"What's so funny?" She inquires softly, feeling his

laughter rattle against her cheek. Did he notice her staring at his chest?

The smile on his face reveals nothing as he spins both of them so her back turns to the glass wall. He leads the dance perfectly. The light-headedness settles back in like an old friend. If he stops, she will drop to the ground.

"This song," he answers softly, bending his head so he speaks in her ear. He twirls her out and brings her back in delicately, looking at her slipper socks. She smiles at the pandas on them, throwing up her leg like Estella suggested. Agent Darcy smiles but it fades away as he tightens his hold on her back. "I struggled to understand the reason behind this song. In my village, being young meant you were irresponsible and foolish. We were raised to pursue manhood from infancy. Why would I want to be with someone who makes me feel young? Foolish? A woman is supposed to complement my strength."

Her heartbeat picks up, meeting his eyes as his thumb rubs the valley of her spine. Dad jokes that Moe ages him, but Moe says he makes her younger. She remembers her father stealing their mother away for hours at a time, taking her on adventures. One of the pictures in their bedroom captured Moe and Dad sitting in an arcade three years ago, riding motorcycles too small for them. Moe wanted it kept in their wallets, where no one could see, but he insisted on displaying it somewhere. They compromised for the bedroom.

"And now I understand." He holds her eyes, cradling her heart without knowing it. Darcy lowers his head closer, resting his forehead against hers. Without permission, her eyes slip closed, lips trembling as his breath dances over them. "The feeling of being naively hopeful and carefree. I feel like I may fly away if I let myself." He confesses, voice lowering as her eyes open again. The mixture of physical exercise and his words steal the response from her tongue. She stumbles on her own feet but he chooses that moment to lift her. "Thank you for teaching me the value of youth. I will not forget it."

"The value of youth?" Emma inquires, trying to force down the swell of snark. This means something to him! She shakes her head slightly as an uncharacteristic sorrow seizes her. "What? The ramen? The school stress? Debt? Being alone? Having no idea what you are doing? If any of it matters? How you're going to get to a place where you are finally content? If that is even possible."

"Feeling like you can be in the moment without the world coming to an end," he answers instead, gently gripping her chin to make her listen. Emma breaks the stare, trying to catch her breath as he melds their hips and slides. They easily dodge another couple with his nimble moves. "Look at me. What time is it?"

"I'm not sure." At one point she watched the clock religiously, trying to convince herself that the passing time threatened her essay. Even the slow march of time could not motivate her. Not when interesting music began and dancing lessons became the activity of the hour. "I lost track."

"I never lose track... or never used to," Agent Darcy whispers, raising one hand to brush a strand of hair out of her face. She watches his eyes while he does and then his lips. It happens before she can stop it, and once it has, she loses her reason to stop staring. His lips glisten in the neon lights. "Being here with you? Time stops. For us. I know that cannot be true, but I choose to embrace the fall rather than fight to find a foothold."

Emma notices the transition to a new song but she does not let go. She doesn't know how. Music fuses them together. Warmth bleeds to the tip of her toes. Darcy presses the side of his cheek to the top of her head, humming to the music.

The pragmatic side of her, which sounds oddly like Moe, tells her to step away. For so many reasons. Primarily his status as a murderer and a basic stranger. However, the romantic in her, fed by hours rom coms and classical literature, tells her to allow the halting of time to consume her. Another day will come and with it, goodbyes will be said and she will need to leave this phase behind her.

Why not take advantage of the moment?

Isn't that what it means to be young?

Irresponsible? Perhaps. Free? Certainly.

She runs her thumb over the dip in his hand, her face slowly making its way against his heart. Her arm wraps around his waist while his drops to her lower back. Agent Darcy squeezes the hand in his hold, running his thumb up the side of her finger. Emma laughs quietly against his bare sternum.

"What is so funny?"

She shakes her head at his imitation of her voice and glances at Agent Estella. Her corrections have now been thrust upon two of the younger looking agents. The girl looks petrified. "I was thinking if she sees us, we're going to be scorned for our lack of framing. I don't think this is how we are supposed to waltz."

"Who said this was a waltz? I asked you to dance." He remarks cleverly, careful not to break the moment. She watches his eyes close and does the same, surprised to find herself drowsy. Lifting the arm from her waist and he adjusts her hair, twisting it off her neck to allow some cool air. The heat pouring off his body adds to the innate desire for a nap.

"How old are you?" Emma asks, surprising herself. He does not tense, but she feels the break in his step. The question plagues her, mostly because of his comment about being 'too'. 'Too' old is not a good enough answer. Not when they constantly hint at being older than they look. Just this afternoon they commented on not being raised with video games... despite virtual reality gaming being the standard as Emma grew up. "I know you said no personal questions... but I will be a little put off if you are forty."

He laughs, too strongly in her opinion. In the back of her

head, Moe lectures her for falling for a man so old. Emma has noticed most people of African descent do not seem to age like Caucasians. Once she met a woman at church she would have sworn was thirty, and then the woman told her she was turning fifty-eight! They laughed together but she stopped trusting her age radar after that.

"Twenty-seven. I was twenty-seven." He answers. Her eyebrows draw together at his tense use. 'Was'? As in no longer is?

"You talk like you are fifty." Relief fills her despite his odd phrasing. Twenty-seven. A seven-year age difference doesn't bother her. Not if they both know who they are and what they want from the world.

You are thinking that as if you will have the chance to know what he wants… this is temporary.

"Age and *time* do not always coincide."

Her face scrunches further as the song ends. It punctuates the silence between them and her confusion. Yes, they do. Time ages you. Age, by definition, means the amount of time that has passed since someone's birth.

"You should return to that essay," he decides, detangling them. The expense of a question. She tries not to feel bereft without him as she watches Darcy scan the room. He notices her dismayed expression, grabbing her hand as she begins to turn away. Pressing a soft kiss between her knuckles, he glances up at her. "I should convince Rosalind to have a dance as well."

Emma watches him leave with a mixture of confusion and despair. This feels too much like goodbye already. It winds her and yet her mind wages war against her heart. She *should* be grateful for the space.

Except he makes her feel so young.

She could dance weightless, limitless, for an eternity.

Time loses meaning in his arms.

CHAPTER 20: THE BUTTON

Someone is stomping down the hall.

Emma nuzzles her pillow, trying to ignore them by sheer willpower. They must be new residents. Her neighbours know to be conscious and quiet for fear of the landlord's infamous lectures on proper hallway etiquette.

Rubbing a hand over her face, she lifts her head to check on Avery. After a long evening of dancing, she punched in her card and died to the world. Emma smothers a laugh at her sister's open mouth and the line of drool dried onto the left side of her face. Both arms stick up against the wall, fingers twitching. One leg slides off the bed, brushing Agent Bingley's head where he sleeps on the floor below her.

He sleeps in the same way, one leg thrown onto the end of her bed and one hitting the mirror beside it. Rosalind sleeps at his side, and though she built a barricade of books between them, one of his long arms manages to extend past the wall to hit her in the face. She sleeps with her arms pinned at her sides, legs straight, his hand covering half her forehead. Nothing looks peaceful about how she sleeps. Especially not the exasperation permanently etched into her face.

Her eyebrows are pulled down by her nose. The distaste-filled pucker of her lips never leaves. Emma chuckles as Bingley shifts and throws an arm over Rosalind's mouth. She still does not move. No one else does either. The room is silent for the first time... in a week.

Emma's pushes herself onto her elbow with a frown, using one hand to rub the grogginess away as a *slam* sounds. It is too early for residents to be awake. The only person typically up and stomping around at 5 AM is Trevor. His boots are loud even when he is quiet but no one bothers him because he saves people for a living. Trevor might be returning from his trip. It has been over a week since he left.

Tomorrow is church.

All grogginess leaves her mind at the thought. Moe will lose it if Emma and Avery miss church. While the deVries' never forced their children to attend, expectations were clear. On her own or not, Emma strives to meet their standards and honour them as best she can. Besides, church is the highlight of her week. She loves working in the nursery or connecting with her friends as they worship.

Pushing her hand against her face, she yawns loudly into the back of it. Hopefully Agent Darcy's heart has been as touched as hers and he will consider the small mercy of letting her go to church. After a week in captivity, they deserve it.

Her eyebrows draw together at the sound of other footsteps joining the first. Not Trevor then. Their shuffle is emphasized by the clink of metal. Emma pulls off her blanket and leans forward, searching the room for Darcy. For the first time, he is fast asleep with every other agent, a book resting against his chest.

The side of his head begins to fall off the office chair as one arm hangs over the armrest. Agent Eyre and Estella sleep close by. Eyre's small snores are the loudest thing inside her small apartment. Outside of it, the march continues, emphasized by quiet voices. It must be a couple agents returning from their off shift. She keeps track of who leaves, when they do, and the agents who come in to take their place. Normally, they are quieter though.

Climbing over Avery onto her regular side of the bed, she reaches down to poke Bingley's face. Someone needs to tell the agents to stop drawing attention to themselves and she refuses to wake Darcy. He looks so cute wrapped in one her blankets.

Despite his previous dead sleep, his eyes shoot open. They take a moment to adjust to the light and her face. She puts a kind smile on her face, opening her mouth but he lifts a finger to silence her. Blinking slowly, he glances at the clock and groans quietly. "Later."

His voice disappears into a murmur of Russian, each word dripping with irritation. Twisting away from her, he punches his pillow, not reacting to the loud *thud* down the hall. Why is an agent knocking on a door down the hall? Especially at this time. Another one sounds, closer this time.

"You need to tell the agents to be quieter."

He mutters something, gnashing his teeth together at her insistent poke. Emma doesn't want to stir him anymore than he wants to be stirred but they might be lost! Shifting back onto his side, he presses his hip into the ground and fixes her with his best glower. "What are you talking about? All the agents are here."

"Then who is in the hall?" Emma questions, her eyebrows drawn together. She tilts her head towards the wall, the *thuds* coming closer. "They sound like new agents. I can hear the tactical gear and guns...."

The blood draining from his face is the only warning she gets. Weight drops against her stomach, clawing at her as the thud sounds against her door. She cannot explain her next actions except to say the voice of God itself moves her to action.

She wraps an arm around sleeping Avery and throws them both off the bed.

Bullets spray through the wall as they collide with the cold ground and soft flesh. Emma curls her body around her little sister, locking her in a vise grip and holding her head to her chest. Gunshots overwhelm her ears as she tucks Avery underneath her chin. Agent Bingley and Rosalind throw themselves on top of the sisters as the agents rush to action.

"Bingley cover!" Agent Darcy shouts, hiding behind the chair. He slides their guns towards them over the floor and loads his own. "Charlie move to hall, Delta cover them. Alpha stay, Beta on standby if abort measures need to be taken."

He rushes towards them on the ground as Bingley and

Rosalind jump to their feet. They are already out of breath, fighting to load their guns and prepare for counterfire. Agent Eyre supplies extra ammo to those who rush into their spots and hands a vest to Agent Bingley when he comes close.

For a moment the gunshots cease. Emma chances a look up and tears up at the bullet holes marring her walls. The bullets shredded them like paper. Her beautiful glass windows are reduced to spiderwebs. *We are going to die.*

Agent Darcy breathes against her head and speaks so quietly she can hardly hear him. "We wait until they breach."

Righteous fury rips through Emma's defenses. She shakes around Avery, not out of fear, but with a protectiveness that scares her. They brought shooters to her front steps. As if her life being endangered by Darcy is not bad enough, he makes her feel protected. Like nothing can touch them.

"Emma?" Avery whispers, fear filling her voice. Emma holds her closely, pressing her hand against the back of Avery's head.

"Close your eyes," Emma responds, stroking her hair. "It's just a bad dream."

"I am going to get you to the bathroom," Agent Darcy whispers, adjusting his gun. It clicks properly into place as he watches the agents. "When I tell you to, you need to get up and follow me—"

Gunshots begin again. Emma watches the bullets fly overhead, colliding with her glass walls. Bullets embed themselves into the glass but it does not give away. The webbing spreads until the entire wall takes on the appearance of snow. *Dear God let the glass shatter. Please draw the police's attention here. Save us. Deliver us. Please Father.*

Agent Darcy pushes them underneath the bed, leaning on his elbows as the light above her bed falls onto it. Sparks fly out from the exposed wires. They catch on her bed set, flames shooting out across her bedsheets.

Emma holds Avery's face against her chest as she forces herself to breathe calmly. She cannot close her eyes. The only way to protect Avery is by keeping vigilant and praying. If people surge into the room, Emma needs to see it. She needs to be ready to do whatever it takes to get her sister out of this alive. *Lord let your will be done and let it be to preserve Avery's life. Jehovah Sabaoth please.*

Debris flies off her walls and then the books follow. She watches pieces of her mirror fly away from the bullets, sprinkling the ground. The particles drop around the bed but they are spared. *Pride and Prejudice* falls at her feet, bullets torn through it. A Bible on fire drops on the other side of the bed, the leather cover melting away.

For the first time, she closes her eyes.

"Emma," Agent Darcy calls, grabbing her foot. He pulls them out by their feet, picking them both up when Emma's legs refuse to work. The bullets stop as he plants her on two wobbly feet. She almost trips over herself and falls back to the ground as he ushers them towards the hall. "Quickly!"

Emma holds Avery up and rushes down the hall. People are shouting. Somewhere in the apartment someone screams. Agent Eyre and Rosalind stand guard by the kitchen, moving apart when they come, and then close in once they are through, creating a shield to cover their backs. Darcy opens the door to the bathroom and shoves them in.

She manages to get one look at the front door. The one thing spared from bullets. Whoever stands in her hall knows better than to open the door. The walls act as a barrier for them. Preventing the agents from being able to see what is happening on the other side. Some holes gape wide enough to provide a glimpse at the wallpaper outside her apartment, but they are too smart. At least she can console herself knowing the agents are good enough not to risk shooting her neighbours.

"Get in the tub," Agent Darcy demands, closing the door partially. He helps Emma into it, careful to hold her hand until she lies down fully. Avery keeps her eyes pressed tightly shut, tears escaping. "You do not get up. Stay there until I come back. Keep your heads down."

He detaches a pistol from his belt, cocking it. Emma shakes her head slightly but he grabs her hand and wraps it around the gun. The strength in his hand forces her tremours to stop. His eyes hold her in place, providing an anchor to bring her back to shore. "Do you know how to shoot a gun?"

"Hypothetically," she whispers, her voice strong but body shaking like a leaf. Avery lies on top of her, legs trapped between hers. If she could, Emma would put Avery below her, but it will prevent her from shooting. "I am not really comfortable doing that."

"If someone comes in here you do not recognize, you *will* shoot them," he states, squeezing her hand in his. Her finger gets caught against the gun, refusing to move. Manually shifting her pointer finger around the gun, he slides it into place over the trigger. The callous' on her hands remind her of the dance. Was that really last night? "It's you or them Emma. Aim for the leg. Their chest will be covered with a vest and it's the second biggest surface area."

"Darcy—"

He extends a button towards her. Grabbing her other hand, he presses it into her palm and places her thumb over the blue trigger. It looks like a bomb detonator. Even considering what it could be makes the pit of her stomach twist. She meets his eyes, shaking her head rapidly. "You do *not* press this unless you have no other choice. If they get through the door and you cannot shoot them, you press this—"

"I think you are overestimating my abilities," Emma whispers nervously, holding his thumb tightly. Shouting begins against outside followed by bullets. She jumps, sweat causing the gun to slide in her grip. Avery opens her eyes, watching their interaction with tear-rimmed eyes. "Please do not leave."

"I am the team leader, they need me." Agent Darcy responds, pressing a heavy kiss to her forehead. He holds the back of her head firmly, brushing his thumb over the curve of her skull. One deep breath. Two. Just as she is filled with the peace of his strength, he withdraws, pulling the bathtub curtain to cover them. "Shoot for the legs. Press if there is no other choice."

"Darcy!" Bingley shouts, his voice soon drowned out by a rain of bullets. An explosion shakes their apartment. "Breach."

Agent Dracy sprints towards the door and closes it soundly. She would get up to lock it, if her legs worked. They are numbed entirely and she can barely breathe properly without letting loose the sob in her chest. Avery breathes in time with her as their agents start shooting. They sound different. With every one of their bullets, an odd sound rings out. Like balloons expanding.

"What do you think will happen if we press the button?" Avery asks, voice shaking. She holds one hand against Emma's shoulder, grasping it like she is falling and Emma's the only handhold. "Do you think your entire apartment will blow up?"

"Should we find out?" Emma jokes shakily, the sweat of her hand making it difficult to keep her finger on the trigger. She readjusts her grip, listening to the ebb and flow of their bullets. Based on sound alone, she can tell when the agents gain the advantage.

Agent Darcy starts shouting, his instructions lost between the barrier of the wall and bathtub. Their bullets and the strange whistle afterwards take over. It begins in her hall and moves out of her apartment within seconds. Soon enough, her apartment is almost silent.

"We should press it," Avery decides, trying to laugh. It is fragile, like her quivering smile. She closes her eyes again as a scream rings through the building. The smell of metal overtakes Emma's senses as she sniffles. "If this is a bad dream, it doesn't matter what happens."

"If this is a dream, it will not work until the last moment," Emma counters, pressing her lips to the top of Avery's head. "Close your eyes and try to go back to sleep."

"Emma... I'm young, not stupid."

She rests her head on top of Avery's, staring at the detonator in her hand. Bullets thud against the wall again and her door shakes as another explosion tears through her apartment. Part of her refuses to believe this is real life. She could be trapped in a bad dream. Losing Avery, being the one responsible for her death, not being able to protect a family member—all fears hidden in the depth of her mind. Nightmares steal from memories and experiences to torture people all the time.

Except when someone else screams, it sounds genuine. Filled with fear and pain. *Please do not let it be one of ours God. Protect them.*

CHAPTER 21: ADULTS ONLY

Emma's heart skips a beat when she hears footsteps down her hallway. Using her free hand, she forces her little sisters head down at her side, twisting slight. Avery closes her eyes tightly as Emma lifts the gun again. She is not sure if they will see her, but she will see them as soon as they open the door. The safety is off, her hands stopped shaking, and her finger brushes the trigger as shadows pass under the door. Riri prays underneath her breath, wrapping one arm tightly around Emma's torso. She holds the detonator in the other tiny hand, waiting for the command.

"You keep your eyes closed," Emma directs quietly, biting down on her lip. The shadow moves underneath the door as whispers sound on the other side. "Get ready."

Avery nods, burrowing into Emma's armpit.

The person shifts on the other side, eliciting a low whine from the wooden floor. Another *creak* sounds over her rushing blood. How many people is she going to shoot to protect Avery? How many rounds are in this gun? She thought she heard one but they were whispering to someone. Her arm aches so she readjusts her hold on the handle, breath rattling in her lungs. It could be Darcy. They do not know how long it has been. Her phone is locked above the fridge, her watch left on her nightstand when off-duty, and she did not think to install a clock in the bathroom.

The minutes bleed into hours.

It feels like an eternity in this tub, muscles cramping, beads of sweat rolling down her forehead.

Avery sniffles.

Too loudly.

It sounds like canon fire.

"Emma? I am coming in," Agent Rosalind begins, her voice soft and sweet. The doorknob slowly twists but the door does not open. "Do not shoot me."

"Darcy said wait for him," Avery calls, her voice shaking. She opens her eyes to meet Emma's. Emma nods and shifts until they are both sitting up.

"Where is he?"

"Chasing down the other team," Rosalind answers, glancing around the door. Her golden eyes meet Emma's as she shows her hands. Knocking the door open with her hip, she spins so they can see her lack of weapon. "I need the remote."

"You can give it to her," Emma whispers to Avery, switching on the safety with numb fingers. Agent Rosalind rushes forward to take the remote when she sees it, exhaling when it powers down. Sliding it into one of her vest pockets, she rip the shower curtain back.

"Any injuries?" Rosalind inquires, offering her hand to Avery. She shakes her head timidly, and with Emma's help, stands. Agent Rosalind surprises them both by lifting her straight up and out. The woman is smaller than Avery in size and stature. Yet, she lifted her like a feather, like Darcy. "These things get out of hand sometimes."

"What happened?" Avery questions, following Rosalind out. Emma's fists clench as the fear drains from her body and leaves her with anger. She considers everything she is going to say to them. Especially when she sees how pale Avery is. Her baby hairs are matted to her sweaty face! "Who was shooting at us? Why?"

"A couple of our agents thought it would be funny to host a paintball rematch in the apartments. We are lucky they did not destroy anything."

"You can't be serious—"

Emma stops, jaw dropping as she scans her apartment. Everything is back to normal. More than back to normal... perfect. Not a book out of place or a sign of her mirror's fracture. The glass windows shine more than ever.

Emma walks past her sister, blinking more than she needs to. The shock of being shot at and now *this* is too much for her brain. Not after the last week and everything they've endured at the hands of the agents. Their surveillance equipment were the first things destroyed in the shootout and now it is all back together like nothing happened. No paper out of place. The same dust marks on the screens. A candy wrapper crammed underneath the monitor stem.

"Paintball?" Avery questions, glancing at Emma for the truth. *I do not know anything....* Her mind struggles with the truth of what she saw and the reality she faces now. What is truth? Because those were metal bullets, *not* paintballs, and her apartment *was* obliterated. "That didn't sound like paintball."

"We have special equipment," Agent Rosalind laughs, a sound so forced it must be painful. She runs a hand over her messy braids and leans against the wall. "We knew they were coming for us eventually, which is why we normally sleep in our gear. I cannot believe they caught our moment of weakness."

Her amused expression drops the moment Avery no longer stares at her. She watches Emma inspect the walls instead.

Not a chip of paint out of place. A lopsided picture would be enough but there is nothing. Not a single indication of the shooting that took place minutes earlier.

"Why couldn't I play?" Avery frowns, crossing her arms. She stops pouting and turns on Rosalind instead, kicking out her legs. "I am fast! And small! They couldn't hit me!"

"It's an adult's only game... too intense."

"Adult's," Avery scoffs, sauntering up to Emma. She leans her face against Emma's chest and smiles widely. "I'm basically an adult, right Em?"

"I wasn't invited either," Emma counters, narrowing her eyes on Agent Rosalind. Her expression does not change. The neutrality further agitates Emma. She pulls at her earrings, trying to ignore the nausea filling her stomach. Every time she closes her eyes, her throat burns. Lying to her sister sickened her a week ago, now it inflicts righteous punishment. "How did the other team know where I live?"

"They saw the drawings on the window last night and recognized Bingley," she answers, jaw locking. Emma's displeasure does not compare to what she sees in Rosalind's eyes. Gold turns to molten. It scalds her. Threatens consumes her. "We were as surprised as you. Fortunately, they clomp around like clumsy elephants."

A shiver crawls down Emma's spine as the horror sets in. If she did not hear them, would she and Avery be dead now? Would the police find them? Or would Moe walk into her broken down apartment and see her bloody daughters in each other's arms? What would their organization say? How would they convince the public it had been a random attack?

Carter talked about government cover-ups all the time. Car accidents that were covert assassinations. Shootings by rival gangs that were actually government agencies. Would Emma and Avery end up on Reddit? Carter would try to figure out exactly what happened. He and RedPanda69 would tear apart every theory and run down every lead. Naturally, the organization would have to kill Carter and RedPanda69 for their knowledge. Some woman would lose her twelve-year-old son in an unfortunate school field trip accident and would never know the real reason she could not see him again.

Carter might be recruited for his brain or end up face

down in the ocean… who would feed Smuckers!?

After 20 years of being an unmovable mountain, Emma's peace shatters with a tiny squeak. Her heartbeat pumps loudly in her ears until it is overwhelming. She sways towards the videotaping equipment, knocking one of the camera's over. In the tidal wave of blood rushing through her head, she barely registers Rosalind's chastisement as she catches the expensive piece of technology. Avery tugs on her hand but her voice is a thousand miles away.

"Emma," Agent Rosalind murmurs, reaching forward. She squeezes Emma's shoulder, breaking through the haze. Avery could have been murdered. In her apartment. Her last memories would have been about this locked apartment and strangers. While she has not complained and she's enjoyed the dancing and drawing, this is not what she's supposed to do. Her life is so beautiful. Filled with people and sports and family. She is going to be a super star. Change millions of lives with her bravery and smile. Spread the love of Jesus as she's been doing since the day she learned to speak. And they almost took that away! "Ms. deVries."

"Avery," Emma utters coolly, pressing a hand to her throat. "I am feeling really thirsty, could you grab me a glass of water please?"

Avery nods obediently, leaving the room at a quickened pace. When Emma's eyes meet Rosalind's, hers are the ones filled with fire. It burns green and yellow. The heat travels all the way down to her toes as she steps forward. A feral part of her comes alive in the guttural way her teeth *clack* together.

"What happened?"

Agent Rosalind clears her throat and crosses her arms. "Paintball. You have seen how competitive we g—"

"Try again."

She glances at Avery in the kitchen, struggling to reach for a glass. When her eyes return to meet Emma's, she presses her tongue into her cheek. Whatever decision she fights with is made when Emma steps closer. "The ones we have been surveilling discovered us. I told Bingley to stay away from the windows."

"You do not get to make excuses for what just happened," Emma spits, her good nature arguing with her. Everything proves too much. She can barely think. Her blood pressure is higher than it has ever been. Anger, unnatural to her, attacks her body and convinces it they must be at war. Sweat coats her skin as the shakes return with a vengeance. All the breathing exercises she learned to calm her emotions as a child are forgotten. "My little sister could have *died*. Because you broke into *my* apartment. You brought them here. So, you will tell me what you are and who they were. If you do not, I am going to start causing problems."

"I just added twenty-three to my body count," Agent Rosalind remarks lowly, a hand drifting towards the gun on her hip. She runs her long nails over the ridges decorating the barrel, eyes flashing. "I take care of problems. Do you need to be taken care of? Does your little sister?"

She tilts her head towards the kitchen, one eyebrow raising.

That's enough.

Emma steps forward, towering over Agent Rosalind. The height difference makes it easy for Emma to lean over her, forcing her to crane her neck. Hopefully she cannot see Emma's shaking hands from down there. "You think I didn't see the fear in your eyes when you saw that detonator? Are you fast enough to stop me from pressing that button?"

Visibly taken aback, she scoffs. "You wouldn't."

"Threaten my sister again and find out."

Don't let her call my bluff Lord. She glances down at the detonator pointedly, dragging her eyes back to meet the smaller woman's.

"*Move.*"

Agent Rosalind's eyebrows rise at the venom in her tone. She blinks twice before sliding out of the way. Clasping her hands behind her back, she watches Emma appraise herself. Neither she nor Avery are dressed. Where are her keys? They do not need to grab Avery's overnight bag; Emma will return it tomorrow. "You cannot leave. Agent Darcy will not allow it."

"Darcy can't stop me if he is not here," Emma counters, walking towards her wardrobe. She rips it open, something throbbing in her throat. If she allowed herself to, she would crawl into the tiny space and disappear into the dark for a couple hours. Wait for the peace to return. Find her truer self in the deep. Free of worry and anger. "I suggest you leave. Or Avery and I will take turns smashing your cameras."

"There are currently gunmen outside of your apartment," Agent Rosalind reports, waiting for Emma to look at her before she continues. There is no superiority now. Her face and voice remain soft as Emma grabs a sweater. "They could be hiding in one of the rooms or waiting in the stairwell. Darcy and Bingley are trying to flush them out of the building and back into their headquarters, but the radio went silent. We do not know if the mission is successful until they give us a body count."

"You're saying it is dangerous to leave?"

"I am saying you will be shot if you leave," she answers, unwavering as Emma scans her over. Could she be lying? Emma trusts everybody implicitly. It's the cause of half her heart's pain. "I was sent back to secure your apartment and make sure you and Avery stay safe. You may not like it, but I am what stands between you and death."

"You are the reason—"

She stops when Avery walks back into the room. The tension is too obvious for the sister to ignore. Her eyes move over the agent first and then Emma. "What's going on?"

"They should have invited us," Emma answers nonchalantly, accepting the glass gratefully. She drains it completely before grabbing a pair of jeans and a sweater. "Get dressed."

"What? Why?" Avery pouts, fluttering her long lashes. She glances at Rosalind but the agent is preoccupied with the windows. Neither of the women are going to back down. "I thought I could go to church with you! You come to the house anyway...."

"We are leaving when Bingley and Darcy come back," Emma states, pressing her hands on either side of her sister's face. Avery's brows drop as looks at the clothes spilling out of her duffle bag. Pressing a kiss on her forehead, she grabs a new bra and brush. "Come to the bathroom with me."

"Why...?"

"Because you need to change too and I don't want you changing in here if they are coming back."

Avery observes her sister with a tilted head. Emma can feel herself unravelling and try as she might to hold herself together, she is a pinch away from bursting into tears. Or simply losing all her hair and dropping into a corner. If this is what it feels like to be high strung or anxious, thank God her normal days are free from the pain. She cannot wait to return to them.

Lord, I need extra strength and peace right now. To walk out of here with Riri. To say goodbye.

"I am sure they didn't mean to be rude."

Emma's eyebrows draw together as she closes the

bathroom door and locks it behind them. Her mind takes a moment to catch up to Avery's words. Caught between undressing and pulling her shirt on, she stares at her sister. "What?"

"I'm sure Darcy and Bingley didn't *purposely* exclude you. They probably didn't know you wanted to play paintball with them."

Emma blinks at her until finally the pieces click. Her heart aches with love as she pulls her sweater over her head. "Oh Ri."

She grabs Avery and hugs her tightly, pressing her nose into the top of her sister's head. *I almost lost her.* The thought makes her squeeze harder.

Avery grunts a little bit, but wraps her arm around her sister, nonetheless. They relax into each other's arms as Emma thanks God. Emotion clogs her throat for a moment, silencing her while she glances at herself in the mirror. She doesn't even look like herself right now.

"That's not why I am upset. I think I'm just a little stressed." Emma sighs, removing her pajama pants and replacing them with her jeans. "I am okay though *schatje*. Thank you for being concerned. You have a beautiful heart."

"I can fight them if you want me to," Avery promises, her voice too serious for Emma's liking. She pinches her cheek and shakes her head.

"No, thank you."

Agent Rosalind waits by the front door when they return. She looks up from the knife in her hand when Emma steps over. Her eyes are narrowed like a cat's, focusing on Avery in the front. Twisting the blade over her fingers, she sheathes it and follows them into the living room.

"Why are they going to the clinic?" Avery inquires, leaning against the glass. Agent Rosalind steps forward to stop her but Emma is soon at her side, watching the street below.

Agent Darcy and Bingley stand outside of the clinic, guns in hand. People walk past them... as if there are not two men holding guns in front of them. Rosalind crosses her arms slowly, ignoring the look Emma gives her.

"Maybe Bingley and Darcy like to be stabbed," Avery observes, shrugging her shoulders contentedly. She returns to Emma's bed, collecting her things from around the apartment. Emma watched her stuff become Swiss cheese in the shootout. Now the book Avery brought, previously gunned down, balances precariously on Emma's desk as it did last night.

Emma wraps her arms around herself, watching them walk into the clinic. *They're going to kill the people inside.* She quickly shakes her head and steps away from the windows. If they are, she does not want to see. How many murders can she witness before the police will lock her away? It is a silly, selfish thought to have but she cannot afford to go to prison. School, the clinic, her desire for a husband and family... does she need to report the murders to the police!?

Can she risk retribution from the agents? Will the police put her into witness protection? Could she describe Darcy to a sketch artist and condemn him?

What is her Christianly duty in this? *Dear Lord, I cannot handle these thoughts right now.* She waves a hand, changing her mind on getting out as soon as possible. This apartment holds too many memories. Being here is akin to torture. All she can imagine is watching Darcy's eyes close as the lethal injection kills him.

"Why are you packing a bag?" Avery questions, reaching over the bed to grab one of her stuffed animals. Emma does not respond immediately, stuffing the pajamas she wore this morning into her backpack. There is dust all over them. Debris. Is that a *burn* mark? On her favourite pajamas?

Agent Rosalind wanders closer, lips pressed together. A good thing considering Emma is not sure what she would do or say, and that worries her. She has no idea what she would be willing to do in this state. No calm voice guides her. It disappeared in the bloodbath.

You're my rock God. I need you.

"I want to spend some extra time with Moe. I feel bad for taking you from her."

"Oh." Avery scratches her head as she looks at her stuffed bag. "I don't know if I forgot something."

"That is how forgetting tends to be," Agent Darcy remarks, surprising both of them. Emma's eyebrows draw together as she glances towards the glass windows and then at him standing against the doorway. "What do you think you are doing?'

"I'm bringing Avery home," Emma answers, focusing on her bag. This should not hurt. His silence delivers the final punch to her chest. It should not hurt. Not this bad. It should not be difficult to say goodbye to this man she barely knows. "You are free to stay as long as you want."

"Hey," Agent Darcy whispers tenderly, stepping towards her. Between the adrenaline still pumping through her veins and the fear hidden in the recesses of her body, she jumps away. Her hip collides with her desk and sends Avery's book off the desk and *slamming* into the floor. It echoes like a gunshot. How many more does she need to hear? If she presses her hands to her ears, will she stop hearing it? "Calm down—"

"Do *not* speak to me," Emma snaps, glaring at him. She clenches her jaw to stop the tears from coming. "You almost got my little sister killed. After I told you how much she's gone through. What our family has gone through—Riri go back to the bathroom."

"What why?"

"Because I am going to braid your hair. You like when I braid your hair right?"

Avery stares at her, mouth open, eyebrows raised, the perfect picture of perplexed. She glances between the two adults, hands shifting towards her hips. A moment later, she settles on a glower directed at Agent Darcy's apologetic face. Marching towards him, she plants her feet and points a finger at his gobsmacked face. "You should not have excluded her from paintball. That's *rude*."

"We could not have known," Agent Darcy whispers as Emma moves past him. His hand reaches for her but stops an inch short. They both stare at it; her silently pleading for him not to. One touch and it's done. The fight will drain out of her. "It was a shock—"

"*You* said we could not have been safer with you here," Emma argues brokenly, twisting around to face him fully. They collide as she lifts her own finger. "You put us in danger. There is no excuse you can give me that justifies what just happened. I *trusted* you."

"We will be gone tomorrow."

What?

Emma's hand drops, the bravado crumbling as she sees the pain plainly written on his face. *Stop it. Stop looking.* Her eyes drop, focusing on the toes of his boots. They are covered in blood. *Remember who he is.*

A mapmaker. An adventure lover. Someone who reads. Who loves spending time in thought. An excellent dancer. A man of God, who spoke about his mother like a saint.

Darcy flexes his hands and takes a deep breath, forcing her eyes to meet his again. The pain is gone. Professionalism slides back into place.

Emma swallows past her own emotion. The light-headedness is no longer affiliated with a warm fuzzy feeling. It just feels like an ache, settled into her bones.

"Give us twenty-four hours to clear out the equipment and tie up loose ends. Once we are gone you will never hear from us again... neither of you will be in danger again."

"You've made promises like that before," Emma sighs, suddenly tired beyond belief. She crosses her arms and shrugs her shoulders. Avery needs her goodbye with Bingley. "Twenty-four hours. If you aren't gone, I-I don't know what I am going to do but it won't be good."

She turns on her heel and flees to the bathroom. Avery waits with a brush in hand and elastics on the counter. Emma directs her towards the toilet and closes the door. She locks it behind her and releases a deep breath when no one comes marching over.

"Did you tell him he's mean?"

"Yes," Emma answers with a half-smile, taking the brush from her hand. She presses a grateful kiss to her little sister's head. "I am okay."

"I hope you can forgive him. He really likes you. He looks at you like Dad looks at Moe."

Emma pauses, her hands hovering over the elastics. She rolls two onto her wrists and brushes Avery's hair before dividing it. "Don't get too attached—"

"And they're fun. I hope I have friends who like to

paintball when they are old... we could decorate that big glass window above the front door for Easter! I am sure we still have the ladder Moe uses to clean it." Avery declares, moving her head from side to side in her excitement. Emma finishes the line to divide her hair and begins the Dutch braid on the right side of her head. "Maybe Dad will approve of me being a building photographer... it's boring enough. Although, I told Bingley once they make a fun playlist—"

"*Schatje*, you cannot get too attached. They are not the kind of people who stick around," Emma explains, choking on her own emotions. She tries to control them but they're threatening to swallow her whole. The deVries' have never been the family who bad-mouths people. Gossiping and slander equally disrespect the children of God. Bitterness and unforgiveness too is characteristic of the unsaved, not believers. However, it's easier to ruin Avery's romanticization of them than explain the truth... Emma doesn't even know the truth! "They do not care about how their actions affect others. This may have been fun but—"

"You can't say that while you're upset! You're not going to like them if you're angry," Avery admonishes, looking up at Emma through her eyelashes and eyebrows. She tilts her head back fully but Emma adjusts it back into place. "What happened to second chances?"

"We don't know them Avery," Emma retorts, her eyelids getting heavier and heavier. She considers taking a seat on the tank to relieve her aching legs. They woke up too early and too violently. Her hip also smarts where it hit the desk. It'll bruise... the only reminder of agent's presence after tomorrow.

"They are your friends though."

Emma pauses, pressing her lips together. She clears her throat quietly and runs a hand over her messy hair. "Yes, well *you* don't know anything about them. I meant the royal 'we'."

"I want Bingley to come see my room," Avery declares, picking her nails. She swings her feet on the toilet and glances up at Emma again as she finishes one braid. "He needs to see my big creeper... and Chocolate. He's never seen a ferret before! Do you believe that? Moe is going to love him. I think Moses will too, once he gets over the awkward phase. Dad says Moses needs more friends." She pauses, her silence saying more than her words. Their eyes meet in handheld mirror on the sink. "They'll like Darcy too. Moses and him are the strong, silent types. They'll sit on the deck while we all play in the creek."

Emma slides to her other side. She begins the new braid, lost in her own emptiness. Her brain is vacant. No thoughts to be found. Not right now. "They do not live in the area."

"Well, they can come visit. God gave us airplanes for a reason," Avery decides, crossing her arms. Emma almost sighs but holds herself back for her sister's sake. Avery's stubbornness and aspirations will always outmatch hers.

Besides, she does not have the energy for this fight. Not today. "Bingley told me he wants to game with me. He hasn't been in a VR box and after this week Mom and Dad will probably buy me the newest model like I asked."

She watches her sister expectantly. Emma's lack of reaction sets her off. The 'deVries' jut begins, her chin higher than her nose. "I'm going to call you the nickname you don't like."

"Ri—"

"No, you're not telling me something. I can feel it." Avery accuses, crossing her arms. She glares at Emma when she finishes the second braid and takes a slow seat on the bathtub rim. "I'm more than your little sister, I'm your friend.'

Emma sighs softly. "I know. It has nothing to do with your maturity or age... it's just hard to explain. Can you trust me?"

"I *do* trust you. But Dad also says you're too nice and people walk all over you."

Daniel deVries shares his wife's fondness for loud opinions. Neither are shy in sharing their 'concerns' about their children with the other children. Her dad said as much to her on more than one occasion "And what does that have to do with this?"

"You need someone to stand up for you," Avery answers, crossing her arms. "I will. I'm taller than half the agents, let me at them. If you give me permission, I can be *really* rude."

"I am an adult. Don't worry about me."

Avery raises her eyebrows with a look so much like her Father's, Emma gapes. "You worry about me all the time."

"Well… I'm your big sister."

"And I am your little sister. We're both sisters so we both worry."

Emma laughs behind closed lips. How is she supposed to argue with that? A couple thoughts trinkle down but nothing solid enough to dissuade her sister. "Touché."

CHAPTER 22: FAT LARD

She cannot sleep. Try as she might, she can only watch the lights from the street curling over the ceiling. Most of the equipment is already gone, but half the agents are not. Agent Darcy sits with his back against the shelves underneath the TV. He was reading, but now the book is neglected, over his knee as he stares out the window.

Emma sleeps better with the world peering in. They opened the curtains after the cameras were cleared out, letting her bathe in the neon lights and fog. It's going back to normal. Her apartment is beginning to feel like her own again.

Why doesn't it feel good?

She should be relieved but instead she feels sick. Like someone carved a hole into her stomach and flooded it with liquid nitrogen. Avery shifts at her side, her warm breath invading Emma's space. When she tries to move, Avery inches closer. Despite her enjoyment of her little sister's company, she looks forward to having her bed all to herself again. Specifically, to be free of elbows in her face.

Curling onto her side, she watches Agent Darcy over Avery's shoulder. He's the only other one awake. His pensive expression gnaws at her. He's upset... she upset him. When she and Avery left the bathroom, they were halfway through packing up. Emma could barely look at him or the other agents, so she hid behind a book and headphones.

If she spoke with them, she'd apologize. As if the shooting were her fault. What if they took her apology as an invitation to stay? Miss them as she may, they need to leave.

Emma picks at the pillow between her and Avery, half-hidden in the mass of comforters and blankets. It's wrong to watch Darcy, especially when he still thinks she is upset with him. God knows she should be. Except with the passing of a long day, she realized their first thought had been her and Avery. Bingley jumped on top of them. Darcy made sure to get them to a safe place.

He sent Rosalind back to secure them. While she would not have been attacked if he were not here, he did not cause it. They did not ask to be shot at. She heard him scolding Rosalind for threatening her. Emma did not tell him what the agent said so she must have admitted it herself. Contrary to his anger, Agent Darcy's voice never rose. His stern voice warned her to never do it again, but no punishment came with it. Agent Rosalind drifted back to work and Darcy ran a hand down his face. Like his hand possessed the ability to wipe away exhaustion.

A guilty conscience doesn't allow a good sleep.

Throwing off the blanket, she slides out of bed, careful not to step on Agent Eyre. Agents surround her bed, sleeping with weapons instead of pillows now. Rosalind rests at the foot of her bed, knife in hand, barely hidden underneath her pillow. One wrong step and she could have a bullet in her foot. The risk gets her sluggish heartbeat going as she makes her way to Darcy.

He finally notices her progression, unfreezing from his hunch. As she sits down across from him, his legs unfurl and the book closes.

Silence dances between them. He gazes at her as she scans the street. When she sees nothing worth watching, her eyes turn up to meet his. They are no longer filled with childhood comfort and warmth. Instead, they remind her of a school field trip to a farm. Looking at the baby cows as they were ripped from their mothers. Emma's teacher kept repeating 'informed consumption kids, informed consumption'. She cried to the pastor a week later, like she was personally responsible for the transgression and he *laughed*. No one is laughing now.

"I should not have gotten so upset."

"You have every right," he responds softly, wrapping his arms around his knees. Leaning his head back against the shelves, he studies her and then looks out to the rainy street. "We disrupted your life. Do not worry, it will not happen again."

"What happened?" Emma inquires genuinely, crossing her legs. She cocks her head to the side, feeling one of her braids slide down her back. Darcy watches the action and sighs.

"Emma—"

"I know those were real bullets. I saw the holes in my walls and watched the mirror crack. People were trying to kill you." Emma states, edging closer. He drops one leg and scratches the back of his head. His legs form a barrier to keep her out but he cannot escape her eyes. "Who are they? What did they want? What have you been looking for in the clinic?"

"You will not understand."

"You guys need to stop telling me what I can and cannot understand," Emma remarks, keeping her voice light as the frustration returns. No, not frustration. It is desperation. Oddly not for answers, but for him and his safety. Ignorance impairs her. She can provide no support without basic knowledge of what they face. The agent's lives were in danger too. What if one of them were shot before they got their armour? All she can do is pray but that's a superpower in itself. "You do not know what I'll believe. I could help. I don't know how, but I know I could. Let me help."

"Emma," Darcy repeats, grabbing her hands. She squeaks when he pulls her closer. The satin of her pajama bottoms allows her to glide over the wooden floor. He opens his legs slightly so that her knees touch his feet. "It is better you remain ignorant. For your safety and for Avery's."

"And where was this concern for safety when you first came here?" Emma questions, squeezing his hands. His brows drop as he blows out an exasperated breath but she holds his attention. "I am not trying to be petty; I am just saying you didn't seem concerned before—"

"Because I saw you, Emma. We saw each other." Agent Darcy whispers, letting go of her hands. He lays his arm over his knee, shaking his head. "And you were right across from the building we needed to monitor."

"There is no way you could have seen me. We were too far away from one another."

His expression shows no amusement. Their eyes meet as Emma's mind spirals. She knew they made eye contact, even though it should have been impossible. With the lights from the street and the tint on the outside of the windows, he should not have been able to see her from outside. In the dark of the night, she barely saw him. Yet, their eye contact started this all.

"I am already in danger," Emma argues, proud of herself for bringing up the point. He is not so impressed. Darcy's eyes remain trained on hers without even a fraction of pride or admiration. Leaning forward she rests her chin against his raised knee, wrapping her arms around the base. "They found me once—"

"They will not find you again."

His voice becomes so dark she feels blinded. There is the anger she tasted when he spoke with Agent Rosalind. Unlike then, he is not trying to restrain it. Instead, he allows it to colour his eyes and expression. She runs her hand over his clenched fists, surprised to find herself so comfortable touching him with that emotion on display.

"You—"

"Yes, I can. You were going to say I cannot control that but I can." Agent Darcy promises, squeezing her hands. He runs his thumbs over her knuckles. By the steel of his eyes alone, she is swayed. It looks like he needed convincing too. When she nods her head, relief fills his eyes. She trusts him completely. The fact slaps her in the face and leaves her speechless. He says everything will be okay and she sees no reason to question it. "We have already dealt with this branch. We need to prune a couple more—"

"Branches of what?"

"I am not going to answer your questions," he states, daring her to challenge him. If she were a smidge more stubborn, she probably would. Except it is after midnight, on possibly their last night together, and she does not want to spend it fighting. She wants to know everything. About why he is here. About him. About the other agents. If he does not want to answer that question, there are hundreds of others. "Don't waste your time."

"How did you get rid of the bullet holes?" She asks, wrapping her arms around her midsection. He stares at the street, shaking his head but she is too curious to stop asking. They are past the point of her fearing him. Sitting in silence is not something she enjoys. "You cannot tell me that much?"

"It will bring more questions and few answers."

"You said I will not see you again. What's the harm?"

"Emma. Those people with assault rifles have friends. They know where you live. If I am not cautious, you will be followed. I do not think you want to be watching your sister's game when a bunch of gunmen break into the arena and shoot everything that moves." His expression remains devoid of all emotion as he stares at her. No, his face may be directed towards her but he is not looking at her. Instead, his mind is a thousand miles away. The cold words and empty expression create a haunting dance down her spine. She cannot think about a scenario like that. Thinking about it produces a burn down her throat. "You want me to stop being cautious? I will. There is nothing I can withhold from you." He laughs shakily, throat working as his fist clenches. "The truth is that I lost focus. I let myself be absorbed by you. By this life. And you reaped the consequences of that. My entire team did. Yet, I'd do it all again for a night in your arms. That is the harm."

His voice loses its strength on the last sentence. Darcy drops his eyes to his lap, shoulders heaving. Tears gathered in her eyes at some point. He's right. There is too much to lose here. Whoever these agents are, they are inherently dangerous. To her. To her family. Emma does not know how she'd protect her family or live with the guilt of hurting them. Everything comes with a price.

It's not fair to ask him to pay it.

"What is your favourite thing to do in your free time?"

His shoulders shake with silent laughter as his eyes return to hers. "What?"

"You asked me what I like to do in my free time. Now it's my turn. I know you read, is that your favourite pastime?" Emma refuses to flinch underneath his peculiar stare. His lips curl up at the sides, causing a dimple in the shadows. A sign of character on his plastic face for once. "You can tell me that without endangering my life."

"I love to read. It is my favourite thing to do. Most people in my village could not read. We told stories to one another, in song or at bedtime, but the elders swatted children who began daydreaming and I could never stop myself. When I heard a good story, that world comes alive in my head. Reading gives me the space to do so... I love to escape to world's I'll never know." Agent Darcy explains, his jaw clenching. He runs his fingers over the pages of his books, looking twice as old in the pale moonlight shining down on the city. "The privateer taught me so he could drink while I read him his letters and responded to them. After I joined the agency, I realized people put their stories on paper and the first purchase I made with my own money was a box of old books."

"Do you enjoy fantasy?" Emma inquires, although she knows he enjoys classical literature. As the team lead, he must be the one who named the agents. Bingley and Darcy, *Pride and Prejudice*. Rosalind, *As You Like It*. Eyre, *Jane Eyre*. Estella, *Great Expectations*. "Far off kingdoms, daring swordfights, magic spells. Dragons. Magic. Knights. Princesses."

"I love the classics," he confesses, crossing his legs. His knees meet hers as he smiles. "Especially from the eighteen hundreds. Seeing what the world was like for different people. This world is fantastic enough for me."

"That does not surprise me," Emma admits, smiling when he meets her eyes. They both dress like they could be historians. Well, Agent Darcy only wears the same kind of colours and fabrics on duty, but she can tell by the way he stands and reads that he would look incredible in khakis and a button down. With a sweater vest stretched over his chest—she better stop before she suggests they go thrifting together. "You strike me as the kind of man who would sip fine wine, lounging on a velvet seat, with your glasses perched on the end of your nose and reading *Great Expectations* like Charles Dickens is some kind of revolutionary."

His lips twitch slightly, part of his hand covering them as he leans his elbow against the window. Emma raises her eyebrows, turning to lean her back against the glass wall. They stare at each other, the tension of the day disappearing with their hidden smiles. "What do you have against Charles Dickens?"

"Pip is a silly name for a protagonist. He treated Joe deplorably and as a pacifist, I thought he could use a smack upside the head." Emma describes, laughing when he does. He nods in agreement as she watches him with fond eyes. She will miss this. Conversation with someone who enjoys reading just as much as she does. Who makes it so easy to hold a conversation and speak about herself. Someone who makes her forget about looking at the clock. "Also, Estella was awful and I cannot believe she ended up being the one for him—"

"You must have known."

"I am a romantic and I did not want them to end up with one another."

"People in that time viewed wealth and status higher than anything else. Dickens tore down the romanticization of the rich and challenged the degradation of the poor. Despite Pip being raised by the 'lower class', he lives a richer life than Estella. He had freedom, fun, and genuine love. His counterpart got the neglect, abuse, and mistreatment often associated with the 'impoverished'. Pip taught her the meaning of joy and she helped him learn the true danger of status. In the end, Pip got exactly what he wanted and Estella got what she needed. They were written for one another."

"I do understand her awful upbringing, but it does not excuse the way she spoke about and treated people."

His eyebrows draw together as he crosses his arms. She lifts her legs, allowing him to lower the other. Gratefully stretching out his legs, Darcy pulls her closer, smiling when her legs form a steeple over his knees. The bottom of her thigh brushes against the rough material of his pants. She shivers slightly, the combined scratch of the fabric and the cool glass on her back becoming too much for a moment. "You do not think those who have undergone great deals of stress and trauma should be treated with sympathy and grace?"

"They should. I am *sympathetic* to her pain but she knew what she was doing. Abuse and trauma are not an excuse to do whatever you want. Everyone experiences some kind of pain in their life. If everyone acted like her, like their hurt justifies anything, we'd have a lot more brokenness in this world. Imagine a world filled with bitter people who have a 'get out of jail free card' for being mean. More and more people would turn out exactly like them and then the entire world would be miserable." Emma explains, shaking her head. Most of the time she waits for others to share parts of themselves and encourages them to share more... but Darcy makes her feel like they are on a level playing field. Like they can explore each other equally. "It is one thing if they do not know better, but when they are taught that what they do is wrong? It shows a lack of character if they do not change."

He nods his head but the smile he flashes at her is lopsided. Is she rambling? Speaking too much overwhelms any attractive quality. Maybe she should not have ranted.... "I am sorry, I did not recognize the metaphor. I agree with you. Too often bad experiences are used as excuses. I saw your special edition of *Pride and Prejudice*, is that your favourite classic?"

"It must be. I read it whenever I need comfort." Emma

laughs, making a mental note to play her favourite board game with him. She watches him cross his ankles and tries to see what book he is reading. "What's your favourite book?'

His laugh starts soft and becomes a touch sinister. Surprised by the sound, she crosses her arms excitedly. "You are not going to like it."

"Now you need to tell me." She adjusts her seat again, sitting astride his legs with her hip pressed against the window. Bringing her knees to her chest, she watches him excitedly. "Should I guess?"

He hands her the book he is reading instead. Emma shakes her head in disappointment as she reads the title. Darcy laughs softly, rustling around behind him. "No, you're joking."

"Have you read it?"

"In English AP," Emma laughs, the sound ending abruptly when he wraps his warm jacket around her bare shoulders. Wetting her lips, she flips the book side to side. "Please tell me... you... do not tell me *Winston* is your favourite." His laugh disconcerts her as she rapidly shakes her head. "Anyone but that—fat lard. Please Darcy."

She chokes on her own insult and then she is laughing with him. He throws his head back, pressing his hands to his stomach as she covers her mouth. Someone groans in the room and more than a couple agents shift. Trying to force the laughter back down, she refuses to look into his eyes.

When their eyes meet, the laughter goes silent. Drawing

out tears from her eyes and forces Darcy to stuff his fist against his mouth. Midnight hysteria settles in as the moonlight glistens off her tears. She drops her head against her knees, cowering beneath the jacket.

"He is not too bad," Darcy pleads, his shoulders still shaking. She wipes away the tears, bringing her head up with a cocked eyebrow. The needed release of tension adds to the hysteria. He leans forward to catch another tear and starts laughing at her silent wheezing.

"He was my least favourite character."

"He is a coward, and selfish, but he is supposed to represent what happens when we stop fighting for one another and for good. It is not his fault Orwell chose to make his existence a metaphor."

"I hoped he would be saved," Emma confesses, wiping away the tears. Handing her a tissue, the agent pats his heart to calm it. Their voices lower more as the agents keep moving. "I thought he would take down the regime and end up with Julia… He was a cheater though. I should've given up hope after that."

"The more you say the less I like him." They both laugh at that. Darcy pats the spot beside him along the glass and smiles approvingly when her hip meets his. "What is 'AP'?"

"Advanced placement. There are the regular classes and then the AP ones." Emma explains, clasping her hands in her lap. "They are mixed with college courses—"

"So, classes for smart people?"

Her face flushes slightly as he smiles down at her. "More for kids who really enjoy a subject or intend to do a lot of schooling. If you take full AP, it removes the first year of requisites, based on your credits."

"Did you?"

"I thought I wanted to be a surgeon," Emma nods, laughing at herself. His eyebrows raise in surprise as she looks at his hand. He offers it to her, relaxing when she begins to draw lines down his fingers with her nail. "I set up my courses to do pre-med. Then I realized that my failure would mean death for loved ones. Even if I was successful… things go wrong. I enjoy being a 'sloth'… Moe says that's what I remind her of."

"Why pharmacology?"

"I enjoy numbers. I know, people think I am crazy. Math is a sure thing and I still have a chance to be part of relieving people's pain. I know what to pray for them when I see their prescriptions."

He slides his fingers through hers, enclosing her palm in his. Callous' cover the pale skin. Little scars and healed rope burns uniquely mark his hands. Emma pulls his hand into her lap, using the other to trace a particularly gnarled area.

"The horse was not happy I caught him."

She smiles, closing her eyes when his head drops on top of hers. "Why *1984*?"

"Because it shows what happens when dangerous men are in power and unchecked. What one moment in history can do to people and time. Dangerous men with power give birth to reckless monsters. And he taught me that history is controlled by those who tell it." Agent Darcy explains, his voice turning grim. Surprised by the conviction in his tone, she peers up at him. She immediately regrets it when their lips end up inches apart. He lifts his free hand, turning slightly towards her to brush his thumb over her cheek. "It gives me perspective on how different people react to control. I know what it is to be controlled by a man. I know I'd fight my best but there are people run by fear who would not. Others are happy to comply with the guarantee of certain luxuries. I consider it a personal study. Eric Blair, or George Orwell, predicted the Cold War; he was a great man. One who opposed absolutism and totalitarian regimes openly while the world unraveled. I was proud to be one of his first supporters."

"Mrs. Ambrose would have loved you... my English teacher. She always challenged us to put ourselves into the shoes of every character." Emma explains, bringing her head back to his shoulder. It flexes under her head as he fixes the jacket on her shoulder. "I struggled with Winston."

"Because you are selfless and protective. You are everything he is not."

Emma smiles and then her eyebrows draw together. "George Orwell died before the two thousands began... how could you have been one of his first supporters?"

"The literary world lost appreciation for him when the last fascist leader lost power," Darcy remarks but she can feel his body tensing underneath her arm.

She should ask.

Except he will not answer. Better to choose a safer question to preserve their small eternity here in the corner of her little apartment. "What made you choose Darcy?"

"People misunderstood him and made judgements based on what they perceived about his appearance and countenance. I am a large black man; it happens too often. No matter where or when I go."

"I am sorry," she whispers, shaking her head. "People can be so cruel. You deserve better."

"You have not seen this side of me yet, but I am spontaneous and fun. At work, I need to be focused... as focused as I can be." He admits, brushing his thumb over her hand. She syncs her breathing to his and closes her eyes again. With her back against the cool wall and the hard floor digging into her hip, she could fall asleep. As long as he kept talking. His accent and warmth lull her. "Most do not know how to handle the transition from serious leader to fun friend."

"And he is protective, sweet, and considerate." Darcy shrugs at that but she sees the little smirk on his face. "Moe was a double major. European History and English Lit. Her collection of classics fills two bookcases. I remember being ten and she wouldn't let me read any of that year's bestsellers until I picked a classic. She argues you cannot enjoy books if you do not see where they started. While I do not feel as strongly convicted as her, she taught me to read and appreciate old language."

"You speak like an Austen character sometimes."

"I always related to Lizzy. I will never be as... outspoken as she is, but I could see her protectiveness and vulnerability. It is easy to hide behind sass and wit when you have a big heart."

"You do not hide behind it."

"Moe can be sassy at times but my Dad is the calmest man I've met. He is very level-headed." Emma laughs, shrugging. "I take after him. Just like Lizzy, the favourite of her Father and arguably the most reasonable."

Darcy laughs. The sound sends butterflies down her stomach as she cuddles up to his arm and smiles into it. Her father refuses to choose a favourite. Emma holds no special regard towards any one person. She knows she and Moses are closer than the others, but she would not say he is her favourite. Both for fear of hurting others and because she does not feel it is true. They are all her favourites... he just knows her the best.

Darcy is her favourite agent. Even the thought of spending time with him warms her heart. It goes cold as she glances at the clock for the first time. Time has never scared her before but suddenly it is ticking away and she desperately wishes she could have more of it.

CHAPTER 23: GONE LIKE THE WIND

No one enjoys the feeling of falling.

Especially when it happens in a dream, leaving the sleeper to wake with a start. Emma's heartbeat calms as she adjusts to her surroundings. The morning sun pours into her apartment, gleaming off the buildings across the street. Horns are honking below. All is as it should be. With that thought, she nearly falls back under… but then she notices the agents are gone.

Shooting up, she presses her hands to her eyes, trying to rub the sleep remnants away. The room is empty! When did she fall asleep? Looking down at herself, she almost tears up. Darcy put her into bed. Last night Darcy shared more about his own faith and childhood. Somewhere between listening to the Bible as he heard it and the way colonization changed their religion, she fell asleep. The stories were designed to be bedtime stories but she didn't intend to fall asleep on him.

The conviction he spoke with moved her. She hung onto every word. To the point she convinced herself on the brink of unconsciousness that she'd never find another man like him. Emma plans her apology, considering what book to give him, when she sees her empty apartment again.

The ache from last night comes back in full force, winding her. Wrapping her arms around herself, she moves towards the uncovered windows. Clear blue skies greet her from above. Light streams unbidden into her apartment. It crawls through every corner of the room, leaving no place for the agents to hide.

They dusted. Her apartment is spotless. No wrappers or scrap pieces of paper... like they were never here.

People walk into the clinic from the street, unbeknownst of her eyes set on them. She would follow the agents there... if she could. They left nothing here for her to remember them by.

"Are they gone?"

Emma glances at Avery and nods her head soberly. The younger girl's face crumbles in a mixture of confusion and exhaustion. She rubs her arm over her eyes and groans.

"Gooood morning sleeping beauty. Seems you need the rest with all that drool on your fa—" Bingley greets, appearing in the hallway. Avery's face lights up as she throws her blanket off. Within moments, Bingley ends up pinned to the wall by a torpedo of pink and black.

The agent laughs good-naturedly, patting Avery's messy braids. She presses her face into his chest even as he disentangles himself. Then Darcy steps into the room. His tactical gear is back on, belted into place, with weapons decorating him. All she sees is the man she stayed up with until the sun started creeping out.

Emma manages to keep control of herself as she imagines jumping into his arms. He meets her eyes with a sad smile.

"I thought you left," she remarks, grateful when he steps past the others and heads towards her. He waits in front of her, allowing her the choice. She takes it happily, wrapping her arms around him. "Were you about to wake us?"

"I wanted to let you sleep."

"You couldn't leave without saying goodbye!" Avery exclaims, shaking her head. Emma nods against Darcy's chest, agreeing completely with her outspoken sister. Her heart broke a little at the sight of her empty apartment. Darcy runs his hand through her hair now, soothing her. *Did he kiss my hair?* She squeezes her eyes shut as she feels his lips press against her messy curls again. The word 'goodbye' burns her tongue. "Come to church with us! You're here anyway. You don't need to go anywhere."

"We have adult responsibilities we must return to, маленькая акула," Bingley states, pulling on the end of her braid. He nods at Emma, offering a hug as well. She steps towards him but their embrace holds no extra warmth or unspoken desires.

"The fool could not think of leaving without saying goodbye," Agent Rosalind mutters, crossing her arms as she leans on the doorway. Emma stands still as Avery hugs her. The agent freezes a little, her chin forced out of the way by Avery's head. Her arms come around to pat her shoulders. Like one would swat a bug. "Okay, that is enough."

"You can come to our family dinner," Avery continues,

turning to Darcy now. He tries to smile for her sake but fails. This is all wrong. Nothing right feels this horrible. Emma leans against his arm, grateful when his hand comes down to hold hers. "Please?"

"Someday," Agent Bingley offers, shrugging apologetically when Rosalind shakes her head at him. Avery's squeal of excitement drowns out anything else. She hugs him again, refusing to let go as he musses her hair.

"Emma needs more friends," Avery remarks, grinning towards Emma. She misses the way Bingley blinks a little faster. His hand comes around the back of her head, splaying there as a tremour snakes through his jaw. Avery is too busy smirking at their entwined hands. Emma does not have the heart to pull away. "And a boyfriend. She is *very* single."

"I have friends," Emma blushes, heat creeping down her neck. Darcy turns his head towards hers, tucking her into his side. She hugs him back, listening to his heart. Allowing this to be real for as long as she can.

"Sure, you do. A racecar does not count."

She shoots a playful glare at Bingley, trying to convey with her eyes how desperately she wishes to help with the pain he hides. The agent ushers Avery out of the room, casting back a 'look'. Emma hardly hides her grateful smile. Agent Rosalind watches them go and then scans over the two left in the room. Slowly, she pushes herself off the wall and twists around.

"I am sorry for being rude. And for falling asleep while you were telling me about your childhood—I cannot make up for it but thank you for trusting me."

The agent pauses, running his hands up her arms to stop at her shoulders. A gentle squeeze and then he lets go. "You were showing your might. Do not apologize for that. As for falling asleep, there is no greater gift you can give me than your time and trust. I got to spend the sunrise with you in my arms... you gave me another memory to treasure."

The silence hangs between them, daring one of them to go.

"She scares me," Emma whispers hearing Rosalind in the other room. Darcy laughs from his belly, hand pressed there as she cracks a shaky smile. "I wish I had the chance to make it up to all of you. To hear all the stories...."

Her words hang in the air as she reaches for his hand. Darcy squeezes her fingers in his, beginning to pull away. Closing her eyes, Emma holds on tighter, knowing just how much she wants to ask him to stay. Not in her apartment... because God knows that's a right saved for her husband.

She wants him in her life.

The late-night discussions she prioritizes over sleeping. Shared laughter. Bumping each other's hips in the kitchen. Rendered speechless when he levels her with the universe caught in his gaze. Listening to his voice and allowing the accent and sincerity to soothe her. The stories he conjured of his own imagination and the ones about her family and way of life which fascinates him.

"I know I told you to leave—"

"Please. Stop. We are not going to make this harder for ourselves." Agent Darcy whispers, grabbing her other hand. Swinging them together, he leans forward, his forehead resting against hers. Emma memorizes the smell of him. The way his hands feel in hers. How his warmth surrounds her. Tilting her chin down, she forces the swell of emotions away. Nothing makes goodbye easier though. Reason and romance wage their war against one another in her mind. "Emma, look at me *skat*."

He lifts his head to allow her the room to meet his eyes. Taking a deep breath, she stares into his face, fighting against the newest surge. Darcy's hand caresses her face as she tries to name the emotions swimming through his eyes. Are they similar to her own longing and despair? She cannot remember the last time her emotions were intense enough to suffocate her. A sneaking suspicion places it five years ago when Avery's screen came back negative for the first time.

"Thank you. For giving me part of yourself. I know we intruded but I will not forget your kindness." Darcy states, squeezing his eyes shut when her hand rests against his stubbled cheek. Part of her calls for her to fight. To find some way without a cost... but time is a valuable currency. One unable to be multiplied. They had their moment. "I cannot think of a better way to spend the time I have. You made every moment worth it."

She nods her head gratefully, eyes closed as he leans forward to press a kiss against her forehead. Her hands come up against his chest, gripping the rough vest. As he pulls away, her mind screams 'no'.

"You will never see me again," Darcy whispers, squeezing her shoulders when she winces slightly. The reminder is worse than anything else. She could bear saying goodbye if she could trick herself into thinking they'll see each other again. Except they won't. As he says it, she can feel the inevitable truth settling into the pit of her stomach. "*Aweh*, it is how you say goodbye in Afrikaans."

"*Tot ziens.*"

He knows what it means. She feels it in the way he hesitates.

Say it back. Say it back.

Pressing one last kiss to her head, he runs his hands down her face and then he is gone.

She watches him walk away, throat closing around the lump of emotion. Following him, she pauses in the hallway, glancing at Avery as she brushes away tears. Darcy smiles when Avery hugs him.

Emma strains to hear what he says.

When the door closes behind him, she is lonelier than ever.

Avery rubs her arm over her face and pinches her nose. "I

need a tissue."

Emma numbly watches her walk down the hall. When she looks back at the door, it is locked—complete with the special utensil her Dad gave her. She lays the back of her head against the wall, barely able to breathe, let alone think.

"Now what are we supposed to do?" Avery questions, returning with a tissue. She offers it to Emma but stops when she sees Emma is not crying. How is she supposed to? This feels like a dream.

Her apartment looks like it has never been stepped in by anyone other than her. The snacks she bought for her and Avery are back on the counter, just as they were the night before the shooting. She blinks slowly, tempted to ask her little sister what day it is. It could have been a hallucination induced by all the sugar they ate. Darcy is too good to be true. Straight out of her own imagination. "Em?"

"Go get your stuff," she croaks, forcing a smile onto her face. It feels fake... fragile even. The corners of her lips quiver, enough to make Avery's eyebrows knit together. "I should get you home. Moe is going to be worried when she sees we did not go to church."

"Are you okay?"

"You have the energy of a rabbit," Emma laughs, squeezing her sister's head as she gives her a half-hug. Just like Bingley. Her mind reels, unable to accept the name or anything else. It brings pain like a sucker punch. "You just wore me out. Next time, I am going to convince Carter to give me a few of his energy drinks beforehand. I'll be bounces off the walls while you sleep."

"Never," Avery grins, running to the bed. Emma watches her go and shakes her head, walking into the kitchen. Where are her keys? She brings her hands up to her chest as she searches the kitchen. Finally, she finds them on the little table, right beside an envelope.

"Ri, who left the envelope here?"

"Bingley," Avery answers, backpack already on. "He told me he forgot to leave it the first time and that's why they came back."

Her heart aches as she reaches down for the envelope. No name. No return address. Nothing but a standard white letter.

Pushing the tab up, she stretches it open and gasps. Or is it a sob?

Avery's eyes double in size as Emma pulls out the wad of cash. A small note is attached with a paper clip. **A month's rent and enough to cover lost wages… thank you.**

A small smiley face is drawn poorly beside the note.

Enough to cover her wages? By her count alone, it is twice what she would have made in the last week. She almost takes a seat… except she sees the worried look on Avery's face. "You got everything?"

"Yes."

Nodding, she slides the money back into place and throws

it onto the basket atop her fridge. "Time to go then."

CHAPTER 24: TAKE CARE

It's raining.

The water soaks into Emma's leather jacket, bursting against the visor of her helmet. She cuts the engine, tension melting out of her sore arms. It was not supposed to rain so heavily this morning. Puddles form on the dirt road, right before the place it becomes stone. Mud covers Avery's entire back, all the way up to the top of her helmet. The rain suit protects her clothes from most of the damage but they are both shivering.

Avery struggles to remove her helmet as Emma stares at the mud up to her knees. Her legs are practically frozen to the vehicle's body. Normally the rain is not cold in her city, but it freezes the inches of unprotected skin on her hands. She cannot feel her fingers.

"Emma!" Avery calls, shocking Emma. She jumps around the bike, foot jerking against the kickstand. Finally, her eyes adjust to the driveway of her parent's house. She presses her hand against her heart. When did they get here? "Are you coming?"

Emma nods to herself, removing her helmet. Her long locks drop down onto the spattered dirt, but she does not care enough right now. Rain is pouring anyway. It washes her clean as she puts her helmet away beside Avery's. Unzipping her jacket, she stuffs it into the trunk beside Avery's rain suit. The chill seeps into her sweater, tunneling towards her heart. She cannot remember putting any of this on.

Shimmying out of her leather pants, she shakes them off as best she can and hides them away too. The mud is going to cake onto the expensive fabric but she'll clean it later. At home. When she's alone....

"She didn't put the red bunny out this year," Avery frowns, stomping her feet on the welcome mat. A swell of panic hits Emma at the sound. Her nervous system is fried. "How long do you think it will take her to notice when I put it out?"

The girl disappears through the front door as Emma pauses on the step. Robotically removing her boots, she slides them beside the Easter display. Jesus sits on a large egg, little bunnies surrounding him with baskets in hand. His wound covered hands hold chocolates in them for guests to take. Like every other year.

"*Liefje,* you're home," Moe exclaims, excitedly rushing forward. She grabs Avery and picks her up, pressing kiss over kiss on top of Avery's head. *Normalcy. I need normalcy.* "You two were not in church."

"The rain," Emma excuses weakly, wrapping her arms around herself. She and Darcy stayed up late. Darcy's voice hypnotized her to sleep before she could set an alarm. "I know, I should get a car."

Moe blinks silently at her, glancing down at Avery. She

squeezes her youngest daughter's shoulder and waves her hand at the stairs. "Go put your stuff away."

Avery looks between them nervously. Emma nods with a hidden smile before making her way to the kitchen. She grabs a glass of water, searching the cabinets for something to eat for breakfast. Heat flows back into her limbs as she moves, burning until she cannot ignore them. Placing the glass beside the sink, she rubs her numb fingers up and down her damp jeans. Moe parades into the room, arms crossed.

"What were you thinking? What possessed you?" Moe questions, neck straining as she keeps her voice low. She follows Emma around the kitchen until she finally stops. Snatching up a banana, she offers one to her mother and shrugs when she reuses. "Emma—"

"I am tired," Emma apologizes, taking a deep breath. She puts the banana down on the counter and takes a deep breath. "I was thinking I wished I had a big sister who would listen. I would have loved to have someone who cared enough to make me feel seen when I felt invisible. She needed to be reminded she's not alone. She has people cheering her on, supporting her."

"We are on her side. You pulling her away and acting like we are the enemy isn't the solution. We work together. We are a family." Moe argues, leaning forward on the counter while Emma peels the banana. She sighs loudly, blowing hair out of her face. "We support each other, we supported you in what you wanted… I don't understand why you felt that way. You had older brothers, Em. And your Mother—"

"It's not the same."

"What's gotten into you?" Moe questions, eyes widening. She puts her hands onto her hips, watching Emma chewing the banana. The food anchors her to earth again. "You cannot cut me out. I won't let you. So, you need to tell how to help." *There is nothing you can do. Nothing I can do.* "Emma?"

"I've been a little lonely in the apartment," Emma sighs, wrapping one arm around herself. Darcy saw her. Really saw her. Understood her. His smell clings to her skin. She desperately runs through every conversation because she does not want to forget his voce. While Avery got ready to leave, she sat on the floor in her empty apartment and it hit her. This is life. For people to come and go. It felt nice to have them in that space. Dancing after the moon reaches its peak. Listening to old records and laughing about them. Going through her book collection to find the best things to read. Playing cards with the agents and Avery. When was the last time before this week that laughter filled her entire apartment? And it will never happen again. Worse yet, it cannot. "It was nice to have someone in the apartment with me. Avery was having fun. She needed to get some space for a little bit… and I needed someone to watch old movies with me. I didn't plan to kidnap her or anything, we just lost track of time—I can't really handle a lecture right now Moe."

"*Liefje*," her mom whispers warmly, grabbing her arm. She rubs the skin hard enough to conduct heat. It pulls Emma back to nestling beside Darcy. "You know you are welcome home."

"I know." Home is where the heart is and it is not this place. The thought registers and brings with it an elbow to the gut. Her heart is with the agents, wherever they are.... "I am just tired. I should go back before the fog comes."

"You are my little girl. As much as Avery or the twins." Moe's eyebrows knit together as she touches Emma's frizzy hair. Brushing a strand behind her ear, she strokes a thumb to catch a tear she didn't notice dropping. "You know you can talk to me about anything, right? Hell hath no fury like a mother protecting her children."

"I know," she promises, desperately flailing as Moe's eyes see through her. More tears are coming and she cannot stop them. Not with the burn gathering at the back of her throat. Or the ache spreading its hand across her jaw. "There is no slaying to be done... thanks Mom."

Words dance on the end of her mother's tongue. She sees it in the way her jaw flexes. Ultimately, she drops her hand with a quiet harrumph. Emma throws the banana peel into the compost and heads towards the door at top speeds. She makes it to the door before Avery intercepts her. Her arms wind tightly around her older sister's waist, forcing her to stay as everything screams at her to flee. "Aren't you going to say hi to Moses before you go?"

"No, I need to beat the storm home," Emma smiles, pressing a kiss to her head. It is dangerous enough as is and if she lets herself cry, she is not going to stop. Exhaustion and heartbreak are interchangeable only to those who cannot see the difference. One look and Moses will crack her open. "Thank you for staying with me."

"Thank you for the best sleepover ever!" Avery responds, grinning. She rocks from side to side with Emma. "Send my tag to Bingley so he can play with me."

Agreeing wordlessly, she slides towards the door. It opens easily with her soft force. The rain has weakened its attack. Wind swells slightly and with it a wave of moisture hits her. A voice carries on the wind, telling her about the storms he witnessed sailors trudge through. Emma pauses, resolve settling in as she twists on her heel. "What did he say to you?" Avery pauses halfway through closing the door, expression like a deer caught in the headlights. "Darcy—before he left."

Saying his name makes it real, but with every passing moment, she is less convinced of reality. Yet she can close her eyes and feel his arms around her again. Hear Frank Sinatra's soothing voice filling her apartment. Remember the exact feeling of the first time the butterflies burst into her stomach.

"He told me to take care of you."

Her heart falls into her stomach as she nods. Of course, he would. Closing her eyes, she forces a smile onto her face and waves to Avery. "Bye *schatje*."

"Bye."

Emma's door *creaks*. The sound echoes in her small empty apartment. She steps through the door and closes it with the back of her foot, staring at the bags on her wrist. Stepping on the back of her own heel, she slides her foot out of one boot and does the same for the other. The mud and rain soak into her socks but the feeling keeps her anchored. Her mail from last Friday sits exactly where she opened it Sunday night.

Her eyebrows draw together as she walks into the kitchen. The fridge has exactly the same things it did last Sunday. Well not anymore with the pho leftovers she slides into it. Rubbing a hand over her face, she leans against the counters and then looks at the cabinet over the fridge.

The chair squeals against her kitchen tiles as she drags it over the fridge. She grabs her phone from inside, blindly patting the top shelf. Where did Darcy leave her battery and SIM?

When she presses the power button to check, it comes to life. Immediately messages ring from her phone, but the sound is overwhelming. Emma tosses the phone onto her table, hands on her hips as the device continues buzzing. The envelope of money is no longer atop the fridge. She leaves the kitchen and walks quickly to the glass jar she keeps hidden underneath her bed. The letters **Travel Fund** have been worn off over the last ten years as she's stashed pocket change.

There is more than enough money to go somewhere but she cannot decide where. On nights she wants to avoid school and nothing else distracts her, she surfs the web. Looking at cruises. Tours of her favourite book locations. Carter doesn't like to travel and Moses works too much, leaving her on her own to travel… where's the fun in that?

Sure enough, the extra money is sandwiched between her other bills. Or is it? She stopped counting the money a year and a half ago when she realized the all-expenses paid trip to Florida with her family for an amusement park circuit wouldn't be happening anytime soon. Not with Cody… Cody!

She hasn't thought about him in a while.

Dropping backwards, she wraps her arms around her knees and takes a deep breath. It feels wrong. Her entire apartment is perfectly back to normal but it no longer her home either. Everything is too perfectly in place. The half-open textbook. Her laptop opened to the same tab. She thinks; It *has* been a week.

"I am not losing it," she tells herself, returning to the kitchen. Her trip took double the time because she lost herself in the distraction. Riding meant she did not need to think about her empty apartment. It stopped her from considering whether this could be a hallucination. Avery saw them too. She did. The thought gave her enough comfort to force some food down.

Her steps are too loud. The fridge cries as she opens the door, looking for something to distract her. She would turn on music if she could bear to look at her phone.

Reaching for a yogurt container, she pauses. There goes the perfect cover. Emma laughs, hard enough to tear up as she grabs what should be cheap fake milk. The fridge has the same products, but they are different brands. Higher quality. Nothing expired like the milk was.

"Darcy." She slides down the wall beside her fridge, ripping open the yogurt package. She read *Pride and Prejudice* again. It is possible she lost herself in it. Imagined a man fitting Darcy's profile and let everything else fall in. In her mind, Rosalind would be Caroline Bingley though.

This is extra protein yogurt.

She shakes her head, getting up to grab a spoon and her silent phone. Light floods from the dark street into her room. As she makes her way to the windows, she shuts off the lights, grateful for the darkness. The red and orange lights no longer feels promising. It displays the danger of the clinic. What is hiding in the building? Are they there? Could she still find them? Is she going to wake up and realize it's been a couple hours? Go back to her life like nothing happened.

That's what she needs to do anyway. She *must*.

Lowering herself with the yogurt over her head, she crosses her legs and sticks the empty spoon into her mouth. How to spend the rest of her evening after such an eventful week? The very thought fills her with unexplainable grief. If the record player were still here, she would play their song all over again.

As she scoops the first spoonful of yogurt into her mouth, grateful for Darcy's taste in fruit, her phone rings again. It flashes for one moment and then the screen is black again.

Finally opening it, she goes immediately to Carter's text string. Dozens of texts create a long blurb of blue. His last one is the one she pays attention to. **Are you okay MaMa? Miss me xoxo?**

He knows how much she does not like the nickname. It is the only one she tells people not to call her. After so many ignored texts, he must be getting scared. **I will explain everything tomorrow. I'm okay.**

She puts the phone back down. Hundreds of other texts fill her phone. Social media notifications. Emails from the clinic with shift offers. Even the thought of responding makes her consider ripping out the battery and SIM card again.

Opening her phone, she navigates to the music app. '*You make me feel so young*' is the first one to come from her search.

The soft music fills her room as she puts the phone onto

the ground. Closing her eyes, she rocks with the beat and imagines herself dancing again in Darcy's arms.

CHAPTER 25: DR. MAMA

Walking into work drops Emma back into cold reality. She unlocks the secondary doors and then the bars afterwards as a cold gust of wind attacks the back of her bare calves. Pushing the chain link aside, she slips her keys into her purse and starts on the other side. The lights are motion sensitive and burst to life as she steps into the warm, dry clinic.

She adjusts the rows of medicine as she passes. Taking out her phone, she starts building a list of what needs to be replaced. By the time she reaches the wrap-around counter, the list appears to be never-ending. Carter stopped texting her last night but he never messages her in the morning anyway. He will show up late as he does with coffee in hand, or sneaky energy drinks, and she'll burst into tears.

Emma opens the gate into the hub, locking it behind her. He rarely goes through it anyway. Carter gets excited at seeing her and his high energy leads him to jump over the gate most mornings. She starts working on the bottles, lining them up for the prescription fulfillments of the morning.

The backstock is dwindling. Someone forgot to order new thermometers. Mina, their other co-worker, left the computer open on her ID with a hundred tabs open. All the little things add to the pit in her stomach.

Emma takes a seat at the desk, staring at her user ID login blankly. Is it too late to call in? She knows the answer but entertains the idea for a moment too long. When she hears the doors open, her heart skips a beat.

"MaMa?!"

"Back here Dr. Friesen," Emma calls, pushing off the desk so the office chair wheels back. He looks the same. There is an odd comfort in that. All hyped up on caffeine as he leaps over the counter and throws his leather satchel onto the ground underneath the desk. Papers and pens spill out, all over the floor. She cannot be bothered. "You will need to stop that when I get my degree."

"Dr. MaMa has a good ring to it," Carter argues, extending a Chai tea to her. She accepts it gratefully, sipping gently. It burns her tongue and hands, but the reminder of being human is much needed after the last week. He bounces in place, tapping a finger impatiently on his travel mug when the silence continues. "Do I have to ask what's up? You went radio silent."

"It should wait until break. We have a lot to do." Emma murmurs, playing with her earring. He watches her do so with his eyebrows knit. Leaning against cabinets, he crosses his arms, unwavering in his intensity. "We have to do our jobs, Car."

"I can multitask," he sings, putting his coffee down. He slides out of the room, searching for a pair of gloves. "We work and talk at the same time all the time. C'mon."

"It's not something I can just come out and say," Emma

whispers back, typing in her ID. Carter mutters something in the other room, disappearing momentarily as she prints off the prescriptions. In the two days since they left, she nearly convinced herself they were never there to begin with. The insanity of the whole situation is too much to handle at the best of times. She fell asleep against her window listening to Sinatra. For six hours the next day, she stared at the street, trying to conjure them like she did before. "You are the only one who might believe me."

Carter's golden head pops into the doorway, one eyebrow cocked into his hairline. "Tell me."

She glances at the clock and then at the bucket of pills in his hands. Moving to his side, she collects a couple bottles, filling the prescriptions under his careful watch. "I saw a shooting down my street—"

"The one from the museum?! They cannot ID any of the bodies or the shooters but I saw someone say—" He stops himself when he notices her silence. Nodding his head apologetically, Carter grabs the next bottle and metaphorically zips his lips. "Please continue."

"And I thought I made eye contact with the shooter," Emma whispers, lowering her voice until nothing and no one else can hear her. Dr. Pepper will be coming in soon, ready to interrogate her about her absence. He is more a worried uncle than a boss, but he will want to know why her name won't appear on payroll for a week. She got nine different emails from him when she finally checked her phone yesterday morning. "But that should be impossible... right? You know how far apart the museum is from my apartment."

"Yeah, that's a couple hundred feet. Around half a kilometer or more, but I've heard stranger things."

"We made eye contact. Before I could call the cops—like I pressed nine and one—he and a group of militants walked into my apartment. They had automatic weapons and their faces were covered with these motorcycle-like helmets. I saw the blood on their hands...." Emma states, shaking her head. She wouldn't even believe herself if Avery had not been there to experience the whole thing as well. God forbid she tells her mother and Moe calls the cops. "I know it sounds crazy—"

"Did they hurt you?"

Her hands drop to her sides as she glances at him. Carter stops counting the pills when he notices. A weight lifts off her chest as she grabs him. His hug feels nothing like Darcy's, but it is warm and comfortable. Reassuring. Even as he pets her head like a cat. "You believe me?"

"You are the most honest person I have ever met Emma. Every word out of your mouth is sincere. You don't pull pranks because they are 'lies'... why wouldn't I believe you?" He questions, snorting as they part. "I believe in aliens. You think I don't know a thing or two about secret militant agencies? I have a whole binder about them—"

"That's the thing though. They started out by asking me

all these weird questions about my life and my parent's life. I had to give my phone to their leader and make him see I didn't call the police. I watched them haul in all these cases and bins and set up cameras to watch the acupuncturist clinic." Emma whispers, watching him nod considerately. No recognition flashes in his eyes. Not yet. She chews on her lip slowly and peeks over her shoulder. They need to open soon. "Everything was going okay for the first few days—"

"Days!?"

"They were with me for a week, Car," she answers, running a hand over her braid. She needs to shower. When she stepped foot into her bathroom with that mission in mind, one look at the tub was enough to unravel. Emma spent half an hour searching for bullet holes. By the time she gave up, her hair was a bigger mess than before but she didn't care enough to fix it.

She struggled to wake up for work. The temptation to snooze her alarm for the first time in years hit her more than once. Darcy returns in her dreams. One dream showed them traveling the sea on a pirate ship. She woke up, startled to find herself on land, in bed. The disappointment pained her. "A *week*. When they left, everything went back to how it was before they arrived. Food products, my keys, even my toilet paper was down to one roll again! Like it never happened."

"So, what happened? You ran out of toilet paper?" He demands, turning towards her fully. Neither of them are working on the pills while they look at one another. As she predicted, but Carter makes her sane again. "And they didn't react well?"

"No, you sent a text. I don't even know which one because I didn't get my phone back until they left, but they were worried about something you said," Emma confesses, desperately hoping he will have a better idea. Carter's paws his face, blowing out a breath as he looks at the ceiling. She can practically see his gears turning. Of the dozen texts he sent, one struck Agent Rosalind. "I promised them you were not a threat, just a conspiracy theorist, but one of them told me I should give you more credit. I think you knew something about them—"

"It must be the dictators."

"The what?"

Carter snaps his fingers, rushing away from her. She maneuvers around the shelves of meds and leans against one to watch him rifle through the stationary strewn underneath the desk. When he finds what he wants, he pulls a binder out of a pile of paper. Not a digital collection, but an actual, old timey binder. Complete with three metal rings. Identical to the one filled with Darcy's maps.

"Come, come."

"Carter, what are you doing?"

"We had another breakthrough on a thread I've been following recently. Remember I told you people were seeing old dictators again?

"When I joked about that man who looked like Hitler?"

"Yes!" Carter exclaims, patting the office chair next to him. She cautiously settles down at his side with the tea firmly clutched in her hands. He flips through the pages like a madman, breathing heavy. One rips but he continues, undeterred, as she leans closer. Emma jumps when he claps loudly, looking at the street, expecting to see someone with a gun there. "See."

He turns the binder towards her, revealing a row of blurry photos. Every picture takes place at night. Admittedly, some of the pictures share a likeness to their tyrannical counterparts. Especially the one of Joseph Stalin. Moe would find the entire thing ridiculously amusing. She enjoyed learning about dictators, considering what her family and country faced during the second World War.

"Car, they do share a resemblance but they can't actually be—"

"But people can break into your house?"

"Technically, they didn't 'break' in. They managed unlock my door without making a sound or breaking it...."

He stares at her, the weight of his unblinking stare dragging on her. She trails off and runs her tongue over her lips. Forcing herself to take a moment to think, she leans back to drink her tea. "You tell me assailants break in; I say okay."

"Because it happened to me. I lived it. It's plausible that a government organization could have decided my apartment was the perfect place for a stakeout," Emma counters, although even saying it sounds ridiculous. She taps her nails on the paper cup. The sound dulls the heat gathering on the tips of her ears. "What are you suggesting? Reincarnation? There is no proof of that."

"No, not reincarnation. Time travel."

Time travel.

Her jaw drops. Normally, she can control herself but she almost can't believe he is being serious. When Carter does not laugh or crack a playful smile, she puts her drink down. "Time travel? There is no—"

"Don't say 'proof'. Just because you do not do research about it, does not mean it does not exist."

"If that technology exists, the owner would be a billionaire. Every news article would cover it." Emma whispers, crossing her legs. She shakes her head, surprised to find herself considering it. When he shares his conspiracies, she happily listens but rarely takes part. A little voice in her head seeds doubt. One moment bullets tore her apartment into pieces. The next her sisters book balanced perfectly on her desk, surrounded by polished books and unbroken glass. "Time travel? Really?"

"Maybe the technology doesn't technically exist *yet*. What if twenty one hundred is happening right now? We might be the past." Her head hurts. "It is rumoured that there is this elite, *military-like* group from the future who is wrangling these dictators and bringing them back to the past where they belong. Maybe they are here because the last dictatorship ended recently and they bring back the civil war." Carter states, throwing his arms up. He pushes the binder into her lap, jerking his chin towards it. "I don't know much; I personally like aliens a bit more."

To appease him, she grabs the binder. The photos do not get better in quality. One after another they show a barely legible tyrant. Some she recognizes from Social AP and her mother. Many she cannot place. Carter watches expectantly the whole time. As if she is suddenly going to believe.

"You are very organized Car. These do look like them, but time travel? Where are the articles? Where are the stocks? The butterfly effects of even the dictator's presence should be noticeable. We still know who they are… you do not think we landed on the moon—"

"I do not think the *first* moon landing was real," he corrects, lifting a finger. "I believe others have landed there. You would be shocked by what the rich and powerful do under our noses. They run this world. If the powers that be do not want the little man to know about time traveler's, the sheep will 'baa' and go about their grazing."

"Is this about the Illuminati again?"

"Explain to me who those people were and why they were in your apartment."

"They were surveilling the clinic—"

"Why?"

"I do not know. The leader refused to tell me because he did not want to endanger me. We were already shot at."

Carter's face blanks as he leans forward. "Shot at?"

"There was an incident," she confesses, brushing a frizzy strand behind her ear. He laughs to himself, taking a drink from his coffee. Or energy drink. It is perfectly hidden in his little cup, leaving her with no idea. "I appreciate your enthusiasm—"

He notices the oddness of her silence mid-sip. Emma pauses on the page, leaning forward with her eyes narrowed.

It can't be.

"What?"

Except it is.

"Can you tell me what that is?"

Carter leans over her hand, removing the picture. They inspect it together underneath the light of his phone. What she sees takes her breath away. "That's the second gasp. What's up?"

Emma fishes out her phone, typing in her passcode. She moves to her pictures, half-expecting not to find it. Fortunately, the agents were so bad with technology, they did not think to check her photos. If they did check her camera roll, they missed the dark photo she took, as she behind her covers.

She slips her phone beside the picture, rubbing the side of her head.

What if Darcy saw it and left it there? What if he wanted her and Carter to find it? Hope swells, fighting for room in her heart with cold panic.

"They're a perfect match," Carter remarks breathlessly, holding up her phone and the picture. The circle-shaped symbol from the agent's equipment. Carter's printout leaves a grainy image with no respect to the actual appearance of the landscape or the people around it, but the symbol stares her down. "This picture was taken on September first, nineteen thirty-nine. The first day of World War Two."

"Agencies can last a hundred years. They started the CIA around that time too."

His eyebrows drop, oddly like Darcy's as he reaches into a folder behind the clear slip of pictures. Within moments, hundreds of poorly printed photos are spread out on the white desk. Dr. Pepper, a lover of organization and cleanliness, is going to be furious—for multiple reasons.

"Do you recognize any of these people?"

"Carter—"

"A group of strangers breaks into your apartment after you witness them murder people who do not exist. They are not in any of systems—you know C.O.N.N.E.C.T. records every birth from around the world. There is no such thing as unidentifiable anymore Em and yet dozens of unrecorded humanoid creatures end up dead.

"They watch an *acupuncture clinic* across from you for a week before disappearing into thin air. Somehow, they manage to make your apartment look perfectly like it did before... as if they can manipulate time around you while keeping you in the current day." Carter describes, punctuating every word with a press of his finger into the desk. "And you are not the least bit curious? You won't even take a look at these pictures? You *coincidentally* happened to take a picture on your phone of the exact symbol found on weapons from World War Two... over a hundred years after the event. Who are these people? Why were they in your apartment?"

"Okay, I will look... but you need to fill prescriptions."

"Absolutely not—don't give me that look. If I try to fill prescriptions right now, someone is going to overdose and die," he scoffs, his legs bouncing. She has never seen him so excited. For a moment she worries he may have moved to something more exhilarating than energy drinks. "Come on, we haven't got all day. When Dr. Pepper gets here, he's going to scalp me and make you clean up the mess."

She laughs but gives in at his eager look. Most of the pictures show half-shots of the symbol. They are not all from the same time though. She can tell as the quality increases that they must have been on phones or high-resolution cameras. It could just be a branch of the government. Most of the pictures appear on the side of luggage. One is graffitied onto an overpass.

Carter's voice is the one that invades her head. Maybe the government figured out time travel and they don't want to share it. What if they have something like the CIA but handling different timelines? She'll do anything to legitimize the agents. Make them the heroes of this story.

Dismissing the thoughts from her head, she begins to laugh. How silly is this? A week ago, she would have waved off Carter and kept him on the job. Now she is enabling his obsession to continue. Emma's laugh dies in her throat. The next picture she pulls out drains her of all amusement and argument.

"You recognize something."

"That's not possible."

She holds the photo in shaking hands as she brings it further towards the light. No way. "It's not possible. This can't be possible."

"What?" Carter questions, leaning forward. "The people? Oh, catch this, I have a picture of that one in a newspaper."

He points to Bingley on the photo and reaches into the folder again. The little newspaper clipping reveals someone like Bingley in the back of a photo. It would not be so concerning if the newspaper were not dated in the 1900s with Joseph Stalin's face pictured front and center. The dictator's head partially covers him. Emma wishes she could convince herself otherwise, but Agent Eyre walks at his side, blush and all. Another picture, later on, shows a hint of ink on the back of his neck.

The paw mark.

"You... look like you've seen a ghost," he remarks, poking a finger into her forehead. She puts both the picture and newspaper clipping down, hands shaking. "Whoa, whoa, whoa, whoa. Take a deep breath. I know how to do CPR but I do not want to go to second base. We don't have that kind of friendship and I'd prefer to keep it that way."

"They were the agents in my apartment. Two of them anyway...." Emma whispers, shaking her head. "It's not possible. They must be distant relatives."

"You're saying this group of people—" he points to the agents standing around a crate with the same symbol on it. Now that she's seen his face, he appears in other pictures. Maybe she forces him to appear. Every curly head belongs to Bingley. Wild mane, Agent Eyre. Black braids, Agent Rosalind. Where is her tall, dark, and handsome man? "Were in your apartment this week?"

"Familial genetics must be strong."

"Do you know what that symbol means Emma?"

She is afraid to look at him. Afraid to ask. Afraid of the answer. Afraid of the desire for this to be real, not a dream. "No."

"It means time. The circle and dots are supposed to represent timelines and concurrent events. They use it at seminars to talk about time travel... they have since the early two thousands," Carter describes, eyes bulging. "You met time travelers."

"That's not possible—"

"I do not pay you to sit around, looking at family photos," Dr. Pepper announces, stepping into the clinic with an air of irritation. He straightens out his lab coat, making a direct line for Emma. Carter gathers the pictures together, yanking the paper out of Emma's hand. A thin cut wells up with blood and burns enough to elicit a *hiss*. "Emma darling, where have you been? This thing falls apart when firecracker doesn't have his extinguisher."

He pauses in his greeting, noticing the paleness of her face. "What did you say to her?"

Carter stuffs his satchel and sits up dutifully. "I didn't say anything."

"I'll believe that when pigs fly," Dr. Pepper scoffs, glaring at the counter in the back with open pills spread over it. His eyebrow raises incrementally as he drags his eyes all the way to Carter. The expression on his face alone saves Emma from implosion. "I see you didn't fill the prescriptions yet."

"We were taking a quick coffee break, discussing the importance of proper CARE," Carter lies, glancing down at Emma. She jumps to her feet, scurrying to the back. "And now we will continue our informational discussion while doing our jobs."

Emma drops a pill bottle, hands shaking as her brain processes the information. Processes seeing Bingley in *three* different centuries. Plastic skin stretched tight over his face without a sign of age. Carter snickers at Dr. Pepper's lecture, closing the door behind them with his mouth opening.

"I don't want to talk about it."

Carter's mouth snaps closed as he nods his head. Except it immediately opens up again as he grabs her hand. "Emma, you had time travelers in your house!"

CHAPTER 26: THE IMPALER

"Hey Emma!" Trevor greets, grinning widely when he catches Emma. She jumps at his hand on her arm, removing her earbuds at his quiet apology. All the tension of the day drains out when Chewy barks at her excitedly. "What's up? I texted you to see if you could watch Chewy on Friday and Saturday but you didn't get back to me."

"I can," Emma agrees, gratefully holding Chewy against her. She rests her head on top of his, horrified when the tears come back. "How were the mountains?"

"Rocky," he jokes, laughing as he crosses his ankles. Her furry buddy plops onto her lap, exposing his belly at the same time as he kicks over her bag. "How was your spring break?"

"Mostly the same. It's not a break for my program." Trevor frowns at the watery smile on her face, playing with the watch on his wrist. It is the time of night when he takes Chewy on their last walk of the day. Something they both look like they need. Chewy wiggles around her, stilling when he sniffs something in her bag. Barking loudly, he nudges his wet nose into her face. "I probably smell like the train. I decided to visit the pier."

Nodding, her neighbour kneels amidst the clutter, gathering it back into her bag. Emma slowly gets up, wincing from the tightness of her muscles. Her sleep has been longer than ever but it's painful. It's like her body forgot how to sleep without others in the room. Agent Darcy's presence soothed her in ways she still cannot explain. Or maybe it is because she is always chasing him in her dreams. Trying to convince him to stay. "I do not want this to come off as rude, Emma, but I work with at-risk people every day and you're looking a little…."

"Haggard?"

"In the nicest way."

"Last week was long," she confesses, running her hand over her face. Leaning against her door, she fishes for her keys with tired eyes. "I am okay. I'm missing out on my beauty sleep."

"I'm a door away. Seriously, I barely sleep anyway. If you need something, just knock… you know where the spare key is if you really need a place—"

"Thanks Trevor, I appreciate it," she responds, smiling kindly as she opens her door. The paramedic smiles, whistling as he walks down the hall. Chewy's tail wags with fervour as he realizes their walk is continuing.

Her apartment is dark when she enters. Pushing the lights on, she throws her keys onto the little table by the entryway and removes her shoes. After such a long day, it is labourious to remove her moist coat. Throwing it onto the hooks, she twists her hair into a bun and walks into the kitchen.

A ring breaks the silence. It scares her, *again*. She never used to be jumpy. Then again, a week ago she never questioned whether time travel exists outside of fiction. Now she genuinely questions every thought. How did she decide time travel only belongs in movies? What about it is unreasonable? The implications of choosing to believe it are monumental. If someone can travel through time freely... they hold the power to change the very fabric of reality.

We need to talk about what happened at work this morning. You can't ignore it.

While she is reading Carter's message, another one comes. **If those people really were in your house, it means time travel exists Ma!!!!**

Brushing a hand over her hair, she puts her phone on her kitchen table and leans against it. Another ring sounds out but she cannot respond. Carter has texted her twenty times since she left her shift. She thought going to the pier would offer some discernment, but it confused her more. A dad was teaching his kid to skip rocks. She lost herself in the ripples.

If time travel exists, everything she knows might not *real*. How does fact and truth exist in a world where nothing is permanent?

Time travel cannot be real. Movies and books contain that kind of thing. Not real life.

The Bible never mentioned it. Suddenly accepting one thing to be true ruins everything else. One loose thread and everything unravels. *God, I do not know how to reconcile this with what you say you are. You are the only one outside of time. The only omnipresent one... where does that leave me?*

Now she questions everything.

Every interaction.

Agent Rosalind's joke about being eons old. Labelling technology as outside of their 'time'. Their fixation on the clock. Darcy's concern about age and time. Cracking jokes about being 'too' old. Not one agent navigated Emma's phone with the usual ease of her generation. She bought it five years ago, used. A normal twenty-seven-year-old would know the different apps and their uses. They would have grown up in the golden age of media and technology.

Darcy mentioned meeting George Orwell and buying his book first. He knows all the classics. Talked about studying *1984* in preparation for work and life. Learning from it to see how to help people... George Orwell died January 21st, 1950. Over a hundred years ago.

The privateer. Cartography. Slave trade. Dictators and totalitarianism. All markers of a world that no longer exists... or does it? Is anything as it seems? The Bible warned about the world being ruled by one leader. One person chosen to rule over all. The nations get closer and closer to it every day. What if they are grooming someone to rule with an iron fist?

Stepping away from the table, she drags a hand down her face. Maybe Trevor is right. Moe told her sometimes the most relaxed people are the ones with the highest stress levels. They keep pushing away their feelings and worries before they all bubble over. Suddenly they have a psychotic break and their brains inherently change until they cannot go back to who they were.

What if she is having a break?

Avery may have never been at her apartment. The agents never came. After trying to catch up on assignments, her brain collapsed. Work, school, life became too much and she just cracked. It is a *reasonable* explanation... more than literal time travel and power conspiracies. She could accept them being a government agency using her apartment for official business. Exposing a drug ring. Or human trafficking. Fraud. Money Laundering.

Please let it be a Ponzi scheme.

Any option is more feasible than them being time travelers who used her apartment to track down ancient *dictators*. Not even reincarnated dictators, but men and women being taken out of their time periods and brought to this one. Why here? Why now? Why her? It doesn't make sense. It's more like she either fell asleep watching a movie with a fever... or someone is playing a gigantic joke on her.

Cody teased her about being gullible as kids. He doesn't have the cruelty to do this, but someone else might.

She drops her hands, groaning when her knuckles collide with the countertops harder than she thought. Holding them, she turns around, her head snapping back. Walking closer to the garbage, she leans in. The smell is rancid... like burned eggs.

Her eyes widen as she rifles through her garbage from the last few days. Underneath it all, empty tubs of ice cream... and burned eggs. The eggs she tried to make for the agents.

It should not surprise her so much, but she crouches down by the garbage and stares down into it. She takes a drag, coughing at the acrid smell as it burns her nostril hairs.

I am not crazy.

The thought liberates her enough to stand up and run away from the garbage. Sliding on her jacket, she jumps into her rain boots and leaves her apartment behind, lights on and all. Emma pauses halfway in the hall, running back to lock her doors. Time traveling henchmen know where her apartment is. The last thing she needs is for them to break in and wreak havoc.

Her feet slip out from underneath her as she sprints down the stairs, but she grabs the banister and reorientates herself. Now is not the time for an accident. All the months of using these stairs gives her the agility to take two steps at a time.

Exploding onto the street, she pulls up her hood and reaches for her phone. It's not there.

Instead of heading back, she continues down the street, turning her face away from the drizzle of rain. Lights from the street reflect off the puddles on the sidewalk. She walks through them without regard, making her way towards the museum.

It is a bad idea, but the police are gone and with them the tape sectioning the street off. People promenade freely inside on the first floor. She leans against the lamp post just like last week, watching the dark upper level and wondering about its potential.

Had this started everything? Emma's fascination with the museum's upper level began months ago but she never stopped to observe it until the days leading up to the agents. It cannot be a coincidence.

Fate and time travel may not mix, but there *must* be a plan. One truth to uphold everything else. God has a plan and it led her here.

She saw the man who looked like Hitler here.

It feels like an eternity ago but it was less than two weeks.

Pushing her hands into her pockets, she rests her head against the power pole and takes a deep breath. It smells of rain and dirt, clearing out her mind and poor nose. The night smells like revival.

This museum holds nothing for her. If the police could not find anything, she certainly can't. Arguably she knows what she is looking for but the agents are careful. Darcy would not let them tag the museum, and if they left their logo behind, it would not be easy to find. Does she really know enough to find them though?

No tug from the Lord convinces her otherwise. Without a gut feeling, she leaves the glass building behind and makes her way down the street. She waits at the light, expecting it to change... but instead Emma's gut pulls her the other direction.

Glancing at the bright light from the acupuncture clinic, she loses track of her thoughts. People shoulder past her to make the crossing as the lights change. She feels it dancing over her face, beckoning her back to the safety of her side of the road. Except the orange and yellow from the clinic sing to her. The sign flickers slightly, wagging a finger.

She's not impulsive. At least not on her own. When others want to start an adventure, she goes with it, but recklessness has a lot of consequences. Sometimes grievous ones which put you into jail like in Carter's case.

Except she cannot think of a consequence right now.

Ducking her head, she walks away from the crossing, against the crowd as they head towards the train and home and away from the clinics and stores. She reaches the street in front of the clinic and stops by a bench.

Taking a slow seat on it, she crosses one leg over the other and stares up at the windows. Shadows move across the light. A group of people walk out of the clinic laughing. Emma grabs a wet newspaper, hoping it disguises her from anyone dangerous. *Lord make them forget my face.* She left her phone in her apartment, along with any book or object she could use to look like she belongs—or call for help if the need arises.

When she peers down the street, her breath hitches. Bingley? Alone? Jumping to her feet, she begins forward, colliding with someone walking out of the clinic. "Sorry—"

The person pauses to right themselves and as they do, her blood goes cold. She never considered how she should feel, looking into the face of Joseph Stalin. Now he stands right in front of her, brushing his long wool jacket as if she ran into him as a personal insult.

Someone rushes quickly from the clinic, giving her a dirty look, before they grab Stalin and march into the night. She begins to follow them… Bingley means the other agents are close by. Emma cannot miss this opportunity. Pausing, she stares at the sidewalk, hoping to see Darcy too. The dictator and his assistant continue down the street, completely unperturbed.

Another person walks out. Distantly familiar. He keeps his eyes down as his handler speaks lowly. Emma steps out of their way and then she is twisting on her heel.

Instead of going to the crosswalk as the law dictates, she sprints across the street. A car honks at her but she is already at the front steps of the apartment. Waving her key fob over the sensor, she steps inside and rushes into the elevator. Her boots are wet and her steps frenzied. The two are not a good mix.

"Hi Emma," one of her neighbours greets with her eyebrows drawn together. She glances at her son, and then scans Emma over. "You look wet."

"I am," Emma responds, hurried as she tries to muster a smile. The woman's head physically moves back in surprise.

She gets out when the doors open to her floor, ushering her son out. Emma taps her foot against the carpeted floor, watching the numbers changing.

Finally, it opens to her level and she begins the fight with her keys before she fully steps out. They nearly slip through her hands from the water on them. Drying her hand off on her pants, protected by her jacket, she slides the key into place and unlocks her door. Another person calls out to her but she cannot be distracted. Not right now.

Stepping inside, she shuts it and nearly forgets to twist the lock. Her boots fly out. The rain jacket joins them on the ground. Rushing towards her living room, she launches herself across the bed. The lights from outside taunt her vision as she searches for her laptop. Raindrops gather on the glass walls, distorting the shine from outside. Normally, she stops to admire the different colours, but her mind is completely focused on her task.

Vlad the Impaler.

The search quickly goes through, bringing picture after picture. Leaning back in her chair, she pushes her hair off her face and then stands. Just to be sure, she searches up Stalin and sees his face exactly as it was on the street a couple minutes earlier.

If it weren't for her extensive social studies education and her Mother's slight obsession, she would not have recognized the Impaler. She has seen Hitler twice. Not just a likeness.

Someone identical to him. Three dictators, all hundreds of years old, walking the streets of Chinatown.

Crazy or not, she knows what she saw.

Her socks glide over the smooth floors as she sprints to the kitchen. Dialing Carter's number, she pulls at her earring and looks at the burned eggs in her garbage. "You finally answer—"

"You need to come over," Emma declares, shaking her head. "Bring everything you have on them. I just saw Joseph Stalin and Vlad the Impaler outside of my apartment and it looks like they're getting ready to jump ship."

CHAPTER 27: TO MY LIZZY

Carter listens to every word as Emma recalls the events of the last week and a half. He nods his head, listening intently, offering insight where he can.

"I know it sounds crazy, but I saw them," Emma insists, shaking her head as she looks at the papers splayed over her kitchen table. Carter chews his ramen and scoffs.

"If you're crazy, I'm crazy."

"We could both be crazy," Emma proposes, taking a seat at his side. She pulls one knee up to her chest as he shrugs. This entire thing *is* crazy. "There is nothing concrete here."

"Not yet, I was continuing my research and asking around when you called," Carter states, reaching into his bag. He throws a baton out of the bag and pouch of zip ties, missing the expression of horror on Emma's face. Other objects follow as he unearths a blue duotang. "I did find one last thing that may be helpful."

"It's another picture."

"A clear picture of the people you recognized. I got a friend to run it through their editing software and found a high-resolution printer." Carter answers, crossing one leg over the other. He leans back as Emma slides it over the table onto her side. The picture is clearer than day. Her memories lack the clarity of a picture. Forgetting small details like the mole on the left side of Eyre's face or the prominence of Darcy's nose.

Bingley is speaking into a phone Emma knows isn't scheduled to release for ten months. It is supposed to have the first holographic display. "You still think they're the same people? If you do, that means we have photographic proof of them being in four different centuries."

"It is them," she confirms, running her finger down Darcy's arm. They stand in a circle, guns in hand, Rosalind looking at something off camera. Whoever took the photo must have been shaking because the original photo was blurry and too zoomed-in. "But this could have been taken yesterday—"

"This couldn't have," Carter argues, producing the newspaper clipping of Bingley and Rosalind. The closer she looks, the more convinced she is. Unlike the photo, it is dated. 1937. A crowd of people and in it, two of the agents. "Is the man on that phone the same one in this newspaper?"

"He goes by Agent Bingley," Emma laughs, shaking her head. Bingley's appearance is unchanged, but there is something about the way he holds himself. The lack of joy on his face. Avery's spreads light wherever she goes but this is a huge transformation. His frown weighs on her soul, forcing her to look away. She points at Darcy on the clear photo. "He is their team leader. He loves the classics. All the agents' names come from his favourite books—"

"Do you have Stockholm Syndrome?"

She waves away his words, holding the clear photo. It's

them. Supposedly the day World War 2 started. Eyre is there, standing in the background as Darcy pensively stares at the ground. They are wearing the exact same gear. *God, what am I supposed to do?*

"I'm scared Carter," she sighs, dropping her face into her hands. Carter reaches out to pull on her ear and then stands up with their bowls, to toss them into the sink. "What am I supposed to do with this information?"

"What do you want us to do?"

Find them.

"Is the acupuncture clinic a front for these people taking dictators?" Emma asks, glancing at her windows. The curtains are now permanently closed. She is not going to risk being seen by people with guns while figuring out her next move. What if they begin to suspect her? "That can't be safe. Having so many violent, powerful people in the same space."

"I am sure they can handle themselves. You said they have guns. Besides, we both know the future has better technology. They probably have invisible armour on or something."

"But...." She stops herself, watching him take a seat in front of her. Carter leans forward, eyes intensely blue. Neither of them speaks for a moment as Emma grapples.

"Tell me what you want."

"I want to find them," Emma confesses, sitting back. With it out there, her shoulders drop. "I do what is expected of me.

I've lived responsibly. Taking as little risk as possible because I thought that's what God wanted from me—I think He's the one who brought them here. Darcy and I, we-we shared a connection. The agents… I don't want to say they need me but I think they do. I think they need me."

Carter taps his finger on the table, scrutinizing her face. He begins to nod as his eyes drop to the contents of the table. "If I found them, what would you do?"

"Go confront them. Maybe join them? Is that crazy?" Emma whispers, laughing. "Of course, it is—"

"You like taking risks, you're just too careful. You talk yourself out of it. What's the worst that can happen? Stop waiting for permission to have your adventure! A little danger never hurt anybody!" Carter exclaims impassioned, tapping her hand. He stands up, nearly tripping on his chair. Collecting the photos and newspapers, he stuffs them into his satchel. "I am going to ask around and see what I can get. I don't know how long it will take. I want to make sure these people aren't… going to hurt you if you go find them."

"Darcy would never," she assures, zoned out as she looks at her oven. How much does she really know about him? Enough to know the pain of slavery and the effects of racism on his life. His love for literature. The way his Mom raised him to know God and treat everyone with respect. The privateer who treated him like a pet. How his subordinates hang onto his every word and follow his commands without question. He earned their respect. Emma's too. "I am so blind sometimes."

"We all are."

Carter taps her head twice, taking his cup of coffee. "Try to get some sleep tonight... for both of us."

"You need to sleep!" Emma calls back as he disappears down the hallway. "And the worst thing that can happen is pretty bad so please for the love of everything be careful Car."

His silence is only punctuated by the slam of her door. Careful and Carter may share three letters but that is where the intersection ends.

Yet, she trusts him.

She snickers quietly, unfurling herself from the table. Cleaning up after the two of them, she begins the water for dishwashing and searches for a hair tie. When she does not find one, she lowers the water speed and walks over to her living room. Searching the nightstand beside her bed, she finally finds one and ties her hair into a knot.

Her hands still when she notices something out of place for the first time. It is so indistinct she would not have noticed it from any other angle.

Her special edition *Pride and Prejudice* is upside down.

Rounding the end of her bed, she grabs the book, turning it in her palm. Light flashes outside, likely from a bus, scattering light around the room from the corners of the curtains. She settles down beside her lamp, looking for anything amiss.

Nothing. All her annotating notes are still in place, the legend laminated onto the first page. Maybe they forgot?

Unlikely. Tears gather in her eyes as she flips to page three hundred and forty-seven. Her edition pre-dates the version's mass produced following the third film installment. What he said to the police officers of being bewitched does not appear in the original.

Her eyes skim Fitzwilliam Darcy's plea to be put out of his misery. Sure enough, written on one of her pink tabs: **To my Lizzy, you have bewitched me body and soul. My feelings will remain forever unchanged. Forever yours.**

She can almost hear him saying it. Laughing to herself, she presses the book against her chest. The sound of water rips her out of the fairytale and sends her running into the kitchen, but she cries tears of joy as her socks soak in a puddle.

We are going to have our forever.

CHAPTER 28: SUPERTATOR

Carter is late. It would not be concerning... if the clinic had not already opened. Fifteen minutes. His record for latest arrival *was* fifteen minutes. The train broke down. He still managed to walk in nonchalantly with a drink in hand and his satchel slung over his shoulder.

Now, hours after opening, Dr. Pepper covers his shift grumpily and she has no idea where Carter is. The dynamic between her and the polite older man is totally different. He works wordlessly, except when dealing directly with clients. Unlike Carter, he makes no attempt at small talk while filling bottles or typing at the computer. Carter asks people about their families and their plans for the day. When the patients share something, Dr. Pepper only politely nods, and begins to work on the next prescription.

His work is efficient and precise. Emma observes him closely as she monitors the phone and assigns orders from the online portals to patients in the CARE system. Mina taps on her tablet in the back, marking one of the orders as filled, and brings a pre-filled canister to a regular waiting off to the side. Together they rarely speak to one another, but there has yet to be a line of people waiting.

"And make sure to be watching your bowel movements. If they do become irregular, come back in and I will write you a laxative prescription." Dr. Pepper suggests, nodding at the young woman who blushes. She rushes away as he steps back and removes his gloves. Emma offers the hand sanitizer, smiling when he thanks her. "Has anyone heard from the good doctor?"

"I haven't," Mina answers, tripping over the new shipment. She tries to look at him over the boxes but they tower over her. Placing the tablet on top of one, she pulls out a box, and nearly drops it on herself with a loud grunt.

"Mina, what did I say… you are going to get yourself hurt. We are not those kinds of doctors."

Dr. Pepper grabs the box from her, suggesting she cuts the big boxes open to grab the smaller ones. Their conversation quiets as they move further from Emma with arms full of new meds. When they step into the backroom, the world goes quiet. The pharmacy's lights make a faint buzzing noise but for the first time all day, there is nothing to do. She runs a worried hand through her hair and glances at the gold watch on her wrist. It is almost lunch and he is still not here.

They go to the bistro down the street for lunch every shift. He never misses his fish and chips.

With no patients in the clinic, she exits the hub and walks into the security camera's blind spot. Under the guise of checking the shelves for restocking, she slips her phone out of her white coat. It takes a moment for her to be hidden enough to check. No messages from Carter… but a dozen from Moe. She rarely texts Emma, preferring to call if she can.

Who is this Bingley person Avery keeps talking about???

You didn't say there were going to be strangers at your apartment ☹☹☹☹

She said you held hands with a man!?

Do you have a boyfriend?

When did you get a boyfriend? Why haven't we met him?

She said they stayed overnight!? Emma Marie deVries you were raised better than that. What example are you setting for Avery?

You can't avoid me.

It is a Thursday so you are probably working... you will call me the MOMENT you get these texts!

Your Father and I are very disappointed. ESPECIALLY BECAUSE YOU DIDN'T TELL ME! I thought I would be the first to know when you found a man. You told me when a boy first called you pretty.

What happened to that girl? When did the lying and sneaking begin?!

Ik ben boos niet. Gewoon erg teleurgesteld.

Em, this is Dad. Moe wanted me to text you in case you were ignoring her. So here I am.

Dad again, Henny isn't pleased with my last text. I want to say I think this is probably being blown out of proportion. We all know girls like a little drama

sometimes. Avery said he was VERY handsome, so good job honey. Proud of you.

He was supposed to tell you to CALL ME!

Emma pinches the bridge of her nose, unsure how to respond. There is too much happening, with Moe interrogating her, Avery sharing more than she wanted, and Carter missing. She still feels ridiculous after their conversation last night. As if they are actually time travelers. Emma would have kissed Darcy, if he tried, and by her calculation, he could be hundreds of years old.

Time and age do not coincide.

'Dr. Racecar' never responded to the picture she sent either. What if he stepped out of the apartment and the smugglers took him?

She leans against the shelves, staring at her phone. Carter could be dead in a ditch somewhere. While Emma doubts it, his proclivity for getting into bad situations where he ends up getting hurt is mind-boggling. Like ending up on private government property in his search for aliens and being held for 48 hours. They did not let him share anything about what they put him through but the guy looked scared for once.

More scared than the time he ran into a gang and 'luckily' got out with a few minor bruises.

These people are dangerous. Dictators. Guns. Powerful forces two young adults cannot compete with.

As a person who normally lets things roll off her back,

she never learned how to deal with stress. Worry drowns her. All the old dread from Avery's time in the hospital comes back swinging. In a breath, she says a quick prayer. The anti-anxiety meds stare her in the face as she leans back against the shelf. She laughs at the irony, closing her eyes to focus on the annoying noise of the lights above her head. *He is in control. God, you know. Help me to walk in that faith.*

Opening her Mom's texts, she sends a message back. **Not avoiding you! Just working. I'll call and explain everything after work.**

A text immediately shoots back. **Can you explain why my little girl is in love with an old Russian man?**

Crushes rarely make sense Moe.

It is not a crush! She says they are meant for each other.

Emma presses her hand to her forehead, trying to remember the peace from a moment ago. She laughs instead. Not just a little this time, but hysterically. Why would she have noticed Avery's odd behaviour? Blind as a bat. Either too consumed in Darcy's stare or her own brain to notice anything around her. She should have realized her little sister didn't like the guy as a friend. **And she will say that about the next man she meets who smiles at her and laughs at her jokes. I was in love with my Sunday school teacher.**

Perhaps not the best thing to say but it'll distract her.

Emma opens Carter's contact and presses on the dial,

glancing at the hub. Dr. Pepper chops one hand into the other as he explains sequence to Mina. He changes their path back to the other room when Mina corrects him.

The call instantly goes to voicemail. Her blood goes cold but she forces away the worry and takes a deep breath. "Hey, where are you? It's eleven fifty-seven and you're not here. None of us have heard from you. You only turn on your voicemail when you're in a sketchy situation… I hope you're staying safe. As soon as you get this call me, please."

She begins to slide the phone back into her pocket when it buzzes in her hand. Excited, she presses on her messages and sees the text is from Moe. **You were in love with Louis Blanche? He's FRENCH.**

I'm at work Moe, I will call you later.

No call, you are coming over. I need an explanation and you need to be reminded where you came from.

Emma tugs at her earring, exhausted all over again. Carter's disappearance, her lack of sleep, Moe's intensity, *time travel*… renders her momentarily thoughtless. As if her brain cannot function anymore past breathing.

Ok

She slides the phone away, jumping when Dr. Pepper calls her. "Over here, I was checking merchandise."

"What do you think about me dying my hair black?" The older man inquires, brushing his hand over the grey. "My wife says I'd look like I belong in a boy's band, but it's my natural colour."

"Was!"

Emma's heart almost drops and shatters when she hears Carter. He runs into the clinic and easily clears the counter in his jump. Dr. Pepper's expression darkens. Instead of saying anything, he pins him with a glare of disapproval and then returns to the backroom.

"Where's MaMa?" Carter questions, out of breath as he looks at Mina. He throws his satchel onto the chair, tugging at his hair. "I thought you were—she is supposed to be working today."

"She's right there," Mina responds rudely, throwing up her arms. "We're missing a box of Adderall; you didn't take it, did you?"

"Eat me," Carter scoffs, dismissing her with a wave of his hand. Emma doesn't understand their rivalry but for now she's thrilled to hear it. He's safe. Free of injuries from what she can see. Carter throws his hands up when they make eye contact and gestures wildly at the counter. "What are you still doing over there!? Let's go lassie."

Emma smiles gratefully, walking towards the gate. She unlocks it, ignoring his gentle whining and stamping. How many energy drinks did he shotgun? "Were you awake all night?"

Her eyes widen the closer she gets. His long blond hair, normally pulled back for work, is a mess on top of his hair.

Half of it fights the constraints of a rubber band and the other half sticks out in every direction. Red lines surround his blue eyes, giving her a clear indication of why Mina would accuse him of substance abuse. Dark bags gather under them. One of the buttons on his top is missing and every other button is out of sequence. On an abnormally dry day for the city, he wears tall polka dot rainboots.

"Yes and no," Carter answers, cackling. He scratches the back of his hair, messing it up further. Emma reaches up to grab a cheese puff from his hair, eyebrows knitting together when he snatches it from her hand and eats it. "I took two power naps and met up with a couple guys wherein we all blacked out because one of them had this really bad—that's beside the point. I figured it out."

"Figured what out exactly?"

"Everything."

Carter grins maniacally at her as he pulls out a collapsible foam board. At first it is no bigger than a cutting board, but then he starts to unfold it. Mina catches the movement and pauses as she watches him adjust the pictures and threads.

"You let him do this," Mina warns, wagging her finger at Emma. She jumps when Dr. Pepper calls her and scurries back between the shelves.

"I am going to feed her to the Syndicate."

"The what?"

"Take a seat kiddo."

He grabs one of the office chairs and pats it for her. Emma gingerly lowers herself into the chair, watching him buzz like a bee. They have been concerned about Carter's 'episodes' before. His excitement sometimes turns into mania but she never knows whether it is a health concern or if he's overly excited and fixated on an obsession with too much caffeine in his system. "Are you ready for me to blow your mind?"

"Absolutely," Emma answers, crossing one leg over the other. She rubs her hands over her slack-covered knees, watching him hop in place.

"There are two groups. Here we have the Syndicate. Overall bad dudes. From my research we have their origin placed as early as the 'Biblical' times. Look at this picture of this man who is depicted in early Ethiopian culture as the 'mastermind' and this picture from *two* months ago." Carter explains rapidly, pointing to the two pictures. One is a crudely taken photo of a vase with designs carved into it. The other is a picture from New York with a man standing in Times Square, his head tilted down. While the vases' depiction gives no indication for colouring or dimensions, they do look oddly similar. "I found this site that supposedly belongs to them. Live streaming of girls—I think they are involved in an actual trafficking scheme, which is how they make their money, and though a couple key members have been arrested or even murdered in this poor guy's case, they run a pretty tight ship.

Seventy-nine separate entities—in a group of, by my count, thousands of time-travelling GOONS—from their 'business' have been questioned but they blame other gangs. A couple still ended up in prison which is how I located a headhunter with connections to the *government*. It comes as no surprise that all of them end up dead within months of being incarcerated."

"Because of the gangs… or the Syndicate?"

"Unimportant," he responds, waving his hand. "What *is* important: they are a trafficking group, but not in the way they want people to think. Sure, they take little girls and sell them to the highest bidder—but that's a front! Behind the scenes, they are going back in time and taking dictators from their timelines. AND-AND-AND they have members who they seeded in these key regions—" Carter grabs a different board, beginning to unfold it as a bead of sweat rolls down his forehead. "With ties to *twelve* different subjugation groups."

"Car," Emma whispers, touching his hand. He blinks rapidly at it as she smiles gratefully. "Can we stay focused on the time travel right now? I'd love to see the other board after."

"Right, right," Carter repeats, tossing the other board behind him. It clatters loudly to the ground, drawing a concerned welfare check from Dr. Pepper. She doesn't have the time to respond before the first board is being thrust in her face. "Look at this painting. It depicts Wu Zetian but look at the person in the background."

"He doesn't look like he belongs in ancient China."

"Exactly!"

Emma pushes lightly against the board, making it move back enough for her to see the photo in the light. The man forgotten in the shadows has a gun strapped to his hip! The artist painted would not have known to be suspicious of something that didn't exist back then. Has a museum seen this? Surely someone will notice... unless they do not want to. Ignorance is a powerful thing. "Are you sure this is accurate to the time though? It could be a recreation—"

"This picture was taken of the original art, kept in the home of the artist, by his great-great—a lot of great-grandchild who posted it to knomore.askquestions.com. Sure enough, the man in the painting matches a man who was *caught* as a member of the Syndicate in EIGHTEEN NINETY-THREE for inappropriate conduct in public. He was shot going into the courthouse."

"Why dictators? Did you figure out what are they trying to do with them?"

"Well, I only have theories—but the anti-liberation cells I was talking about? They are fighting for a reestablishment of a 'strong', 'united' party across Central Asia." He points to a list he wrote out, except his handwriting is illegible. Emma presses a hand to her mouth as he stares at her expectantly. Finally, he realizes and shakes his head rapidly. "Fine, well, a couple thoughts. They are taking dictators out of their time periods in hopes of ruining the space time continuum. There is an event they want to avoid and they think by taking the dictators out of their time that it will work—EXCEPT they are taking the dictators *after* they lose power. Notice how we still remember being taught about these leaders in school and their heinous crimes. It's not that we suddenly think they are good. The Syndicate is not trying to change how history remembers these dictators or change anything... at least from my research. I didn't find proof of events we can no longer remember. We still know about the Holocaust and Holodomor and the Missile Crisis."

"Okay, where does that leave us?"

"Well, *my* favourite theory is that they're doing genetic testing on the dictators. They are going to extract DNA from each of them and create a superhuman with charisma, arrogance, and a complete lack of moral code. With its entire purpose WORLD DOMINATION."

Silence hangs between them. Carter taps his notebook as if it solidifies his point. "We went from changing the course of history to cloning and world domination."

"This is serious stuff."

"You actually think they could be... stealing DNA from dictators and trying to make a 'supertator'?"

They both snicker slightly at her words, but Carter is the first one to break it. "Either that or they will release them into their respective countries again. Some will revolt but imagine a leader, who many thought was great, returns and says they were reincarnated to save the country. Especially someone like Joseph Stalin who all the girls in my social class thirsted over.... All you need is a large event, to bring every country to the brink of destruction, and offer strong leadership—look at what happened during our last plague."

"Supertators or purposeful terrorism."

"Which brings us to Dies Iter," Carter states, taking his laptop out of his satchel. He opens it and types in his password with a grunt. Even at his fastest speed, the password takes half a minute on its own. "'What is Dies Iter' you ask?"

He looks at her pointedly as the screen comes to life. Emma leaves over his shoulder, grinning. "What is Dies Iter, Dr. Friesen?"

"Loosely translated in Latin, it means time's journey, or timeline. Only *one* record exists of the two words put together as a title, and it was found in a phone call conversation between a known Syndicate agent and what he thought was an informant but we believe was actually a member of Dies Iter, breaking into their ranks. Someone in the NSA flagged the conversation for being suspicious," Carter explains, tapping the spacebar on his laptop. A slideshow presentation begins with the symbol of Dies Iter. Slowly their name builds up underneath it, with an **Est. ???**. "These guys were difficult to find. I could probably show you hundreds of Syndicate members, but there are only seven pictures involving Dies Iter.

You have seen most of the ones including human beings. I assume they are more careful about staying hidden because—"

"They are like a police force for the timeline," Emma whispers, leaning forward now. *Or is it timelines?* He nods eagerly as she stares at the pictures side by side. Overtime, the quality and colour changes but their faces do not. She can always find them in the photo. Darcy specifically. He is only in two of them. One with the others at his side, and the second on a dock, standing behind two men shaking hands. He looks younger there… the privateer! He must be the man he stands behind. This isn't a photo of him out of time, this is a picture from his life! "So, they are the good guys."

"Arguably, if you believe in good and bad," Carter remarks, smirking proudly as she sits back. He preens when she claps softly. "From my sources, the clinic is a known Syndicate front. How else could they discard the sharps they use for genetic testing and blood drawing? It would be easy enough for a clinic to hide 'waste' material and dispose of it 'correctly' and raise no eyebrows. I don't know if they actually do acupuncture there. Apparently showing up with no appointment is 'unacceptable'. That's where I was this morning. I wanted to see them with my own two eyes."

"Did you?"

"Nope. I assume they exclusively bring them out during the night. It's easy to mistake someone for a historical figure and convince yourself 'it couldn't be' when it's dark outside."

Carter sighs, lips popping out. He grabs more pictures out of his bag, adding them to his little presentation. The Syndicate. Pictures of the dictators. Dies Iter. "Based on my own intelligence, I believe each of the Dies Iter's members are chosen because they represent the countries of the different dictators. Even for twenty-fifty, the group is oddly diverse. In age, in looks."

"Agent Estella was Italian; she must be Mussolini. Agent Rosalind must be Wu Zetian. Agent Eyre... she's not German, but she mentioned something about being Jewish and she did sound slightly Slavic." Emma explains, shaking her head slowly. If they are taken from their time and brought on as agents because of their country of origin, Agent Rosalind would be *thousands* of years old. The oldest of them... *eons* older. "Agent Bingley, the Russian, must be Stalin."

"Presumably. He's the only one that we've seen but considering Russia's long rap sheet of totalitarian leaders? Lenin, Ivan the Terrible, Gorbachev, Bloody Nicholas, Brezhnev, Putin... really the list goes on and on. Tyrants, absolutists, monstrosities are better words than 'dictators'. The things I saw while doing this research? The school system protected us too much." Emma's eyes glaze over. Who is Darcy assigned to? A Dutch settler? Someone else? "I found all of this within the span of twelve hours and should be immortalized as the smartest man on Earth. I accept a standing ovation and three dozen red roses."

"Why put some of it on your computer?"

Carter glares up at Mina as he slams his laptop shut. He guards it close to his chest, glaring at her. "Because I ran out of room *Mina*. Don't you have a job to do?"

"You all do," Dr. Pepper remarks, arms crossing as he walks towards the desk. His nose scrunches together as he looks at the half-clear photos and strings attached to the white board. "Don't you have better things to do with your time, Dr. Friesen?"

"I am revolutionizing truth sir," Carter counters, about to drink his coffee. Dr. Pepper takes it from him, walking right back to the room he came out. "Now I found out what they are and who... I don't know where to find them. Dies Iter hides remarkably well. I went through every search engine I know, got in contact with every person I thought might have a clue... nothing. No indication of where they were last seen or when."

"I think I saw Bingley last night. I went for a walk before you came over, that's why I called you."

"I may have someone who knows someone who can get me CTV footage of the street," Carter offers, his eyes brightening. "I can cross-reference that with other cameras and see if I can find a last known location."

"You're brilliant Car," Emma whispers, standing up. She claps again, grinning when he bows with flourish. "Truly. I'm sorry if I haven't seen that before. I'll make it five dozen roses and a fruit basket."

"Don't get mushy on me now. You're going to pay it back to me." Carter assures, patting her head. He is two inches taller than she but acts like he is a giant in comparison. The real giant, her giant, is waiting out there. "We're finding this thing together kid and I'm coming along for the ride."

"Aren't secret agencies kind of... against civilian interference?" Emma inquires, helping him pack away the board. Dr. Pepper sends Carter a dirty look, as he greets a customer off to the side. She didn't hear the bell to the front door. "What happens if they erase our memories or something? That can happen right?"

"We find them again," Carter snorts, shouldering his satchel. He glances at the distracted doctor and shimmies away. "You need to believe a little in fate and destiny. Say it with me 'there are no coincidences and therefore no consequences'."

"I don't think—"

"No think. Just say."

"And if we cannot find them?"

Carter points his finger at her across from the desk, trying to hide his getaway from Mina and the doctor. "None of that. If I come up with no leads, we try something else. We found time travelers Emma. I am not sure about you, but I am not willing to just let that knowledge slide off my back and keep going about my boring nine-to-five."

Emma meets his eyes, surprised. She never thought he

was bored. Honestly, she never contemplated her own boredom either... until she uncovered an entire other world hiding underneath her knowledge. Exhilaration now pumps through her like blood. Maybe she hasn't been able to sleep because for the first time she can remember, she wants to jump out of bed and do something exciting. Something irresponsible. He notices the spark in her eye growing and begins to nod his head excitedly. "There are no coincidences."

"There are no accidents!"

"There are no accidents."

"No consequences."

Mina leans over the counter, gritting her teeth. "You're going to lose your job—"

He whoops and then he is running before Dr. Pepper can finish his conversation.

Emma feels weightless again. Her boots barely touch the sidewalk as she glides to her apartment. Instead of hiding in her pockets, her hands swing at her sides like they used to as a kid. She might start dancing. To no music, simply the rhythm of her heartbeat.

The sun stays around longer now. Warm weather returns

to the city, bringing out the rich green colour of the trees and grass. She thinks about the cute sandals she will get to wear soon. Then her mind moves to Dies Iter. Carter and Bingley are going get along well. Agent Rosalind will think they're insufferable together... but she might enjoy Carter's sharp mind.

She doesn't know what will happen with Darcy... or how long it will take to find them all again. The agents may try to convince them to give up, but Carter and Emma made up their minds. She is not afraid.

Her gait slows when she comes to the front of her apartment and sees the clinic. No one is going into it. There is usually a steady stream of people. Grabbing her phone, she checks for texts from Carter. Nothing. No indication of any investigation with the clinic.

Adjusting the bag on her shoulder, she glances at the others walking down the street. She could go into it. Check it out herself. If they asked about appointments, she could schedule one for tomorrow and come in. Except there is something wrong.

Her gut twists.

Freezing on her side of the street, she slowly brings her hand to her stomach. The lack of people going in and out cannot be a good sign.

She runs into her apartment and up the stairs, careful to keep her steps quiet. Instead of putting the key in immediately, she twists her doorknob. It does not open. The hallway is empty and yet the hairs on the back of her neck lift.

A security camera in the hallway blinks. Did the red light go out?

Someone is watching me.

Sweat gathers on her hands as she kicks her door in.

The apartment is untouched. Dark because she turns off all her lights. Her heartbeat hammers in her ears as she flicks on the hallway light. Nothing.

Emma does not remove her shoes as she sprints into the main room. Sliding onto her hands and knees, she begins to pull bags and boxes out from underneath her bed. Bringing one of the bags to her wardrobe, she pulls it open and for no concrete reason, starts packing.

The last box fits perfectly in Moses' truck.

"Is that everything?" he questions as she closes the tailgate. Emma nods breathlessly, melting against him. Between the frenzy of packing up her place in two hours and loading it into his vehicle, she's pooched. Moses throws his arm over her shoulder and squeezes once. "So, you're sure this doesn't have to do with the people Moe says 'invaded' your house?"

"No... I don't really feel comfortable with one of the neighbours," she states, glancing at the clinic. Someone is standing on the top level, looking down at the street. They meet her eyes, and then they are gone. "Moe won't be too upset—"

"She's not my concern." He puts his hands onto his hips, watching Emma twist her hair into a cleaner bun. "Moe is going to be thrilled. She's been talking about dragging Cody back and getting all her 'ducklings' back into the nest."

He shudders, smiling when she does. A car honks behind them, an angry woman gesturing at the **no parking** sign. "City folk."

"No kidding," Moses muses, walking around the hood. He waves his hand at the driver but pauses to look at his sister again. "You know... if you wait a couple weeks, I might have a place we can live together."

Her jaw drops, pride swelling in her chest at his flush. "You were being serious about moving out?"

"Don't tell Moe or Dad yet, I haven't mentioned it to them," Moses laughs, scratching the back of his neck nervously. He throws his keys from one hand into the other as he opens his door. "We all have to sometime. Right? It's weird my little sister moved out before me."

"You like living at home."

"Yeah... but I'd also like to have a room dedicated to my

collection and you know how they feel about that," Moses smirks, laughing as he climbs into the vehicle. Emma smiles to herself as she opens the door. Someone catches her eye as they leave the clinic. Wearing tactical gear, the woman could pass as a Dies Iter member, but it's not anyone Emma recognizes.

Their eyes meet and the soldier pauses. She tilts her head slightly to the side, eyes narrowing. Emma nods with a smile and swiftly climbs inside, snapping her seatbelt into place. Moses pulls away from the curb before the woman can cross the road completely. He mutters something about city drivers but smiles at the person who tried to stop him from getting onto the road.

Emma glances at the rearview mirror, pressing a hand to her stampeding heart. God knew. She made the right choice.

CHAPTER 29: GLORIOUS PURPOSE

"Why is there stuff in my front foyer?" Moe questions, marching down the stairs. She opens the door further for Moses and Emma as they haul her bedframe inside. The desk is the heaviest thing but this is the most awkwardly shaped. Emma did not have the time or tools to anything apart. "What happened?"

"Water is out in the building," Emma groans, lowering the frame to the floor. Moses raises an eyebrow but wisely stay silent. If she tells her mother the same story, Moe will think Avery was in danger. No need to cause undue stress. Besides, her lease is up in three months and she didn't know whether to renew it or not. The pharmacy hasn't made an offer of employment and she didn't want to stay where rent is the highest without a guaranteed income. "I decided after everything with the power outages and misplaced mail that I need to find a new place to live… is it okay if I stay here for a while?"

"Stay as long as you need to," Moe agrees, rubbing her shoulders. "Oliver! Joseph! Summer! Winter! Daniel! Help move Emma's things back into her room."

Moe picks up a box, heading up the stairs as Oliver runs down. Her dad comes out from the study, eyebrows drawn together in surprise. Instead of looking worried or upset, he reaches out for her and presses a kiss to her head. "Welcome back home sweetie."

Emma fights with her box, grateful when Winter helps her get a grip. None of them question her or her parents as they bring the boxes back to her old room. Avery joins them as the boys almost drop her desk. She pokes her head into the sage-green room eyebrows, knitting together, until she notices Emma staring out the window. Sidling up alongside her older sister, she pulls on her sleeve. "What are you doing here?"

"I'm moving back in... for a little while."

Avery squeals, throwing herself at Emma. She laughs, running her hands through her long black hair. The hug helps bring her back to the present, soothing the cold fist around her heart. Moses didn't ask her why she kept checking the mirrors, or why she looked over her shoulder a dozen times. The entire trip here she expected to see an army of angry people riding after them with guns blazing.

Maybe she should have asked to stay at Carter's place.

"Why?" Winter finally asks, crossing her arms. She scans the room, jumping out of the way at Joseph's shout. He shuffles into the room, making a beeping noise as a grunt comes from the hallway. Oliver and Moses struggle with a huge box of books, muttering to one another as they pivot to get it into the room. A book spills out onto the floor as they high five. "It's not like I'm not happy to see you but this is weird. You're super organized."

Emma wraps her arms around her younger sister, praying for God to keep her clueless. Keep all of them clueless. *No coincidences, no accidents, no consequences.* "I've had a couple problems with the apartment—"

"Did you break up with that guy?"

"Emma doesn't have a boyfriend," Moses remarks, grabbing the book off the floor. His certainty breaks at the silence. Everyone is crammed into this small room, looking at her, expecting her to say something. What is she supposed to say? He is not her boyfriend but her soulmate but she doesn't believe in soulmates and he's definitely a couple hundred years old but it's okay because he is a time traveler? Leaning against the desk, he meets Emma's desperate eyes. "I haven't heard about any boys."

"I bet she broke up with her boyfriend," Summer whispers to her twin, pouting her lips. "Before we got to meet him, what a sin—"

"I don't have a boyfriend to break up with," Emma assures, running her hands through her hair. She looks at her family, looking at her, then each other, and drops her arms. "Seriously. My apartment has a lot of problems, and with no water, I cannot shower. It's not appropriate to go into work with greasy hair."

"If you say so," Summer sings, snapping at Oliver when he pushes her away. Dad corrals them, stretching out his arms to prevent Summer from saying something else. He waves his hands until the pesky siblings leave, exiting himself to get back to whatever project he was working on in the study. Avery gazes up at her worriedly, hanging on her arm.

"Did something else happen?"

"Something else?" Moses inquires, his eyebrows drawing together. Moe is already unpacking her boxes, folding her clothes for the wardrobe.

"Nothing happened," Emma promises, squeezing the side of Avery's face. "I'll join you for game time after Moe and I finish up in here."

Avery narrows her eyes, torn between her older siblings. She knows a dismissal when she hears one. Still, she waits for Emma's nod towards the door before she starts backing away. Bringing two fingers up, she points them at Emma and then Moses, and back at herself.

With her out the room, Moses and Emma gather around the box of books.

"The neighbour you don't feel comfortable with...."

"Not my boyfriend. I met a guy, but we're not exclusive, and it's a little complicated." Emma admits, laughing quietly. She leans her head against his shoulder as he brings one arm up to hug her. "You know how I like my life uncomplicated."

"Yeah. If this is your solution to make it *less* complicated, you should have said something." Moses jokes, pulling away. His considerate smile drops as he bumps his forehead into hers. An apology is on the tip of her tongue but Moses doesn't need it. All he needs is for her to bump his head back. When she does, he nods, and steps away. Casting one glance at their mother in her corner of the room, he throws up a finger gun. "We will start… perusing, together tonight?"

"Sure," Emma agrees, smiling after him. "Thanks Pea One."

"Anytime Pea Two."

Moses steps up behind Moe, pressing a kiss above her blonde bun. She watches him go with a warm smile. "He thinks he's so sneaky."

Emma laughs, thanking her mom as she shimmies the desk over the carpet. "He's sweet."

"He's a coward," Moe corrects with a smile, crossing her arms as she finishes one box. She watches Emma fight with her office chair, and stop beside the massive box of books. Her shelves came with the apartment… so she doesn't have anywhere to put them. *Dad probably kept the old ones.* "A sweet coward. He thinks Dad cannot handle it. Two of my babies have already left, what's another one? But he and your father have a special relationship."

"They'll see each other at work every day."

"Unless he needs to spread his wings further," Moe shrugs, picking at some lint on a pair of pants. She tosses them aside, reaching for the next. "I know how adulthood works."

"I did not leave you," Emma promises, joining her side with the clothes. There is no point unpacking her books if they have nowhere to go. Besides, she and Moses might have a new place in a month. "I needed to be closer to work."

"You left," Moe corrects, shaking out a silk dress. She scrutinizes it and holds it against her chest, searching for Emma's floor length mirror. It leans against the wall, a fake ivy broken apart on top of it. A horrified gasp leaves her mouth before she slides it onto a hanger. "For a while you did not come to visit every Sunday, and then you did again. Cody left, but he'll come back too."

"Cody is different."

"He was born independent, but you all have that same drive in your own ways. It's my stubbornness and your father's ambition. Cody wants to prove he is as mighty as he thinks he is. Moses wants to show he is a different person than Dad. You wanted to prove to yourself you could do anything you put your mind to," Moe explains, shaking out the clothes. Emma takes a sweater from her hands, frowning at a little stain on the shoulder. *Is that permanent?* "Oliver will try to show there is nothing wrong with also going into the family business. Summer will date too many wrong men. Winter will distance herself to show she can. Joseph is going to end up in prison, mark my words. Avery... *Heer red ons*, will do exactly what people tell her she cannot simply because she wants to show them where faith can get you."

"You're worried about Summer?"

"That girl puts grey hairs on my head," Moe sighs, not

laughing when Emma does. "I try to equally distribute my worry to each of you, but she gets a special portion. You all take after one of us more than the others so I can predict what you are going to do—mother's intuition. I don't know where that girl came from but she surprises me every day."

"You do not need to worry about me—"

"But I will. I used to worry about you more than anyone else," Moe confesses, laughing slightly. Her eyes begin watering, both horrifying Emma and making her own eyes mist. "Before Avery got sick, before you finished elementary school. You were the quietest person in the family but you made friends so easily. I worried you were depressed, or a little... special."

"Moe."

"I know, I know, mothers worry about silly things *schatje*. Sometimes it doesn't even make sense to *us* and we are the ones worrying."

"What changed your mind?" Emma inquires, gathering her socks in her arms. She refuses to fold them or let her mother. "Avery getting sick?"

"No," Moe admits, chuffing. "Dad and I were heading to the hospital one day, without you all, to visit Avery. You came running out—almost got hit by the car—to give us this head scarf you knew Avery would like. I told you we weren't going to bring it, because it could interfere with the equipment and their monitoring."

Emma drops the socks into their drawer, smiling fondly out the window. "And I moved to stand in front of the car."

"Even when your Dad inched forward you did not move. You stood there with your arms folded. I realized right then and there: where it counted, you had my strength in twofold." Moe answers, not noticing how emotional Emma is getting. She looks off to the side, rubbing away the tears though she suspects her mother knows. As mothers do. "Now, you did apologize the moment we got back and told us you understood if you needed to be grounded or punished... your dad and I had a good laugh about that. We still do."

"I love my family."

"You're a good girl. A good friend. An even better sister." Moe agrees, squeezing her shoulder. "Maybe one of our best, which is why I don't worry when stuff like *this* happens. I know you honour God, and you have a good head on your shoulders."

"And that's why you texted me a dozen times this morning?"

"That had to do with this business about Avery and some *Russian*. If you insist on dating in the continent, it should be Holland. They need some work but you will not find more respectful, good men," Moe declares, shaking her head. She finishes off the box with a *humph* of approval. "It is time for coffee and *speculaas*. Are you coming?"

"I would never say no to *speculaas*."

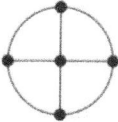

"May I ask you something?" Emma inquires, leaning forward on the stool as she holds her mug. Moe glances up from her cutting board and nods once, before returning to her aggressive attack against the celery. "As someone who extensively studies history, what would time travel mean for us?"

"That is less of a historical question, and more of a scientific one," Moe counters, lifting the knife. "You should ask a Physicist."

"Okay, but what if someone were taking people out of history? Like Hitler... what if someone removed Hitler before he became Chancellor and brought him here? Or an ancient civilization?"

"Then the Holocaust would never have happened. This reality would cease to exist. You and I would not be talking about him." She tilts her head to the side as she looks at the cutting board. Gathering the celery, she throws it into the soup pot for supper tonight. "Or it should. I suppose there could be an argument made that another would step into his role, but it would not be him then, would it?"

"What if they took Hitler, faked his suicide and now he's

here… in our time? Say every dictator is. You studied them. I know you find tyrants fascinating. I've read some of the publications you have and articles from colleagues. You guys have studied the traits they share," Emma continues, crossing her arms by the coffee. Moe stares at her, taking a slow sip from her own mug. *She's already looking at me like I've lost it.* "What do you think would happen? Would they just murder each other?"

"These men and women were known for their lack of sympathy, entitlement, and racism. Many of them would not recognize others as having a true claim to any power. I doubt they'd resort to a brawl, but poison would end up in a few cups." Moe answers, coming around the island. She presses the back of her hand to Emma's forehead, shaking her head when she is no warmer than normal. With all the people Moe works with, Emma expected her to provide a little more insight. It's hard not to show her disappointment. "Is this another one of Carter's theories?"

"It is a fun thing to consider, I thought you enjoy playing with ideas."

"Well, I am not sure the concept works Em," Moe remarks, staring at her spread of vegetables. The carrots are chosen as her next victims, chopped to pieces in two swipes. "What would be the aim? They gained most of their power by manipulating impoverished people with the promise of a brighter future. Dictators came into power because of food shortages and the cost of war. After our longest bout of international peace, what need would they promise to fill? Nationalism went out of style when I was a kid and I don't see it returning."

"I guess so."

"I will say one thing," Moe begins, hand pausing. She puts the knife down and meets Emma's eyes. "I would never want to be in a room with all of them; that's for sure."

Emma stares at her roof, unable to sleep. Carter texted her with a frowny face when she asked for an update. Refusing to pressure him more or cause a fuss, she spent the rest of her day with Avery and Chocolate, before going to 'sleep'. Well, the little rat spent most of his time locked in his tube system because he tried to bite Emma. Most animals love her. She cannot figure out why the little rat despises her so fully, but she likes to believe it is jealously.

Slowly, she rolls onto her feet and walks over to the boxes of her books. Taking *Pride and Prejudice* out, she slips to the ground underneath her window, and opens it to Darcy's note.

She doesn't even know his real name.

Bingley called him 'Z' but there are so many names with

a z.

It cannot be easy to find people who put so much effort into hiding. Time travelers… they can jump through time and erase themselves or redo something if they realize they have been caught. He must want to be found. Why else would he leave the note? She is not imagining their connection.

Of all the deVries', she may be the least creative after Cody. How could she imagine something like this?

The next problem, if Carter cannot find them, is figuring out where to start. She noticed the camera in the hall, directed towards her door. Could she get Trevor to call in his favour and get access to the footage to see Dies Iter? Darcy must have come back to put the envelope of cash in her glass jar. What if he left something else?

All she knows is pressure has been building on her chest for days. Cody always talked about this 'glorious' purpose outside of their little town. She never understood it but now she is beginning to wonder if this is what he felt like. Restless. Disturbed. Never able to stop thinking about what he calls his 'one path'.

She knows one thing for sure and that is she will see Darcy again. When and where does not matter, but they will see each other again.

They *need* to.

CHAPTER 30: I SEE

Bingley glances at Darcy for the eighth time since they got into the black sedan. He taps his fingers against the steering wheel, tempted to say something. Rosalind meets his eyes in the rear-view mirror. She shakes her head, disturbing the crusted blood up the side of her face. They cannot die but age-old exhaustion wears on their bones. The wound on Darcy's arm is healing slower than normal, a sign he needs to get back to his time and refresh.

"That could have gone better," Bingley finally declares, ignoring the heated glare directed at him. Agent Eyre laughs helplessly from the backseat, holding a cold compress against her eye. One of the Syndicate members tried to rip it out of the socket. They are getting crueler. Last week changed everything. Dies Iter procured information that will lead them to the last of the Tinkers. "A quick refresh and then the next one?"

"You know protocol," Rosalind snaps, teeth bared. Her bad mood is constant, but it's been worsening. The inevitable is coming. No one wants to face it. Bingley nods compassionately, biting his knuckle as he stares at the road. "We always go back."

"Long enough to regenerate," Darcy states softly, glancing at her. "Not too long—"

"We will all go back *permanently*. Once our mission is

over. Do not forget what we are here for," she hisses, wincing slightly when her torso twists. Both men immediately tense, relaxing when she does. If Rosalind shows her pain, it means something is broken. Normally they cannot break bones... but they've been gone for too long. "Delusion gets people hurt."

"It's not delusion," Eyre mumbles, her voice nearly lost in the purring of the engine. Bingley purposely slows down as she speaks, straightening to see her in the mirror. Her eyes watch the city passing by, wide and unblinking. They try to absorb as much as they can, while they can. "It's hope."

"False, foolish hope. You forget yourselves." The muscle around her temple moves as she swallows. "It is your job to keep them in line, Agent Darcy. Not me."

He presses his lips together, staring at the sky instead of at her. Normally he is the one making jokes on their way back to headquarters. Trying to lighten the mood. Encouraging the team with everything they did right. With the danger gone, the day over, and only the party left to be had. The pensiveness began long before Emma, but she exacerbated it. He is getting caught in his own thoughts. Enough to cause a risk to the team and his own life.

Bingley covered his back, but he could have gotten sent back... and HQ rarely allows setbacks like that. The two of them always have each other's back. In everything but blood they are brothers. "Stop causing problems Na."

It is a tempting idea to give in. To make the new

memories disappear and cling to the old. To stop caring. Bingley faces the conundrum every morning when he looks himself in the mirror. Watching the world age and change around him in impossible ways.

"I will not allow a single week with a pretty girl and her little sister to pull this team apart. We functioned as a well-oiled machine. Hadassah was seconds from being sent back because you two were mourning the loss of your connection to this time," Rosalind sneers, leaning forward. She points a finger at Bingley but he keeps his eyes on the road, not entertaining her petty insults. For all his resolve, the vein in his neck pops out, pulsing with his veiled temper.

"You are right Na. I have not been a proper leader." Darcy clenches his hands together, eyes closing. "I am sorry, it will not happen again."

"No, not 'I am sorry'," Bingley mocks, cursing in a line of Russian so thick Darcy cannot understand. He slams his foot on the break, careening to the side of the road, not listening to the insults flying from Rosalind's lips. She jerks against her seatbelt as he slams the stick into park. "I am not sorry. We are not machines. We have *feelings,* that is what separates us from these монстр."

"Shut it Alexander—"

"No! For the first time we feel alive. Tell me you did not feel alive and I will get back onto that road and drive straight into the checkpoint," Bingley challenges, turning around to glower at Rosalind. She sucks in her lips. The weight of his stare drops onto Agent Eyre, who promptly tries to melt into her seat. Their team leader is silent, looking out the window again with a forlorn expression on his face. Such a strong man should not be brought low by something like *this*. "A woman like Emma does not exist in every era, Z. You either take hold of your life or you let people who are using you destroy it. I know what I would choose if I found someone who fits me like she fits you. Aren't you tired of being a puppet?!"

"It is not that simple—"

"She will understand. I am sure of it. She deserves the chance to choose goodbye." Bingley argues, cursing the watch on his wrist. It beeps in warning, flashing the countdown to checkpoint. He pulls back onto the street, shoulders tense as he mutters to himself. A car behind them honks at the intrusion and gets a flash of his tallest finger in response. "You underestimate her—"

"Alexei."

"No, let me finish. You say the car means no roles. You do not tell me what to do. I tell *you* what to do. You act like she cannot understand or she would not want you over her lifestyle, but you do not see. I *SEE*. I see an empty apartment. I see rows of books and movies filled with great adventures like yours. I see someone who desires more, like all of us do. None of you can tell me you did not see that same quality in her eyes. The ones we all have that made Dies Iter choose us!"

Bingley snaps, slapping the steering wheel. He shakes his head vehemently, cutting another person off to get on route. The driver honks and flips him off but Bingley punches the window threateningly and silences them with a glower. "Or maybe you are not as worthy of her as I think you are. We are not the brave fighters I thought. My mistake."

"Alexander—"

"You have waited thousands of years for her. Where is your romance!? Where is your fight!? Where is that passion a good leader needs?"

"Alexander!" Darcy shouts, slamming his hands on the dash. Bingley shuts his mouth, breathing loudly through his nostrils. He rolls his neck and shoulders back, eyes shuttering. The lecture is going to be as intolerable as this traffic. "Turn around."

"What?"

Rosalind's voice is drowned out by the screeching of the car. Bingley does not give him a chance to change his mind. Within moments he is speeding so quickly down the street that it is a miracle he does not hit someone or something. The smell of burning rubber fills the vehicle as he cackles evilly.

"HQ is not going to forgive this insubordination!"

"They cannot replace me, or Hadassah, sorry to say it's different for the two of you, but I take the blame."

Rosalind brandishes a knife, waving it at him. "That's not the point—"

Bingley waves her off, pulling to the side of the road with a cry of delight. Her head comes within inches of the window. Darcy unclips his seatbelt, brushing off the blood. He removes his semi-automatic, keeping the pistol at his side. Giving him an enthusiastic thumbs up, Bingley whoops as his best friend runs towards the love of his life's apartment building.

Darcy waves his watch over the sensor, sprinting down the hall and to the stairs. It took him one glance to memorize her apartment number. As he reaches her level, someone steps out into the hall. The agent nods at them, affectionately recognizing the dog. Chewy and his paramedic.

They pause, watching Darcy make his way down the hall. Neither do anything to stop him from approaching Emma's door. Out of breath, he lifts his fist and knocks once.

"She's gone."

It takes him a moment to realize the man is talking to him. "Pardon me?"

"Emma? She's gone. Packed up all her things and loaded them into her brother's truck. I don't think she's coming back...." Trevor explains, clearing his throat uncomfortably when Darcy stares at the door aimlessly. Chewy, on the other hand, greets him excitedly. His wagging tail clobbers the agent's knees as Trevor holds him back. "If you give me your name, I can tell her—"

"No, I will be gone by then," he remarks, thanking him with a nod. Trevor walks away timidly, glancing over his shoulder. His eyes stay on the ARMED, large, sad-looking man as he slips out his phone.

"I know someone who looks like Lenin, not completely but if we shave his head and do some light makeup," Carter offers, sipping his coffee. He smacks his lips as Emma presses the library books into her chest. "Take a couple pictures, add a location, and set the trap. Your mom still helps with the local theater so they have accurate sets and costumes, right? We take an *ushanka*—"

"If their entire jobs rely on gathering and guiding these people, they can probably tell the difference between the real thing and a fake."

Carter purses his lips and gestures between the two of them. "See, normally in a brainstorming session, there is more than one brain adding to the conversation."

"Sorry." She is. More than he knows. Theories and the incredible are his forte. Trying to keep up with his brain is a full-time job. "I haven't been sleeping well."

"I can tell."

"Carter," Emma begins softly, stopping. Shifting the books from one arm into the other, she faces him fully. It is difficult crammed between two full bookshelves with her arm full of books. She touches his arm to grab his attention from the coffee cup. "When a girl says that you should show concern."

"But you're not a girl. You're Emma."

"True, *but* it's good practice."

"Do you ever think about their forbidden section? I read somewhere every library has one, you just need to know where to look."

"Time travelers is enough adventure for me right now," Emma assures kindly, smiling at Elena. The pretty library assistant smiles back, glancing up at Carter. If Emma were more violently inclined, she'd elbow Carter. He's more interested in staring at the walls and bookcases for a hidden clue than the pretty girl in front of them. "The book was excellent. Thank you for the recommendation!"

"If you loved that, I have three others you may enjoy," Elena offers with a smile. "Do you have five minutes?"

"Definitely."

She sashays out of the closed in desk area, disappearing into the dark library. Emma stares at Carter until his eyes fall on her. He reels back, eyebrows jumping, as he holds the coffee cup to his chest. "What?"

"She thinks you're cute."

"Oh."

"She's gorgeous."

"She looks like you," Carter remarks with a little laugh, flushing. His eyes widen slightly as her face cracks into a tiny smirk. "Not to say you aren't beautiful... I am sure you are. I just like girls who aren't so intimidating."

"I am intimidating?"

"Externally."

"Externally?"

Carter's face turns so red Emma immediately feels bad. She begins her apology when her purse begins to vibrate against her hip. No, not her purse... her phone.

Brushing her shoulder kindly against his arm, she fishes her phone out as the smile becomes fuller. It drops the second she sees Trevor's text.

Hey, some large dude with a gun just showed up outside of your apartment??? I didn't tell him you were coming to watch Chewy.

Then another comes right after.

He said he'd be gone before I could call you, but I can make sure he is gone before you show up?

I don't want to get in your business but I have a cop buddy who can help out if you need a restraining order.

Her blood drops to her feet as she grabs the desk. Carter mentions something about the molding breaking between the sci-fi section. She dials Trevor's number, refusing to get her hopes up but the feeling of butterflies is rapidly returning.

"Hey Em—"

"What did the guy look like?"

"You sound scared. I meant it when I said I have a buddy. I can call him right now—"

"No, no that's okay. I just need to know if it's my friend...."

"Uh tall, Black, slightly British, wearing body armour with a GUN strapped to his thigh. Did I mention the gun? What have you gotten yourself into?"

"I am going to be right there! Can you tell him to wait?"

"Did I mention he smells like blood? I work with a lot of blood... I already left the complex—"

She hangs up, apologizing to no one. Handing her library card to Carter, she grips his arm. "Dies Iter is at my apartment. Scan the card. Get the books. You should get her number because I know she's nice and you both like thrift stores. Please."

"Wait, I want to come!"

His voice disappears under a wave of people shushing him. They give her dirty looks as she sprints through the library. She pauses by the door and apologizes to the old couple trying to make their way inside. Emma holds it open as propriety dictates but her legs are shaking. *Hurry up. Hurry up. God please tell him to wait!*

"Thank you dear," the woman drawls, gripping her forearm.

She smiles kindly and then she is running again.

"What are you doing back out here without Emma?" Bingley questions, eyebrows drawing together. He leans against the outside of the car, arms crossed. "No way she said no—"

"She was not there."

"Impossible."

"I went inside," Darcy remarks, gripping his watch. He glances at the timer counting down, massaging the back of his neck. "We are not going to make it out of this city before the jump."

"Good, then we're waiting here."

"We cannot leave this car on the side of the road. It will be towed, or worse the Syndicate will steal it." Rosalind sighs, crawling out. Eyre slides over the seat to stand with them, chewing nervously on her nails. "We cannot leave that kind of evidence."

"Then we burn it," Bingley shrugs, turning towards the vehicle. Darcy catches his arm, shaking his head slowly. "Then you can drive and disappear from behind the wheel."

Rosalind refuses to catch the keys. She lets them hit her chest and roll off onto the sidewalk. The resentment in her eyes becomes a raging fire. Bingley raises his eyebrows warningly but she will not rise to his bait. "If she is not here, she will not be coming. You hope for a miracle but we disappear in... two minutes."

Rosalind turns around expectantly, her arms raised in a silent taunt. They do not see her hopeful eyes when her back is turned. Her heart beats a new rhythm against her ribcage as her eyes move through the crowd. Her hope vanishes when she turns back to Bingley. Locking her jaw, she crosses her arms, and glares at her reflection in the SUV's tinted windows.

Bingley fixates on the front door of Emma's apartment complex as if she could suddenly burst out.

"Hey!" a loud voice greets. They all turn at the same time. If Bingley looked over his shoulder, he would see Rosalind's surprised but optimistic expression. It falls when she sees a tall man jogging towards them with a dog, instead of Emma. "You were the guy waiting for Emma, right?"

"Yes, have you seen her?"

He looks at Bingley, bewildered. The first thing he notices is the gun slung over his back. Bingley waves his watch-clad hand over his eyes, stashing the gun in the car before he comes back to it. A handful of cool things are created in the future, but the 'Short Term Memory Eraser' is his favourite. He uses it more than recommended. "Uh, what was I saying?"

"Emma," Darcy answers firmly, tempted to shake the

man. He steps forward, patting the dog's head. "You were telling us about Emma—"

"Oh right, she asked me to tell you to wait. I think she was on her way to take care of Chewy."

Darcy looks down at his watch, shaking his head. One minute. "How close was she? What direction was she coming from?"

"I don't know... if you need somewhere to stay, you can come up to my apartment."

"No, thank you," Darcy sighs, running his hands over his head. He clasps them behind his head, trying to breathe past the stitch in his side. It is her eyes when he closes his own. Her laugh filling his head as he says goodbye to this place. "But she's safe?"

Trevor's eyebrows draw together. "What?"

"Why did she leave her apartment?"

"Oh, she said she and her brother might be moving in together and need a bigger place," Trevor answers, shrugging his shoulders. Chewy sits excitedly, waiting for the treat from his owner's pocket. "She didn't tell you any of this? When I spoke to her, she sounded... relieved, and more excited than I've ever heard her."

Darcy walks in a circle, shaking his head. A weight lifts off his chest. The Syndicate did not get to her. She got out of the apartment before they could find or threaten her. When their ambush went sideways, he worried someone escaped.

Knowing the kind of people they hire; his girl didn't stand a chance. He briefly considered breaking protocol and risking everything to make sure his lack of discipline didn't cost her anything else.

At least he knows she is safe.

"Sorry!" Emma apologizes, out of breath as she sprints. She brushes against someone again, not apologizing this time. If she wore sneakers and pants to the library like a regular person, this would not be happening. She insisted instead on platform boots and a long floral skirt. The skirt slaps against her knees as she pushes herself faster. Years of running up her apartment stairs prepared her for this, and she is still out of breath.

Pausing slightly, she leans against a newsstand. The screens flicker to life, offering different headlines to read. One yells at her to pay the coin fee.

She pushes off the stand and runs again, removing her jacket as she does. With a little foresight, she would have left her purse and jacket with Carter. Now they slow her down. Every step forces the purse to smack her hip.

This is like the worst nightmares. Going as fast as

possible. Desperation fueling every pump of your arms. Yet, you make zero progress.

The crosswalk light flashes red at her. Sliding to a stop, she rests her hands over her head, and then her heart stops.

Darcy's eyes meet hers across the street.

His eyebrows curve warmly around his eyes as his own hands drop from his head.

Bingley cheers, jumping up and down beside Rosalind

She breaks the law.

A car honks at her as she sprints onto the road.

Rushing across the street, she pushes her way between two people and almost calls to him. Her legs burn as he starts sprinting towards her.

His bounds are twice hers, eating up the space between them.

Inches from each other, she watches his expression contort into surprise. By the time his body should have collided with hers, only shredded clothes are left to fly in the air. She catches a strip of his vest, heart hammering in her chest, as she stares into nothing.

OMA
MY EDITOR & ROLE MODEL
(September 26, 1938—November 6, 2022)

My Oma, Hendrika, immigrated from Holland at 12 years old. Her family wanted to escape the aftershocks of Nazism in Europe and so they sought Canada as their safe haven. She quit school in the ninth grade to start working, to provide for her family, and though she mourned the loss of her education, she knew family came first.

She met my Opa Morris at church and they began our clan. Her youngest daughter gave birth to me, a middle child with way too much anger for such a little body. Through my childhood of angst and pain, she was a bright light. This incredible woman of God saved me from my eating disorder, taught me how to believe in myself, and showed me what faith really means.

Despite struggling her entire life with bipolar, Oma brought joy and laughter everywhere she went. I do believe she is one of the many who inspired me to start writing. I fondly remember her bringing books over to the house and forcing me to sit still at her side so she could read me a book (sometimes even books about how farts cure cancer).

She was the first person to put my words on paper. I was MORTIFIED when I showed up to our yearly family reunion and saw chapters of my WIP printed, in a neat stack, on a table. Those papers did not stay there. Oma went around to every one of my family members, insisting they read it, and boasting about how talented I already was (I think I was 13 at the time).

I mean it when I say she was my hero. Around the age of 40 she lost my Opa Morris, other members of her family, got braces, returned to finish school alongside one of my aunts, and got remarried to my Opa Rick. Though she was sometimes uncouth by Canadian standards (if she said you looked like a prostitute it was a compliment because it meant lots of men want to sleep with you), she never spoke a harsh word with a desire to harm in her life.

She joked as we got older that she'd die before she could hold my book in her hands. April of this year (2022), I showed her up by arriving at her house to surprise her with my printed book. She edited this book. Her handwriting covers the text block I referenced when keying in edits. During the editing stages, she called me frequently to correct my spelling of Dutch words or to provide encouragement with something she really liked.

I got to watch her reaction as she finished this book; the first person ever to do so. I dedicated the book in part to her because I knew she'd laugh at the cheekiness... I never got to tell her that before she passed away on a random Sunday after a long battle with the health of her heart.

She was the first person I called to ask her opinion on my pen name. The first person I called when God said, "hey quit your job, drain your bank account, and publish this book". Through it all she provided me with endless encouragement, wisdom from God, and I know without a shadow of a doubt that she's laughing in heaven watching me sob while writing this because she's flying with the angels (if her theories are to be believed).

I know she is proud of me. I want to let you know, dear reader, that my Oma would have adored you. She'd demand you call her Oma (unless she assumed you were older than her), probably ask an insensitive-like question because she desperately wanted to know you, and give you a hug that smelled of bergamot and love.

I want you to know no matter where you are in reading this that Oma is proud of you. For fighting the battles, you are. For finding beauty in the little things. She loved you though she never met you and I hope her legacy affects you as positively and strongly as it affects me. You are worthy of love. No matter the condition of your life, body, mind, or spirit. She loved you as Jesus did when he died on the cross, and I pray you will never forget it.

Her greatest piece of advice to me was "do the next good thing". If you're hopeless and lost, just do the next good thing. I think in this instance the next good thing is to go have some *speculaas* with tea or a coffee and take care of your heart because it is precious and she was an expert in taking care of everyone's.

To you and to Oma, *dank u wel en tot ziens*.

(I do want to note that Moe is NOT based off my dear Oma, though there is a similarity or two. Oma would be absolutely appalled to think I viewed her as such an abrasive persona and I most certainly do not. She loved to argue but I cannot remember her being truly angry or petty.)

ACKNOWLEDGEMENTS

I am going to begin this acknowledgement with two things:
A) I have too many people to thank and I am undoubtedly going to forget about someone. So as a blanket statement, thank you to everyone who has provided encouragement over these last fourteen years. A special kind of thank you to everyone who opposed me (except for my fifth-grade teacher) and taught me how resilient and strong I am and gave God the opportunity to be glorified.
B) this book would not exist if I did not have a wild dream about my 12-year-old sister and put it on Tik Tok. I follow a master list of book ideas and choose a set schedule of which ones to write in a year (most of the ideas waiting on that list for multiple years at the point I write them), but VIT was a surprise. This book came out of nowhere and when I uploaded the dream to Tik Tok (June 2021) stating I did not intend to write it, I never expected to be here.
So, thank you. To every commenter, liker, sharer on Tik Tok who practically forced me into writing this book. With over a million views and thousands of comments, I know many did not follow the entire journey but I thank you nonetheless for even viewing the four-part video series.
Binners, thank you for being the inspiration to this book. I believe God saw that you needed your big sister and thus VIT was born. Our last year together has been filled with monthly

sleepovers, video games, secrets, and a couple petty 'misunderstandings' because I am a grumpy old woman. I hope you never doubt how much I admire your strength, humour, and bravery. I am so proud to be your big sister and greatest cheerleader.

Kendra, I'd paid for therapy considering all the crap and whining I put you through during the process of editing/publishing this novel but I'm broke. So instead, I will acknowledge the fact that you put up with my constant self-deprecation and self-pity and never failed to encourage me. I took your words to heart, I AM ASHLEY GRAHAM.

And on a serious note, thank you for being my rock during Oma's death. I don't know what I'd do or where I'd be without your presence in my life… look at you making me cry all over my laptop. Worst best friend ever (but actually you're awesome).

Anneke, I am not doing the sappy stuff yet (I'll wait for the documented adventure of Wificus or perhaps EoD), but I will say I ADDED the vein(s) in Chapter 14 for you. Hope you enjoy.

My best friend's best friend I included the you know what in Chapter 19 for you. I know it's your thing.

And to you know who because you know who you are, I added the toes in Chapter 17 just for you.

Stephanie, thank you for not calling me insane when I told you my plan to quit my job and drain my life savings to publish…

your validation of my own brilliance helped a lot. I'll never question my antics again.

Megan Nicole, you are awesome. I cannot put into words the gratitude I felt when you sent Timmies or a message of encouragement. Thanks for being one of my cheerleaders and for giving birth to an adorable child whose pictures made my long days better. I adore you.

Ravendoor Roomies, thank you for putting up with my slight slacking off when it comes to chores and for being willing to sit on my office floor as we craft words together. Thank you for letting me bounce ideas off you guys and for celebrating every milestone with me. You saw me through the initial decision to run to $0 and provided advice and a listening ear so many times. I couldn't do this without you two.

Mom, you are a constant inspiration and pillar of strength to me. Thank you for telling it to me straight when I spoke about my struggle between giving it my all or playing it safe.

Dad, thanks for losing sleep over my decisions and undoubtedly praying for me when the Dad worry set in. I appreciated your Biblical wisdom and the shoulder you allowed me to cry on more than once.

Opa, thank you for taking up Oma's torch. You reminded me how much Oma adored the book and being part of this process right when I needed it. I'll never forget your strength and loyalty.

Kaitlyn, even though your constant inquiries about how editing was going stressed me out and convicted me (because half the time I was gaming when I shouldn't have been), I am so grateful for you driving me to success. You have been one of the greatest contributors to my love of books and stories, thank you for encouraging my writing and enabling my reading by making me buy books you want to read!

Gabriel, we've had a lot of ups and downs in our relationship but you have been the #1 supporter of my books since day 1. The way you hounded me to send you an email of my newest book the day it was written always made me feel special. I appreciate you so much and I hope you know I'm your #1 supporter too.

Mrs. Ngata, I think you've read a version of every book I've ever written. INCLUDING THE BOOK WRITTEN ENTIRELY IN BOLDED CURSIVE!? You are a saint and I am so grateful for your sincere input on my books and publishing journey. Thank you so much.

Pastor Michael, your discernment of the Holy Spirit in responding to my request for prayer released me from strong chains. I know I would not be here if you did not allow God to speak through you as I stood there, shaking, nauseous, and unsure if it was finally time. I cannot thank you enough.

Auntie Sen, I did not know whether I'd have the strength to leave. Your grace and mercy in your treatment of me and my sudden departure helped me to achieve the peace I needed to move forward. Not only that but you have been a constant

Godly influence in my life. I know we spoke about the possible plot hole I might have in one of these books and I'm proud to say that I had already written myself out of it without realizing. So, rest assured, these books should not have anything disruptive in terms of story flow.

My church twin (Ashley C if that wasn't clear), I remember being a pre-teen and telling you I'd be a famous author one day. You never blinked an eye and you've supported me in prayer and words since. Thank you for seeing me.

Paije, when I dropped out of university to pursue writing you were the only person to check on me. You've been with me ever since. Thank you for believing in me.

Arielle, I'm sorry I skipped our coffee date to edit. Next month it's my treat.

Everyone who donated on GoFundMe, from words of encouragement to $1000, you showed me that waiting for my audience is stupid—you're already here. I love and appreciate you all so much and could not have made this book without your generosity.

Melody, we've never met. You stumbled upon that first video about my dream and I guess it got you hooked. A year and a half later and you are still in my comments on every video, encouraging me, reminding me that this book has a reader waiting for it. I hope it, and the two others, live up to your expectations. If you happen to throw it at a wall, please film it and send it to me so I can have my evil cackle moment.

A special thank you to Boston Pizza, Lord of the Rings and Sophie Lark's Anastasia. I consumed likely a hundred pounds in hot wings over the duration of writing and editing this book (sponsor me BP's). I have waited A YEAR for my annual Lord of the Rings marathon; Aragorn is my boo. And Anastasia is my present to myself because I did it. After 14 years, I am a published author. And you reader, made that happen, so thank you. For taking a gamble on a book with a cover I put together in four hours on Canva a week before the release… so *really* thank you.

Finally, thank you Lord. For giving me the dream and this talent and passion. You are the reason I am sitting here, able to write this. This year has been one of the worst yet and through it all You continued to display Your never-ending faithfulness and enduring love every day. I was diagnosed with PCOS in November of 2021 and at the worst place my health has ever been and You drew me out of it. You cleared my mind and helped to heal me. Wherever You take this book God, wherever You take me, may we glorify You.

ABOUT THE AUTHOR

Ashley Godschild began writing at the age of 9/10 when her elementary school teacher gave the class one hour to write a four-page short story, and by the end of the block, she had twelve pages and claimed the story had just begun. By the age of 12, she finished that story. By the end of mandatory education, her backlist reached past 30 completed projects... even though she deleted everything and decided to start over from scratch. As of this publication, she intends to write over 200 books (76 different series') and the list continues to grow.

Ashley enjoys reading (avidly), scrolling aimlessly on Tik Tok, spending time with her family and golden boi, and can rarely be found anywhere outside of her home in Canada. You might be able to catch her gaming or attending church, but better not blink or she'll be gone like a wraith. Her proudest achievement is the callous' on her knees from spending so much time in prayer and if you want to see Gollum in real life, you need only watch her eat hot wings. *Vacancies in Time* is her debut novel, and it would not be possible without the bountiful grace of God and support of her loved ones.

Find her on most social media platforms: @our_novel_guild or @authorashleygodschild

Made in United States
Orlando, FL
28 July 2024

49661681R00261